STALINGRAD IN THE CROSSHAIRS

OR

THE DUEL THE SNIPERS

W. T. WALLENDA

STALINGRAD IN THE CROSSHAIRS

\-

OR

THE DUEL
THE
SNIPER

Imprint:

©2025 – W. T. Wallenda

Cover and back cover:

Cover picture:
Drawing from PA-0060-Landser vor dem Einsatz
© W.T. Wallenda – Privatarchiv Author
all rights reserved by the author

Back cover:

Sophia Wallenda - Stalingrad 1
© W. T. Wallenda
all rights reserved by the author

other contributors:

Cover design and publishing:

BoD · Books on Demand GmbH,
In de Tarpen 42, 22848 Norderstedt, bod@bod.de

Print:

Libri Plureos GmbH
Friedensallee 273, 22763 Hamburg

ISBN: 978-3-7597-2239-3

In the noise of arms, laws are silent.

Marcus Tullius Cicero

If all men went to war only out of conviction, there would be no war.

Leo N. Tolstoy

This story is based on the legend of the duel between the Russian sniper Wassili Grigorjewitsch Saizev (*23.03.1915 - †15.12.1991), who was declared a hero of Stalingrad, and the probably fictional character of the German sniper instructor Major Erwin Koenig.

The German officer is given a biography and his fictional story is told very realistically against the background of the Battle of Stalingrad.

The plot and the protagonists are fictitious, with the exception of historical figures.

Drawing of P.A-0060-Landser vor dem Einsatz
Landser before combat deployment
© W.T. Wallenda – Original Photo
Privatarchiv Author

PROLOGUE

The twelve-year-old boy had been lurking in the undergrowth for almost two hours, tirelessly observing the large clearing. The settlement of Yeleninka in the Agapovka district, where his parents' farm was located, was more than an hour's walk away. It was snowing. He felt at home in the silence of the forest. He was free here. It was his kingdom.

Hunting had always been his passion. He mastered both types of hunting. The stalking and the lurking. He could startle his prey and kill it quickly, but he could also wait for hours to aim and shoot at the right moment. The qualities that characterized him were perseverance, patience, and an irrepressible will to hunt down his target.

No doubt they were waiting impatiently for him at home, but he didn't want to return home without a kill. He had to finally shoot the wild goat he had been after for so long and bring its meat home to feed his family. Nothing could stop him, let alone frighten him. He wasn't even afraid of the approaching darkness. Why should he be? The bears were hibernating, and he would keep the wolves away with his shotgun. If necessary, he could make a torch. Wolves feared fire.

"I want to shoot this goat before the wolves get it," he had said to his brother and left.

"You must be back before it gets dark," he was told.

With a broad grin, he turned and replied: "Don't worry. I'm only in the forest."

Now the silence of the forest surrounded him. The rifle lay calmly in his hand. In the distance he heard the howling of the wolves.

They are far away. That's good!

In the middle of the clearing was some hay. He had brought it from the barn and used it as bait. It must have smelled heavenly to the grass eaters. He looked up to the sky.

Soon the sun will be gone.

This goat had challenged him, but it had run deeper and deeper into the forest. He had accepted the challenge and followed it stubbornly. The goat's trump card was time, his trump card was his old rifle

9

and his almost inexhaustible endurance.

A muffled cracking sound in the underbrush told him that something was approaching the clearing. His senses were heightened. His right hand slipped from the warm glove. The butt of the rifle was pressed against his shoulder, his right finger pressed into the trigger guard.

Cautiously, as if sensing him, the wild goat moved toward the hay.

Breathing shallowly, he aimed as he had been taught. His forefinger reached the pressure point. He was on target. Exhale, hold your breath. The shot cracked, the butt slammed into his shoulder. The bullet tore through the goat's heart and it collapsed. The snow around them turned blood red.

"Yes!" rejoiced Vasily Saizev, shouting his joy into the silence of the forest. "I chased them and I won! Papa will be proud of me, and everyone will eat their fill."

Little did the boy know that fifteen years later he would be hunting again. But not in his home forest in the Chelyabinsk region, but in faraway Stalingrad on the Volga. He would wear the uniform of the Red Army, and his prey would not be wild goats, but German soldiers.

This young boy, named Vasily Grigoryevich Saizev, would become the most feared sniper in the Red Army.

German snipers were also used at Stalingrad, but only one man had the skill and tenacity to take down Saizev. Major Erwin Koenig.

On the day a Russian sniper shot Major Koenig's son, fate took its course and the German officer began hunting Saizev.

The two most skilled sharpshooters of the armies fighting in Stalingrad roamed the ruined city to find each other.

The hunt ended in a duel between two equal opponents, after which neither of them ever fired at another human being again.

While the Soviet propaganda machine stylized Saizev as an icon and advertising figure of the Red Army, cleverly concealing the fact that the hero of Stalingrad did not fire a single shot after the duel with Major Koenig, the German officer covered his tracks to turn his back on the insane battle forever. All that remained was the myth of the sniper Major Erwin Koenig.

Sophia Wallenda - Stalingrad 1
© W. T. Wallenda
all rights reserved by the author

STALINGRAD IN THE CROSSHAIRS

–

THE DUEL THE SNIPER

1

"If you think you've seen everything there is to see in war, you haven't been here!" the company commander shouted to the beardless lieutenant lying next to him in the trench.

The young officer nodded silently and tied an aftershave-soaked handkerchief to his nose. It was an ineffectual attempt to mask the disgusting, sweetly foul smell of rotting flesh that the wind carried over to them.

The company commander kept staring at his wristwatch. It wouldn't be long before the signal to attack. His heart was racing, his pulse was pounding. How many times had he raised his fist and shouted the order to charge? How many times had he jumped up with his men and charged forward? And how many times did he have to write hard words on white paper after the battles to tell the bereaved at home that their sons, husbands, brothers or fathers had fought bravely before they died a soldier's heroic death and gave their lives for the German people and the final victory?

What bloody nonsense! That's not heroism, that's mass slaughter! You mothers and fathers at home, be glad you can't see us die here, were the next thoughts that crept through the captain's mind.

The officer's palms grew damp. The reporter lying to his right fiddled with the radio. Finally, he tapped the shoulder of the 20-kilogram device and raised his thumb to indicate that all was well. "The switch is fixed," he shouted to drown out the wailing Jericho sirens of the attacking Stukas.

For days there had been a fierce battle in Stalingrad for Mamai Hill, known militarily as Hill 102. It stood like a monstrous watchtower between the southern city center and the large factories in the north. Whoever owned it controlled the city with their artillery. They had a clear view of the city center, the railway station, the factories and Stalingrad's lifeline, the Volga River.

Dramatic scenes took place on the river. Red Army soldiers were ferried across on ships and barges of all kinds, and had to sail through the deadly fire of German artillery. In places, burning oil slicks floated on the water. Black smoke robbed them not only of their sight, but also of their breath. If you sucked it in, it burned your lungs.

NCOs in earthy brown uniforms led the men, while officers shouted orders. The banks on both sides of the river resembled ant hills, swarming with insects.

Ships were hit, their hulls ripped open, planks burst, water entered and capsized them. Soldiers swam for their lives. The lucky ones were able to cling to a piece of driftwood. Most of them drowned. Bodies were floating around. Their lifeless bodies floated on the waves of the Volga, whose spray broke on the bows of the ships. The Soviet soldiers were in agony. They were helplessly exposed to the enemy's fire and the Volga's water. The shells whizzed incessantly, lowered their flight path and exploded. However, not only the river was targeted by the German artillery, but also the part of Mamai Hill occupied by the Russians.

Huuiiit - Wham

Splinters and shrapnel whirled through the air, digging into positions, trenches, bunker ceilings, and the flesh and bones of Red Army soldiers digging in to fight.

Once the height of 102 was taken, one would inevitably be the master of Stalingrad.

With this knowledge, the 295th Infantry Division had been

storming the Red Army positions for days. Yesterday evening they had almost succeeded, taking the lead with heavy losses. But the Russians had kept pumping new soldiers into the battle through the Volga lifeline, and after a counterattack in the morning, they had pushed the Germans back. Now the next counterattack was imminent.

At first, the corpses were removed during lulls in the fighting. This chivalrous last service was withheld for some time. The fighting became more intense and bitter. With great difficulty, the medics were able to rescue the wounded from the field of death. The fallen remained lying. Since the last Russian attack, the corpses had piled up.

The captain closed his eyes. He suspected what was waiting for him. The shells from the howitzers not only crashed into the barbed wire and the occupied Russian trenches, they also exploded en masse among the piles of corpses, shredding what was left of the human appearance of the dead.

The company commander knew that they would have to wade through a mixture of stinking blood and bones to reach their objective. He had seen the piles of corpses between them and the Russian trench through his binoculars, and it was clear what the explosive force of the shells that had detonated between them had done.

A chill ran through him. Goose bumps spread over his entire body. The officer's stomach rumbled. He swallowed the nausea and looked at the young lieutenant who lay trembling next to him.

That's not a bad idea with the scarf, he thought to himself.

Squadron after squadron of Stukas thundered over them. They dipped their noses and the deafening wail of their sirens sounded. For the German soldiers, it was liberating music; for the Red Army soldiers still holding the eastern slope of Mamai Hill, it was nothing more than the nerve-wracking announcement of death.

The pilots took aim at their targets, released the bombs, fired from their guns and pulled up the noses of their Ju 87s.

The air raid was the second wave of the attack. It was preceded by a heavy artillery barrage. The third and decisive wave was the infantry attack.

The captain clutched his submachine gun. A stick grenade was in the belt. He would lead his men to victory or go down with them. He had too many letters to write in his short time as company commander. The 295th Infantry Division was a top division and always on the front lines. Hard on the enemy. The price was human life.

His thoughts drifted home to beautiful Saxony-Anhalt. His son Rolf had graduated from high school last year. The captain knew that the Wehrmacht would come for him, since Rolf had long since been drafted. He went on the offensive, advising him to volunteer and choose an officer's career. This might have prevented him from being drafted and sent somewhere.

"If you do that, then try this way," he had advised him, and Rolf had listened. "As an officer, you might be able to stay here in Germany. Or you could come to France. That would be good too."

Rolf finally received his call to the Reich Labor Service and did his six months of compulsory service in East Prussia. His application was then accepted and he began his training as a flag officer.

They should transfer you anywhere but to Russia! I want to spare you that, my son. Damn war! What's happened to the world? I hate it! How did it come to this?

One of the bombs exploded very close to their positions. The detonation was loud and made the earth tremble. They pressed themselves firmly to the ground. The air pressure not only threw up dust, stones, and earth, but also tossed around shredded human parts. When a piece of stinking intestines and a rib with a flap of skin next to it landed in front of the lieutenant, he lifted the handkerchief he had tied to his mouth and threw up.

The requested group of assault engineers was getting ready. They would blast their way through the Russian wire tangles.

"Oh God, if you exist, help us survive this," the captain pressed his lips together.

The last group of Stukas finished the attack and the artillery shifted its fire to the Volga. A red flare shot up. That was the signal. He took another deep breath, then jumped up and shouted: "Attaaaack! Forward!"

At the same time, the stormtroopers jumped to their feet and rushed forward. Machine guns rattled, trying to stifle any possible resistance on the Russian side.

Rrrrrrrrr rrrrrrrrr

The captain gasped. He was close behind the engineers. His men followed with a loud "Hurraaaa!" on their lips. They screamed their fears from their souls.

Mamai Hill began to come alive. Soldiers rose and ran up. At the top and on the occupied flanks, Red Army soldiers crawled out of cover and took up defensive fire. Russian artillery joined in. Machine guns rattled and tore the first holes in the attacking ranks. Again and again, hit soldiers fell to the ground. Some lay motionless, others writhed in pain.

The way up was difficult. There was no cover. The reality was worse than the captain had imagined. The terrain was littered with body parts. Shrapnel of various sizes had to be walked around or through. A mixture of blood, human parts and bones collected in them like in a soup kettle. You had to try, but you couldn't avoid everything that was disgusting. Again and again, boots sank into this blood soup, or the chest of a fallen man was stepped on, crushed, and stinking foul gases were expelled with muffled noises reminiscent of gasps.

The company commander saw one of the sappers fall.

Shot in the head, he registered.

The soldier collapsed like a wet sack. Immediately after, the next sapper fell to the ground, hit. The officer pointed his machine gun in the direction of the Russian trenches and fired two rounds, then raised his hand and waved it vigorously at the storm troopers.

"Cover the engineer attack! Barrage fire! The machine guns are supposed to protect them, damn it!" he shouted to his reporters, who both tried to keep up.

The howling of several Katyushas could be heard.

Huuuiiiiii huuiiiiii

"Full cover! Stalin organ!"

They threw themselves to the ground. The captain rushed into a larger shell hole. He smelled burning. He avoided looking around.

Wham wham wham

Impacts could be heard. The warheads of the missiles crashed into the ground again and again. Fortunately, most of them missed the lines of the attackers. The referees passed on the order they had received earlier. When the radio operator tried to repeat the order, he was shot in the head.

The second!

The captain suspected it. He raised his head in a flash and looked around. "Out! Run!"

They rose and ran toward their target. The machine-gun fire was shifted. The engineers only managed to fight their way close to the Russians' wire tangle with two more breaks in cover. The noise of battle raged. Men yelled, wounded men screamed. Medics rushed around, helping where they could, applying bandages or waving for their medics to carry the seriously wounded to safety on stretchers. The captain gave a tactical signal to the platoon leader of the second platoon. He acknowledged and was shot in the neck. Then the young lieutenant collapsed, mortally wounded.

This is the work of snipers! Those damn bastards!

Wham - wham

Two loud explosions were heard. The engineers had blown up an alley.

Where is that damned sniper?

He had to abandon the idea and keep running, leading his men through that alley.

Then come and get me, you damn sniper!

The officer raised his fist. "Forward!"

A machine gun hammered away, firing a barrage. A second and a third machine gun joined in. Soldiers trickled through the alley of the Drahtverhaus. The sappers blew open a second way. One of the men got his uniform caught in the wire mesh. He struggled for twenty seconds to free himself, cut the wire with a pair of pliers, and when he finally got free, a bullet shredded his lung.

More and more Landser poured into the Russian position. Bitter trench warfare ensued. On the left flank, a light machine gun was pushed over the edge of the trench. An attacking squad ran directly into the fire. Two men were killed instantly, two were seriously wounded, one slightly.

One of the storm troopers had gotten close enough to throw a hand grenade. Panting, he unscrewed the safety cap, then took a quick look. He grabbed the trigger, pulled the cord, lifted his torso, and hurled the grenade in the direction of the firing machine gun. Rolling in the air, the stick grenade flew relentlessly toward its target, descending, landing in the trench, and detonating just three meters from the machine gun.

Boom!

With the detonation, the soldiers jumped up and covered the last few meters to the trench. The machine gun was blown away. The two gunmen were lying on the ground in pieces. Three Red Army soldiers ran into the trench. The first soldier opened fire from his PPSch 41, shooting from the hip as he ran. Most of the bullets hit the trench wall, but three or four hit a fellow soldier in the chest.

"He got Willi! Ivan's coming from the left!"

Panic was in his voice. The young private, who had warned of the impending danger, knelt down, raised his 98 carbine and fired a shot. At the same moment, the Russian with the Shpagin stumbled over a dead man. He lost his submachine gun. Now the other Germans also fired, killing the other two Russians. The stumbling man remained lying. He slowly raised his head and looked into the young corporal's eyes. He had fired and was pointing at him with trembling hands. The Red Army soldier waited for the fatal shot and looked at his enemy. He looked deeply into the eyes of the corporal. The barrel of the carbine wobbled considerably. Up and down, left and right.

The corporal whined nervously: "Ruki vverkh! Hands up, damn it!"

"Shoot him down!" they shouted.

"Get your fucking hands up," the innkeeper slobbered, more than excited.

The Russian wondered for a moment if he should try to grab his submachine gun and kill as many Germans as possible. The PPSch 41 lay on the ground not a meter away from him. He squinted at it for a moment. Pictures of his children flashed through his mind. His wife smiled at him. It was then that he decided to surrender. He knew this young German soldier would not pull the trigger. Otherwise, he would have done so long ago. The decision for death or captivity, for death or life, was made in a split second. He had made his and slowly raised his hands. He knew that here and now he had no other choice.

"I have a prisoner!"

Meanwhile, the trench warfare continued. The defenders fought tenaciously, not retreating a single meter voluntarily. A Red Army soldier emptied his carbine, hit a Landser in the abdomen, turned the rifle around and hit the attacker in the face with the butt. You could hear bones breaking. The eyes took on an unnatural color. The look was broken. It was the look of a dead man. The soldier fell backwards and lay twisted.

The man behind the fallen man fired, but in mortal fear missed his target. As he fired, the Russian shattered his shoulder with the butt of his rifle. Only the third German was able to stop the Red Army soldier with a shot to the chest. He staggered, spitting blood, but raised his Mosin Nagant carbine again to strike. Before he could bring the weapon forward, the compatriot's next shot pierced the Soviet's neck. Blood gushed from the wound with every heartbeat. The Russian dropped the carbine and grabbed his neck with both hands. A minute later he had lost the battle.

"Medic! Over here!" yelled the shooter, kneeling beside his comrade with the shattered shoulder. "Hang in there, Heinz. They'll get you out of here in a minute!"

A sergeant ran up to the captain. His uniform was covered with blood.

"Captain, we need reinforcements. The Russians are counterattacking on the right flank. We may have knocked them out of the trenches, but we can't hold this position for long!"

The next volley from a Stalin organ whizzed in and plowed the ground. This time the strikes were dangerously close.

Huuuuuuuuuuuuuuuuuuuuuu ... wham wham wham wham

"Get down!" was shouted.

Another volley came roaring in. The sergeant squinted up,

ducked even lower, but knew that this volley would pass over them without danger.

The captain had a similar reaction. "How many men have you lost, Mueller?"

"The platoon has shrunk to group size! We need support immediately or we'll all die," he added vehemently.

The veteran soldier's expression worried the officer. Mueller was not one to give up easily or to complain without cause. The Twelve could be counted on blindly. The company commander recognized fear and panic.

The reporter fumbled with the knapsack radio. The radio, which weighed about 20 kilograms, had a range of up to 25 kilometers with its 2 watts of power. He raised his hand and shouted to the captain, "I've got the battalion's battle staff on it. Tell them to hold the line!"

The officer nodded and turned to the dispatcher. "Run to Sergeant Brückmann immediately. Have the grenade launchers move to the right flank immediately! Now!"

"Understood, Captain!" the young soldier shouted and ran off, crouching.

"Pass the word to the battalion staff that we urgently need replacements. The reserve company must come here immediately!" he shouted to the signalman, trying to drown out the noise of the renewed battle. Then he tapped a second signalman on the shoulder. "Run over to Lieutenant Funke. Tell him to cover the left flank with his men. I also want all machine guns in position immediately. The lightly wounded are to go with the medics through the ranks of the fallen and support them."

"Got it!"

He turned back to the reporter. "And now report to the battalion that we absolutely need artillery support. Tell them to keep the eastern slope under fire. The Russians are stubbornly holding out there."

The man at the radio immediately went to work, flipping switches and pressing buttons. At short, regular intervals, he pushed the button and tried again to reach the battalion's command staff. "This is Saturn Two .... This is Saturn Two .... the enemy is counterattacking ...

21

strong infantry units are forming on the right wing in section four-one. .... We need backup and artillery support .... I repeat .... the enemy..."

The transmission impulses found their way through modern technology. The words crawled over coils and wire coils down copper cables to the antenna. The radio operator hoped that the man at the receiver would be able to pick them up on this wavelength, listen, take notes, and pass them on.

The artillery shells whizzed over their heads and crashed again into the eastern slope of Mamai Hill. They turned over the earth, burying corpses and bringing up parts of men that had already been buried. The smell of burnt flesh, powdery smoke, and warm blood filled the air. There was also the constant stench of decay. Many of the fallen had been lying around for days, and there was no hope of a humane burial at this time.

The dark veil of death hung over the city.

They lay in the trench, waiting for the counterattack. The captain peered through his binoculars. He looked at his wristwatch. The glass was dirty. He moistened his finger and wiped it, then ran the sleeve of his uniform over the glass again.

Damn Russians! Where are they hiding? They can't survive such Ari attacks! Where do they get their fighting spirit?

Reduced to the strength of barely two platoons, the men had pretty much reached the end of what was bearable.

"Any news from the battalion?" he asked the reporter.

A shake of the head. "Nothing."

The officer knew he wouldn't be able to hold the position for long without reinforcements. "Damn it! Where's the reserve?"

The enemy rose. Red Army soldiers ran toward their position like a brown, flaccid wall. The Russian machine-gun fire rattled incessantly and gave a barrage.

"Urääähhhh ..."

There it was again. That battle cry that cut to the bone. Whipped up by officers and fired up by political commissars, they crawled out of their shelters, gathered like a pack of wild animals and attacked, driven by hate, fear and rage. They shouted as loud as they could.

"Uräääääähhhhh ..."

The defensive lines waited for the order to fire.

"Don't fire yet! Tell the grenade launchers to get ready!"

Nerves were on edge. Mortal fear spread and crept into the minds of the men. Some of the soldiers were shaking, some were wetting themselves, others were vomiting.

"Prepare to fire!"

More and more projectiles whizzed over them, piercing the earth or the corpses lying around. The first hits had to be taken.

"They're damn close already," Sergeant Mueller urged.

"Just a moment!"

The roar of the charging Russians became louder and louder: "Uräääääähhhh ..."

The salvation: "Now!" was shouted.

The German soldiers opened fire. Machine guns fired volley after volley from their barrels. The first ranks of the attacking Red Army soldiers were seized and crushed as if by an invincible fist. Blood spurted, and men fell dead or wounded to the ground. The third rank threw themselves for cover. The screams and cries of the wounded mingled with the din of battle.

A squad leader of the light grenade launchers watched the impact of his explosives and directed the fire. "20 right - 40 short - open fire!"

Plop - plop - plop - wham wham wham

Grenade after grenade whirled through the air, lowered its trajectory, and died in the crowd of attacking Soviet soldiers.

After the fifth volley, he was shot in the head.

"I need more ammo!" yelled a machine gunner as his gunner II inserted the last belt.

Then he pressed the butt of the LMG 34 into his shoulder, aimed at the brown human mass rolling toward them, and pulled the trigger.

Rrrrrrt ... rrrt ... rrrrrrrt

The bullets were chased out of the barrel and flew toward their targets, piercing the attackers' kneecaps, thighs, stomachs, and chests.

"Right!" the shooter heard. "Swing around now!"

Then there was a boom so loud he could not hear. At the same time, he felt a strong air pressure that ripped the gun away from him and threw him to the side. His entire body felt numb and warm. He lowered his eyes in shock and saw only blood, bones, and a torn uniform. Then he collapsed.

"Right machine gun taken out by hand grenade!"

Sergeant Mueller saw some Russians jump into the trench. He swung his submachine gun around and crooked his trigger finger. Again and again he swung the barrel around and fired bursts until the magazine was empty.

The captain was about to give the order to retreat when he heard a loud "Hurraaaaaaaa".

"They're here. The second company has arrived and is about to counterattack," the executioner shouted.

Two groups of men met. Field-gray uniforms against earth-brown. Bayonets flashed, spades with sharpened edges were swung. Melee broke out.

The captain knew what to do. "Forward, comrades! Attack!" he shouted this hated order as loud as he could, clambered over the edge of the trench and charged at the enemy.

"Forward!" he heard Mueller say, and he knew the men would follow him. They would run, shout, and fight. They would rush to the aid of their comrades in hand-to-hand combat and use this counterattack to beat back the enemy.

"Hurraaaaaaaa!"

He felt a bullet whiz past his head, raised the submachine gun and emptied the clip. Then he reached to his side, drew the 08 pistol from its holster and charged forward. A Red Army soldier ran toward him with his mouth open. He held the rifle out like a spear. The bayonet was in place. The captain fired two shots from the 08 and the attacker fell to the ground. Just as the officer turned, he received a blow to the shoulder from the butt of the rifle. A sharp pain shot through him. He dropped the pistol and dropped to his knees. A Russian soldier, his face contorted with rage, raised his carbine for the fatal second blow. Anticipating the fatal blow and unable to react, the captain closed his eyes. A loud scream, distorted with pain, brought him back from his seconds of lethargy. The Russian staggered. Blood spurted as a soldier pulled the bayonet from the Red Army soldier's neck. The soldier looked at the captain for a moment, then charged.

The officer fumbled for his pistol, took it in his fist, and rubbed the sore spot on his shoulder. He was about to get up when he felt a blow to his right knee. As he lay there, a bloodied Russian had kicked the German officer in the knee. The captain stumbled. The Russian got up and pounced on the German like a wounded panther. He grabbed the captain by the throat and squeezed. Again and again he uttered incomprehensible words. Only then did the officer realize that the Russian's jaw was broken.

The Soviet literally dug his fingers into the German's throat. While the captain's left hand grabbed the Russian's forearm and tried to pull him away, his right hand pointed the barrel of the .08 pistol at the attacker's body. The captain could not breathe. He had to act quickly and pull the trigger before everything went black before his eyes. He wanted to live!

The index finger curled. A shot rang out, then another. After the second crack, the chokehold loosened. The Russian gasped, collapsed lifelessly over the officer, burying him beneath him.

Breathe!

He struggled for oxygen. The weight of the Russian made it extremely difficult to breathe. He tried to roll the dead man off him, but it didn't work.

Screams, yells, wails. Gunshots, rattling metal, gurgling noises and shouted orders suddenly became muffled. Everything began to spin. Stars danced around. The Russian moved a little. The captain breathed deeply. He needed oxygen, too much to die and too little to live. The urge to breathe grew. Another feat of strength followed. With the strength of desperation, he finally managed to push himself out from under the corpse. Panting, he gasped for air. He was drenched in sweat. His shoulder hurt and it was getting dark. Breathing became gasping, stars flickered before his eyes. He succumbed to unconsciousness and fell over.

Example photo

PA-0-13 Fliegerangriff / Air raid
Privatarchiv Author

all rights reserved by the author

2

Until well into August 1942, there was little sign of war in Stalingrad. Although the Germans were advancing rapidly, the Russian troops were not in the city but in the surrounding countryside. The construction of defensive positions was also slow. As a result, life in Stalingrad was almost as it had been in peacetime.

Life in the city on the Volga was vibrant, and its suburbs formed a vegetative contrast to the vast steppe leading to it from the west.

Cherry and peach trees burst with green and bore masses of fruit. In the villages, chickens and geese ran around the thatched houses. Panje horses grazed peacefully or pulled the loaded carts of the simple farmers.

Besides the railroad, the Volga was the main artery to Moscow. It was as wide as a huge lake and flowed lazily along the city for 15 kilometers. Ships docked in Stalingrad's harbor, brought goods and people into the city, filled their bellies, and sailed on.

The huge granary, built near the Volga, could be seen several kilometers from the city.

The "Barrikaden" artillery factory, the "Lazur" chemical factory, the "Red October" steel plant, and the "Dzerzhinsky" tractor factory, which was completed in 1930, but whose production had been switched to tanks, especially the T-34, brought prosperity to Stalin-grad.

Housing estates were built for the workers, and parks were used for local recreation. There were cafes, shops, cinemas, and hospitals. Stalin, who gave his name to this southern Russian metropolis, implemented his first Stalin Five-Year Plan here.

Sunday, August 23, 1942, was a gloriously warm and sunny day. The sun was shining over Stalingrad, and Katja Kalikova was happy and in a good mood as she put a scarf over her packed picnic basket. Their destination, like that of many other Stalingrad families, was the Mamayev Kurgan, the big green hill on the Volga. From here they had a wonderful view of the city and the river. Pure idyll in the best of weather.

"I would rather go to the little bay on the Volga and swim. I'm sure my friends will be there," Grigory begged, looking at his mother with big eyes.

"Not today, Grisha." She often liked to call him by his nickname. "We'll meet dad at Mamai Hill. You were looking forward to the picnic."

The eight-year-old stomped his feet angrily on the ground. "But it's summer and..."

"...and I've prepared a chicken. Look," Katja countered in a quiet voice, lifting the dishcloth over the picnic basket.

Grisha peeked inside. "Yummy! Oh yes. Picnic with chicken. What else you got in the basket?" he exclaimed happily, and the boy stuck a hand into the picnic basket.

"Slow down, Grisha, not so fast," Katja laughed.

When the boy found Russian rolls among the bread, he forgot all about swimming in the Volga. "When is daddy coming?"

"He said he wouldn't stay long. You know, he has to visit some of his patients in the hospital, and then he'll come straight to us."

"And maybe he'll go swimming with me and Boris later."

Katja laughed. "Yes, Grisha, that can definitely happen."

"A great day."

Boris, Grisha's younger brother by a year and a half, came into the kitchen. "Are we going swimming?" he asked.

Grisha grinned. "We're going to do something much better. We'll go to the Mamayev Kurgan and play Cossack fortress. The enemies will come up the Volga in their sailing ships, and we will sit on a watchtower and watch them. We'll eat chicken and buns, and if the pirates attack, we'll beat them back with our sabres!"

"Hurray!" cheered Boris, "we are the brave Cossacks!"

Katja Kalikova came from a small village near Stalingrad. Her ancestors were Don Cossacks, and the handsome Russian embodied the wild and racy like no other.

The nurse met her husband, Pyotr, when he was a medical student and she was a student nurse. They became a couple and got married. He graduated, and after graduation they both got jobs at the Stalingrad hospital. The young couple could afford a good apartment and they felt very much at home here. With the birth of their sons, Grigory and Boris, the young family's happiness was complete.

Mamai Hill was busy, and Katja was glad that her favorite spot was still free. It was here that she had kissed Pyotr for the first time. She would never forget that night. He took her in his arms, told her that her eyes were brighter than the stars, that his heart was hotter than the sun, and that his love for her was as endless as the universe. She absorbed every word. And when their lips touched, her heart beat three times faster than normal.

Katja stood still. Her sons were close behind her.

"Here again?" asked Grisha, dropping the blanket. He knew his mother would say yes, because they always sat here. Only once, when the seat was occupied, they went to the other side. Where you could see the veld. But the boys liked this place better. From here you could see the Volga and the ships. This spurred the imagination of the two brothers and they had one adventure after another in the game. Here stood their imaginary Cossack fortress, which they defended with sabres made of willow branches.

"Yes, children. We'll stay here. Give me a quick hand with the blanket so you can play."

"When is father coming?"

Katja looked at her watch. "We have to wait a little longer. But I can give you a little piece of cake and then ..." She couldn't finish the sentence. She was drowned out by a loud: "Yes ... yes ... food for the brave Cossacks".

A little later Katja sat on the blanket and read a book. Bees flew from flower to flower. Birdsong accompanied the laughter of children frolicking about. A few feet away, a young couple dreamed of true love. They whispered and giggled. Katja put down the book, lifted her head and smiled as she saw the couple flirting fervently. Then she looked at her sons. Boris and Grisha were jumping across the meadow, slashing at imaginary pirates with their willow sabres, and cheering when their little Cossack army managed to put the pirates to flight.

Katja enjoyed the sun. She put the book down, stretched and changed her sitting position. Her stomach rumbled and she wondered how long it would be before Pyotr arrived. The young mother was about to reach for her book again when she suddenly felt uneasy.

Somewhere nearby a loudspeaker was screeching. A tinny voice could be heard over and over again. "Citizens - Air Alert!" Then a siren sounded.

At first, the Sister was annoyed by this disturbance of the heavenly idyll. Lately, the false alarms had become more frequent. She didn't want to be bothered by the alarm and continued reading, but as soon as she started, she stumbled. This time was different. The announcements didn't stop. They kept echoing: "Citizens - air alert!" - followed by the deafening wail of sirens.

Katja became nervous. Dozens of people were hurriedly packing their things and leaving Mamai Hill. She checked her watch again, then looked for her boys. They were gone. There was a slight fear.

"Grisha, Boris," she called.

Nothing. Katja got up and put on her shoes. "Grisha, Boris," she repeated louder now.

"Mama, over here. Come on, quick!"

She turned around, relieved. She had found her boys. Both children were standing at the top of the hill, pointing toward the steppe. Katja ran up the hill. The view was clear. The sun was making the horizon shimmer a little, but she thought she could see a large cloud of dust in the steppe that seemed to be heading toward the city.

"What's that, Mom?"

The piercing wail of the sirens continued to be interrupted by urgent warnings: "Citizens - air alert!"

Boris pointed to the sky. "Look!" he said, and that was enough to give the sister goose bumps all over her body. She was surrounded by sheer panic. People were staring at the sky, running, leaving their belongings behind. Women were screaming, men were calling for their children.

Over the rising din of the screaming people, a low hum could be heard, steadily increasing, as if someone was turning a dial. Katja stared at the crowd, which had started out like a swarm of insects and had quickly grown to the size of a flock of birds. The Russian knew they weren't birds. They were airplanes. German planes. They were heading straight for the city. Katja turned white as a sheet. Her heart was pounding, her pulse was racing. At that moment, panic gripped her as well.

"Give me your hands and run, children!" she cried.

"Mommy, the chicken!"

"Run!" Katja screamed, grabbed her sons' hands and ran.

They raced down the hill. Not all the visitors to the Mamayev Kurgan had realized what was happening. The little family ran past a group of young men who were singing drunken songs and laughing as they opened another bottle of wine.

"Flyers!" she shouted to the people.

The young men waved back. "What's your hurry, pretty lady? Come on, let's have some fun."

Katja ran on, pulling her sons with her. An elderly couple had taken a nap in the sun, woke up and just stared, shaking their heads in disbelief. Others, realizing the seriousness of the situation, began to pack hastily.

Katja knew where the nearest shelter was. That was their destination. Boris began to cry. Grisha kept turning around, threatening to stumble, but his mother's strong hand prevented him from falling.

Not only on the hill, but also in the streets of Stalingrad, the warning words from the loudspeakers were not taken seriously at first. Only when the hum of the bombers' engines grew louder and the anti-aircraft guns in front of the city began to fire, did the people of Stalingrad realize that they were under attack.

600 bombers of the 4th German Air Force flew towards Stalingrad and darkened the sky. Aircraft of all types, but mainly Heinkel He 111 and Junkers Ju 88 bombers, attacked the city on that sunny Sunday afternoon, dropping their deadly bombs.

Tons of high-explosive and incendiary bombs fell on Stalin Square. The explosives swirled down on the houses, hitting them and bringing death and destruction. Buildings collapsed thunderously. Scorching fire swept through the streets. People fled to the Volga to escape across the river. All the boats and ships filled up in a flash. Those who couldn't find a place tried to swim to the other side of the river.

The huge oil depots of the factories were hit by several bombs and set on fire. The burning oil poured into the Volga. The floating carpet of fire caught ships full of fleeing civilians. They could not escape the terrible death by fire.

Meanwhile, the heat of the fires raging and coalescing in the city sucked in the air. Whirlwinds of fire formed and again swept through the ruins with unimaginable destructive power.

The bombs of the next wave of attacks exploded in this inferno. The German Luftwaffe launched attack after attack. A huge wave of destruction swept over the city on the Volga.

The inferno lasted for three hours. Then Stalingrad was nothing but a burning pile of rubble, its soot-black veil of death shooting up for miles and visible far into the steppe.

The peaceful, happy, smiling Stalingrad, as we had known it until that moment, had ceased to exist. 40,000 people fell victim to the air raid. They were burned to death, torn apart by bombs, crushed by collapsing buildings, or buried in cellars. More than three times as many people were injured.

At the same time, German soldiers were advancing on Stalingrad. The first suburbs on the Volga River had already been reached when the flames of the city erupted. The soldiers saw the burning Stalingrad and believed in a quick victory.

Katja Kalikova huddled against the wall. Boris sat on her lap, and Grisha, pressed close to her, sat beside her. The shelter was overcrowded. The air was suffocatingly thick. It smelled of sweat, urine and fear. Prayers were being said. Children cried, babies cried. The ground shook again and again. Detonations could be heard and the extent of the destruction could be imagined.

Pjotr. Where are you? Please live!

Katja's thoughts were with her husband. She suspected the worst, wanted to be weak, cry, scream, punch the walls and run out, but she had a job to do. She had to protect her two sons. Grisha and Boris were all she had. They were her love. She had to protect them and get them out of the city. She had to be strong.

A thick lump formed in Katja's throat. She closed her eyes. A tear rolled down her cheek and seeped into her light blouse. Grishka saw it and squeezed his mother's hand. Boris just sat there motionless, staring ahead.

"Is daddy coming?" whimpered Grisha.

Katja returned his firm handshake. She couldn't answer. Her voice broke, but Grisha knew what this handshake meant. He was the man of the house now. He had to take care of his mother and brother. He, who only two hours ago had been a Cossack fighting pirates with his willow sabre, now had to feed his little family. Grisha took a deep breath. His stomach rumbled, he felt the roll cake trying to find its way up, suppressed the feeling of nausea and swallowed the thin spit that gathered in his mouth.

I do not surrender. I am a man. I will protect Mom and Boris!

He hugged his mother even tighter, put his other hand on his brother's knee, closed his eyes and began to cry softly.

Example photo

PA-0060-Landser vor dem Einsatz
Landser before combat deployment

Privatarchiv Author
all rights reserved by the author

3

The hard-fought battles for Hill 102 brought disillusionment to the German commanders. Contrary to initial reports, the fall of Stalingrad was far from imminent. On the contrary. The Soviet resistance was extremely stubborn and growing by the day.

The city was to be held as long as possible by the Russian defenders. This tied up the German troops while the Russian commanders in Moscow worked feverishly on a counteroffensive.

Stalingrad had long since been reduced to rubble. Hardly a house remained standing. The battle took a new turn. It would become a war of rats. Every part of the city, every street, every building, every floor was to be fought over bitterly. Not a single yard was surrendered without a fight.

The Russian snipers were particularly effective on Mamai Hill. Among them was the son of a peasant from the Urals, Vasily Saizev. He was not only very accurate, but also full of ideas.

At his suggestion, a new sniper movement was created in the 62nd Army. Snipers and their scouts were deployed in groups in the regiments. These small groups positioned themselves along the front lines and repeatedly inflicted casualties on the German troops. They would usually set up one to three camouflaged hideouts, lie in wait for a target, strike, and immediately move to the next hideout.

This approach decimated the enemy and destroyed their psyche. Sniper teams quickly earned a reputation for terror. They were invisible, they lurked where no enemy was suspected, they were silent, and when they struck, they brought certain death.

The 295th Infantry Division had not only suffered heavy casualties in the battles for Height 102, but had also lost an enormous number of officers to the use of Russian snipers. Saizev and his men had shown themselves to be masters of their deadly craft.

The captain's company suffered more than two-thirds of its losses. On the same day, it was removed from the front line and transferred to the stage for rest and refreshment.

While the company staff stayed with the troops in a collective farm in a suburb of Stalingrad, the platoons were housed in the nearby Balka, a natural erosion gorge.

The office was located in a small outhouse. The second room was used as a storeroom and also as a living room for the company sergeant.

The writing room was heated by a small stove. Three tables were converted into desks. There was a typewriter on each one. Letters were also piled up on the first table. All of them had a black border.

As soon as they got up, Sergeant Major Schmidt had lit the fire and put on a kettle of water. Schmidt was a lively little fellow whom everyone respected. Freshly shaved and eager for a cup of hot coffee, he took the boiling water from the stove and carefully poured it into a filter.

"Mhmm ... smells good," he muttered and set the kettle aside. His eyes fell on the letters and he shook his head. His good mood had suddenly vanished.

The door opened and the captain entered the study.

"Good morning, Captain Koenig," Schmidt greeted him.

"Good morning."

"Coffee will be ready soon."

"Thank you."

The officer hung his cap and coat on a nail on the wall, walked to the largest of the three desks, and sat down. He lifted the typewriter to the center. To his right lay the broken identification tags of the fallen, to his left white typing paper. He took a sheet and fed it into the machine.

"How's the shoulder today?" asked Schmidt, pouring water into the filter again. The smell of freshly brewed coffee wafted in.

"It's better, but I can't lift my arm any higher than this ..." at the same time he made a movement that ended with a face contorted in pain.

"Is letter-writing any good?" the Spike said, indicating the amount of work involved. "I could also..."

"Schmidt, they were my people. I fought with them. They fell and I survived. I must write these letters myself." He emphasized the word "must" extremely. "It is not easy, and every single letter is difficult for me, but if I were to delegate this work, it would be like a denial of the highest honor from my point of view."

"I see," the company sergeant replied, placing three cups on the table and pouring.

The door opened and a corporal entered. He limped in and greeted the other two soldiers.

"Good morning, Otto. You set your watch by my coffee," the spit returned the morning greeting.

"As soon as my leg is healthy again, I'll run away from your coffee," the corporal laughed. "I always say take a spoonful less and it will taste better, but no..."

"Coffee just has to taste like coffee. You can also use Mu-cke-fuck for colored water," Schmidt grinned and served the coffee.

Captain Koenig took a sip. The corporal was absolutely right. The coffee wasn't exactly good, but it was a wake-up call. It was strong and black. The officer put down the cup and picked up the next brand.

"Lieutenant Erich Kleindienst," he read aloud.

Pictures flashed through his mind. He relived the terrible hours of battle. The young lieutenant was right next to him when he was shot in the head.

"A sniper," the captain muttered. His thoughts immediately turned to Germany and his son.

It could have been Rolf. My God, I hope my boy doesn't have to go to Russia. Damn snipers!

More sniper hits caught his eye.

They also got the engineer. And many others. There are only two officers left in our company. Lieutenant Funke and me.

Captain Koenig leaned back. He had noticed something. He thought about it, made a quick note and pushed the lieutenant's badge aside.

The enemy was outnumbered. They fought hard and stubbornly and definitely had very effective snipers.

They're not just firing wildly at us, trying to kill as many as they can, but they're choosing their targets carefully, killing where it hurts.

Sniping has always been Koenig's hobby. His father was a gunsmith at heart and introduced him to guns as a child. As a boy, he hung on his father's every word when he talked about the front lines in World War I. And the little boy found the stories about the snipers particularly exciting.

"My son, you couldn't even walk on the thunderbolt without fearing they'd get you. They literally stole our sleep," he said.

When Erwin Koenig was 17 years old, he received the news of his death. His father had been killed at Verdun. For Kaiser, people and fatherland.

Erwin's mother, a teacher of German, Russian and English, never got over her husband's death and took her own life two years later. It was to her that Erwin owed his foreign language skills, some of which he taught himself.

After leaving school, Erwin Koenig decided to study engineering and married his wife Ilse while still a student. Their son, Rolf, was born in 1924.

Koenig quickly rose through the ranks of his company. His language skills allowed him to work in Russia and England. When Ilse died of severe pneumonia eight years later, he stayed in Germany with Rolf and gave up his corporate career.

Rolf went to boarding school and was a model student. Erwin was very proud of his son. His son loved guns as much as his father and grandfather. The two spent their weekends in Grandpa Koenig's old workshop, tinkering with guns and repairing hunters' weapons.

They were also among the best shooters. They won several tournaments and gave shooting demonstrations at smaller village festivals.

Then the war broke out. Erwin Koenig, a lieutenant in the reserves, had to enlist. Initially assigned as a platoon leader, the eloquent engineer quickly attracted attention.

Even as a platoon leader, Koenig distinguished himself in battle and was quickly promoted to first lieutenant and finally captain.

Koenig was transferred to the regimental staff. There he served as an assistant commander, where, among other things, he was instrumental in training the regiment's own sharpshooters.

Koenig had never forgotten what his father had told him about the deadly sharpshooters of World War I, and he attached great importance to the phenomenon of sharpshooters spreading fear and thus weakening the enemy's psyche.

He talked to the weapons master, had captured Russian sniper rifles shown to him, and studied how they worked. He demanded a lot from the selected snipers, but nothing he did not demand of himself.

Some of his individual training sessions went too far for his superiors. Even though they were aware of the snipers' effectiveness, they were given little respect and were still disparagingly referred to as sharpshooters. They embodied something sneaky, mean, and disreputable. No senior non-commissioned officer, and certainly no officer, took up the telescopic rifle. Except Captain Erwin Koenig.

He taught the men his way of looking at things and instructed them not only in weapons, but also in tactics and camouflage.

Soon rumors began to circulate about him, and behind closed doors people talked about one or two heroic deeds that never happened. Erwin Koenig had a reputation as a noble marksman without ever having fired a shot at an enemy. He became a phantom, and the word spread quickly.

This reputation and the general opinion about the sharpshooters should bring him back to the fighting troops.

One day the regimental commander said to Captain Koenig: "If you want to reach the rank of major, my dear Koenig, and possibly aspire to a good post in Berlin, I advise you to prove yourself again as a leader of a combat unit. Only there will your medals and your reputation as a good officer grow. I thought we might appoint you company commander for six months and then make you deputy battalion commander."

"Major?" came the hesitant and surprised reply.

"I like your abilities, Koenig. Not only are you a talented linguist, you're also a real expert with weapons. We need people like you back home. Especially where important decisions are made regarding the choice of weapons, etc. You would also spend more time with your son.

Erwin Koenig didn't have to think long. He had a longing for Rolf, a longing for home, a longing for peace. He wanted to wake up in a soft bed in the morning, to bathe whenever he wanted, and to go to a

39

restaurant for a meal when he was hungry.

This was in the spring of 1942, and he agreed. Weeks went by and suddenly he was told: "One more city, one more battle. We'll get Stalingrad and you'll be home for Christmas, Captain Koenig."

Now he was sitting here in the steppe before Stalingrad and had to write more letters of condolence than ever before. He had seen hell on earth and knew that this battle was far from being won.

Koenig picked up the fallen lieutenant's badge again. He turned it between his fingers and finally placed it in front of him.

"Schmidt, I need an appointment with the old man!"

The first sergeant raised his head. "You mean the Battalion Commander, Captain?"

"No, I mean the regimental commander."

Schmidt reached for the bakelite receiver of the field telephone.

"Ask for Lieutenant Colonel Harras. He knows me and will see me."

The first sergeant, who had the rank of sergeant major, shook his head. "As if I could speak directly to the lieutenant colonel. I'll get the outer office!"

"You'll be fine, Schmidt."

While the spit tried to make the call, Captain Koenig typed the beginning of the next sad letter on the white sheet of paper.

He knew what the parents wanted to read. They wanted their sons to be heroes.

This young lieutenant was a hero to them!

Again, the captain saw the young officer before him. He will not write to his parents about how Lieutenant Kleindienst trembled beside him or how he had to vomit because of the disgusting stench. He will write them that he was brave. His parents made the greatest sacrifice a war can ask. They gave up their child.

I don't want to sacrifice my child, he thought to himself and typed the first words on the paper.

Click, click, click, click...

The sound of the typewriter resembled the monotony of grief. Each stroke will bring a tear of despair. This letter will be read a thousand times, and a thousand times it will evoke deep sadness and incomprehension.

Even worse than the battle itself was the task of informing the bereaved of their loved one's death.

Captain Koenig tried to take enough time to find the right words for each of his men. If possible, he tried to add something personal. But that often didn't work. In the end, his name would be at the bottom of a letter that no one wanted to receive. A letter that, with its few grams, weighed so much that it could crush people.

Dear Mrs. Kleindienst,
Dear Mr. Kleindienst.

I hereby fulfill my heavy duty to inform you that your son, Lieutenant Erich Kleindienst, was killed in action at the age of 20.
While attacking a Soviet position on Mamai Hill, he heroically charged the enemy at the head of his platoon. Thanks to his courage and fighting spirit, we achieved a decisive victory in the Battle of Stalingrad.
Erich was shot in the head and died instantly. He didn't have to suffer.
Your son was buried in Stalingrad with full military honors. As soon as time permits, I will send you a photo of his grave.

Sincerely yours
Erwin Koenig
Captain
Company Commander

Koenig wrote ten more letters that morning. The loss rate was immense. Finally, he pushed the typewriter aside and got up.

The field telephone rang shrilly. Schmidt picked it up. "1st Company office, Schmidt. ... Who is this? .... Oh, it's you. You old sewer rat. When did you join the Utilities Department? ... You'll have to tell me more about that. Now to the point. What's going on? ... No... this is a surprise. Great. So I'll send someone over ... over."

The spit hung up. "That was my old comrade Heini Kanzelbauer. We're getting cutlery. I'm supposed to send someone backstage to pick up the stuff."

"Then send Sergeant Mahlmeister away in his Opel Blitz. That's good news."

"Otto, will you jump out and..." Schmidt choked off the sentence when he saw the grim look on his comrade's face.

The corporal stood up and muttered: "Jump? If you want to make fun of me, please do it another way. I'll limp away and tell that fat bastard Mahlmeister. But only because I've run out of tobacco for my pipe."

"Can you manage that, Corporal Remmler?" Koenig asked.

"Play, Captain. I need to move my leg anyway."

Koenig nodded in agreement.

The field telephone rang again.

"What's going on now? Everybody wants something from us right before lunch. It's a real milking of the mice," the sergeant grumbled, just as you'd expect a grumpy, bad-tempered, respectful company sergeant to do. He picked up the phone and grumbled into the receiver: "1st Company, Schmidt!"

Silence. A jolt went through the sergeant major, and Koenig had the feeling that Schmidt was standing at attention as he sat down. He grinned.

His tone changed from grumpy to polite.

" ..... Regimental staff? ... yes, First Lieutenant ... as an exception ... tomorrow at 11:00. He has fifteen minutes. Thank you, sir First Lieut.... "

Schmidt was astonished.

"He just hung up. The guy's pretty arrogant," he slipped out as he hung up the phone.

Koenig laughed out loud. "That was Lieutenant von Klemmstein. He really is a special person. Don't take it personally. It's an honor in itself that he called himself."

The company sergeant looked down at the note he had made during the conversation. "I'm sure you heard, Captain. Tomorrow at 11:00 - and you have exactly 15 minutes."

"Thank you. Make sure a bucket truck (*Light, all-terrain military car*) is ready on time. And by on time, I mean on time!"

42

"Don't worry. The bucket will be there!"

"Good! By the way, after dinner, I'd like to go to the military hospital and visit our people. Will you come with me?"

"Gladly!"

"And Schmidt, I want us to distribute all the market goods as soon as they arrive."

Schmidt frowned. Thick wrinkles formed under the oddball's half bald head. "If that's a reference to the last bottle of cognac, Captain, I have to say in my defense, it didn't open and I thought before we gave it back..."

"...we'd keep it for ourselves," the officer finished and smiled at the first sergeant.

He turned around, opened the trunk behind his desk and reached inside. Then he placed the bottle on the table. "Here it is, Captain. I didn't drink it, if that's what you think."

The company commander stared at the brandy in amazement. "I didn't think so."

"You see, old Schmidt may be a grumpy old man who still has a lot to teach the young stubble-hoppers, especially discipline, but I don't take anything away from my men. I'm saving this good stuff for something special."

"You see, Schmidt, that's one of the reasons I like you."

The Spike stood up. "Then I'll get our food from the kitchen bull."

"I actually wanted to eat with the team, Schmidt."

"If we go to the military hospital later, boss, it'll be too crowded." Schmidt pointed at his watch. "It's only a few kilometers, and I know you. As soon as you ... Excuse my language ... start talking, it'll take time."

Koenig laughed briefly. "Then go and get our food."

"With pleasure. I can't wait to see what the kitchen bull conjures up from the cauldron today. I've known him since school. We come from the same village," said Schmidt, putting on his coat. He put on his cap and walked out of the office.

A cold wind blew into the house. Captain Koenig went to the stove and added a few logs. Then he rubbed his hands over the warming fire.

The 6th Army was still well supplied and it was certain that the Red Army would be pushed across the Volga before winter set in. Except for a few bridgeheads, Stalingrad was occupied by German troops. Although the enemy put up considerable resistance, the next offensive was being prepared. All hope lay in it.

However, the leadership of the 6th Army also began to have serious doubts, as the German combat units had suffered heavy losses. In particular, a relatively large number of officers had been killed. As a rule, combat strength was only two-thirds of what it had been, and in some units even less.

In the course of its reconstruction, the Wehrmacht had changed some fundamental things compared to the old Reichswehr, which also distinguished it from the army structures of its opponents. These differences increased the fighting power of the Wehrmacht.

Soldiers largely came from the same areas. This deepened camaraderie. Saxons served with Saxons, Bavarians with Bavarians, and so on. Many knew each other or were even distantly related. This sense of belonging made them stand up for each other more than before. People were willing to sacrifice more for comrades to whom they felt connected than for a stranger.

The second point was the drill on the weapon. Every Landser could disassemble and reassemble a pistol, a 98 karabiner and a machine gun blindfolded. They knew how to handle their weapon in any situation, and if it jammed, it could usually be repaired in a few simple steps.

Orders were known down to the lowest ranks. If an officer fell in battle, the sergeant took over, and if he fell, a lance corporal could also carry out the order.

And a psychological weapon, as Captain Koenig called it, was also changed. The rations. Whereas in the First World War there had been different rations for enlisted men, NCOs, and officers, in the Wehrmacht everyone received the same food.

What the field kitchens conjured up from the cauldron was served to everyone, from the common soldier to the general. This created unity.

The rations were delivered to individual troop units upon request and after the numbers had been announced. When the supplies worked, morale was good. In addition to the basic rations delivered through official channels by the divisional issuing offices, there was also a kind of self-supply of fresh produce from the surrounding area. This was officially purchased or bartered. The troops were forbidden to requisition.

In fact, food was taken from the Russian population to feed the German troops. The starvation of the Russian people was accepted.

Some Landser helped the Russian civilians, others took what little was left. Good and evil lived side by side.

The Kübelwagen fought its way through the streets of the suburbs of Stalingrad in the constant cold rain. The corporal driving the all-terrain military vehicle had to shift up and down, accelerate and brake again and again. The speedometer needle kept moving back and forth. The windshield wipers struggled to wipe away the rain. Captain Koenig was in the passenger seat and Sergeant Schmidt was in the back. He had joined the officer to personally deliver some papers to the regiment and also to use the time to catch up with old contacts, as he put it.

Meanwhile, Koenig was looking forward to meeting Lieutenant Colonel Harras, who was not only the regiment's assistant deputy commander, but also his friend. They had met years ago and kept in loose contact ever since. He wanted to make what he considered an important suggestion.

Once again, the private had to pull over. Field police were directing traffic at an intersection, waving through a couple of ambulances and medical trucks coming from the front. As they passed, a troop transport rolled into town. One of the field gendarmes came up to the bucket truck and motioned for the driver to roll down the side window.

"Hey, soldier, where are we going? This could take a while," came from a grumpy sergeant. The breastplate wobbled in front of the raincoat as the military policeman bent down and looked inside the bucket truck. Rain pattered and cold air poured into the vehicle. "Your pay books and orders to move!"

Schmidt was just about to start in his spitfire manner and fire off a few salty words when Captain Koenig took the floor:

"Sergeant, I am Captain Koenig. I have an appointment with Lieutenant Colonel Harras at 11:00, and if you delay me one minute, I will have you transferred to my company. We lost two-thirds of our men in the last battle, and I'm sure I'll get every man I ask for. So wave us through immediately, or give me your pay book as soon as you've checked ours!"

The field gendarm (MP) was taken aback. He didn't know how to react. He was used to giving orders, but the appearance of this officer unsettled him. He took the soldier pay books, leafed through them without really looking, and handed them back. For a moment he even considered holstering his submachine gun and letting them both out, but something indefinable in the captain's voice frightened him. He handed back the pay books and said, "Right away, Captain!" He walked straight to the middle of the street. There he shouted a few words to his two comrades, and less than thirty seconds later the bucket truck was rolling away.

Schmidt couldn't help but wave to the sergeant from the car. The corporal grinned.

Just two kilometers further on, a slide began. The road here was dirt, and the rain had made it muddy. Mud splashed up as they almost got stuck. The corporal cursed, but managed to get the bucket truck through this part of the route without any major problems. At a quarter to eleven, he parked the bucket truck in front of the regimental command post.

"Well done," Koenig praised.

"Gravel driver," grumbled Schmidt. "My bones are aching. I think you used to move beer barrels."

Koenig laughed. He opened the door of the bucket truck and got out. The rain had eased a bit, but was still so heavy that the captain quickly put on his officer's cap and walked to the entrance of the requisitioned house without waiting for his company sergeant. A soldier standing guard outside saluted him. Koenig nodded casually and waved him off. "Thank you, soldier. Tell me, where can I find Lieutenant Colonel Harras?"

The guard opened the right half of the large, heavy oak door and pointed down the long corridor. "At the far left, Captain."

The building seemed to have served as a town hall or school. It was not residential. There was a lot of activity. Koenig saw a bustle in the hallway. A detector emerged from one of the rooms, slung his pouch around his neck, and buttoned his long leather coat as he walked quickly. Another Detector disappeared into the office across the hall. Typewriter keys pounded letters onto paper, telephones rang.

Schmidt came running up. He cursed the weather, wiped his half bald head with the flat of his hand, and pulled on his cap. The corporal who had opened the door for Koenig was about to close it. He paused and looked at the sergeant. His gaze lingered a little longer on the two butt rings on his sleeve.

"Shitty weather, damn it! Where do I find the post office? And where do I find Sergeant Konschewski?"

"I, uh ... this is the regimental command post, Sergeant Major. The field post office is not part of it ..."

"You wise guy, are you going to lecture me about where things are in the Wehrmacht? I know where the field post office belongs, but that's not what I asked! Ask me again! Where do I find the post office and Sergeant Konschewski?"

The private swallowed. His Adam's apple was moving up and down. He wondered what to say to the spit in front of him.

Captain Koenig stopped and turned around. "Schmidt, a little quieter, please."

"Captain, I was just asking this private a little question," the hot-tempered company sergeant grinned.

"It's not our company you're looking at, it's a guard from the regimental staff."

The private was grateful for Koenig's little help. "The field post office is diagonally opposite," he pointed across the street, "and First

47

Sergeant Konschewski has been our new weapons master for four weeks. He can usually be found in the smithy."

"There you are, young comrade," said Schmidt rather politely, looking over his shoulder at Captain Koenig. "I'm over at the post office and would like to see the armourer. This is an old comrade of mine ..."

"Wait for me at the field post office. I'll accompany you to the armorer."

"Yes, Captain."

Schmidt turned, pulled his cap down over his face, and ran across the street, cursing loudly.

Captain Koenig walked down the corridor to the back and entered the office he was shown. It was an anteroom to Lieutenant Colonel Harras' actual office. A sergeant was reviewing reports, and Lieutenant von Klemmstein was standing on the wall in front of a situation map. He was sticking pins in certain places and stretching threads of different colors between them.

"Good morning, gentlemen," greeted Captain Koenig.

"Good morning, Captain," the sergeant groaned, standing up straight.

Well drilled, Koenig thought.

The first lieutenant turned briefly, recognized the senior officer, put the thread aside and saluted him too, clicking his heels together, extending his right hand and shouting, "Heil Hitler, Captain!"

Koenig merely nodded and returned the salute by raising his hand briefly and immediately lowering it again, looking more like a limp wave than a proper military Hitler salute.

"I have an appointment with Lieutenant Colonel Harras!"

"Captain Koenig, I'm glad to see you again," the first lieutenant said.

Koenig looked at the map. The sergeant sat down and resumed his interrupted work. "White threads, blue threads, green threads and red threads," said the company commander.

Von Klemmstein looked at his watch. "Three minutes to go. We take everything very seriously. If you work precisely, you won't make any mistakes."

Koenig looked at his counterpart. What an ass! I disliked that guy from the start and I still do! He's a snob like no other. I don't like him, he thought.

Now the first lieutenant replied to Koenig's remark about the different colored threads. "The threads all have their meaning. These are our battalions. Red is for the Russians."

"It's all a big mess. It looked just like it did in my grandmother's sewing box," said the senior officer, somewhat smugly, glad not to be under Klemmstein's command.

Koenig recalled that von Klemmstein joined the troops as a young lieutenant and was immediately able to avoid front-line service. His father was a high-ranking government official in Berlin, and his contacts were sufficient to get his son on the stage immediately. Koenig also recalled how, after two glasses of wine, von Klemmstein admired the company commander's Iron Cross at his promotion ceremony to first lieutenant, which Koenig happened to attend.

"Would you like one?" he asked him at the time.

"I'm sure I'll have enough decorations after the final victory," was the answer.

"You'll get them on the battlefield," was Koenig's reply, and von Klemmstein stood like a watered poodle in the midst of his superiors. To divert attention from himself, he had changed the subject with a toast to Adolf Hitler and the final victory. Koenig was certain that the lieutenant had not forgotten this verbal slap in the face.

Koenig looked at the officer's chest. "Still no Iron Cross? I have lost many officers and need capable men. Join me and you can earn a few medals in no time."

That had done the trick. The old wounds had been torn open. Hatred glittered in the first lieutenant's eyes. The sergeant buried his head deep in his papers, as if to say he hadn't noticed.

"Everyone has to serve where they are assigned," von Klemmstein countered, walking to his superior's door and knocking.

"Come in!"

Klemmstein opened the door and stuck his head through in a slimy, submissive manner. "Excuse me, Lieutenant Colonel. Captain Koenig is here. He asked for a short interview. I'll remind you that your time is very short. I'll have the bucket truck brought around. You must

49

be at the division in a few minutes!"

"Thank you, tell him to come in."

Von Klemmstein turned to Koenig. "The lieutenant colonel has a few minutes for you now."

Koenig squeezed past the first lieutenant, grinned, and greeted the deputy regimental commander: "Hello Richard! How are you?"

"Erwin, my friend. We haven't seen each other for a long time. Come in. What can I do for you?"

Von Klemmstein positioned himself at the door frame and wanted to eavesdrop, but Koenig closed the door without being able to refrain from the quiet remark: "Excuse me, this is confidential."

The greeting was cordial. The men shook hands. "Congratulations on your new position," Koenig began.

"Only temporarily. Our real second-in-command is seriously ill. As soon as he recovers, he'll take over again. Come, sit down. I'd like to offer you something and talk longer, but I'm on my way. I have to get to Division. We're preparing for a decisive strike against the Russians. Things are heating up. How can I help you?"

Koenig quickly recounted his last mission and the conspicuously high casualties caused by Russian snipers. Then he made his suggestion to the lieutenant colonel. "... and that's why we have to react and fight back in the same way. We have to push our sniper unit and use it in a targeted way. And that's why I suggest we just copy the Russian. Only if I confront the enemy with the same tactics, the same toughness, the same fighting spirit, can I beat him. He emphasized the next sentence, giving it explosive force. "Sniper combat is different from regular soldier combat, Richard! We've lost a lot of blood. Too much blood. We must fight fire with fire!"

"You've already mentioned the key word. We've lost too much blood, Erwin. That's why I can't agree to your proposal. Our regiment will be used again. I'm going to the last big debriefing after our talk."

Flashes of thought exploded in Koenig's mind. They had suffered such heavy losses, and yet the regiment was thrown back into battle. He felt that Stalingrad was different from all previous battles. He had seen the tenacity of the enemy. The war with Russia was hard and brutal. It was horrible and anything but heroic. War was always and everywhere cruel, but in Stalingrad it would be hell. Captain Koenig took a deep breath. "Give me the opportunity to rebuild a powerful sniper unit as a z.b.V.. I promise you effective success!"

"Erwin, I want to be completely open and honest. We have lost many, too many officers. We've lost too many men altogether. Winter is coming, and our main goal, to drive the Russians across the Volga, has not yet been achieved. We can't afford to lose a single man, and certainly not officers like you."

"Richard, I was out there fighting. I have seen the effect of the Russian snipers and how our people tremble in front of them. The daily sniper war takes place in the minds of the soldiers. It's an enormous psychological pressure. They are insecure, afraid. The Red Army's sniper operations eat away at the nerves of our men.

Lieutenant Colonel Harras listened carefully to his friend. Koenig was a good soldier and an excellent officer. He trusted him. A quick glance at his watch was followed by a nod. "Good, Erwin. I'll think about it. But first there's the last big offensive. We are convinced that this time we will drive the Russians completely out of their positions and crush them on the banks of the Volga. Chuikov won't be able to hold out much longer."

Koenig remained stubborn. "Can I at least do a little planning for myself?"

"What do you mean?"

"I'd like to look around the armoury and take what I can use."

Lieutenant Colonel Harras took a blank piece of paper and wrote a few words on it. Then he signed it and handed it to King. "Here, take whatever you need, but I'm telling you right now, you'll be leading your company into battle again soon. This time the stakes are high. We must push the Russians across the Volga before winter sets in! We'll think about your idea during the winter break. You'll see Stalingrad through the crosshairs soon enough."

The king took the paper and skimmed it. It was an order to the Master-at-Arms to provide Koenig with everything he requested.

"Thank you, Richard."

"My old friend, we'll talk about your proposal later. If we set up our winter quarters here, we will certainly have enough time to prepare militarily for a final strike in the spring. Perhaps your idea can be incorporated into that."

Koenig remained silent. The echo of Harra's words kept reverberating in his mind: Stalingrad in the crosshairs.

There was a knock. Harras looked at the door and called: "Come in!"

Von Klemmstein entered the office. "The driver is here, Lieutenant Colonel. You must leave immediately."

"Thank you."

Von Klemmstein left the door open. Koenig couldn't help but say: "And Richard, we could really use men as capable as von Klemmstein as platoon and company commanders at the front."

Harras made a questioning face as he got up. He went to the checkroom and slipped into his coat. "You can't be serious. Von Klemmstein is a slimeball and a failure, but he's also an excellent statistician. If I sent him to the front, he'd be killed within a week, and someone in Berlin would be all over me," he said very quietly, holding out his hand. He wanted to make sure that the first lieutenant in the outer office couldn't hear him.

Koenig remained serious, but also spoke in a whisper. "A week?" he grinned almost maliciously. "He wouldn't last a day. Not a single day!"

They left the office together and headed for the exit. There was still a lot of activity in the corridor and the adjacent rooms. The guard at the entrance greeted them and opened the door. The rain had finally stopped. Harras and Koenig said goodbye with a friendly handshake.

"When we've pushed the Russian over the Volga and are well fed in our winter camp, we can drink a cognac in peace and talk about old times."

"We'll do that, Richard."

The lieutenant colonel got into a bucket truck. The driver, who had held the door open for him, slammed it shut, walked around the vehicle and got in. Harras rolled down the window again. "Erwin, I almost forgot to tell you. Your son is coming here for front-line parole.

Von Klemmstein arranged it with my predecessor without my knowledge."

Koenig froze.

"I'll see to it that he comes to us, then I can get him a good post, and with luck he'll be back home in the New Year without having seen a Red Army soldier."

"Thank you," the captain pursed his lips. He wanted to ask when his son would arrive, but the driver had already started the engine and left.

The company commander was shocked. He would have liked to go back to Lieutenant von Klemmstein's office and punch him in the face, but that wouldn't have helped anyone.

Rolf is coming to Stalingrad.

Now exactly what Koenig wanted to prevent had happened. All hope was in Harras and his influence.

My good comrade will see to it that Rolf doesn't have to go into battle! Von Klemmstein, you rat, I'll get even with you. And if anything happens to my son, I'll hold you responsible!

With a mixture of anger, despair, fear, and apprehension in his stomach, the company commander crossed the street and walked purposefully to the makeshift field post office.

He had already anticipated that he would not receive immediate approval for his plan, but he knew Harras well and knew that he would consider the proposal carefully. Knowing that his son, Ensign OA Rolf Koenig, would be coming to Stalingrad, he had to succeed in quickly implementing his plan to train the regiment's own snipers and deploy them effectively.

The sound of aircraft engines grew louder and then died away. A swarm of German fighters buzzed above Koenig. He raised his head and saw the ever-shrinking silhouettes of Me Bf 109s that would soon land somewhere on an airfield.

His comrades fly their boxes in all weathers, he thought respectfully.

Koenig was about to enter the post office when the door opened and First Sergeant Schmidt stepped out. He was carrying a messenger bag full of letters. "Sometimes I really am too good for these troops," he laughed. "Now I'm taking work away from the soldiers and transporting field mail. But the boys will be happy. There's something from home for some of the men."

"Have you read the names yet?"

"No, I wanted to see my old buddy Konschewski quickly. I hope there's still time. That's why I came here."

"That's the weapons master."

"That's what the guard said."

"That fits. That's exactly where I need to go."

"Then follow me. I've been shown the way to the forge."

Unlike most of the other houses, the smithy was not thatched. Either the former blacksmith could afford to use shingles, or it was simply due to the fact that there were always fires burning in his workshop, iron glowing and sparks flying. The building was huge, and provided enormous storage space. A large, barn-like gate stood half open. Two Opel Blitz cars were parked in front of the shop. The tarpaulin of one of the trucks had been folded back while it was being unloaded. The driver stood smoking next to the cab, while three Landsers and a Russian hired hand carried weapons of all kinds into the smithy.

"Damn, Jesus Christ crucifix again! I told you, the defective carbines on the left and the booty weapons on the right! You're all dumber than a kilo of commissary bread," boomed from the smithy.

Koenig poked Schmidt in the side. "But your comrade is not very good at eating cherries. When it comes to swearing, you're an orphan compared to him."

Schmidt laughed out loud. "That's old Konschewski. That's how I know him!"

The truck driver recognized Koenig's rank as an officer, tossed the cigarette butt to the ground, stubbed it out, and stood at attention. Then he saluted. "Good day, Captain."

Koenig saluted him back and said casually, "If you're going to salute me, please put on your headgear."

The Landser fumbled. "I... uh..."

"Shut up, or you'll talk yourself into a corner. Just put your hat on," Schmidt winked.

"Yes, Sergeant Major," the soldier exclaimed after seeing the piston rings on Schmidt's sleeves.

The armorer stepped out of the forge. "If it isn't the voice of old warhorse Schmidt," he laughed, patted the hiwi on the shoulder and repeated: "Looted weapons on the right, the rest on the left!"

Konschewski saluted Koenig as well, then extended his hand to the company sergeant. The sergeant towered over Schmidt by at least two heads. He was a burly fellow with a broad back. Schmidt's hand disappeared into Konschewski's as if it were a child's. "How are you, old man?"

"Fine, but I'd better get right to it. Captain Koenig wanted to see you."

The master-at-arms looked at the officer. "You are Captain Koenig? Captain Koenig?" he emphasized in the second question that immediately followed.

"I don't know what you mean by that, but I am Captain Koenig."

"Erwin Koenig?"

"Don't ask such a stupid question, it's him," Schmidt whispered quietly.

Konschewski held out his hand. "May I shake your hand? I've always wanted to meet you personally. I've heard a lot about you. You're the master of all sharpshooters."

"Don't exaggerate."

"Honestly. You're a hero."

Koenig smiled inwardly, wanting to clarify that while he was an excellent marksman, he had never seen action as a sniper, but then he decided to remain silent. He still had a lot of work to do in the regiment's sharpshooting department, and this reputation might come in handy.

"You're not just called that, you're the king of snipers. The Russians shudders when they hear your name. And you always lead your men from the front. I have the greatest respect for that."

"Don't exaggerate," Koenig replied with a sympathetic smile.

"How can I help you?"

"I have a letter here from Lieutenant Colonel Harras," the

officer said, handing it to the armourer. "For your records, in case anyone has any questions about the whereabouts of some weapons and ammunition. I need several things from you."

"Gladly. What is it?"

"What kind of sniper rifles do you have here?"

The master gunsmith's eyes began to light up. "Fifteen 98 carbines, about ten ZF 39 scopes, and just as many ZF 41 scopes, all with maintenance kits and tools. And then I have the best ever. The ZF 42 from Zeiss. Also 160 mm long, but only 6 lenses and therefore a great 4x magnification. I have exactly 5 of them, Captain. Then I have a couple of Russian Mosin Nagant rifles. They are robust and good. The Russians can do that. They make really good, sturdy rifles. The Shpagin submachine gun is also very reliable."

Koenig interrupted. "You're digressing. Let's stay on topic. I prefer the Karabiner 98 anyway."

"Good weapon!"

"What about ammunition?"

The first sergeant grinned. "My predecessor was an old fox. He stockpiled both steel-tipped bullets, which incidentally have been out of production for some time now..." he noted, "... heavy, pointed bullets, a few cartridges with phosphorus, and also bullets with tracers. The nitro powder of the tracer ammunition glows up to 900 meters."

Schmidt looked at Armsmaster and Captain Koenig as they spoke. Both were completely engrossed. "I think you two are going to be very good friends," he murmured. "May I ask in between if we can go inside? It's uncomfortably cold out here."

"Gladly," the sergeant major said, immediately turning back to Koenig. "I'll show you the weapons."

Konschewski turned and walked away. Koenig and Schmidt followed.

"Hey, Sergej," he called to another assistant who was working on a broken carbine in the forge. "Get me the best sniper rifles and the ZF 42."

"Right away, First Sergeant," the Russian helper replied with a heavy accent.

"I happen to have a pot of hot coffee on the stove in the back."

"Later, I want to take a look at the weapons first," said the King. "But you can have a cup with Schmidt now. The Russian can show me the guns."

"Thank you, Captain. The assistant's name is Sergej."

Koenig went to the man who was willing to help. The master-at-arms took his buddy aside. "I'll have a shot of juniper to warm you up. Shall I pour you one?"

Schmidt grinned. "I wouldn't mind a little sip. Makes the *Muckefuck* taste better."

"It's not *Muckefuck*, it's real bean coffee!"

The blacksmith's shop turned out to be a veritable weapons paradise for Captain Koenig. He chose a Mosin Nagant with ammunition and three Karabiner 98s. In addition to the Mauser rifles, he took every type of ammunition in stock. He also chose two of the latest 42 riflescopes and one of the small 41 riflescopes.

He also found a compass, various camouflage items, a combat knife, a padded branch fork as a rifle rest, and two binoculars with makeshift visors. Koenig was extremely pleased.

"You are a sniper, Captain?" Sergej asked after a while.

Koenig nodded and answered in almost fluent Russian. "I trained our snipers."

"You speak Russian?"

"Yes, I learned my love of languages from my mother. Are you a sniper?"

Sergej laughed. "Then I wouldn't be here. Snipers don't get captured. They get killed. You know, Captain, we Russians have a lot of sharpshooters. Men and women. That's what makes the Red Army so strong. With you women are nurses, with us they fight. Our sharpshooters hunt and shoot German soldiers. They kill as cold as ice. I met one of them. His name is Saizev. Vasily Saizev. His name means hare. He's a simple hunter from the Urals and one of our best sharpshooters. He has long since been awarded the title of Noble Sniper and the Order of Valor that goes with it."

"Noble Sniper?" Koenig asked.

"If you have 40 proven kills, you are a Noble Sniper."

"How do you know this Saizev?"

"I gave him the first sniper rifle. I was a sergeant in the Red Army. 62nd Army, 1047th Rifle Regiment, 284th Rifle Division. As a weapons sergeant, I often had to deal with the snipers."

"Why did you defect?"

"I am honest. I fought against you Germans because you invaded our country. But what I experienced in the Red Army was terrible. They were chasing young men to their senseless deaths. If someone retreats without orders, even if it is tactically correct, he is considered a coward. If someone disobeys discipline and shows weakness, the political commissars say he is aiding the enemy, and this applies to both soldiers and civilians. And then there is a summary trial. They are shot. I've seen half children shot in cold blood just because they took cover. They ran towards the enemy without weapons and were told to take weapons from the dead. Some of them were afraid. That is understandable. There were many, too many, sentenced to death by their own courts. I saw young men pleading for their lives, howling with snot and water, crying for their mothers. I heard a sniper boast that he shot a woman because she talked to a German soldier. She may have been begging for her life, Captain. He just shot her. When our position was overrun, I decided to stop fighting for the Red Army. I may never know if I was right or wrong, but I could no longer stand for this injustice.

"You speak good German, too. Where did you learn it?"

"At school."

"That Saizev. What kind of a man is he?"

"He is cold as ice and has the patience of an angel. He is a master of stealth, and when he aims, he hits. He is highly respected and has such good ideas that many of them are implemented by the officers. Saizev has made it and has gone from being a simple hunter from the Urals to a hero of the Red Army".

"Thank you, Sergej. Please bring me a box or something where we can put all the equipment."

As the hiji left to carry out the order, Koenig whispered a name: "Vasily Saizev.

Sergej brought a box and packed.

After the captain had found everything on his personal list, he

58

walked contentedly into the corner of the forge where the two sergeants were sitting and talking loudly.

"Sergeant Konschewski, I've picked out a few things."

"How are you doing? Did Sergej take notes, too? I mean, so that the papers fit."

"He did. He's a good man. Knows his stuff."

"Yes. He was in the Red Army. He was something of a weapons master there, too."

Captain Koenig pointed to the stove, to the coffee pot there. "I would like a cup of coffee, too."

The Master-at-Arms got up and went to the stove. "But of course, Captain."

"And Konschewski..."

The first sergeant picked up a cup, reached for the pitcher and poured. "Yes?"

"You can give me a drink from your bottle, too. I mean the one you have behind the stove, down on the right, by the wood."

Schmidt's face turned red and Konschewski almost spilled the coffee. "You saw that?"

"Just pour it."

The burly master-at-arms bent down, poured an extra-large gulp into his coffee, and walked back to Captain Koenig. "Here you go."

"Cheers, gentlemen!"

After that, they drove to the sutler's shop. With a truck in tow, they finally returned to the company command post. There they unloaded. While Koenig inspected his weapons and accessories, Schmidt checked the sutlery and decided on its distribution. Meanwhile, Lance Corporal Remmler sorted the field post.

"Man, how bad. Here's a letter for Hans Zentner. He died two days ago from severe injuries," Remmler muttered to himself. In the end there were four letters in a separate pile. All for Landser, who was dead. "What should we do with the four letters?" he asked.

Schmidt leaned back and scratched his head. "Throw them away. I want the senders to think the men read the letters before they fell."

Remmler got up and walked to the stove. He opened the door and looked back at Schmidt. "Do you really think so?"

"Put them in."

The letters went into the embers, and blue and yellow flickering flames quickly ate their way up. Remmler added a piece of wood and went back to his desk. "I have to take three letters to the hospital, and one is for the boss."

Koenig had just mounted a ZF 42 and looked up. "For me?"

"Yes, the sender is your son."

"I'm sure he'll let me know he's coming here."

Schmidt and Remmler couldn't believe it. "What?"

"I found out this morning. Frontline parole in Stalin grade!"

"I should have been struck by lightning while I was poo-pooing," grumbled Schmidt, apologizing immediately. "That just slipped out on the spur of the moment. I'm sorry."

With the return to battle imminent, Captain Koenig had the sutler's goods distributed to the company that very evening. There was tobacco, cigarettes, drops, scho-ka-kola, razors, wine and liquor.

The men cheered Captain Koenig when they learned that he had picked up the sutler's goods with the personnel list before the last casualties were deducted, and that there were generous rations for every soldier.

That night, the officer lay awake for a long time. As he listened to the cheerful singing of his celebrating soldiers, he thought of Rolf. He had told him in a slightly coded way that he was on his way to see him. To write it openly would have been forbidden. So Rolf had written that he was going on a long journey by train to complete an internship that preceded the end of his training.

Rolf, you don't know that you're going straight to hell. I hope they find you a quiet place on the stage.

He kept thinking about the last sentence of the letter.

Dad, I'm looking forward to seeing you again.

4

Immediately after the air raid, Katja had rushed to her husband's workplace and, together with her two sons, desperately searched the ruins of the hospital for her husband. Try as she might, she found nothing. There was no sign that he had survived. And try as she might, Katja had to admit that her beloved Pyotr had probably died in the ruins of the hospital.

"Comrade sister, nobody got out," a fireman had told her.

The building had not only taken a few direct hits, it had burned to the ground. It was at the epicenter of the gigantic fireball. Even if someone had made it to the basement, they would not have escaped death. The air was searing hot, and breathing it burned the lungs. The searing heat paved the way for the deadly fire roller to sweep through every nook and cranny. Everyone in the hospital was doomed to die.

Katja finally had no doubt that her Pyotr had died in that hospital. Killed by German bombs.

Although she no longer had any hope, she searched all the makeshift hospitals in the following days, but even there she looked in vain for the love of her life.

"There is no doctor here," she was often told.

"Mrs. Kalikova, unfortunately your husband is not here."

Eventually, she sat down, looked into the tear-filled eyes of her two sons, and gave up the search.

It had been a terrible war so far, but not her personal one. The fighting was far away, and she lived in peace with her family in this city on the Volga.

With the German invasion and the complete destruction of her city, everything changed abruptly.

While many civilians fled from the bombed and burned ruins, hiding in the sewers or on the steep slopes of the Zaritsa Gorge, digging caves, Katja returned to her house with Boris and Grisha. Not only the old house, but also the road leading to it was completely destroyed and strewn with craters and piles of rubble. They had to climb over piles of rubble to get to the ruins where they had a large apartment until recently.

The property had taken a direct hit. One wall of the house was completely torn down and more than half of it had collapsed. The roof and the two upper floors were gone. The bricks, beams, and remains of the wall had buried the rest of the building. Katja and her children had stared for a long time at the huge pile of stones where they had lived happily. Then they had walked around the ruins twice, until Grisha had accidentally found an entrance to the former staircase. As if by a miracle, some heavy roof beams had been wedged together in such a way that if you crawled through an opening about 60 centimeters wide, you could reach the entrance as if through a hollow path. Only a small part of the staircase on the first floor had survived the attack. The stairway to the upper floors was completely destroyed. The apartments on the first floor were also inaccessible, only access to the basement was clear. This circumstance, along with the huge stroke of luck that the great conflagration had not completely reached their house, offered the prospect of safe shelter.

"Kids, maybe we'll get lucky and the basement will survive the bombing unscathed."

"What are we going to do, Mom?" asked Boris, squeezing Katja's hand tightly.

"We're staying here, children! We're going downstairs to look around," she had told her boys.

There was still a last spark of hope that their Pyotr might return one day. It was that tiny little light that let her sleep at night and gave her new strength in the morning to get up and fight for survival.

She had gone against the tide of people. She didn't want to live in a hole in the ground like an animal. She wanted protection and security. Here, in her old house, Katja would feel safe.

Grisha stared down the basement stairs. "Mama, it's pitch black down there. We have no light."

Katja looked around, spotted a broken support beam from the former banister, and picked it up. She weighed the piece of wood in her hand and was ready to use it as a baton in an emergency. Grisha also looked around and wanted to arm himself, but Katja shook her head.

"You take Boris by the hand and look after your brother!"

Grisha held out his hand to Boris and decided to defend him with his life. He was a proud Russian and he would represent his father. He, the eight-year-old Grigory Kalikov, whom everyone called Grisha, would protect Boris and his mother. He had respect for the cellar, especially when there was no light, but he was no longer afraid.

I am a man now!

Just last month, going down to the basement to get something for his mom or dad was like a big adventure for him. Grisha preferred to go down to the cellar with Boris or, if necessary, armed with the wooden sword his father had carved. They never knew what to expect, because Grisha suspected that something lived down there. Almost every time he ran up the stairs on his way back, he had the eerie feeling that this invisible something was reaching for him. Now he was not afraid anymore. He squeezed his younger brother's hand and stood close behind Katja. "Don't be afraid, Mom. I'll protect you."

"Hello?" Katja called into the darkness. "Is anyone here?"

She stared down the stairs and saw nothing. Her left hand went to the wall. She took a step onto the stone stairs and another. Everything was dark. "Hello? This is Katja Kalikova. Is anyone here?"

Creaking. At the end of the cellar corridor, the door to a room was opened. The light of a flickering candle fell into the hallway, illuminating it slightly. Shadows danced on the wall. Katja was startled. Grisha stood rooted to the spot behind his mother. He and Boris stared into the hallway. Katja clutched the piece of wood tighter. She took a deep breath and took the next step forward.

"Who's there?" she heard a familiar voice.

Relief.

"Mother Yenkova," Boris cried, tearing himself away from Grisha, pushing past Katja and running down the stairs.

"Boris! Stop right there!"

"Mrs. Kalikova. We are here."

Katja was relieved to recognize her neighbor's voice.

The old couple, Lydia and Fyodor Jenkov, who lived in the apartment below them, had fled to the cellar during the big attack and had been hiding there ever since. Katja learned from them that all the other residents had fled or died. During the heavy bombing, the couple had taken everything that seemed important to them out of the apartment and put it in the basement.

"And here we are safe for now," the old woman finished her story.

Katja and her sons went to their own cellar. There wasn't much in the 20 square meter room. A few sparsely filled shelves. A small workbench with a few tools and the old bed frame with the straw mattresses that Katja had long wanted to throw away, but Pyotr said he wanted to use it to build something for the children. Now she was glad he had kept it.

In the days that followed, Katja had tried several times to escape from Stalingrad, going down to the Volga with her sons every day to get on one of the ships and reach the other side of the river, but the plan proved much more difficult than expected.

Crowds of people crowded the port day and night. Soldiers were transported to Stalingrad, the wounded were brought back. Military transports were given priority. Thousands of families waited, hoping to embark and leave the burning city. The ring closed by the 6th Army became tighter and tighter. The civilians were afraid of the enemy soldiers, afraid of the war, afraid of dying. They were homeless and didn't know how to feed themselves. They sought their salvation in escape.

Departure was controlled and managed by the NKVD, the People's Commissariat for Internal Affairs. This was often done very arbitrarily. If one of the commissars didn't like a face, the family had to stay. Chaos reigned.

Nevertheless, the bellies and decks of ships of all shapes and sizes were filled with civilians. They cast off completely overloaded and sailed to supposed safety. Some of them capsized. Katja once saw a smaller boat just sink in the middle of the Volga. It tipped over, filled with water, and sank. Most of the 30 or 40 people who had crowded into the boat drowned. A few managed to swim to shore or were pulled out by the crew of another ship. It was terrible.

On another day, she saw how hardship changes people. When

one of the sailors gave priority to an older man over a pregnant woman simply because the latter had slipped him a gold watch, the situation escalated and the sailor was attacked by several waiting, angry women. The captain ended the fight by drawing his pistol and firing a shot into the air. Soldiers became aware of the situation and came running. They shot both the sailor and the man trying to buy passage.

When the German artillery began to fire more frequently on the great river to fight the Red Army's supply route, Katja finally gave up her plan to leave Stalingrad via the Volga and decided to stay in the city for the time being.

She trusted that the Red Army would quickly liberate the city, which bore the name of Father Stalin, from the German invaders.

The few supplies in her cellar were quickly used up, and the sister suspected that she was in for some very hard times. She immediately began to gather essential supplies. Together with Boris and Grisha, she rummaged through the ruins in search of non-perishable food, medicine and bandages. The small family also took things like tools, nails, and knives to exchange for food when the opportunity arose. Katja scoured the rubble for blankets and clothes, candles and matches.

The din of battle that could be heard all around them, sometimes louder, sometimes fainter, but never completely fading away, became a constant companion. With it, the small family became accustomed to death. Again and again they came across dead soldiers.

Pure desperation, love for her children and unbridled anger at the Germans for killing her beloved Pyotr gave her the strength to fight for survival and not to despair.

In the days that followed, Katja learned that people become animals when their very existence is at stake. She learned that she had to be fast and greedy to get her prey. She learned to overcome her disgust and to search the pockets of the dead for useful items. She also learned to look around before crawling into the hard-to-find entrance to her basement lair. She learned to move quietly and deftly through the ruined landscape. In short, she learned how to survive. She distrusted everyone. She hid from her fellow Germans, from Red Army soldiers, and from the other civilians left behind in this hellish city.

Once she found a badly wounded medic. He was dying, crying

65

for his mother and holding his stomach. It was a blond young man who looked at her in a feverish delirium and imagined that she was his mother. Katja took pity on him and sat down beside him to help. She put her hands on his open stomach wound. As a trained nurse, Katja knew that the torn abdominal wall meant death for this man. Nevertheless, she used her hands to push the stinking mixture of intestines and blood back into the body, which was getting colder and colder. She hummed a lullaby. At one point, she stroked the dying man's hair with her bloodied hand. She waited until the soldier breathed his last, then took the first-aid bag, rummaged through the pockets of his uniform, and went to her sons, who were waiting on the sidelines.

Another day, she saw a woman being dragged into a corner by two male civilians. While one raped the woman, the other took everything the Russian woman had taken that day. Katja thought about helping, but what could she do as a woman? They would probably rape and rob her as well. God knows what would happen if her sons came to her aid. The two criminals might beat her to death. No! She was powerless. And she was afraid for Grigory and Boris. The Stalingrad of today had nothing in common with the city on the Volga that she loved so much.

Stalingrad was not only a place of death, which ruled with cruel severity, but also of hatred, contempt for humanity, hunger and suffering.

They returned to their hiding place.

"Boris, Grisha. You can't trust anyone anymore. From now on it's just the three of us. We can't tell anyone where we live. Promise me that you will always stay together," were the words with which she greeted her sons.

"Yes, Mom," replied little Boris.

"Mom, what about the Jenkows?" Grishka wanted to know.

"They are our only friends, but they never leave the cellar. They guard our house," she replied, and last night flashed through her mind in horror.

She remembered what she had been carrying since yesterday. She reached into the right pocket of her coat. She felt cold steel. A guilty conscience spread. Could she have helped the woman? She repressed the terrible scene and thought about her neighbor.

Yesterday, while Grisha and Boris were sleeping, Mother Yenkova knocked on the cellar door. She just stood there, holding out a thick, warm blanket to Katja. Her look was kind and loving, as always. "This blanket is for the children. My Fyodor and I are old. We won't survive the winter if we stay here. We'll rest for a few days, then we'll go to the river and hope that the big crowds will have gone by then," she had said. "We will also leave you all our supplies. I have dried mushrooms, lots of pickled vegetables, and a few jars of honey. Fyodor and I won't need much more."

"Mother Yenkova. You can't get through by the river. I've been there. More than once," Katja had told her. "The NKVD controls and decides who gets on the ships. And the Germans are shelling the Volga all the time. It's terrible! Stay with us. Together we will hold out until the Red Army defeats the Germans."

Katja earned a smile. It was a gentle smile, but the old Russian woman's look seemed broken. "Our decision is made. I'm 79 years old, and my Fyodor is 82. We still have enough strength to go down to the Volga, but not enough to survive a winter without a stove. Take everything when we're gone. And..." she reached under her apron and pulled out an old army revolver, model Nagant M1895. "It has seven cartridges in the cylinder, Fjodor has another seven cartridges in this cloth," now she reached into the wide pocket of her apron and pulled out a piece of cloth tied into a pouch. "These are bad times. If you have to defend yourself, or if you see no way out..." she didn't finish the sentence, took a deep breath and continued: "This is Fyodor's revolver from the last great war. He was a captain in the artillery," she said with a proud look. "Take it. It can save your life and especially the lives of your sons."

Katja took the revolver and the bag of bullets.

"I'll show you how to load it and how to change the cylinder," Lydia Jenkowa began to explain, pointing to the toggle lever on the right side of the gun. "Tilt it down and you can push the cartridges into the empty drum. You can also remove the cylinder by pulling out this part here at the front."

Katja watched intently and finally tried everything under her neighbor's supervision. Every move was perfect. It was easier than expected.

"You see, Mrs. Kalikowa. It's not that difficult."

"Thank you. Thank you," said the nurse. At the same time she thought that fourteen shots would be enough.

Eleven Germans, then my two sons, and the last bullet for myself.

She closed her eyes and pushed the last thought out of her mind. Then she tried again to persuade the old Russian to stay. "Mother Yenkova, it's warmer here in the cellar than outside. It's a well-built and very protected cellar. It's guaranteed not to freeze."

"We made our decision a long time ago. We'll leave the day after tomorrow at the latest. Good luck!" She held out her hand to Katja and squeezed it firmly. "And get everything we have over there. It's all yours," she said, letting go and stroking Katja's cheek with her cold hand. "Oh, and I have this for you," the good-natured old woman added, handing Katja an envelope. "It contains 300 rubles. That will get you from here to Moscow, and you should even have some money left over to live on."

"I can't accept that," Katja replied, but Mother Yenkova pressed the envelope into her hand, turned and went back to her husband.

Katja closed the door, hid the envelope and the revolver on the top shelf, and crawled into bed with her sons. The nurse pondered her neighbors for a long time before finally falling asleep.

The next morning, when Katja went to the Volga to fill the ten-liter canister with water, she thought the Yenkovs were still there. When she and her sons returned from their daily romp through the ruins half an hour ago, Katja instinctively felt that she would not see the Yenkovs again. That was something she now had to tell her children, who both loved the old couple as if they were their own grandparents.

"Grisha, my darling, the Yenkovs will be leaving soon. We'll be alone here."

The eight-year-old nodded in understanding, but tears came to his eyes, which he wiped away with a quick movement.

Boris, on the other hand, reacted angrily. "They shouldn't go," he cried, and ran out of the basement room into the hallway. He ran straight to the Jenkovs' cellar and stopped there.

"Mother Yenkova, Father Yenkova, stay with us," he called

loudly.

Silence. There was no answer. Katja and Grisha came to Bo-ris, who tried again, drumming his small fists against the wood of the door. "Mother Yenkova, Father Yenkov!"

The knock caused the door to open a small crack. Katja feared the worst when she realized that the cellar door was unlocked. She pushed against it and pushed it all the way open. The room was empty and dark. There was no light coming from the cellar window shaft either. She was buried.

"Grisha, run and get our flashlight," said Katja, and the older of her sons ran off.

A moment later the flashlight's cone of light circled the floor and the sleeping area, which consisted of a homemade wooden platform with mattresses on it. On top were two neatly folded duvets with matching pillows and sheets. Katja spotted a note on the top. She went over and read it.

"Dear Mrs. Kalikova, this is all yours now. Take care of Grisha and Boris. They are two beautiful boys of whom you can be proud. My husband and I are going on our last trip. Good luck and all the best, F. and L. Jenkow".

With tears in their eyes, the cone of light then moved over a wooden shelf of jars. They found pickled vegetables such as cabbage, cucumbers, and peppers, jars of honey and jam, and two shelves full of dried fruits and mushrooms. There were even three bottles of vodka on the top shelf. Two warm winter coats hung on the opposite side. Katja found sewing materials and scissors, a hammer, some nails, a handsaw and a small axe. In the far corner were three 10-liter canisters of water and a 20-liter canister. Next to them were some towels, a large wash bowl, and two sheets. A bucket with a lid served as an emergency toilet. There were also some old newspapers for toilet paper.

Then there was a small box, slightly larger than a shoebox, on the shelf. Katja pulled it out and opened it. The old couple kept medicine and bandages in the box. Katja saw two rolls of bandages, tincture of iodine and painkillers, a screw-top jar of homemade ointment for inflammation, and dried herbs for tea.

Not only did they think of everything, they really saved us, Katja thought, and began to cry quietly. They volunteered to go to the Volga to save us. Thought after thought came to the sister. I must go to the river and find them! But no! I cannot leave my sons alone. It was her free decision.

Katja knew that the supplies would guarantee survival for at least six to eight weeks. If they used them sparingly, maybe even ten or twelve weeks. That would be enough for the Red Army to get enough troops across the Volga to drive the Germans back into the steppe.

Mother Yenkova and Father Yenkov. I wish you good luck.

For the next two days the battle noise was extremely loud. So Katja decided not to go on a raid. She stayed in the basement with her children. To make use of the time, she played school with them and tried to teach them.

In the evening, the three of them snuggled up in the Jenkovs' warm quilts, and while Boris and Grisha fell asleep, Katja listened to the never-ending dull roar of artillery, the firing of machine guns, and the crash of shells, which fortunately did not fall near their house.

On the third day, after her neighbors had left, the noise of the fighting died down. Katja decided to go out again. This time she decided to leave without her sons. Early in the morning, while Grisha and Boris were still asleep, she took the revolver from its hiding place on the top shelf. She checked the cylinder.

Seven bullets!

She left the cloth with the seven spare bullets on the shelf. The sister decided to put on pants.

It makes me more agile.

The day before she had sewn Pyotr's old work pants. The material was strong and wouldn't tear so easily when she had to crawl through the rubble. She wore a blouse under her thin coat and a knitted vest over it. It was cold for this time of year. Although the sun warmed the air as soon as it reached its zenith, the cold east wind never let up. A scarf hid her long hair. Katja slipped into her sturdy shoes, which she had fortunately stored in the basement during the summer to save space, buttoned her coat, and wrote a short note to her sons.

Grigory and Boris

Stay here in the cellar. I'll be back soon.
And wash yourselves! I love you

Mama

The masculine clothes could not hide Katja's beauty. Her steel-blue eyes shone brighter than before, and her determination conjured something unapproachable in her gaze. She looked like an Amazon lost in the turmoil of war.

Katja crouched down and walked through the tunnel-like hollow path to the exit, pushed aside the corrugated iron they had placed in front of the hole as an additional screen, looked around to make sure, and crawled out of the hiding place. Then she covered the entrance again and marched off.

She was carrying a backpack and an empty bag. The revolver was in her right coat pocket. She had a screwdriver and a small axe in her backpack and a knife in her belt.

The other day she had seen the carcass of a horse. Some stray dogs were fighting over the bones and eating the entrails. The flesh of the dead animal had long since been cut off. If she made a similar find, she would cut out a large piece of flesh. Maybe she was lucky and another horse or cow or some other edible animal had fallen victim to the artillery attack that had forced her to stay in the cellar for the past two days.

That was why she had left early this morning, before sunrise. In an hour or two, the streets would be full of people sneaking through the rubble in search of food. The first to find it would be the winner. The winner in the battle of life and death. And she would fight. Nothing and no one fights more determinedly than a mother looking after her cubs. She was the lioness of the pride. A pride without a leader.

Katja ventured farther than usual this time. The area around her hiding place had already been completely plundered. She needed to find a new area.

71

The sun rose slowly, and after an hour's walk over rubble, through ruins and along shattered walls, the rising sun pushed aside the gray of dusk. The destroyed Stalingrad looked different from the vibrant city Katja knew. Orienting herself by landmarks, she passed a shop where she had once been a customer.

Ah, now I know exactly where I am.

She saw two young men crawling out of one of the ruins, brushing the dust from each other's coats. While one man's coat was much too big, the other's seemed to be much too tight. Katja ducked to avoid being seen. Instinctively, she reached into her coat pocket and her right hand gripped the handle of the revolver.

Stay calm. Not everyone is a rapist.

She took a deep breath and kept walking. Only one street away was a barely destroyed house. Katja sat down on the pole of a downed power line across from that house and watched it for a few minutes. She wondered if it would be worthwhile to go in and look for usable things.

Probably not. Since it didn't look destroyed, there must have been quite a few people in there looking for it, she finally thought, getting up and wanting to go on. Then she heard voices that made her freeze. German soldiers! They must be close by. She could even make out some of the words.

"Group ... civilians ... our leader!"

Katja ran across the street, pressed herself against the wall of the house she had been watching for a few minutes, and finally slipped through the open door.

It smelled disgustingly sweet and foul and she immediately put a hand over her mouth and nose. She suppressed an incipient gag reflex and stood still until her eyes adjusted to the dim light.

The German soldiers were approaching. Their footsteps grew louder and a conversation could now be heard clearly. The men stopped in front of the house. Katja didn't move. She was afraid of bumping into something and attracting the attention of the hated intruders. Her heart was beating fast, her pulse was pounding. They were talking. Katja concentrated and dug out her German school vocabulary to understand as much as possible. She listened to the conversation with a mixture of fear, anger, and curiosity.

"Hans, we haven't been there yet. Go there with your men and if you find civilians, lead them to the wide road."

"Man, the other day we liberated the rows of houses from Ivan, now everyone thinks there are still civilians there. That's nonsense! There aren't even a few rats hiding here anymore."

"The order is to evacuate the civilians. And that's what we're doing!"

"Why didn't Ivan evacuate them himself?"

"Why are you asking me that?"

"Because you're our new platoon leader!"

"I'm a sergeant like you, and just because I'm replacing Lieutenant Funke doesn't mean I know everything."

"It's okay!"

"Well, it's not the civilians' fault. We get them out of the rubble and that's it."

A third voice joined the conversation. Katja was afraid that the soldiers would also come to this house. She looked around in panic. There was a lot of rubble on the floor. Should she go upstairs?

No! The stairs might creak.

She decided to stay where she was.

Grisha, Boris, I'll come back for you, she thought, still gripping the revolver so tightly that the white of her knuckles stood out. She was ready to fight, but not ready to die. Not until she had brought her sons to safety, to the other side of the Volga.

"If we get the Russian civilians out of here, it means nothing but that we are advancing again!"

"Of course we're going to do that, Kurt. We need to push the Ivan across the Volga once and for all so we can set up our winter quarters in peace."

"Sounds good. I'm hoping to get some time off for Christmas. My Traudl and the children are waiting for me. I haven't seen them since February."

"It's going to be tight with the vacation."

"Don't do anything stupid!"

One of them laughed. Another, standing further away, shouted: "Hey, you two! Stop right there! Stoj!"

They had spotted the two young men!

Katja's chest rose and fell quickly. The smell became more and more pungent and she felt the fear of being discovered creeping deeper and deeper inside her.

Loud footsteps. The hobnailed boots of the lansers made an inimitable sound when they hit the hard stones of the road.

You bastards, are you going to kill us civilians too?

No shots were fired. The Germans were gone. They must have followed the two Russians.

Are they all gone?

Katja waited a few minutes, then she was sure that no one was standing outside the house. She went through the first floor as carefully as possible, but found only empty and, above all, destroyed furniture. Her first suspicions were confirmed.

Just as I thought, everything here has been looted.

Even without the hope of finding anything useful, she decided to go upstairs and look for useful things there as well. Besides, she felt safer in the house than out on the street, where the Germans were probably looking for civilians to evacuate.

Evacuating from the battlefield is good, but unfortunately you're taking us in the wrong direction!

The stench grew stronger. Katja knew it was the stench of decay. She suspected that an animal carcass was lying around rotting, but on the second floor, the bootleg of a German was sticking out of a room into the hallway. Undoubtedly, a dead person was lying here. Nervously, and although it wasn't really appropriate in this situation, she pulled the revolver out of her coat pocket and held it protectively in front of her with a slightly shaking hand. She took a step forward and saw the body of the soldier, shredded by a hand grenade. Now Katja knew where the pungent smell of decomposition came from. The dead man's flesh was already black, and all the open areas were covered with mosquitoes. Larvae buzzed around in the eyes and open wounds. The Russian woman gagged, but once again forced herself not to vomit.

Come on, old girl, you've seen worse as a nurse!

The body had probably been overlooked after the fighting. It had not been removed from the house and, like all the other corpses, had been placed in a paper bag and buried outside the city. Now he was rotting in a house in Stalingrad. Katja climbed over the legs and quickly realized that there was nothing to be gained here. When she looked at the fallen man again, she realized that the dead man was lying on his haversack.

No, thought Katja and started to go back into the corridor, but then she suddenly saw the faces of Grisha and Boris in front of her.

What am I doing, she thought next.

She put the revolver back in her coat pocket, bent down and, disgusted, grabbed the corpse by the uniform to roll it a little to the side. A blast of foul gas shot toward her. What felt like myriads of flies circled around her. Holding her breath, she grabbed the pack with her left hand and pulled it forward. Then the body tilted back to its original position. Katja pulled out her knife and cut the strap of the bag around the fallen man's shoulder.

I hope it was worth it!

Katja left the room and quickly walked downstairs. She breathed through her mouth and tried to keep her nose closed. She had to get some fresh air. She stopped at the front door and looked outside. The Germans were nowhere in sight. She walked out into the street and greedily sucked the cool, fresh morning air into her lungs. She felt as if she had risen from the bottom of the Volga after a dive. Her lungs filled up, blew out the stale air, and filled up again. Katja looked around, disappeared around the corner and sat down on the ground in the shelter of a pile of rubble to inspect her prey. She eagerly opened the haversack and was amazed.

The contents proved to be extremely useful. The dead man had an Esbit stove with a full box of fuel tablets. Then there was some stale bread wrapped in paper bags and a few spices she could use to make a good soup.

Hot food!

That would be good for her sons and herself. The soldier also had storm matches, a round tin marked "Scho-ka-Kola," the fortifying chocolate, a can opener, a tin of liverwurst, and a tube of cheese.

She tucked everything into her backpack, leaving the bread sack, which reeked of decay.

Satisfied with her haul and frightened by the German soldiers, Katja decided to go back to the hiding place and cook something hot for her sons. She got up, went out into the street, and made sure there were no soldiers around. Then she scurried across the street, past the store, remembering the last time she had waved to the owner, laughing and with a full basket, and made a little detour around a crater. Just as she was about to step over the next pile of rubble, the sister stopped dead in her tracks.

"Stoj!"

Katja closed her eyes. Her right hand went quickly into her coat pocket. But she immediately pulled it out when she recognized four German soldiers. One of them pointed a rifle at her. She wouldn't have had a chance. A feeling of helplessness spread. One of the men beckoned to her. Katja tried to smile and said in broken German, "Guten Morgen.

"We have orders to evacuate the city. Civilians must leave the combat zone for their own safety. Please go two streets away. There you will join the other citizens of Stalingrad."

Katja understood enough to know where to go and that the city was being evacuated. That didn't bode well for Grisha and Boris. She had to get to her children. No matter what the cost. She nodded politely and started to move in the other direction. "Family! Children!"

"Stop! You go that way!" came the commanding tone this time.

If they think I'm a spy or hiding something, they'll search me. And if they find the gun, they'll shoot me on sight!

Katja smiled again, turned around and walked in the direction she was told.

In the next side street there were more German soldiers. She had to walk close to them. One of them slipped Katja a piece of bread. "Here! You look hungry!"

He was young, perhaps in his early 20s, and had reddish blond hair. His eyes were kind rather than hateful. Katja was confused.

The Germans are like animals. If you fall into their hands, they will massacre you, they always said.

Well, they were her enemies. They had killed her beloved Pyotr, and even if she had felt something like humanity in this one German,

76

they were still invaders and responsible for the chaos the city was in now.

"Thank you," Katja replied, taking the bread and putting it in her bag.

People crawled out of the ruins, following the soldiers' orders. Some even came from the sewers. Fear was on all their faces. Fear and pure desperation. They followed the instructions of the foreign soldiers, and when Katja and the other civilians came to the big access road, she saw hundreds of Stalingrad people forming a stream of refugees from the city, moving like a slowly crawling snake.

Katja didn't want to join this line of people. She wanted to get back to her sons, but the way seemed blocked. She had to get in line so as not to attract attention. Her mother tried not to panic.

Think about it! You need to stay calm and make a good plan to get out of here and back to the boys.

Katja looked from left to right. Soldiers stood at regular intervals along the road. Some of them looked at the stream of refugees with disdain, others showed heart and gave something to the people. Some Russians were pulling handcarts, others were carrying suitcases and bags, and still others were carrying nothing at all. They had nothing to save but their lives and the clothes on their backs. Katja watched the scenes and moved from foot to foot. She walked slowly, let herself be overtaken, and only picked up the pace when she thought one of the Germans would notice her walking and look around for an opportunity to escape.

There is good and evil on both sides. No! They are evil. They came and destroyed my home. They killed my husband. I hate them! When one of them slips something to a Russian, he just wants to clear his soul and ease his conscience.

Katja decided to move to the side at the next unclear spot, perhaps to pretend that she had to relieve herself, and then hide in the ruins and make her way to her cellar hiding place at dusk or at night.

She knew she was very lucky not to have been searched, because she could see the soldiers occasionally looking into the refugees' bags and backpacks. Some were also patted down. If they found the revolver in her coat pocket, they would shoot her. The Russian was sure of that.

I have to be careful. Very careful!

Katja continued to look for a suitable place, but then everything turned out differently than she had imagined. Thunder could be heard in the distance. It was as if a thunderstorm was brewing, but this rumble lasted much longer and did not stop. It was coming from the artillery. The air was filled with howling from one moment to the next.

Huiit - wham

"Artillery attack!" shouted one of the German soldiers, throwing himself to the ground.

The first shell was thrown into the middle of the stream of refugees and had a deadly effect. Human bodies were torn apart, shrapnel and stones swirled around. Severed body parts swirled through the air.

Screams, panic, fear of death.

With the sound of multiple shells of various calibers, covered by swirling concrete and street dust, and accompanied by a storm of detonations from the exploding explosives, the stream of refugees rushed frantically into the ruins and among the piles of rubble, seeking shelter.

Katja ran as fast as she could. She ran for her life, jumped over small craters, crawled along a wall, and finally found a small alcove into which she squeezed.

Huuiiitt - wham

Again and again explosions, again and again screams. She relived the heavy bombardment of the summer Sunday that ended her beautiful life and killed her beloved husband. Death walked around her, swinging his scythe and laughing. She trembled with fear and an indescribable rage rose in her. She knew they were Russian shells. The barrels of her own guns were firing, knowingly or not, at the civilians fleeing the city of Stalingrad. Bloody bastards!

The artillery attack lasted less than ten minutes, then the fire was transferred. But those ten minutes were enough to kill scores of women, children, and men, and to injure hundreds more. But this horrific scenario had also allowed Katja to steal away from the stream of refugees and wait here, in her little alcove, until it was dark, and then return to her sons.

5

"We have just been withdrawn from the battlefield, suffered unprecedented casualties, and are already being sent forward again?"

The atmosphere was heated as Captain Koenig announced to his platoon and subordinate leaders that their next combat mission was imminent.

"I'm going to take over a platoon," he said impressively, stepping in front of the men. "We all need to clench our ass cheeks. Anyone who can hold and fire a rifle will march with us. We are the best company in the battalion. The battalion is the best in the regiment, and the regiment is the best in the 295th Infantry Division! If any of you think you have to chicken out now that it's the last fight before winter break, I'll scrub the latrines with you!"

The Skewer talked himself into a rage. The appearance of the rather small and chubby looking soldier was awe-inspiring. Even Captain Koenig did not interrupt his company sergeant. He knew that the men had the utmost respect for their sergeant, and when he, the little man with the high reputation, who normally sat in the office and made sure that the store ran and that the people could go on vacation, get their mail, or be supplied with sutler goods, took up arms himself and sat at the head of the troops, it had an effect.

"... and then, when we have chased the Ivan across the river, we will put up Christmas trees here, have the best wine, schnapps and beer delivered from home, build a few houses and wait for spring behind a warm stove. And if I ask you now if you are ready to go into battle again, there is only one answer I want to hear from you. A loud and terrible hurrah! The Ivan should hear it all the way to his positions and be scared shitless!"

Silence.

"Men, are you ready for this last important battle?"

"Hurraaaaaaaa," came from the throats of the excited men.

The dead and wounded of the last battle were forgotten. The fear of dying was suppressed. They had heard only the words Christmas, warm stove, and home. They were tired, exhausted and at the end of their tether, but for this one battle they would pull themselves together once more.

"Hurraaaaaaaa," they repeated, and Captain Koenig patted Schmidt on the shoulder. He stepped in front of the spit and said in a strong voice in casual Landser jargon: "Today the kitchen bull has plenty of meat in the cauldron. There's goulash! We managed to get a few bottles of red wine. One bottle for two men. Enjoy it men, thank you, dismissed".

After dinner, Koenig called his platoon leaders and their deputies into the office. The captain had reorganized the entire company due to manpower shortages, pulling all combat-ready men out of the ranks and replacing them with wounded or sick soldiers who could not fight.

"Sit down, gentlemen," he began the briefing, explaining his personnel measures. The men were a bit surprised. No one had expected Captain Koenig to take such steps to replenish their ranks.

"This is the right sign for our exhausted soldiers," said Sergeant Major Schmidt.

Koenig nodded in agreement. "And now to our mission. I was with the regiment a few days ago and made representations on another matter. Our problems are well known, but we are close to our goal. If we can drive the Russians across the river for good with this hard, concentrated blow, and occupy this area as well," his hand pointed to the map of Stalingrad lying on the table in front of them, "we will have peace!" With his right index finger, he circled the Russian-occupied triangle in the city's industrial zone with the adjacent Mamai Hill.

"Captain, where will we be deployed?" asked Sergeant Schneider, who had replaced the fallen Lieutenant Kleindienst.

"Our air force will prepare the attack and bomb the enemy. We will attack with two panzer and five infantry divisions. The Red Army won't be able to withstand this force."

"I'm sorry, but that's what we thought at the height of 102. Will we be used there again?"

Koenig looked at the questioner. It was Sergeant Mueller, a brave soldier whom Koenig had personally nominated for the Iron Cross First Class for his service in the battles at Mamai Hill. The company commander realized that fear was involved in this question. The horrors of that battle were still with him.

"No!" the company commander replied briskly.

There was a palpable sense of relief.

That's the paradox of war. They are happy that we are being sent to a different section, even though death lurks there just as much, Koenig's head whirled.

"Our division is in the industrial area and is advancing here," his finger slid across the map, pointing to one of the factories. "We're going to take the Lazur chemical plant with supporting forces and occupy this railroad loop, which is simply called a tennis racket because of its shape. Further south, the Russians are entrenched at the foot of Hill 102 and in the Balkas there. We will push him out of the Dolgii-Balka and the Krutoi Gorge and drive him to the Volga".

Silence. The men stared at the map of Stalingrad. Sergeant Schneider pulled a pack of Juno from his breast pocket, pulled out one of the cigarettes and put it between his lips. He looked around and offered his comrades a cigarette as well, holding the pack out to them in turn. Sergeant Gabler, a tall, thin man with straw-blond hair and freckles who had been in charge of Platoon III for a week, took a Juno and pulled out his storm lighter. He turned the wheel and a small orange-blue-yellow flame danced. They lit their cigarettes one after the other, inhaled the first puff and blew out the smoke. The cigarette smoke rose and formed a small cloud that hung over the conference table.

It was Sergeant Mueller again who broke the brief silence. "This won't be easy. The regimental staff already knows that we're crawling along on our last legs, don't they?" he once again draws attention to the desolate fighting strength.

"They know that, and they know that our battalion is one of the most dedicated. That's why we're the reserve."

"The bottom line is that we are deployed where there are the most fires. We are the fire department!" Sergeant Schneider interjected, taking a drag on his cigarette and blowing the smoke out through his mouth and nose.

"What about the support you mentioned earlier?" Mueller followed up.

"In addition to the troops that will be deployed near us, we will be reinforced with assault rifles and armored personnel carriers!"

If there was anything like relief in such tense moments, it was what the men felt.

"That sounds good."

The General Staff of the 6th Army knew that they were not only fighting Chuikov's 62nd Army, but also against time. The Red Army had to be pushed across the Volga before winter set in. Despite the heavy losses and the fact that the deployed divisions were exhausted and had lost a considerable part of their combat strength, preparations were made for a decisive blow. The goal was the industrial district of Stalingrad, whose rear lay on the Volga.

Here, in the industrial north of the city, Chuikov had set up his headquarters. This was where reinforcements arrived and the Red Army was supplied. If you compared the destroyed city to a body, it was paralyzed. Only the heart was still beating, keeping the battered body alive. It pumped and beat and could not be stopped.

Chuikov had minefields laid around the factories and anti-tank barriers built. The area occupied by the Russians protruded like the tip of a spear into the destroyed city.

The Russian commander was aware of the importance of Mamai Hill. Anticipating the German attack, he launched several diversionary attacks and threw the bulk of his troops into the battle for Hill 102.

It was still dark when they reached their starting positions. Medics and doctors were preparing for the worst and setting up dressing stations. Sankas and trucks rolled forward incessantly, some returning empty. They were carrying ammunition and soldiers.

With the rising sun came the Stuka squadrons. With their curved wings, their silhouettes stood out clearly from the other fighters and bombers. They flew over the Landser, lowered their noses, sped toward their targets in the approaching Russian anti-aircraft fire and, accompanied by the wailing of their Jericho sirens, dropped their deadly bomb load.

Captain Koenig carried his sniper rifle on his back, which

earned him more than a few quizzical looks. There was a lot of whispering behind his back.

"Move aside," was shouted from the rear to the front, and the men of the company moved to the right to clear the road for passing armored personnel carriers.

The detonations were muffled at first, but with each street the HKL battlegroup approached, the roar of explosions and Soviet defensive fire increased.

The faces under the dented steel helmets looked tense. Some men were shaving, others were growing beards. While Sergeant Major Schmidt had considered holding another roll call before the mission, seeing discipline as the basis for success, Captain Koenig felt that the soldiers were so exhausted and tired that they should not be dragged any further and stopped it.

They marched single file through the ruins of Stalingrad. The shadows of the planes rushed over them. One group flew back to the airfield, another to the enemy.

Wrommm

The engine of an armored personnel carrier hummed again, pushing past the marching infantrymen.

"I wouldn't want to sit in a tin can like that in battle. You're at the mercy of the enemy."

"Nonsense! They've got two MG 34s and can really turn up the heat. And you're safer in the belly of that steel body than out here."

"Don't talk so much. Save your strength," an older corporal warned.

"That one," a private pointed to an SPW, "has ammunition for the assault rifles. The steel colossi are already up ahead. They'll clear the way for us."

The young soldier beside him nodded wordlessly. He had begun to pray again that night, after the fighting on Mamai Hill and his first hand-to-hand combat. His hands trembled at the thought of combat, and he would never forget the face of the Russian he had fought to the death. His opponent was as young as he was. The steel helmet slipped from his head, too big for him, and the shaved skull shone in the sun. The Russian had drawn a bayonet and was about to ram it into the soldier's stomach, but the soldier had managed to trip the Russian and they both fell to the ground. The bayonet landed in the dirt. The Russian's hands grabbed the German's collar, his hands went around the Red Army soldier's neck and squeezed. He strangled him. A year ago he had finished his apprenticeship as a locksmith. He wanted to marry his girlfriend and make a career in the steel mill. Then the draft came and he ended up here.

In the barracks, he dreamed of heroism and a decorated chest. Now he had experienced death first hand and had aged years. Yes, he had quietly decided to pray again, and he began to hate what he had once worshipped so much. Hitler and all those talkers from Berlin.

Let them march in person and conquer this shitty city. I want to go home and get married and work. I want to go back to my little apartment and my garden, where we always sit in the summer.

He felt a thick lump form in his throat, reached for his canteen and took a swig before answering. "Yes, these things will clear the way for us."

"Company halt!" ordered Captain Koenig, raising his right hand.

The men marching behind him stopped or sat down as they could. Some lit cigarettes, others rolled them.

A few of the compatriots reached into their packs and pulled out something to eat.

The signalman acknowledged a radio message. "Captain Koenig, the company commanders are to report to the battalion commander immediately. He has his command post in grid square B 11, that's ..."

"Thank you, I know where that is. Schmidt, take over for me until then," Koenig commented, putting down his backpack but keeping the sniper rifle with him as he walked to his immediate superior's command post.

The battalion commander was surrounded by officers. Dispatchers were running, others were arriving. Field telephones rang loudly and radios crackled. Small voices could be heard, some calm and collected, others shouting in panic.

"Second in need of immediate backup," a radio operator shouted.

One of the officers standing around the major, who had recently taken command of the battalion, went to the man on the radio. "What's going on?"

"Second Battalion is calling for reinforcements."

"Oh," the captain waved him off. "That's Lieutenant Colonel Pleicher. He always thinks he has too few men." He thought for a moment and asked: "Or has the regiment officially ordered us to help?"

"No, Captain, I just heard the radio message."

"Then let's slow down with the release of our reserves. The dance is just beginning."

As soon as this was said, the hectic pace increased noticeably. The last of the Stuka bombers moved away, while the tank and infantry forces simultaneously advanced with full force against the Soviet positions.

A buzz of voices, the telephones and radios were literally on fire. One of the men on the radio tried to drown everyone out by shouting: "The Fourth Battalion is making a big bang. The whole first wave of assault guns got stuck in mine barriers. They need sappers!"

Koenig looked at the orderly chaos for a few minutes, then took the sniper rifle off his back and went to the battalion commander. The company commanders of the other two companies were already there, as was the lieutenant of the engineer platoon. When the company commander of the machine-gun company arrived two minutes later and joined the battalion leaders, the major began his briefing.

"I don't want to waste any time. We will move up to the so-called Tennis Arm and reinforce our forces there.

This was followed by instructions as to which company was to advance where, at what strategic points the machine gun company was to position itself, and the information that the engineers would be used as assault engineers this time. The engineer platoon leader tried to protest, but quickly realized that there was no point in protesting.

The reserve was called up just before noon. Despite the massive bombing by the Stuka squadrons, the resistance was enormous. By the time Captain Koenig and his company infiltrated the front, the tennis racket battle had been raging for hours. Grenades of all kinds exploded, machine guns rattled, bullets and shrapnel whirled through the air.

"They were crawling out of all the holes. Suddenly there were Red Army soldiers everywhere," the first sergeant, who was acting as company commander, explained, since all the officers had been killed or wounded. "We took this pile of rubble of a block of houses this morning, then flew out again, and have now reoccupied two-thirds of it. We really need to hold the whole block and set up a VB (*Abbreviation for forward artillery observer*) for the artillery."

Huiit - Wham

Both of them ducked as a couple of shells rushed in and landed near them.

"I see you have a sniper rifle."

Koenig nodded.

The sergeant kept looking at the officer's pigtails. "Are you Captain Koenig? The instructor of our snipers?"

"I am."

"Thank God. We have a big problem here in this section. The Ivan has positioned several of his snipers in the rubble in front of us. We're safe here, but if we move between the houses, they'll shoot us down. We've already lost seven men to these bastards. I hate those nasty bastards," as soon as he had finished, he looked into the captain's eyes, thought about his last sentence and corrected himself: "Well, I mean the Russians, not you. When I tell our boys that you are here and that you have your rifle with you, they will attack with renewed courage."

Koenig considered what to say in response, but decided to remain silent and carry out the order. He turned to his executioner. "Have the grenade launchers fire at the apron. Have the machine guns fire a barrage. I. and II. Platoon attack from the flanks, III Platoon stay in reserve!"

The radio message was immediately relayed and confirmed.

"Attack in two minutes! Mortars and machine guns - open fire!"

Shortly thereafter, the grenades from the launcher unit whirled through the air every second. At the same time, the rattling of the machine guns began.

Rrrrt... rrrrt...

Plop - plop - plop - plop - wham - wham - wham

Rrrrt... rrrt...

Koenig had moved up a bit from his position and was looking at the target and the ruined apron through his binoculars. With the impact of the first shells he shouted: "Attaaaack!"

"Hurraaaaaaa!"

The captain jumped up and took off. He didn't make it all the way to the front of the line, but he was well ahead.

The astonished first sergeant exclaimed, "What a son of a gun," and raised his fist as well. "Attack!"

His exhausted men plucked up courage and charged over boulders and stones.

They were met with defensive fire. Shots were fired from the rubble in front of the ruined house and from the building itself.

Carbines and submachine guns. Not a machine gun, Koenig realized and shouted as loud as he could: "Come on! Come on, men!"

His light grenade launchers and machine guns still covered the apron.

Rrrrt... rrrrt...

Plop - plop - plop - plop - wham - wham - wham

Rrrrt... rrrt...

The soldier running in front of him fell to the ground and lay motionless, the soldier next to Koenig threw his arms up in the air and roared loudly as he hit the ground hard. "Ahhh!"

A bullet whizzed hot past the company commander's ear. He raised his MP, stopped, and fired two rounds without seeing a target. "Forward," he whipped his men.

A Russian, well camouflaged between two piles of rocks, jumped up, emptied his carbine, and collapsed, mortally wounded, as he tried to charge into hand-to-hand combat. On Koenig's right, four Russians met six German soldiers. Roaring like animals, they clashed and fought to the death.

The first Landser reached the ruins. Among them was First Sergeant Schmidt. Panting like a horse, the stocky soldier wiped the sweat from his brow and pulled a stick grenade from his belt. He unscrewed the cap, pulled the ripcord, mentally counted two seconds to make it virtually impossible to throw the grenade back, and hurled it through a completely shattered window into the ruins. He immediately pressed himself against the wall.

Thud

Dust, splinters, and other debris were thrown out by the pressure of the blast. The window frame, already damaged, was completely shredded. More grenades flew into the ruins.

Someone threw an egg grenade at them from an upper floor.

"Grenade!" someone yelled, and everyone ran for cover.

thud

The explosion was deafening. Schmidt's eardrums threatened to burst, even though the first sergeant had covered his ears. Shrapnel sailed through the air and clattered against the ruined house.

"Damn dogs, when will you give up? Are you going to fight forever?" he shouted angrily, jumping up and shouting: "Men, get inside!" Then the Landser charged into the ruins at the front.

Captain Koenig was also hiding. The shrapnel had narrowly missed him. He had seen from which window the grenade had been thrown, aimed his MP there and waited. When he saw the arm of a Russian come out from behind the ledge, he pulled the trigger and emptied the entire magazine. Two or three of his rounds hit the Red Army soldier's arm. The hand grenade he was about to throw at the German attackers exploded in the room. The cloud of explosions was littered with dust, shrapnel, pieces of uniform, skin and flesh.

More and more Landser trickled into the destroyed building.

"Halt! The second platoon will cover the left flank from the outside, the third platoon will move up and cover the right flank. Keep the machine guns in the barrage, close with the grenade launchers!" the orders thundered.

The radio operator had to repeat them several times over the radio before they were finally acknowledged.

There were several more exchanges of fire inside the building. The detonation of another hand grenade ended the resistance and the ruins were taken.

It hissed above them. Grenades hissed through the air, descending and exploding in the wreckage.

Huiit - Wham

This time it was Russian artillery firing.

The Sergeant Major and Captain Koenig had positioned themselves on the second floor of the ruins, peering through the window at their next target.

"It's always like this. When we advance, the Ivan let their artillery know. They take the area under fire and their snipers force us to take cover. Then their infantry advances and pushes us out again. It's a vicious cycle, Captain."

Koenig dropped the binoculars, moved sideways away from the window, and leaned against the wall. There was a pungent smell of gun smoke. "I want a brief situation report, especially how many men we've lost. And I want the platoon leaders to report to me!"

The noise of the fighting subsided somewhat, but not completely. Meanwhile, the shells from the Russian artillery were coming dangerously close to them.

Huiiit - Wham!

"Damn it! They must have a VB sitting nearby who can tell them everything!" hissed the officer, annoyed.

"He can only be sitting in the water tower. Have you seen the to-wer? That thing's all alone and abandoned, as if the Stukas left it there on purpose," said the first sergeant.

"It would be suicide to hide there. I wonder, if he really is on the water tower, why doesn't he retreat?"

"He has the best view! We have to take him out! I'll attack with some men."

"No! He's guaranteed to be covered by one or more Russian snipers."

The first sergeant glanced out of the window, but immediately pulled his head back. "That's possible."

Koenig took a deep breath. He had to do it himself. Hurried footsteps could be heard and tore him from his thoughts. Sergeant Major Schmidt, Sergeant Mueller and Sergeant Gabler came running up the stairs.

Koenig missed Schneider, but he didn't have to say anything because Schmidt gave a full report. "We lost seven men, four are wounded. Sergeant Schneider is dead. Shot in the head!"

"They're here," whispered the first sergeant of the other company. "You were right. There are snipers over there."

"Take care of the wounded!" the officer ordered.

"It will be done, but we can't go back, the damn artillery shoots pretty good. If our gunners worked the same way, we'd have fewer problems."

Koenig deliberately ignored the comparison. "We will immediately prepare for a Soviet counterattack."

"Aren't we advancing?" asked Sergeant Gabler.

"We have to take out the Ivan's VB first, or we'll have a disaster on our hands. I'll take care of that myself."

Huiit - Wham

This time a whole volley of grenades crashed down next to the ruins where they were trapped. The pikeman jumped at the detonations and yelled loudly: "Aye, sir," turned and ran back down the stairs. Sergeant Gabler followed.

Koenig had made a decision. He picked up the sniper rifle, carefully pulled the cover off the sight, and checked the magazine and the load.

Five rounds. Pointed bullet with a hard steel core. I will save my men from you!

Erwin Koenig entered the corridor of the ruins and went up one floor. He had enormous respect for the Russian snipers and avoided standing in front of the windows. Once upstairs, he looked for a room with a good view of the water tower. Then he took his binoculars and watched the tower from just over a meter away from the window. He searched every square inch and discovered the hiding place. The artillery observer's knee was sticking out from behind one of the large support struts. Koenig had only noticed it because the forward observer had moved.

I've got you!

The captain set the binoculars aside and picked up the sniper rifle. He adjusted the sights to the correct distance and fired. Adrenaline shot through his blood. His pulse suddenly began to beat extremely fast. Koenig felt every beat of his heart and his hands grew clammy. Beads of sweat ran down his forehead. The sniper lowered his rifle and wiped his brow. He was nervous. He had had to kill many times during the war. But this was combat. A fight to the death. This time was different. As a sniper instructor, he had often told his shooters. He was fully aware of the theoretical process, but theory and practice were two completely different things.

Concentrate! You taught the snipers. You did it perfectly on the training ground. This man is killing your men. Take him out!

The feeling of watching a person through the scope, taking aim, and killing him with a well-aimed shot was different from shooting at targets. He had to admit that to himself at that moment. He took a deep breath and was glad to be alone in this room.

Huiiit - Wham!

The next volley of grenades rushed in and detonated with a crash. That was the push the officer needed.

You will not send any more of my men to their deaths!

He took the carbine, went to the window and knelt down. He put it back on. Koenig pressed the butt firmly into his shoulder. He felt the wood of the stock against his right cheek. The muzzle was against the windowsill. The sniper instructor searched the scope for his victim and found him. The knee was still visible.

This is going to hurt!

He was at the target. Take a deep breath, exhale, inhale and blow out part of the lung volume again. Hold your breath. He became calm. Freezing cold. Erwin Koenig had the tunnel vision you get when you focus on something while shooting and have the target in sight. He curled his index finger to the pressure point. He was the hunter and his quarry was still on target. K pulled the trigger. Muzzle flash and recoil were one. The Russian VB screamed loudly and fell off the water tower. The impact must have been hard for him. The Red Army soldier was badly injured and could hardly move.

Take him out, was the only thought Koenig had.

As he retreated, a bullet whizzed past his head, just millimeters away. In a split second, he ducked under the ledge and crawled sideways. Leaning against the wall, he took a deep breath.

"I've turned off the VB! Stay down, there are snipers out there!" he yelled to his men.

"Hurraaaaa!" he yelled upstairs.

He knew this would cement his hitherto unjustified reputation as a stone-cold sniper.

Koenig left the room and went into another room. There he sat down by a window, picked up his binoculars, and watched the ruins for more than half an hour. Only when the artillery fire stopped did he put the binoculars down.

Schmidt and the first sergeant of the other company called to him. "Captain Koenig, we have to take the next house. The battalion staff is getting impatient.

"Tell the platoons to get ready. But I need another ten minutes. There's still an enemy sniper out there, and I've located two possible positions where he could be lurking."

"What should we do?"

"Schmidt, we're going to lure him out of his shell with the oldest Landser trick in the book. One of us will lift his helmet with a stick in front of the window. If he shoots, I'll get the Russian!"

"Where will you be?" asks Schmidt.

"I'm looking for a place in the attic. I have the best shot from there. I can't stay here."

The roof was badly damaged by several shell hits. The captain crawled over bricks and under beams. There was a small window in the gable and a larger hole in the masonry to the right, caused by a shell hit. Koenig peered through the 40 cm hole and had a good view of the terrain. Once again, he used his binoculars to observe possible sniper positions. As the company prepared to attack, Koenig prepared to fire. "Let's go!" he yelled down. He took the rifle and aimed it at one of the two hiding places.

"I'm ready too," called Schmidt, who had taken on the role of decoy. "I'll lift the helmet in exactly one minute."

Koenig counted silently.

...forty-five, forty-six ...

The company was ready to attack.

First Sergeant Schmidt had slipped his steel helmet onto the bayonet and lifted it. He moved the helmet along the window in such a way that an observer would think a soldier was crawling from one side to the other.

A shot rang out. The helmet was pierced in the middle by a bullet and thrown to the side.

Koenig heard the bang, saw a tiny flicker, held the gun two centimeters above the flicker, which he judged to be a muzzle flash, and pulled the trigger.

Through the scope he saw the barrel of a rifle lying on the stones.

No movement! That was a hit.

He had killed him. The officer turned and stared at the ceiling beams. His pulse was racing and his hands were wet. This was the second targeted kill in quick succession. He had deliberately killed two people.

Am I freezing cold? Has the war turned me into a monster?

His thoughts raced, but before a kind of depression overcame him, he justified his actions.

No! I saved my men's lives. A soldier goes to war for his country. He kills people who want to kill him. I hate war!

The king pushed his thoughts aside. They had to go forward. He shut off his thinking and replaced it with soldierly automatism.

"Target eliminated!" he yelled to Schmidt and went down. Halfway down, he gave the order to attack and heard Schmidt pass it on.

"Attack! We're storming the warehouse!" the company sergeant yelled, whipping the soldiers forward. "Charge, men! Our captain shot the sniper!"

The shouts of "Hurray!" from the soldiers rising from the rubble seemed louder than ever to Koenig. The company charged. The first volleys tore holes in the front lines, but they fought their way yard by yard to the next house.

Machine guns fired at the window openings, giving the infantrymen a barrage. Koenig left the ruins and joined the attack with the second wave.

Hand grenades whirled through the air.

The captain ran up a pile of rubble, tripped over a piece of chain-link sticking out of a concrete block, and barely broke his fall with his left hand before hitting the boulder hard.

Boom

A grenade exploded near him. Shrapnel and rocks of various sizes flew through the air. Men screamed. Within seconds, he was literally engulfed in a cloud of dust. It was hard to breathe. One of the stones hit his helmet. Shrapnel whizzed by just above him. He knew then that the fall had saved his life. The dust cloud cleared. He lifted his head to see three or four dead comrades. Torn bodies with gaping wounds. Two soldiers rolled around, wounded. One of them was his messenger. Koenig crawled over to the first soldier. A large piece of shrapnel was sticking out of his thigh. The wound was bleeding heavily. His right cheek was also completely slashed. The whole side was dark red from the gushing blood.

"Take it easy, soldier. It's not that bad," he tried to reassure the shocked soldier, clumsily but effectively applying a bandage to his head and cheek. "You have to leave the splinter in, otherwise you'll bleed to death! Do you understand?"

A blank look. A quick nod.

"The medic will pull it out. A pressure bandage must be applied immediately, otherwise you will lose too much blood. Stay lying down!"

The soldier nodded again. He seemed to wake up from his shock and tried to answer, but with the bandage on and the large gash in his cheek, he didn't try.

Koenig glanced around hastily. He searched for medics scurrying through the battlefield behind them, tending to the wounded. "Medic! Over here!" he shouted without seeing one. He held up his hand and waved. "Saaaaaniiiiiiiii!"

Another soldier knelt beside the second wounded man. One of the rearguards came over, picked up the radio, checked it, and looked for Koenig. He spotted the company commander and came over to him. Koenig stood up. "Stay still, the medic will be here soon," he said to the wounded man, grabbed his submachine gun lying on the ground, and

stormed back toward the building. The executioner with the radio followed close behind.

Once again, it was Schmidt who had led his platoon to the warehouse. He used the same tactics as before, throwing hand grenades
through shattered windows and bullet-riddled or barricaded entrances,
then storming in after the detonations.

Koenig was able to cover the last 50 meters quickly, gave the
order to secure the flanks, and followed Schmidt into the large wa-
house. He held up his left hand and pointed to two fin-gers. "Two
squads come with me," he said, then made a motion to the right and
one to the left, indicating the direction of march.

Corporal Gabler ordered a lance corporal and his machine gun
crew to take over the right flank guard and bring their machine gun into
position, then waved the rest of his battered platoon over.

"Körner and Rösler, get your squads over here! We're going into
the building!"

The big warehouse had three floors. The first floor was clear.
Gunfire stopped on the second floor. A man from Schmidt's platoon
reported that it had been taken. Koenig ran upstairs. Several signs of
combat were visible. Bullet holes and scratches from shrapnel scraped
along the walls were everywhere. Fallen soldiers lay about. In addition
to five dead Red Army soldiers, there were two fallen soldiers. Two
wounded men came toward him on the stairs, supporting each other.
Shots could be heard from the top floor. At first just one or two, then
a continuous exchange of gunfire that suddenly stopped.

Koenig hurried up the stairs. Half the group followed him. The
two wounded men pressed against the wall to make room. "Ivan's on
the top floor. The second floor is enemy free," one of them hissed at
him.

The company commander had received the information as he
ran up, nodded briefly, and called upstairs: "Schmidt, where exactly are
you?"

Instead of an answer, Koenig heard the sounds of fighting. Gro-
ans, curses and even a bloodcurdling death scream.

"Ahhhh...!"

A shot was fired. The captain reached the third floor. At the

95

end of the corridor was a large storage room. There, First Sergeant Schmidt and four of his men were wrestling with Red Army soldiers. One of the soldiers tried to thrust his spade at his opponent's head, but missed and hit the wall. The Russian, who was lying on the ground and could only escape the fatal blow by turning quickly, raised his upper body, wrapped his arms around the soldier's pelvis and buried his head in his genital area. There he bit. The German soldier roared loudly and hit the spade with the sharpened blade several times from above against the Russian's shoulder and back. He let go, whimpering, and lay there covered in blood.

"He bit my cock!" roared the Landser, dropping the spade and putting his hands in his crotch.

The half-group behind Koenig also reached the ground. "Forward! Watch out for the side rooms!"

They hurried down the long corridor and reached the large storeroom without making contact with the enemy. Schmidt was in hand-to-hand combat with a burly Red Army soldier. The lively little spitfire slipped out of an embrace, suddenly made a quick move to the right, parried a punch, grabbed his opponent by the collar of his uniform, spun around and threw the Russian to the ground with a shoulder throw. He then reached under his opponent's armpit and held him down, panting. The Russian cried out in pain.

"I've been an active wrestler since I was in high school," the Spit spat. "Give up or I'll break your shoulder joint!"

The Red Army soldier showed no more resistance and surrendered as Koenig and the other soldiers burst into the room. Schmidt loosened his grip and finally let go of his opponent. The Russian immediately raised his right hand to indicate his surrender. His face contorted in pain, he indicated that he could not raise the other.

On the gable of the room was a large double wooden shutter. Goods and supplies could be hoisted into the large room through this opening by means of a pulley. Sergeant Gabler went over and opened one of the two wings a crack. He peered through carefully. "You have a good view from up here. But I don't like what I see. The Russians are gathering. We'll probably have to fend off a counterattack soon," he said. His freckled face glowed bright red from the exertion of rushing into the building and running up the stairs.

"Move to the side. There are snipers out there."

"They got him, Captain."

"The Russians have whole sniper units out."

Gabler immediately stepped aside.

Koenig patted his company sergeant on the shoulder. "Well done, Schmidt."

He stuck out his chest proudly, still panting. "Take him away before I throw him through this hole in a fit of rage," he said.

Two men then searched the Russian and finally led him downstairs.

Koenig also peered cautiously for a moment between the two wooden shutters. "Retrieve the fallen and tend to the wounded. Where is the executioner?"

"I'm here, Captain, my second man stayed downstairs. The device has taken a blow, but he thinks he can fix it. A splinter crashed into the case of the tornister radio. Probably didn't do much damage though."

"He has to hurry." Koenig turned around. "Schmidt!"

"Captain," the Spitfire replied.

"If the radio isn't clear in ten minutes, a dispatcher will have to make his way to the battalion command post. First, we need relief, and second, the coordinates for our field artillery need to be relayed. We must keep the enemy under constant fire!"

"Got it!"

The battle raged with extreme ferocity. Important rows of houses were taken by the German attackers under heavy resistance, partially retaken and reoccupied by Russian troops, only to be pushed out again by German soldiers. The Soviet 62nd Army, under massive pressure, had to send more troops across the Volga to hold its positions. Thus, the 39th Guards Rifle Division and the Siberian 308th Rifle Division joined the battle.

The German General Staff of the 6th Army was also aware of the importance of capturing the industrial district. Therefore, General Paulus ordered the 94th Infantry Division and the 14th Panzer Division to join the battle.

The enemy clashed with merciless ferocity. The battle area resembled a landscape of ruins. Not a single building had survived the constant bombing and artillery fire.

The area around the main and loading station was also in chaos. Destroyed locomotives, wagons, work equipment and blown up tracks had to be overcome in order to advance. They provided cover and protection during the retreat, but were also considerable obstacles to the advance.

The destruction in the large machine halls was almost even worse. All the machines and turbines had been blown up, damaged or buried under stone walls. Tons of tangled cables and iron grids had to be overcome to get from one hall to the next, from one building to the next, or even from one floor to the next.

Every yard had to be bloodily fought for, only to be just as bloodily defended an hour later. The most hated and feared of all types of combat could no longer be avoided. The nerve-wracking and nightmare-inducing melee. No matter what uniform the soldiers wore, they were all accompanied by sheer horror and pure fear.

Seeing the whites of the enemy's eyes was the military term for hand-to-hand combat. This term was also used for the awarding of the Close Combat Medal, created by Adolf Hitler in November 1942 as a result of the tough fighting on the Eastern Front. It was awarded in three stages starting in December 1942.

For soldiers on both sides, it simply meant fighting to the death.

Kill a man with your bare hands or die!

The peaceful farmer from Bavaria, the good-natured worker on a Ukrainian kolkhoz, the dockworker from Hamburg or Murmansk, the hunter from the Urals, the fisherman from the Baltic, the bricklayer, the painter, the farmhand, all of them who had never done anything wrong in their normal work and life, had to attack another human being, dressed in the gray of the Wehrmacht or the earthy brown of the Red Army uniforms, smash his skull with a spade, plunge a knife or bayonet into his stomach, or strangle him with their bare hands, lest they suffer the same fate.

Stalingrad became an icy school of killing and hatred. If you wanted to live, you had to be ready to kill. If you wanted to kill ruthlessly, you had to hate abysmally. A moment of charity, pity, or mercy at the wrong moment meant one's own death. The enemy was no longer just a small, moving dot in a crowd, running towards you like a living, homogeneous mass, at which you fired your rifle. The enemy in Stalingrad had a face, eyes and a voice. Man was brutalized.

The radio was repaired by the referee. The radio messages reached the battalion headquarters and were passed on to the regiment. Captain Koenig's company was moved to the rear by the HKL that same night, and the entire battalion the next morning.

Example photo

PA-0-G-russische Dorfbewohner
Russian villagers
Privatarchiv Author
all rights reserved by the author

6

It had taken two days from the moment Ralf Koenig received his marching orders to the moment he threw his knapsack onto the straw-lined storage area in the railroad car. The young officer cadet felt like an adventurer on a journey. A cannon stove had been set up in the center of the wagon. There was coal and kindling all around. Koenig was as proud as his traveling companions. Only a sergeant and an older corporal, who had also boarded the wagon, looked serious or sad.

Rolf Koenig believed that it was the difficult farewell to the family that was pulling the men down emotionally, and he could understand it a little. But he would see his father.

Finally!

The train ride had been exciting and fun at first, but with every mile they traveled, the excitement faded.

Tsch ... tsch ... tsch... clack ... clack ... clack

The puffing of the locomotive and the clacking of the heavy iron wheels as they rolled over the sleepers were sounds they heard almost around the clock.

After two days of travel, the vast land of the East opened up. The fields became wide, the faces of the people who worked there changed.

The troop transport stopped at regular intervals at smaller stations. The guards were exchanged, the straw was changed, fuel for the stoves was brought, food was distributed. When they had crossed Poland and entered the vast expanse of the Soviet Union, an anti-aircraft gun was mounted on one of the wagons.

"Partisan territory," the sergeant murmured when a young soldier asked him what was going on.

The trip took just under a week, and Rolf Koenig had made friends with everyone in the car. Even the grumpy sergeant and the very talkative lance corporal. He had become aware of Rolf Koenig when the latter, out of sheer boredom, started telling stories about Julius Caesar and the Roman Empire in the evenings.

The lance corporal, on the other hand, told of his experiences at the front. If one of the stories seemed unbelievable, all eyes would turn to the sergeant, who would nod, usually while smoking a pipe, and say: "He's not talking rubbish! That's exactly how it happened!"

Then it was mostly quiet. Later, as they snuggled into their blankets on their straw beds to go to sleep, they thought about what it would be like at the front. Most of the way was already behind them. They would soon reach their destination. They were not there yet, but they were close. This troop transport had traveled almost 3,000 kilometers without incident.

Only twice had it been depressingly quiet during the otherwise cheerful journey, during which they had sung songs and played cards at the beginning.

The first time there was talk of a partisan attack, and the more Rolf heard the story, the more brutal it became.

A large group of partisans blew up a railroad track and attacked a troop transport.

In the first version, the train was stopped for two days before the track could be repaired, and there was talk of several casualties. In the last version, the partisans killed all the soldiers and mutilated the bodies.

Rolf Koenig gave more credence to the original version.

The second time the mood was depressed was when they were being cared for at the station, while a hospital train was on the opposite track. Some of them went on board and came back with pale faces. When they were told at school and in the barracks yard about heroism and the glorious German soldier, they believed it. It was clear to them that they would either die on the battlefield or return home as heroes with medals on their chests.

No one could imagine the former. Everyone thought that their neighbor might get hit, but they certainly wouldn't fall.

Nobody told them that you could be maimed at the front, that you could lose your legs, arms or eyesight, that you could go insane and possibly spend the rest of your life in a mental hospital.

But the young soldiers quickly forgot all that, and now they were almost there. Gawping, the young soldiers crowded around the large open sliding doors. Brakes squeaked, wagons bumped against the buffers of their front wagons, and they came to a halt.

"Pick up your marching packs! Everything out and in line!" came a sergeant's voice. "Show what you've learned! The lottery life in the barracks is over! You're real soldiers now and you can show what your instructors have taught you!"

Rucksacks tumbled out of the wagons, soldiers jumping in after them and picking up the luggage. They got their bearings, found their groups and trains, and lined up. The hustle and bustle at the loading dock resembled an anthill, but it quickly took shape.

The sergeant walked up to the sergeant. They greeted each other with a handshake. As they talked, the sergeant kept yelling: "Zack, zack! That's faster, you lame bastards!" or a: "What kind of lame bunch are you? I'll teach you proper drill before you go to the front!"

Then he would smoke a cigarette and gesticulate with his hands, sometimes more, sometimes less. By the time he threw the butt on the ground and kicked it out with the soles of his nailed boots, everyone was in line. The sergeant lined up last. The sergeant walked down the line, raised his hand, and motioned to an officer standing farther back. He walked over rather leisurely and greeted the new arrivals. They were told that the troop transport was stopping here for their protection due to active air activity with the enemy, and that they would have to walk the next thirty-five kilometers to the forward command post. A speech followed in which the captain explained that Stalingrad was about to be taken and that the recruits and those returning from leave would probably only have to serve for a few more days, if at all. After that, they would have to set up their winter quarters and enjoy a quiet life. Some of the new arrivals were disappointed. Rolf Koenig didn't care. He looked forward to seeing his father again.

"Here you will be sent to your units," the officer finished.

The sergeant spoke. The captain crossed a track and climbed into a waiting bucket truck.

"You can get your other rations at the forward control center. Pick up your gear. Turn left, march without a step!"

Rolf grabbed the heavily laden pack, to which were tied the rolled blanket, the tent sheet, and the winter coat, and strapped it to his back. A steel helmet and a haversack hung from the side. He hung the carbine across his chest so he could rest his hands on something. He had imitated the sergeant, whose MP 40 hung across his chest.

The troop of a little over two hundred men moved out. The sergeant marched alongside Rolf Koenig.

"Herbert, what did the sergeant tell you?" asked Rolf, after the sergeant showed no sign of saying anything about the conversation.

The veteran soldier made no move to answer, whereupon Koenig moved a little closer. "Come on, tell me! I want to know what to expect."

"The Russians are tough. We have huge losses, and the Dagos can't handle the Romanians. Both should cover the flanks."

"The captain says it won't be long now."

"Every night the track UvDs come right up to the stage. As long as the Ivan is still sending them through the air, we haven't reached our goal."

"Airstrip UvD?" Koenig asked.

"Polikarpov U 2 - old biplanes. They fly slowly and low. Their engine is no louder than a sewing machine, so they are called that. We once nicknamed them Taxiway UvDs because they inspect our taxiway on time like bricklayers and occasionally drop small bombs by hand."

"That doesn't sound too good, what you're saying."

"Boy, the battalions in Stalingrad have been bled dry and are nowhere near the finish line."

"But that sounded different before."

"Can I trust you?"

Rolf Koenig thought about it. He hoped the sergeant did not want to make a revolution and was not involved in military subversion. "Yes, of course. Why not?"

"Because you'll be promoted to lieutenant after your trial period at the front! And some men lose their backbone when they are promoted to officer!"

"Wait a minute!"

"Don't be afraid. I'm not a revolutionary. I'm a realist. I led my group into battle before my leave. There are only two of us left. I can't go along with all this euphoria any longer. I'll do my duty here, but don't expect me to praise those," he looked around and whispered to the

104

others, "fat-eating asses in Berlin. Let them lie here in the dirt, lice-ridden and hungry, and then fight when the enemy attacks, whether you've been asleep for one, two or five hours."

"I see," said Rolf, wondering if he should report this conversation to his father. He decided he might and changed the subject. "How far do we have to walk?"

"That's what he said. 35 kilometers!"

"And after that?"

The sergeant grinned. "Then, fortunately, there will be trucks waiting for us. It's another 50 kilometers to Stalingrad."

With only one rest stop, the march felt like a forced march for many, probably due to the full and therefore heavy packs.

Drenched in sweat and with empty canteens, they arrived at the front headquarters. Field gendarmes were directing the traffic, a group of soldiers half the size of a company was distributed on trucks. Reporting officers rode off on their motorcycles, and the commander of a tank, reeking of exhaust fumes and smoking accordingly, had lost his way and asked one of the chain dogs, as the field gendarmes were called, for directions to the repair area.

Two large field kitchens kept the supplies moving. There was a hot meal and cold rations for two days. Rolf Koenig again sought the company of the sergeant, who was sitting away from the bulk of the troops, eating his stew with sausage. When Koenig sat down, the sergeant looked up briefly and said: "They don't get any rest from you either," dipping a piece of commissary bread into the stew and taking a bite.

"What bunch do you belong to?"

"Why?"

"If we were in the same unit, we could work together..."

Before Koenig had finished speaking, the sergeant named his unit, whereupon the ensign grinned.

"Not quite, but you'll be with me for a long time. I'll be in the fourth company."

"Eat, or the lukewarm stuff will get cold. Then you won't be able to enjoy it."

An hour later they were being loaded onto trucks. Several Hennessy, Mercedes, and Opel Blitz trucks drove over a bumpy and barely passable road. The men on the backs of the trucks cursed and held on tight.

"We have the sewing machines to thank for this. They ripped up the whole route. We were able to fill most of the holes with helpers, but..." the co-driver interrupted as the military convoy came to a halt.

One of the men peered through the tarp. "Field marshals!"

Two military policemen armed with MPs stood on the road. One of them was talking to the driver of the vehicle in front. A message was slowly passed from the front to the back.

"This will take time. The Russian is very active. You can sleep for a few hours," the first sergeant with the glittering shield on his chest had told the leader of our squad.

The sergeant grabbed his rucksack and jumped from the loading area. Without saying a word, he found a good spot by the side of the road, unrolled the tent, lay down in it, and covered himself. Before Krueger could do the same and roll himself into the blanket, he heard the sonorous snoring of his neighbor.

At night it began to rain, and the Landser preferred to return to the back of the truck. The tarps kept the water out. They were able to continue their journey before sunrise.

"Do you hear that?" one of the young soldiers asked the man next to him.

"Hear what?"

"The rumbling and thundering. What's that?"

"I don't know."

The sergeant stuffed tobacco into the bowl of his pipe, pulled out matches, and seconds later the bowl glowed orange-yellow. The blue haze drifted mostly into the Opel Blitz's cargo hold, dancing in the faint, gray light of the slowly rising sun under the tarp until it slowly dissipated. The smell of tobacco was sweet and not unpleasant.

"This is Stalingrad, my boy. It welcomes us. It's the shells hitting here and there, turning over the stones and looking for meat."

"At six in the morning?"

"The front knows no time. Get used to dying 24 hours a day!"

"Talk about something else," came from the back.

The sergeant stared at the smoke of his next puff and remained silent.

More and more vehicles and soldiers appeared. They rolled past bunkers and a field bakery. Koenig saw a truck being loaded with commissary bread.

A short time later they had to stop. Several ambulances and trucks with the Red Cross on a white background passed by.

"The wounded from the front," said one of the men.

Silence. Worried faces.

The truck jerked to a stop, and twenty minutes later they reached their destination. The sergeant grabbed his pack and said: "We're here now."

The men were to serve their time. They were in a suburb of Stalingrad. Street signs pointed in different directions. On one, Rolf Koenig read: Berlin 2768 km, on another it said: Entering Stalingrad is dangerous.

A lieutenant with an eye patch went to the front of the bucket car. Shortly after, two sergeants, two lance corporals and a sergeant joined him. They were given final instructions, then marched out to the new arrivals at almost double speed. Each of them called out a unit and the men went to it.

Rolf Koenig heard his battalion being called and went to the sergeant. Of the two hundred or so men who had come to Stalingrad with him, 38 belonged to Koenig's unit.

The sergeant had the men line up in order of height and walked down the line. He studied their faces and shook his head. "We need twice as many soldiers, and experienced ones at that. What are we going to do with a bunch of kids?" he probably asked himself, because he didn't speak directly to anyone. When he reached the end of the line, he walked back to the center, took a step back, and counted. As the number was called, heads flew to the left, as they had learned to do, and when the last person in line whispered his "38!" the sergeant nodded in satisfaction. "There's order at the Barras, even during the war," he said, turning and pointing to a couple of barracks. "You can make yourselves comfortable there and recover a bit from the journey. That means getting your uniforms and weapons in order! Tomorrow morning, exactly 15 minutes after breakfast, there will be a roll call. I want to see clean weapons, clean gear, and clean uniforms. Even if you've walked through feet of mud to get breakfast and wash up. I want your cups to shine!"

A low murmur and groan could be heard.

"Just like the barracks!" said someone from the left.

"I thought this crap was over for good," whispered Koenig on the right.

The sergeant put his fists on his hips and stood with his legs apart. "Most of you are moving to the HKL tomorrow night! We'll meet up with the food transporters and go with them. Then I'll assign you to your units. And now I need your marching orders."

The big search began. The first papers were picked up. The sergeant collected the marching orders one by one. Then the men went into the bare barracks. Each of these simple wooden houses could sleep 20 men.

Koenig gulped when he saw the spartan furnishings. Straw sacks lined the walls, and in the center was a rough wooden table, its top resting on four wooden trestles. There was no electricity, but there were two kerosene lamps on the table. To the left of the door was a cannon stove, but it was not lit.

Seven soldiers were already quartered in the barracks assigned to Koenig. Three were lying on their bunks, four were sitting at the table playing cards. When the new arrivals entered the room, they interrupted their game. One of them, a lance corporal who had been awarded the Iron Cross, stood up. Koenig guessed it was someone returning from leave.

"Welcome to Stalingrad. What unit do you belong to?" he greeted the men, glancing over them and lingering on Koenig. "You look somehow familiar to me. What's your name, comrade, and where are you from?"

"I am Rolf Koenig," the ensign replied, extending his hand and approaching the corporal with a smile. "I don't remember seeing you before."

The corporal had hands the size of toilet lids, and Rolf Koenig's

108

hand literally disappeared into them. He expected a firm handshake and thought his hand would be crushed, but there was no firm squeeze.

"First of all, we're on a first-name basis here, unless you're a big-wig and you're still too far away from that. Second, did you say Koenig?" he added questioningly.

"Yes."

"That's how I know that face. Could it be..." the lance corporal mused.

Koenig grinned and interrupted the Lancer. "He is my father."

"Captain Erwin Koenig is your father?"

"Yes."

"Respect. He never told me his son was coming here."

"You, uh ... you know him?"

"Your father is a living legend. He's the man we need here."

Koenig was a little irritated. "A legend?"

"He is the sharpshooter of all sharpshooters. When he goes into battle, he finds his target and takes it out. He is by far the best!"

"But he's a company commander!"

"Now he leads a company, but before that he trained the snipers in our regiment."

"Yes, he was on the staff and was an officer there. I know that."

"I am in his company and damn proud of it. Your father is the kind of man who leads from the front. Do you understand that?"

"No."

Another of the card players cut in. "He's not one of the wimps. Excuse the expression. Captain Koenig is a real soldier. He never asks for more than he would do himself, but it's a hell of a lot. So when you serve under him, it means you are always on the front line. He teaches fear to the enemy."

Koenig was a little taken aback that his father was something of a hero. It made him proud, of course, but he wanted to talk to him about it first. A hero. I don't believe it. My dad is supposed to be a war hero, he thought.

"Let me give you some good advice. Take care of your equipment and make sure everything is in order. Remember that the Iron Ratiation can only be consumed on command, not when you're hungry! And make a proper camp. The noncommissioned officers will really get you going here before we move on to the HKL," said the corporal.

His fellow card player confirmed it: "Two of us had to take a special watch, and one of us got an aggravated arrest with a record, just because he forgot to oil his weapons."

"Thanks for the tip."

The officer candidate set up his gear next to one of the sleeping areas and made himself comfortable. Before he lay down, he cleaned and oiled his weapons to avoid attracting negative attention during a possible inspection.

The wake-up call was harsh. Rolf Koenig's bones were indeed shaken by the journey. Contrary to his initial fears, he had slept relatively well on the simple straw bed.

Since the rooms they were staying in were not heated, it was correspondingly chilly. Only cold water was available for washing, which didn't make shaving any easier. When the young midshipman visited the latrine, he knew that there were no luxuries in combat.

A beam had been erected in front of a long trench. You could squat on it. The waste fell into the trench. When it was full, it was filled with earth again.

The famous thunderbolt!

Breakfast consisted of lukewarm coffee substitute, fresh commissary bread, some butter and jam. Nevertheless, it tasted excellent, and the young men felt like old front-line soldiers as they sat at the tables in their barracks after the food had been served, with the rumble of artillery in the background.

The roll call, which took place on time, was similar to basic training, and in no way inferior. As the old-timers had predicted, some of the young soldiers were harshly spoken to and assigned to punitive duties such as night watch or latrine duty. The majority had to prepare for a scheduled combat exercise, and some of the newcomers, including Erwin Koenig's son, were assigned to a hand-to-hand combat exercise. But things turned out differently.

"The entire combat exercise with position building and shooting is canceled for you. You have to get ready to march in the early afternoon," we were told.

"You now have 20 minutes to write a few lines home. We'll pick up the field mail afterwards."

Almost everyone took advantage of this opportunity, and the sergeant didn't push when the twenty minutes were up. As if he had no watch, he sat down in front of the hut, took a pack of tobacco from his jacket pocket and began to roll a cigarette. Koenig, who had no one to write to, sat down next to the ensign. He looked at the ensign and held out the tobacco. "Machorka *(strong Russian tobacco)*. This stuff sucks, but when you get used to it, you won't like any other tobacco."

"No thanks, I don't smoke."

The pack disappeared into the side pocket of his uniform. A match flared in the palm of his hand, and as the tobacco burned and the end of the cigarette glowed with the first puff, a strong-smelling haze spread. The sergeant blew out the second drag and spoke. "Some write euphorically, others depressed, and others about trivial things. I know all about that. You have no one?"

"No, everyone is dead except my father."

"I know who your father is."

Both were silent for the next few minutes. Step by step, the embers burned their way forward, and finally the last stub of the cigarette was flicked aside. The sergeant stood up, patted Rolf Koenig on the shoulder and said softly: "Stalingrad is different. This city will devour us. I really hope we can chase the Russians across the Volga, otherwise ..."

"Otherwise what happens?"

The sergeant let the question go unanswered. Instead, he turned around and shouted in the purest spit: "Put down your pens, soldiers! Fold the letters, write the field post numbers on them, put them in the envelope and hand them in. The courier will take them later. Fall in in five minutes!"

As Koenig and the other soldiers lined up to march to the HKL, a new order came. The sergeant seemed nervous, but continued to try to project calm. "The fighting is fierce. When we were at the exercises, everything was turned upside down. We're not moving out now, we're moving food and ammunition supplies forward in the early hours of the morning. The Ivan is putting up more resistance than expected. Go to your barracks. New marching time is 3:30 a.m.!"

The lance corporal who had lined up next to Koenig simply said: "Typical Barras. Another short night ahead. I bet we won't sleep until the day after tomorrow. No matter what you want to do now, lie down and try to get some sleep.

Koenig followed the advice of the experienced front-line soldier and did indeed fall asleep shortly thereafter. At 3:00 a.m. he was rudely awakened. The lance corporal stood beside him and whispered: "Wake up! Get ready!"

They left punctually at 3:30. Spread out on two Opel Blitz trucks with camouflage lighting, they rolled off in the direction of Stalingrad.

"We just have to watch out for those damned runway *Polikarpow Po 2*, called *Mule* oder *UvD on patrol*. Those crazy Russians fly those things at night, too. They drop flares and little bombs after them."

One of the young recruits had been listening intently, staring up at the dark night sky. "But when they fly over, our anti-aircraft guns fire."

The corporal turned to the young soldier. "Their engines are quiet. You can hardly hear them. Besides, they turn them off and glide a short distance, much like gliders. That's their trick."

Koenig and the other young soldiers felt queasy. One of them even put his cigarette back in his pack. "I'd better not start a fire," he whispered to his neighbor.

The two trucks reached the city limits and stopped. The passenger of the first Opel Blitz got out and came to the back. "End of the road. You'll have to walk from here."

The men climbed down from the loading platforms and strapped on their backpacks, while the food carriers unloaded cans and large food containers. "You can help us. We've got some cold rations this time, and don't forget the boxes of ammunition and hand grenades," a private whispered, and everyone pitched in.

Rolf Koenig took a deep breath. It was early morning and dawn was breaking. He lost himself in the atmosphere of the dying city.

This is the smell of Stalingrad, the city that bears the name of the Russian commander-in-chief, the city we're going to take, and the city where I'll see my father again after a long time. Stalingrad, I'm here!

The ensign bent down, grabbed the handle of one of the large food containers, and nodded to the other porter. "Let's go!"

"You probably don't know where you're going, boy," said the Landser.

"Yes!"

"Then don't grin like that. This is a bit of a suicide mission. Every time we take food and ammunition to the front, the boys are in a different house. The day before yesterday, for example, we almost supplied the Russians with food."

Rolf Koenig was astonished.

A man from the rear explains. "What he means is that the front is a bit spongy. Sometimes it goes forward, sometimes it goes back."

"But we already know where our men are, don't we?"

The lance corporal called impatiently to the front. "Get moving. I want to be there before the damn sun shines everywhere and we're walking around like on a platter."

The small group set off. The streets around them were already a mess. Trucks rolled around, a few field policemen stood together in a crowd, apparently just receiving their orders, a badly damaged armored personnel carrier chugged past them at a walking pace. Even at dawn, the scratches and bullet holes from recent battles were still visible on its sides. There was a rumble in the distance.

"That was a big suitcase," said the food carrier who was carrying the bucket with Koenig.

"Do you know the way?" asked the midshipman, who was beginning to feel queasy.

"Sure, if the boys are still where they were yesterday, it's no problem. It's only three kilometers, but no truck can get through. That's why we're going on foot."

"Quiet!" hissed the sergeant who led the small squad and had taken the lead.

After only a few hundred meters, Koenig realized how difficult it was to carry the food container while keeping an eye out for craters and boulders or walking over piles of rubble. They passed a small prisoner assembly area. Four soldiers were guarding about ten Russians. They were the first enemies he had consciously seen up close. The Red Army soldiers looked frightened and shaken. Two of them wore dirty bandages.

"The Ivans are being taken to the rear. Some of them are overflowing. There's more food and we could use the help," the porter said, panting as he climbed over a fallen power pole.

Koenig placed the food container on the pole, climbed over it, and lifted it back up. "How ... much longer?" he panted. His arm hurt and he wanted to change sides.

A machine-gun burst was heard. Two explosions followed. Then there was a small exchange of fire, ended by another detonation.

The sergeant stopped.

"Not much further," the porter whispered.

The queasy feeling in Koenig's stomach grew, crawling through his veins and taking hold of his spinal cord. Goose bumps stretched to the back of his neck.

"House to house fighting! They come in the morning or at night. That's what one of the men told me. They attack with four to eight men. They throw a few hand grenades, storm into the house and shoot at anything that moves. Sometimes they roast us too."

"Roast?"

"Flamethrowers!"

Koenig's throat tightened now. The thought of being burned was somehow incompatible with what the instructors had told them in the barracks.

The porter continued. "And there's hand-to-hand combat. They put a spade over your head and a bayonet in your stomach."

The sergeant turned. "That's enough, Meier!"

The porter grinned. "I'm just telling you what it's like there!"

"The ensign will find out for himself, he doesn't need your help!"

114

The lance corporal stepped forward, put down a box of ammunition and asked: "What's going on? Why aren't we moving on? It'll be light in twenty minutes."

"Because the front is blurry from here, comrade. I want to make sure our boys are still over there first," came the reply. At the same time as the sergeant, he pointed to a ruin. "Two days ago there was what looked like a company command post. Further to the right is a Pak position, but I can't see it anymore."

"Then we'll go over and take a look."

"I'm still giving the orders here, comrade. And I say I will wait a few minutes and see if I can lead you across this small open space."

"I'll go first, too. No problem," the lance corporal suggested.

The sergeant looked at the soldier, saw the Iron Cross ribbon in his buttonhole, and nodded. "All right. Two men. You and who else?" he asked, looking at the men.

Koenig cleared his throat. "We could go with you."

The porter looked askance at Koenig, but there was no objection.

"All right, you three go ahead. I'll secure you." As soon as he spoke, he picked up his MP 40, peered around the corner of the pile of rubble they were standing behind, and waved. "Looks good!"

They had about twenty to thirty yards to cover across a relatively open stretch. The lance corporal grabbed his box, gave the sergeant an almost contemptuous look, and started off. Koenig and the porter grabbed their food containers and followed at a distance of five meters.

Koenig clutched the handle of the canteen. He was panting. Sweat trickled down his brow.

"Come on, boy, we're almost there," the porter groaned.

Koenig thought about answering, but he was out of breath and wanted to conserve his strength. So he remained silent and enjoyed the moment. He felt like a hero right then and there.

Dad will be proud of me, was the last thought in Rolf Koenig's mind.

It is doubtful whether he heard the shot fired by the Russian sniper while he was aiming at the ensign's head. The bullet entered through the eye and found its way to the cerebellum. Rolf Koenig was dead before his body hit the stony ground.

7

Captain Erwin Koenig's company was relieved at night. "Keep close to the west side, along the road you came in on, it's safe there. The Ivan didn't get that far. But it did get through to the neighboring battalion at the crossroads. Their reserves are poor bastards. They've been ordered to go house to house and throw the Ivan out again to clear the front. I've also heard that some Russian snipers have probably snuck through and are hiding," reported the men who had reoccupied the positions. "Take care of yourselves!"

"Snipers? Damn it!" Schmidt replied.

Koenig joined them. "Are all the wounded recovered and taken care of?"

Schmidt took a stance. "All the seriously wounded and those unable to walk have already been taken away, the lightly wounded are going back with us."

"Have the numbers been reported to the battalion?"

"Yes, Captain!"

"Tell the men to fall in, we leave in ..." he raised his left arm slightly and looked at the glowing hands of his wristwatch, "... in exactly six minutes!"

"At two o'clock. Got it!"

Although Koenig's company had lost fewer men than he had feared in the recent house-to-house fighting, the overall casualty rate since the beginning of the Battle of Stalingrad had been extremely high.

The combat strength of a normal company at the beginning of the war was still 2/2/178 men, with a combat strength of 176 men.

Koenig's company had shrunk to 79 men, decimated by more than 50%.

The retreat went smoothly. Unnoticed by the enemy, the company retreated while fresh troops took over the positions. Only at the end of the tactical change did the Russians take notice and fire a few flares, casting a macabre light over the rubble. Now and then their machine guns fired a few rounds, forcing the battle-hardened Landsers to take cover, but not causing much panic.

But a single shot, fired about ten minutes after the last machine-gun salvos, with the flickering light of a burning flare, brought anxiety to the ranks of the German soldiers who had pinned down Koenig's company.

"Sniper!" was shouted, and everyone hid as best they could. The fear of being caught in the sniper's crosshairs was like a malignant fever that suddenly spread like an epidemic.

Captain Koenig, however, was no longer aware of it. He was already too far away and led his company back to the starting position. The adjutant of the battalion commander was already waiting for him.

"Well done, Erwin," he greeted him.

"Heinz, what are you doing here in the middle of the night?"

"I was waiting for you."

Koenig stumbled and looked questioningly at the battalion chief's representative. He pulled a cigarette case from his coat, opened it, and offered Koenig a cigarette. But he shook his head, replied, "Oh, yes, you don't smoke," and put the case back in his coat pocket.

Koenig suspected that this reception did not bode well. "We haven't been relieved to finally get to the stage for a refreshment, have we?"

The adjutant shook his head slightly. "No. We were given a special assignment."

"We? A special assignment?"

"The battalion got the order," he explained. "The boss thought long and hard about it, but we can't do without you and your men. We need every man and your experience."

"Do you have any idea how exhausted we are? My company is bled dry, Heinz. We're finished! We can't take any more!"

"You can rest during the day! There'll be a decent meal before you leave."

Koenig followed. "Spit it out!"

"One of the prisoners reported that it is possible to reach the Volga and thus get behind enemy lines via the withdrawal channels, especially the main channel that runs along the Krutoi Gorge."

118

The captain immediately realized what would happen to his company. "You're not serious!"

The adjutant ignored the remark and continued speaking unperturbed. "Our battalion will advance with a strong battle group and fall on the Russians' backs. We'll have them in the bag!"

"And that's supposed to happen next night?"

The adjutant walked up to Koenig and looked around cautiously, like a thief in the night. He wanted to make sure that the conversation could not be overheard by a third party. "We are all at the end. Either we manage to push the Russian across the Volga, or ..."

"Or what?" Koenig whispered back.

"Or I see black."

They both stared at each other until Koenig broke the silence. "Does it really look that bad?"

"Paul threw everything he had into the fight. We have to make it now or we'll suffer a similar fate as Moscow."

"You're not prepared for General Winter? What about supplies? Where are the replacements? Where is the winter equipment?"

"Erwin, now slow down. If we get into Ivan's back, we'll have him in a pincer."

"Your word in God's ear. I'm just wondering how I'm going to tell my men. They assume we're finally getting to the stage."

"A few more days, then we'll be standing on the Volga and waving to the Russian sitting on the other side."

They shook hands.

"You have to march a little further. The trucks are further back."

"The main thing is that they wait for us," the company commander replied, yawning and finishing the sentence with, "and then take us quickly to our quarters. I'm dog-tired. Can you give me the details of the mission? When do we leave?"

"At night," came the blank answer. "I don't know the details yet. But I'll send for you for the final briefing. Get some sleep first."

There followed a brief conversation about possible tactics and speculation about troop redeployments. Then the two officers said their goodbyes and Koenig went back to his men. He took a deep breath. "Men, now two more kilometers on foot, then trucks are waiting to take us to our quarters. We'll get a good night's sleep, then we'll put something in our harnesses and tonight we have one last big mission."

A murmur and whisper went through the ranks. Everyone had been expecting to be taken to the stage for a refresher. Koenig put an end to the emerging discussions by saying, "Whatever our mission may be, men! We'll get through it together, and when we're victorious, there will be a long lull in the fighting. I'm sure of it. Now, let's march!"

The whispering faded and finally stopped altogether as the troop began to move.

Katja was desperate. There was nowhere to go. The streets and paths leading to her old apartment, and thus to Boris and Grisha, were impassable. There were soldiers everywhere, blocking her way and sending her back.

"Combat zone!" she was told.

"Civilians must leave Stalingrad at the other end of the city."

Or: "There is an absolute danger to life here! No way through!"

German pioneers had also posted signs everywhere.

Watch out for mines! Watch out for snipers!

Besides the soldiers, she avoided other civilians. Since she had seen two men attack a woman, she could no longer trust the other Stalingrad soldiers who had stayed behind. The nurse didn't want to generalize, but she also didn't want to take any risks.

She had to eat the fried herring that a fallen Red Army soldier had wrapped in a page of Pravda in his haversack. Otherwise it would have gone bad. But in addition to the Esbit stove, she had found other booty, two cans of beef, and more stale bread. There was also soap and some toothbrushes in her bag. Both were probably from a store, and the looter must have lost them on his way through the destroyed town. She had also found an old horse blanket that smelled bad but kept her warm at night.

It was the fourth day she had been away from her boys and Katja was very worried.

I hope Grisha is taking good care of little Boris.

Then she remembered that Grisha was still a child. He was only eight years old and had to hide with his brother in the basement of their

120

old house. Doubt and hopelessness brought her to the brink of self-destruction more than once. She would play with the revolver and spin the drum.

Just one shot and the suffering would be over.

Then Katja drew new strength from her unconquerable love for her mother, and also from her anger and hatred for the Germans who had destroyed her life, and tried to get through to her house.

Today her fighting spirit was back in full force. She had made good progress at dawn and had found a safe hiding place for the day in one of the ruined houses not occupied by soldiers. The Germans had marched past and artillery shells from both sides flew over her.

Katja was very hopeful that she would be able to take her sons into her arms the following night.

I'm sure they didn't wash and eat the jars of sour cherries first. And if they did, I won't scold them, she grinned.

The night was colder than the previous three. Katja had crawled into a secluded corner of the house and pulled the blanket over her nose. She shivered and guessed that the first snow would come soon. An icy east wind whistled through all the cracks and open gaps in the wall. It had been like this once before, she remembered. It was about six months after Grisha's birth. They were still lying on the banks of the Volga and swimming in the river, but only four weeks later they were trudging through snow and ice in the Siberian cold.

Katja was overcome with sadness when she thought of Pyotr and how he walked through the cold water with the baby in his strong arms. Grisha laughed and squealed with joy and wasn't afraid of the river at all.

"Pyotr, I miss you," she sighed and tried to sleep.

The cold and the hard ground were one reason why Katja only dozed instead of sleeping soundly; caution and the will to survive were the other. When, in her half-sleep, she heard the typical sounds of clattering soldiers' equipment and the trampling of boots, she was immediately wide awake. Men were talking. The first scraps of words grew louder and finally she knew they were Germans. Her stomach clenched, goose bumps spread from top to bottom and eventually covered her entire body. The sister lay still and dug up all her school German to understand as much as possible.

"Quiet .... Hide and seek ... Watch out ...!

What are they doing here? Are our soldiers coming to attack? Are they looking for civilians?

Question after question went through her head. She was afraid. Her right hand slipped into her coat pocket and gripped the revolver.

Boris, Grisha. I'm coming to see you.

She did not want to join the other civilians and be evacuated from Stalingrad by the Germans. She didn't want to leave without her sons, no matter what the cost.

"There's no one here!"

"What if they find us?"

"Then we'll be scattered!"

Katja tried to make out the voices. The soldiers spoke quickly, quietly, and in a dialect. That made it difficult to understand. From the voices she deduced that there were at least three men.

What am I going to do?

Desperation crept up on her again. This time the shivering was not caused by the cold, but by fear. Katja began to calculate her chances if she used the revolver.

I can shoot one or two with a revolver, but three? The soldiers are armed. They react quickly, and if I shoot the first one, the other two will open fire on me.

She thought feverishly if there was another, better hiding place in this ruin. Then she thought about hiding the revolver under some rocks. That would be safer in case of a search. But then she would be helpless.

The voices came closer. There were three more men. One sounded like the commander. His voice was commanding. The other hardly said anything, and the third seemed a little more cautious or anxious. There was an uncertainty in his voice.

Cones of light moved around. Katja knew she would be discovered in a few moments.

Instinctively, she pulled the weapon from her coat pocket and placed it under some stones next to her sleeping place. Then she pushed her prey into an opposite alcove.

If they were really looking for something, they would be satisfied with the bag.

As a precaution, she put some sandwiches and two cans of beef in her coat pockets. When she was done, the soldiers entered the room. She pulled the blanket up to her chin. The cone of light caught her.

"Someone's lying here!"

Blinded, she closed her eyes and opened them slowly.

"Who do we have here?" exclaimed the one with the commanding voice.

Katja was terrified. She sensed that something bad was coming and cursed herself for having hidden the revolver.

Three soldiers stood in front of her. She could only make out their outlines. One was tall and strong, the other two were a little smaller and much younger than the tall soldier.

One of the men ripped off the blanket and yelled at her: "Get up!"

Katja got up and lowered her head. She wanted to avoid eye contact.

"Pretty thing!" said the tall one. He was the one with the deep, commanding voice. "Search her!" he added.

One of the soldiers patted her down, found the cans and the bread, and took them from his coat pockets. He lifted both into the flashlight's beam. "Look here! That's from us! This bitch has beef and bread!"

"Dirty people!" the big man groaned.

The searcher put the things on the floor and continued to grope Katja's body. He took his time with her buttocks and breasts. "Well built!"

"Has she got anything else in her pockets?" the one with the commanding voice wanted to know.

"No!"

"Then look in the bag beside her and under the blanket!"

At that moment Katja was glad that she had hidden the revolver. She realized that a carbine and a submachine gun were pointed at her. She could have shot one of the soldiers, but then she would have been shot herself.

While the German went through her things, she thought about what could happen to her now. She could be evacuated or shot on the spot.

Or they could rape me and kill me!

She looked at the men. They were soldiers. Far from home and sexually starved. They definitely hadn't had a woman in a long time.

Maybe they had been to a brothel, but even that didn't satisfy their lust.

The hard grips of the Seeker had given them away. His strong hands had literally kneaded her buttocks and breasts. She feared the worst.

They'll rape me and leave me there. I know they'll do it, she kept thinking.

She was shaking like a leaf.

"Peace. Hitler is good!" she stammered.

"Esbit stoves and ready-to-cook stuff. All from us!" said the one who was looking through the things.

The leader of the three came very close to her. She recognized his face in the dim light of the flashlights. It was an unsympathetic, violent, and terrifying face. The unshaven soldier had bushy eyebrows. He also had bad breath and looked very unkempt. Katja was desperate.

"Where did you get this, you Russian bitch? Did you spread your legs for it, or are you a partisan who slit our comrade's throat?"

"I'm not a partisan! Nurse!"

The Landser grabbed Katja's chin with his left hand, held it between his thumb and forefinger, and pushed her head back hard, forcing her to look up at him at an angle. "You are pretty. I think we're going to have a lot of fun!"

"Emil, we were going to find a place to hide. What if she screams and someone hears her and finds us here?"

The seeker interrupted the frightened man. "Shut up, Michel! Emil and I will take care of this tramp. I haven't had a woman for a long time. And she's going to have some fun before we..."

"Before you what?" replied the worried one.

The leader of the three Germans let go of Katja's chin and turned to the worried one. "Michel, you can go outside the door and keep an eye out for anyone coming, and you, Emil," he said to the other, "hold her if she's shy."

"Why do you get to go first? I spotted her!"

"Because we do it according to rank. Just like soldiers should. First me, then you, and if the little one wants, he can have a go after that!"

As soon as he had spoken, he grabbed Katja by the coat and tore it open. Then he pointed the barrel of his submachine gun at Katja and swung it slowly from top to bottom and back again. He motioned for her to undress. "Get out of those clothes, you whore!"

Katja shuddered and shook her head. "Nyet!"

The soldier put the submachine gun aside and unbuckled his belt. He took it off as well and stood in front of the Russian. Then he said to Emil: "She is shy. You keep her in check, I'll do the rest."

"I'm going out for a cigarette," said the young Landser.

When Katja had translated the words she could understand from German into Russian, and the young soldier left the room with a sad expression on his face, she had an inkling of what was to follow. And she also knew that she would not be able to endure it without resistance. She could not surrender to this monster without a fight. Her hands clenched into fists, her breath came fast. She would fight back. Now!

The German's fist struck her hard. She fell and lay on her back, slightly dazed. Then the German opened his pants, dropped them to his ankles, and knelt between her legs. He had his bayonet in his hands.

Katja reacted too late, wanted to roll away, but it was impossible. She felt the strength of the soldier, heard the lustful laughter of the second, and her hands desperately searched for something to hit. Her left hand gripped a rock. As she jerked her arm forward to strike, the second soldier grabbed it.

"Oops! Why so wild?" he laughed, placing the flashlight on a stone, grabbing her wrist and holding her tight.

The leader let out a grunt as he pulled up Katja's outer clothing and saw the white breasts. "We're going to have some real fun!"

"Njeeeet!" the Russian shouted loudly and shrilly. "Njeeeeeet!"

125

Stalingrad was never completely quiet. There was always a cannon being fired somewhere, a flare whizzing upward, or the sound of gunfire. While the soldiers could cover two kilometers on the road and even in the field in a very short time, it took longer in the destroyed city on the Volga. They had to climb over piles of rubble, concrete blocks, the remains of walls, fallen poles, and protruding iron struts. It was already a challenge during the day, but at night it was a difficult undertaking. There was always the danger of encountering a Russian shock troop that had broken through or, what many found even more stressful, being targeted by a sniper.

They had made it about halfway when Captain Koenig felt pressure on his bladder. "I should have gone before, now I have to go to the side and step out," he said to Schmidt, who was marching next to him.

Schmidt laughed. "That's because the freezing cold east wind blows so icily against your kidneys that you produce more urine than usual."

"What nonsense!" replied Koenig, laughing.

"But that's what I tell myself. Because I have to go again."

Koenig raised his hand. "Stop, a short break."

Schmidt led the way. "Come over here. It's good here," he said, standing by a small pile of rubble. Then he turned around. "Damn, I can't do this with half the company watching!"

The Sergeant Major climbed over the small pile of rubble and down the other side. Captain Koenig followed him with a grin. "I don't remember you being this mimosa."

After they had both relieved themselves, Schmidt, who had been thinking long and hard about what to say, was about to speak when a soft but clearly audible scream was heard.

"What was that?" asked Schmidt.

Captain Koenig raised his index finger to his mouth. "Shh!"

A second scream was heard.

"A Russian woman! That was a no-no, or what do you say?" asked Schmidt.

Koenig climbed up the scree and could see the glow of a cigarette two houses away. "Ten o'clock! Cigarette butt. I saw it glowing. Get a group and

then follow
me!"
"But what if..."
"Now!"

Schmidt ran up the hill and down the other side, panting and cursing. "Bloody hell, damn you! I hope it's not Iwans. I'm in no mood for a firefight. I want to go to my bed!"

Koenig ran through the tangle of rocks, rubble, and craters. The Smoker was clearly visible. His face glowed orange-red with each puff.

Idiot, if I were a sniper, you would be my victim, thought the officer, who quickly approached and quietly walked the last few meters. Again he heard a panicked "Njeeeet!

This was followed by a gasp: "Now hold your arms really tight!

"Punch her in the face if she doesn't hold still."

"I still need her mouth!"

"But you can do it without teeth!"

In between, a woman's whimpering could be heard. Anger boiled over. Koenig left the MP 40 hanging from the side of his belt and the sniper rifle slung over his shoulder untouched, pulling the .08 pistol from its holster instead. He recognized a young Landser standing in front of a ruined house, smoking. From behind him came the clatter of equipment as Schmidt's squad approached. The smoking soldier raised his head, listened, and finally looked in Schmidt's direction.

They are coming and he hears it, Koenig realized, and before the soldier could warn his comrades who were doing something in the house, Koenig stepped out of the darkness and held the 08 to the completely surprised soldier's forehead. At the same time, the officer put his finger to his mouth. "Shh!"

The soldier nodded and dropped his cigarette.

Koenig whispered: "How many men are in the house, where are they, and what are they doing? Answer quietly!"

"Two men, second room on the right, they ..." he began to stammer, "... they ... they're raping a Russian woman. But she could be a partisan, because ..."

Koenig grabbed the soldier's carbine and threw it aside, into the darkness of the night. "You turn around, raise your hands and stare at the wall. If you move from here, I will find you and personally sentence you to death by court-martial. Understood?"

"Y... yes..."

Without waiting for Schmidt or paying any further attention to the Landser, Koenig entered the ruins. He saw the faint light of a flashlight and walked quickly to the room. A Landser was sitting beside the head of a blond Russian woman, holding both her arms. Another had probably just forcibly undressed the woman. He was laughing and pushing her legs apart. His lower body was exposed, his member unmistakably stiff. The woman struggled, but she had no chance. The soldier pushed himself into position and was about to penetrate the woman when Koenig fired a shot into the ceiling and yelled: "Hands up or I'll shoot you right now!"

Startled, they both immediately raised their hands. The Russian woman pulled her legs up and clutched them, crying and staring at her rescuer.

The tall man began to speak. "Captain, this may look different than it is. This is a partisan and we..."

"One more word and I'll shoot you on sight, soldier. You're both under arrest! You are a disgrace to the Wehrmacht!"

Schmidt and three men burst into the room. "We've secured the one in front of the door. What's going on?" he asked, falling silent as he realized the situation.

"Disarm all three and tie them up. You will be brought to justice," Koenig ordered, walking over to the Russian woman, taking the blanket and draping it over her shoulder. Then he spoke to her in Russian. "Are you all right? Has it happened already?"

Katja was silent and shook her head. She was crying. "No. You got here just in time."

"I will bring these men to justice. They will pay for what they have done!"

"Thank you!"

The german Officer looked around. "What are you doing here?"

Katja wondered what to say. Something in the German's eyes expressed trust. Maybe it was just her imagination because he had saved her from being raped, but she decided to talk.

"Please, I don't want to go back to the other end of Stalingrad. My name is Katja Kalikova. I am a nurse and I have two sons. They are 8 and 6 years old. My husband was killed in the big bombing in August. I need to see my children. They are in our house. In the basement."

Koenig listened intently. Then he took out a notebook and wrote down some things. "I need details from you so I can make what I saw watertight. Give me your name and some sort of address."

Katja complied.

Koenig reached into his haversack and pulled out some commissary bread and some sweets. "This is all I have with me. Take it, get dressed and go to your children."

Katja stared at him incredulously.

"I also have a son. My wife is dead and he's all I have. I understand, Mrs. Kalikova."

"Thank you!"

"Take this flashlight, too," Koenig said, pointing to the lamp of the arrested soldiers. "You may need it." Koenig now saw that Katja's face was bruised and swollen from the beating. "Does it hurt?"

"It will go away. The other one, that would have really hurt," she pointed to the left side of her torso. "Especially here, in the heart! Thank you."

"Captain Koenig. Erwin Koenig," he said, noticing how much Katja was shaking. "I will leave now with my men. Are you sure you want to stay here?"

"Yes."

"Good luck in this city, which we have unfortunately turned into hell. I'm sorry for everything."

"I think you're a good man, Captain Koenig."

"It is the times that have made us enemies."

"You wear the uniform of my enemy, but I cannot personally consider you an enemy."

Koenig nodded, rose, and was the last of his men to leave the ruins without a word.

As the sun rose, the soldiers pulled their blankets over their heads and most of them fell asleep immediately. Koenig thought for a long time about Katja and the fate the war had brought upon the people. He cursed everything and finally fell asleep, completely exhausted.

The new order had already leaked out with the dawn. The orderlies had whispered it to the food carriers, who had in turn whispered it to the cooks in the field kitchens, and it had been secretly passed on to the soldiers when the food was served.

A strong task force, including Captain Koenig and his men, was to go behind the enemy lines through the drainage canals along the Krutoi Gorge and attack the enemy there.

Captain Koenig had gone to the last briefing with this half-knowledge. In the presence of the battalion commander, the commanding officer explained the planned procedure, first explaining the tactics of the overall operation with the neighboring forces and then going into detail about the task of the battle group.

The meeting was almost over when a dispatcher appeared and was let through to the battalion commander. He saluted and whispered in his ear. Then he handed him a piece of paper. He saluted again, turned and walked away quickly.

About ten minutes later, the orderly ended the meeting by saying: "...and I'll be available for individual questions afterwards."

The battalion commander stood up and addressed the assembled officers. "Gentlemen, the war is taking its toll. Every day we have to write bitter lines to the bereaved. It is up to us and our fighting strength to ensure that the men who fought and died bravely did not give their lives in vain. Only those who have to bear the pain know how bitter it can be. Captain Koenig ..."

Koenig was a little startled to be addressed directly by the boss. Surprised, he replied: "Here!"

"I regret to inform you of the sad news that your son, Ensign Rolf Koenig, was killed in action here in Stalingrad. He was accompanying food transporters to the HKL to report to his unit. He fell victim to a Russian sniper".

The battalion commander continued to speak, but Erwin Koenig's words were muffled. His mind had long been elsewhere. He had a big lump in his throat, his heart ached worse than ever, tears came, his stomach tightened. Pictures flashed through the officer's mind. He saw Rolf as an infant in his mother's arms. He saw the laughing boy running through the meadows. He saw them flying kites in the autumn, and he saw him standing beside his mother's grave, crying.

Why, he asked himself. Why Rolf?

Koenig felt a tap on his shoulder.

"My condolences!"

"Terrible!"

"I'm very sorry!"

All these words bounced off. They came with the tears running down the captain's cheeks. Thoughts of revenge.

You took the most precious thing I had. You will pay for this.

It was only after a few minutes that Koenig realized he was alone with the battalion commander and the executive officer. The other officers had gone to their units to prepare for the attack.

The battalion commander pulled a flask from his coat pocket and held it out to Koenig. "Take a sip. This is the finest cognac from France. It's no comfort, but it'll do you good."

Koenig took the bottle and took a sip. He felt the brandy in his mouth, he felt it running down his throat, and it became warm in his gullet and stomach.

"Go ahead and drink," the commander nodded, and Koenig took a second strong swig before handing the bottle back to the commander, who drank from it.

The orderly cleared his throat and began to speak: "My son was killed outside of Moscow. He didn't survive the winter. They shot him in the military hospital. They couldn't keep him warm. He just froze to death. I know how you feel. But I don't know whether to blame the Russians or our leadership.

"My so ... son ... he ... was ..." The expected nervous breakdown came as he spoke. Captain Koenig howled with snot and water. He squeezed out the pain with his salty tears.

"We're not sending you on this mission! You're in shock. Captain Koenig, you stay with me today," the commander decided and said to the orderly: "He will be part of our staff for the next few days. Make sure you find a replacement to take over Koenig's duties."

"By your command!"

"And you will not leave his side!"

The orderly nodded. "You think he's suicidal? Then I don't know if..."

The battalion commander looked sharply at his counterpart and interrupted him. "I don't think you should leave his side right now and find a replacement for the mission, nothing else!"

The commander swallowed. You could see his Adam's apple moving up and down. He nodded again. "By your command."

8

The first day it was a feeling of freedom when their mother wasn't there. Grisha and Boris explored the entire cellar, poking their noses into every corner and even finding one or two seemingly valuable items in the other cellars, such as a nail, a pair of pliers, or a heavy hammer. They dragged their booty into their own cellar and were proud.

"Boris, we are now stranded pirates and we have to get everything we need to survive from the shipwreck," said Grisha to his little brother, and they regained their childhood for a few hours.

They fought against the Mongols, who occupied this region, and declared the bed to be a boat, in which they sailed on the great river and experienced all kinds of adventures.

The brothers were happy that morning. When they got hungry, the pirates plundered an imaginary village and captured a jar of pickled cherries.

"Mama said we'd get a stomach ache if we ate too many," Boris said in awe as he looked at the half-empty jar, but was still hungry.

Grisha waved it off, laughed and just said: "The parents only said that so we'd use it sparingly."

"Don't we have to save money now?"

Grisha thought for a moment, looked at the glasses and shook his head. "Not today, Boris. Mama will probably bring something to eat. We'll eat the whole jar today."

The afternoon belonged to the boat again, and the hours flew by. Only when the two children got tired did they realize that their mother had not yet returned.

They washed and brushed their teeth. This was to make up for eating the jar of cherries. Mom wouldn't scold them so much and would probably be a little proud of them. With these thoughts they went to bed and cuddled up.

Grisha noticed that the younger Boris was trembling. "What's wrong, little brother?"

"I'm afraid mom won't come back. Just like dad."

"She will come back."

Silence.

"Then it's good."

"I'm here to take care of you."

"Thank you, Grisha."

Grisha took a deep breath. Pictures flashed through his mind. He would never forget that terrible day when the Germans dropped the bombs. Especially not the image of the elderly woman holding her daughter in her arms. But the daughter had no legs. Grisha grabbed his brother's hand. "And you take care of me too, Boris."

Boris returned the handshake. "Yes, pirate's honor!"

It took a while, but eventually they both fell asleep.

When their mother did not return the next morning, Grisha had to comfort his brother. "She must have taken so much loot that it will take her twice as long to get back as it did to get there," he said.

That made sense to Boris. "Do you think she'll bring bread and sausages? Or a roast?"

"Definitely!"

This time the brothers decided not to wash. They both thought that they had only washed and brushed their teeth that evening. That would be enough until the next evening.

Their stomachs were growling and they wanted something healthy to eat. They decided on some dried fruit and also opened a jar of sauerkraut. Their father had told them that the old sailors often got scurvy and died. Then they found out that sauerkraut was very healthy and far fewer sailors got sick.

"That's why we eat sauerkraut with dried fruit. Then we can set sail and play pirates again."

The morning was saved.

At noon there was more sauerkraut, and when nature took its course, the buckets in the cellar were full. Both boys wanted it to be clean and, above all, odor-free. They decided to take the full toilet bucket outside and empty it.

"But Mom said we should stay down here," Boris had hesitantly objected at first, but Grisha had insisted, so they took the bucket and marched upstairs.

"Besides, the fresh air is good for us. You know how Mama always said that we should go out into the fresh air to grow big and strong."

With this argument, Grisha had won again and convinced Boris to come along. "You're right! That's what Mom and Dad always said."

Grisha took the warm winter jacket and slipped into it. Boris put on the thick red sweater he had gotten for his birthday a year ago. He had been offended at the time, saying that red was a girl's color, and then Dad had put on his red shirt and said. "Red is the color of revolution. Red is the color of our flag, red is Russia, red are his sons!"

From that moment on, the boy loved that sweater. A year ago it was a little too big. Now it fit perfectly.

"Looks good," Grisha winked, grabbed the bucket and went ahead.

Boris turned off the light in the cellar, took the flashlight, turned it on and shone it into the hallway. The cone of light hit Grisha, who had stopped. Boris closed the door to the cellar and approached Grisha. The closer he got, the worse it smelled. His brother was right. The bucket had to be emptied!

Mom will be proud of us.

Grisha had secretly armed himself with a knife and tucked it into his belt under his thick jacket. He preferred to keep it quiet, so as not to frighten Boris unnecessarily. He knew his brother. The little boy would have pestered him with questions about why he had a knife and he didn't and what it was for. And that was exactly what Grisha wanted to avoid.

They quickly crossed the basement hallway and trudged up the stairs.

"You can save the battery and turn off the lamp. It's bright enough here."

Boris followed his brother's advice. They reached the top. Grisha stopped and listened, just in case. Mama had always done the same. Everything was quiet. They left the bombed building. In the tunnel of rubble, which perfectly hid the real entrance to the house, only Grisha had to duck his head a little. Boris could walk upright. He just

135

had to be careful at the sides, where iron bars or squared lumber protruded from time to time. Both boys moved very carefully, not wanting to tip over the toilet bucket, let alone spill the contents on their clothes.

"It's like a castle and a moat," the older man explained.

Boris listened intently and said: "Or the secret passage. Because the Mongols are besieging our castle."

"Yes, exactly, or a secret passage," Grisha confirmed.

Boris beamed. A thirst for adventure arose. He and Grisha were also good friends. The six-year-old loved his big brother, and he knew one thing for sure. When he grew up, he would be just like Grisha, and Grisha would definitely be just like his father. The six-year-old took a deep breath and pushed the thought of his father to the back of his mind.

They reached the corrugated iron. Grisha stopped and listened for a while to make sure that no one was here. When he couldn't see anything out of the ordinary, he pushed through the sight barrier. The air was cool and felt good. It was very stuffy in the basement. They could hear gunshots in the distance and the muffled sound of artillery. They crawled out and took a deep breath. Then they walked a few meters to the side, to where the manhole cover must be, into which they had seen a fat rat scurrying last summer. Grisha found a smaller crater and emptied the contents of the toilet bucket into it. He breathed through his mouth to avoid the smell. He covered the remains of the excrement by filling the small crater with stones and debris of all kinds. His mother had shown him how to do this, telling him that it was very important to leave no trace.

"We have to wash the bucket with water. How do we do that?"

Boris was still standing at the entrance. "Let's take it with us and go to the Volga."

Grisha stared at the wet, smelly bottom of the bucket and grimaced. "We'd better take an empty canister. We'll get some water and then rinse out the bucket here."

"But you go and get it."

Grisha went back to Boris, put down the bucket and held out his hand. "Agreed. Give me the flashlight and watch out. If anyone comes, you have to push the metal sheet in front of the entrance immediately."

Boris nodded. He was now the gatekeeper. As he waited, doubts arose.

Will Mom really be angry when she comes home and we're not there?

He weighed the pros and cons and decided to leave the decision to Grisha. He would get into more trouble, after all, he was the older one.

It's nice to be the younger brother. It saves you a few scoldings.

Grisha returned with a 10-liter canister. Boris greeted him with: "Do you think it's good for us to run around? Mom will be very angry."

"But when she comes home and finds a clean toilet bucket, she'll be happy."

"What if we just walk around the ruins of our house? Maybe we'll find water here."

"But we've already looked everywhere with mom," Grisha objected. "There's no food or water here."

"You remember when we were on the Volga with Mama. There were so many people and soldiers. And the Germans were firing grenades," Boris objected, his doubts growing.

"We're not going to the port, we're going to where we used to go swimming. It'll probably be quiet there."

Boris thought for a moment. His pensive features relaxed and he grinned. "That's a good idea." His small hands grabbed the corrugated iron and pushed it in front of the entrance. He looked at it and was pleased. "Nobody will find the tunnel!"

The adventure of searching through the rubble and water for the castle could begin. They had already seen many things during the little forays they had accompanied their mother on. Dead men and animals. Burned and rotting corpses. It had smelled bad, too. The children had been frightened by the first dead bodies, but eventually they had become numb. It was still unpleasant and frightening, but now they would dare to reach into the pockets of the dead. They had talked about it last night, boasting about their planned exploits in advance.

"I'll use a stick to see if he's still alive. I mean, if he's not burned or something. Then I'll see what's in his pockets," Grisha began.

Boris followed him. "I dare to do that too. And if you do, I'll stand next to you with a wooden club, and if the dead man grabs you, I'll hit his hand."

"Dead people can't touch."

"But if he does, I'll hit him."

Grisha had grinned. "And I'll do the same for you. We always look out for each other!"

Children who grow up in the countryside take the sight of forests, meadows, cows, deer, rabbits, and foxes as normal. City children, on the other hand, are familiar with cars, streetcars, the bustle of crowded streets, small winding alleys, movie theaters, and many shops. It is their familiar world. A world they were born into.

For the children who lived in Stalingrad during this difficult time, however, death and destruction had become part of everyday life. Just as the children in the country saw many animals, the children in Stalingrad saw many dead.

In one of the streets lay a dead soldier, bloated with foul gas, not far from an old woman who had collapsed from weakness. A few meters away, a lifeless hand protruded from the rubble. These were all sights we encountered in different variations. Then there was the stench of decay that smoldered everywhere.

As hunger and suffering increased, people's spirits grew cold. People became accustomed to death, plundering the pockets of the fallen or taking off the boots of the dead. The threshold of disgust also sank lower and lower, and people killed rats or mice to boil them later in soup.

Death and disgust lost their horror. Animals of all kinds were now seen as only one thing. Food! If you had to choose between life and death, and you chose life, you cooked whatever you could eat, provided you had found firewood. Eating meant life. Not eating meant death.

The children and civilians of Stalingrad were not going to hell, they were living in hell.

The brothers moved cautiously. Grisha led the way with the empty canister in his hand, and Boris followed close behind. The road to the Volga used to be easy. It led past beautiful houses and a few small shops, and was always taken with joy and good humor. You followed the main road, made two turns and you were there.

Now the town had a new image. Everything had been destroyed. Hardly a house was left standing and the streets were littered with craters, rubble, stones and debris. Still, Grisha found his way around. Now and then she saw people. They all had a strange look on their faces. There was no friendliness, only fear. There was a sparkle in their eyes that warned them to be careful, and often the features of the people of Stalingrad showed a certain deceitfulness. With the destruction of the city, the destruction of humanity had begun.

An older woman waved at the two boys and asked: "Hey, you two. Do you have anything to eat?"

"No!" they replied almost simultaneously.

"Come on over. I've had enough. I can give you something."

Boris had stopped and was inclined to go to the nice woman. Grisha, however, was very suspicious.

The old woman smiled. There was something grandmotherly about her. "Come over here. I have some soup on the stove in the back of my house."

Boris looked at Grisha. "Some hot soup would be nice."

Grisha ran back, took Boris by the hand, and pulled him along. "Come on, Mama said not to trust anyone."

"But she looks pretty nice."

"Nobody makes soup here and gives it to strangers!"

The old woman stood up and walked over to Boris. "Let the other one go, my son, and you'll get twice as much!"

Grisha tugged at Boris's hand. "Come on!"

Boris hadn't eaten anything hot in so long. "There are two of us. We're stronger than Grandma. Let's go there for a moment. If she doesn't have any soup on the stove, we'll go back."

He wanted to break free, but Grisha held him tightly. Suddenly there was a warning shout. The brothers looked at each other. They both looked first at the old woman, who came closer and closer, then back.

"Stop!" someone repeated. "Don't go to the old woman. She's crazy."

A boy emerged from a hiding place. Grisha recognized him. It was Sergej, one of his former schoolmates, who lived just one street a-way. "Sergej," he called to him, waving. "It's me, Grisha Kalikov."

"I recognized you. Come over here. Quickly."

The old Russian woman came closer and closer. "My dear boys. I'll take good care of you. Don't listen to that street kid over there!"

Grisha shouted at Boris. "You're coming with me now!"

Boris swung his head back and forth between his brother and the nice woman. She was only two meters away from them.

Sergej shouted loudly: "Get lost! She's completely crazy!", bent down, picked up a stone and threw it at the Russian woman. Then he shouted: "Get out of here, you witch!"

Grisha panicked when the old woman, smiling broadly, opened her coat and took out a small axe. "I slaughtered a horse with it and made a hearty soup. Come on, my boy!"

Boris opened his eyes wide.

"Run!" warned Serguei, and Grisha pulled his brother's arm so hard that he staggered. Grisha panicked. This time, the feeling of fear was much worse than on the cellar stairs, when he was fleeing from the ghost whose invisible hand was trying to grab him. This time he was fleeing from a human being, and now he knew what real fear was. Fear. A lot of fear.

Both of them immediately started running as fast as they could. They jumped over rocks and craters. Then they climbed onto the pile of rubble where Sergej was now standing and kept throwing stones at the old woman.

"Get lost, you witch. Get out of here! This is my friend and his brother!"

As the stones landed closer and closer to the old Russian wo-man, she stopped and brandished the axe. "I'll get you yet! All of you! I'll get you all, you bastards!"

Panting, they reached Sergej's house. Only now did they turn around. The old woman was still standing threateningly with the axe in her hand, cursing and swearing.

"I was so scared," Grisha gasped, and because Boris thought it was really brave of his brother to admit it, he also admitted that he was scared. "And so was I."

Sergej patted them both on the shoulders, one after the other. "The old woman lost her whole family. She sits there every day luring all sorts of people into her supposed house. But she lives in a hole in the basement."

"And what does she do with them?" asked Grisha, not taking his eyes off the Russian woman.

"I don't know. Maybe she kills them and cooks them."

Grisha was shocked: "Yuck! A cannibal!"

"What's a cannibal?" asked Boris.

"Someone who eats human flesh," replied Sergej.

Boris grabbed Grisha's hand. "The woman is evil."

"We'll go back another way later," the older man decided.

Sergej patted Grisha's shoulder again, as old friends do when they haven't seen each other for years. He had probably learned it from the soldiers. "You stayed here too? Where are your parents? And where are you going back to?"

Grisha told them about the bombing and that their father was missing. He told them about the air raids and that their mother hadn't been back to the hideout for three days, but he didn't say where the hideout was or that they still had some supplies hidden there. Boris preferred to remain completely silent and let his brother do the talking.

Sergej listened intently. Then he told the story. The family was on the Volga River on the terrible Sunday of the bombing. They stayed on the beach into the night, and no one was injured. Later they wanted to cross the Volga to the other side, but it was impossible to get a place. Then the Germans came. They thought his father was a deserter from the Red Army because he had put on a dead soldier's coat and shoes. They locked him up with the other POWs. He, his mother and his two sisters now lived with many other homeless people in the Zaritsa Gorge. They dug themselves a big hole in the steep bank.

"... and all the children who are picked up by the Germans without their parents are put on a train and taken away."

"Taken away?"

"Yes. No one knows where."

Silence. Each of them seemed lost in his own thoughts. Grisha watched the old woman. She had turned and walked back to the stone she had been sitting on when she had approached him and Boris, babbling softly to herself. She sat down again with a friendly grin. The hatchet had disappeared under her cloak. The woman's behavior reminded Grisha of a spider that sits in its web and then quickly runs over the deadly sticky threads when a fly gets caught in it. Disgusted, he turned back to Sergej. "And why are you sneaking around here?"

His classmate grinned proudly. "I've discovered something. There's a lot of wheat in the big grain silo down by the Volga. All you need is a small bag, a bit of courage, you have to know the way, and then you can take some of the singed grain. I've been there three times. At night or early in the morning, because that's when the soldiers are most tired. Then you can sneak past them. "

"Isn't that dangerous?"

Sergej laughed out loud. "What is not dangerous in our city?"

That made sense to Grisha. "Would you take me there one day?" he asked spontaneously.

Sergej looked at the brothers. "Just you?"

Boris stood in front of Grisha. "I'm not staying alone. I'll come with you!"

She shook her head. "This is not for little ones. You have to be really careful," Sergej said dismissively.

Boris grabbed Grisha's hand. "You're not leaving me alone, brother. You said you'd take care of me."

Grisha smiled gently. "Don't worry. I'll go with you as soon as mom gets back."

The sound of a machine gun was heard. Then there were some loud bangs.

Rrrrrrrt ... rrrrt

Wham wham wham

"They're close and advancing," Sergej warned.

"Our soldiers?" asked Grisha with hope in his eyes.

"No. It's the Germans. The bang came from one of their anti-

142

tank guns. Our brave Red Army soldiers are quieter."

"Can you show me the way to the grain silo?"

"You know the silo."

"Yes."

"Then you'll find your way there. The front changes every day."

"Then why don't you come with us now and show me where I have to sneak along at night?"

Sergej thought for a moment and finally agreed. "I can do that. I wanted to go there anyway. You can also earn some bread by fetching water for the Germans."

Balancing themselves so as not to lose their balance, they slid down the pile of rubble with more than a little luck. Once down, they shook some dust off their clothes, then Sergej led them unerringly through the ruins. He bypassed the area where the fighting was coming from and explained. "That's where they're fighting."

As they took turns scurrying through the ruins and sewers, Sergej kept telling them what to look for, what to do, and what not to do. Among other things, he told the brothers that drinking water was a problem for the Germans, who were in their trenches and hiding places in the ruins. They themselves were not allowed or able to leave their positions, and their supplies were not functioning properly. "... and when their tins are empty, they get thirsty. The Volga is not far away, but our Red Army soldiers see the Germans and our sharpshooters shoot them".

"And you help the stupid Germans?" Grisha asked in amazement, climbing up an iron ladder behind Sergej. It led up from the sewer. Grisha was glad. He preferred the corrosive air of smoldering fires to the usual sewer smell, which reminded him of a mixture of rotten eggs and dog feces.

"There are good Germans and bad Germans. You have to stick with the good ones. When they're thirsty, they give you bread or something to eat, and you take their canteens, go down to the Volga, fill them with water, and bring them back. That's all. Water for bread. It's not aid, it's an exchange. An exchange so that I don't starve. I think it's fair."

Grisha thought about it for a moment. From this point of view, his classmate was absolutely right. It was an exchange, and this exchange

143

made it possible to go on living. They didn't starve.

Sergej came to the top. Instead of a heavy manhole cover, the lid of a wooden barrel lay over the entrance. The boy pushed against it and lifted it slightly. He looked outside and finally pushed the round piece of wood completely aside. "The coast is clear. Come on up!"

After Sergej, Grisha and Boris climbed out of the shaft. The entrance was in a kind of man-made depression, and the shaft reminded the boys of the hole in a funnel. They were surrounded by piles of rubble. Boris smelled Grisha's clothes and wrinkled his nose. "You stink terribly."

Sergej laughed out loud. "You get used to it."

Grisha shook his head. "Definitely not our mother. That could cause trouble when we get home."

Sergej waved her off. "Then just wash the clothes in the Volga," he winked. Then his look became serious again. He pointed in one direction. "On the left is the rubble of the bombed-out houses, on the right the Germans have cleared the streets with heavy equipment so that their tanks can drive on them," he explained the formation of this funnel-like depression.

"And how did you find the entrance here and remove the heavy manhole cover?"

Sergej lifted his head confidently. "I didn't have to lift it. It was already there. I guess adult civilians or some soldiers were already using this way before I discovered it by chance."

The boy closed the entrance and placed a few stones and a larger piece of cardboard over the wooden lid so that the entrance would not be visible to the naked eye. He looked at his work with satisfaction, then said: "Follow me. We'll be there soon."

They climbed up the two-meter pile of rubble. Some small stones rolled down. Sergej stopped before they reached the top. He held up his hand and whispered: "Careful!"

Grisha and Boris stopped. Sergej looked over the top of the pile and waved to his two friends. "Everything's all right."

They crawled up the last stretch on their stomachs and lay flat on the rubble. They surveyed the area. "Look, the Volga," Boris grinned.

The river ran wide and mighty through the city. Not a soul was to be seen on the banks of the Volga for miles around. Secretly, all three boys wished they were safe on the opposite bank. The mighty grain silo rose from the rubble like a gigantic defense tower. To their left, a group of German soldiers stalked through the rubble. They rushed from one ruin to the next.

"They are pioneers. You'll recognize them by the equipment they're carrying. They're the same ones who set booby traps in the ruins. Watch out for wires when you go into the houses," he warned.

Boris and Grisha's hearts pounded with excitement. "Is what we're doing dangerous?"

Sergej laughed. "You'll get the same answer as before. What isn't dangerous in our city?"

"You know what I mean. Can we get into fights here?"

Sergej thought for a moment. "It's possible, but that's what you usually hear." He pointed at the large building. "So now you know where the silo is."

Grisha nodded.

"You'll find grain there. If you follow the path I showed you, you won't get lost. You just have to be careful when you come out of the canal and then crawl carefully up here. It's very important to check the situation before you slide down here.

Grisha listened intently, while Boris watched the German pioneers with rapt attention.

"And now we'll go to the German soldiers, who will give us something for fetching water. Come along!"

To the astonishment of the two brothers, Sergej slid back down the rubble and climbed back up on the opposite side. They followed him.

When they reached the top again, the three boys slid down the other side. In front of them was a road that was largely free of debris.

"Trucks and tanks could drive here, but the Germans only do it at night and without lights. I think they're afraid of our artillery. But they're even more afraid of Saizev and his snipers!" Sergej's eyes lit up as he uttered the last sentence.

"Who is Saizev?"

Sergej stood still. "You don't know Saizev?"

145

Both shook their heads.

"He's a famous sniper. I've heard Russian soldiers talk about him."

"Russian soldiers? Where did you meet them?" Grisha doubted his classmate's statement.

"You'll meet them if you sneak a little further back through the houses. But you have to be careful. The ruins are sometimes occupied by Germans, sometimes by Red Army soldiers".

"Why didn't you go with them?"

Shrugged. "They won't take you. Some asked where my mother was, others wanted to know if I had an older sister, and the higher ranking soldiers wanted to know if I knew where the Germans were and how they were armed."

The more Sergej talked, the more Grisha's doubts grew. He secretly began to admire his classmate.

They shook the dust off their clothes and walked along the road for a while. Suddenly Sergej turned to the side and they trudged over the rubble. When they passed a burned-out German tank, they stopped for a while, and the boys excitedly examined the monstrous wreck. Grisha and Boris climbed around the steel grave.

"It must have been shot down by a T-34," said Sergej.

"What's that?" Boris asked his brother.

"Our best tank," Sergej replied and walked on. His friends jumped from the wreckage and followed him. Their friend led them through two ruins, with Grisha carefully watching out for possible wires. He didn't want to walk into a booby trap. When they left the second ruin, Sergej suddenly started talking loudly.

Grisha was surprised and asked: "Have you gone deaf? Or why are you shouting like that?"

Sergej laughed. "No, I'm not, but we can't sneak up on them or they'll shoot us. They have to hear us and know we're kids."

Boris jumped at the word "shoot. He instinctively grabbed his big brother's hand. He felt uncomfortable and was already looking forward to their cozy basement apartment and the soft, warm blanket. And surely their mom would be back soon. He missed her and Daddy so much. He squeezed Grisha's hand tightly and felt reassured when

146

Grisha returned the handshake.

They didn't see him, but he was there, for he spoke to them. The sound of the language was choppy and frightening. "Stop!"

All three stood rooted to the spot. Sergej spoke. He actually spoke a few words of German.

"Bread? Hungry ... we'll get water... Volga!"

A German soldier emerged from the rubble in front of them. He held a rifle, the barrel pointed at them at first, then lowered. Two more soldiers emerged from the ruins beside them. One was smoking a cigarette, and another was holding a rifle, but not aimed at the three children.

"Indeed, we have hardly any water left. Seriously, shall we give them some to fill their canteens?"

The children didn't understand a word, but they sensed it was them.

"Russian pack! They can take a few hits," grumbled the smoker.

The first soldier to get up approached the three friends. He wasn't as grumpy, and he certainly didn't seem as grumpy as the Grumpy Bear, as Grisha secretly called him. There was even something friendly about him. The Landser reached into his haversack and took out three candies.

"Drops. They taste good."

Sergej shook his head in the negative. "Bread good!"

The grumpy bear took a last drag on his cigarette, tossed it to the ground, and stubbed out the embers. "The hungry are not satisfied with anything." Contrary to appearances, however, he reached into his haversack, pulled out a crust of commissary bread, and broke off a piece. Then he reached for the canteen, unscrewed it, took a sip, and turned the bottle upside down. Only a few last drops fell to the ground. "Empty!" he said, "If you fill it with fresh water, I'll give you this piece of bread." He demonstratively lifted the broken piece of commissary bread.

Five minutes later the deal was done. Each of the three children had three empty water bottles around their necks. Some bread, a piece of chocolate and three drops were waiting for them.

"If you mess with us, I'll shoot you," the grumpy bear threatened, pointing to his carbine.

147

The other one laughed. "They don't understand you anyway, Ernst. Besides, the poor bastards just want something to eat. Look at those skinny guys."

"One of the boys fetched water for us the day before yesterday. You can count on him," said the third Landser. "But they're scrawny beanpoles, I'm almost afraid they'll collapse under the weight of three full canteens!"

Everyone laughed out loud and watched as the three children ran toward the Volga.

"Back to your posts," shouted a sergeant who had joined them. "Or do you want the Russian snipers to shoot you down?"

Seconds later, the soldiers were back in cover.

Sergej made two or three turns, choosing a small detour to the Volga. "It's no good if the Red Army soldiers see us. It's better if we go this way," he explained hastily.

"Why?" Boris wanted to know. The little boy was panting, but he was able to keep up with Sergej's pace.

"Tactics," Sergej laughed. "I don't want to give away my bread source. The soldiers will probably be in position here for a few more days, and that means safe bread for us. But only if I get the order to fill the canteens."

"That's really nice of you to share your bread source with us," Boris said happily.

"Nine jars are very heavy to carry. Besides, it's quieter when there are three of us. And you must promise me on your most sacred shrine that you'll find another source of food later."

"Word of honor," Grisha swore.

"Ehr ... en ... wort," Boris repeated, panting.

The way to the river was difficult. There were only a few people to be seen, and they were behaving strangely. They huddled in corners and niches. Two women were washing clothes on the bank. They seemed unaffected by what was going on around them. Somewhere a machine gun rattled again. Boris and Grisha raised their heads as a fighter passed overhead. The rumble of heavy artillery could be heard in the distance.

Suddenly it was there. The Volga. Lazy and yet powerful. Familiar and yet so strange. Almost terrifying. In the summer, it was their pure bathing paradise, and Grisha learned to swim in it. They would sit on the bank, wrapped in towels, and mom would unpack delicious food. Now the Volga looked gloomy. It seemed cold and desolate.

Sergej had chosen a part of the bank that was easy to reach. He quickly knelt down. Determined, without looking around, Sergej took his three canteens from his body, unscrewed one of them and dipped it into the water. Bubbling, they filled up. "Make sure you only fill them with clear water. If you put the bottles in too shallow a place and touch the bottom, dirt and sand will wash up. If the Germans get dirty water, they'll make you feel it at the next meeting. I heard once that they accused one of us of trying to poison them. They shot him.

Grisha knelt down beside Sergej and imitated him. "I don't believe it. Did you see it, or is it just a story?"

"I only heard it," Sergej replied in a whisper. His first bottle was filled. He screwed it shut, pulled the leather strap around his neck, and picked up the next bottle. He quickly unscrewed the top.

Now Boris filled his bottles too, and Grisha looked at his younger brother from time to time to make sure he was filling really clear water.

"How was it with this Saizev? That sounded exciting."

Sergej lifted his head and looked at Grisha. "The soldiers tell each other that he is the hero of Mamayev Hill and that he shot a lot of Germans in the battle there. He's a crack shot, and they say that Saizev hunts silently. The Germans are afraid of him and he will liberate Stalingrad".

Grisha laughed out loud. "Just one man?"

"He's a hero!" replied Sergej and exchanged the canteens again. Now the boy filled the last bottle. Gurgling, it ran full.

"But he's just a man with a gun!" Grisha emphasized the words one and one.

"Our sharpshooters are the best in the world," Sergej replied. The last bottle was filled. He stood up and hung this canteen around his neck as well. "Hurry up!"

Grisha looked at his friend. The sun was shining on his face.

He looked a little rakish. Almost the way Grisha had always imagined the pirates to look when he and Boris fought against fantasy armies.

A shot broke the silence. Sergej fell to the ground as if hit by an invisible fist. A bullet entered the side of his head and came out the other side. Blood, bone fragments and brain matter sprayed out, staining the water and the riverbank red.

Grisha stared at his friend in shock, then jumped up and waved madly at the other bank, shouting loudly: "No! We are Russians! Don't shoot!"

Boris began to cry. He let go of his last canteen and it drifted away, swaying.

Grisha turned his head, saw Boris crying and shouted at him: "Run!"

At that moment a second shot rang out. Boris's little body jerked and was thrown backward.

"No!" cried Grisha. "No!"

An unprecedented pain ran through him as he saw his dead brother lying in front of him. Blood spurted from his chest. Bori's clothes turned red where the heart had been. The boy's face was pale, one eye open, the other closed. His gaze was broken, but he smiled.

"No! Boris! You bastards! We are Russians. We belong to you!"

Anger, tears, pain. Grisha knelt down and grabbed Boris's hands. Snot came out of his nose. He cried bitterly. "Stand up, little brother! I beg you! Get up!"

He didn't notice that a firefight was breaking out around him. Two machine guns were firing, covering the area where the two shots from the Russian sniper must have come from. A grenade launcher unit pointed its barrels in the same direction, and shortly thereafter about twenty grenades whirled through the air.

During this barrage, two soldiers came running up, grabbed the canteens, shouted some words at Grisha that he didn't understand, pulled him violently along, and ran back.

The Russians returned fire. Grisha didn't notice anything. He sat behind a house wall until nightfall, right where the German soldiers had left him.

"You'll be safe here," someone had said.

Grisha just sat there for hours, staring ahead. The silence was broken only when he cried.

At night, a German reconnaissance party went out and found the bodies of the two children. Grisha watched as they laid his brother and Sergej in a crater and buried them. One of the soldiers asked the names of the two dead men in half-understandable Russian. "Boris and Sergej," Grisha breathed in a shaky voice.

Later, the German hammered a small wooden cross with a plaque into the ground at the head of the grave. The names of the two boys were carved on the small wooden plaque. This was the only decoration on the grave.

The next morning, more German soldiers arrived. The grumpy bear, whom Grisha didn't like at first, held out his hand. "Come with me, little Ivan. You can't stay here!"

The boy didn't understand a word of what the soldier said, but his voice sounded right. The soldier waved, and Grisha stood up. His gaze was cold. The Germans had killed his father, the Russians his brother. The pain was immense and he felt only one thing. Anger. Pure rage. This anger turned into hatred. Thoughts of revenge arose. Only one name came to Grisha's mind, a name that was synonymous with his brother's death. Saizev.

The sergeant arrived, looked at the grumpy bear, then at Grisha. "What's wrong with him? Why is he still here?"

"Where should he go? He's in shock."

"We can't take him with us."

"At least a bit to the rear, so he doesn't hang around the front."

The sergeant thought about it, then nodded and said: "All right. A commandant's office has been set up. Civilians are registered there. We'll take him there."

When he was gone, the grumpy bear pulled Grisha close to him. He put an arm around his shoulder and whispered in his ear: "I don't know if you understand me, little Ivan, but I advise you to run away when I shout at you. I don't trust these commandant's offices and their chain dogs. You're a poor bastard. You've lost friends or even family. Maybe it was your brothers who were shot there. Run away! Run away!"

151

Grisha looked at the peasant questioningly. He reached into his haversack, pulled out a quarter of commissary bread, and pushed it toward Grisha. "Take it! And now run! Get lost!" he shouted.

Grisha was startled. He didn't know what was going on, but he put it all together. The boy guessed that the grumpy bear meant well when he sent him away. Grisha said: "Spasiba - thank you," turned and started to run. He ran as fast as he could. He wanted to get away from here. Away from the place where his little brother Boris had been shot. He wanted to go to his mother. Grisha hoped that she was home by now. Would he still be able to see her? Self-blame arose. If only they had stayed at home.

Determined, he ran over piles of rubble and crossed a ruin. He had memorized the way well and finally climbed up the pile of rubble and down the other side until he stood at the entrance to the dry sewer. Grisha didn't realize that he had torn his hands and knees and was bleeding. He removed the cardboard and the stoppers, pushed the lid aside, and scurried into the manhole. He grabbed the wooden cover, pulled it back over the opening, and climbed down the ladder.

On the way home, he sat down twice and cried. He wondered if he shouldn't run away so he wouldn't have to tell his mother that Boris was dead. But then he decided to act like a man. Grisha got up and walked the rest of the way home without stopping.

As he had done during the siege of Leningrad, Stalin showed complete severity in the city that bore his name. His orders were to kill every civilian who collaborated with the Germans, without exception. Even when the Russians carried out the invaders' orders under duress, the Russian dictator showed no mercy. Anyone who served the Germans, whether voluntarily or under duress, was to die. Man, woman, child, or old man!

When the Red Army found out that Russian children were filling German canteens, snipers mercilessly carried out Stalin's orders and shot them.

Collaboration with the enemy, even if one was used as a human shield under duress and was recognizable as a civilian, was punishable by death.

9

Like an invisible frosty hand, the Siberian east wind pushed the icy cold ahead of it and threw it over Stalingrad. It crept silently through the streets, formed a fist and held the city in its icy grip. Thermometers were constantly dropping into the minus degrees. The snow arrived in early November. At first the flakes fell sporadically, but eventually the whole of Stalingrad was buried under a blanket of white.

Meanwhile, the fighting in the city became increasingly bitter and fierce. Exact front lines were in many places no longer recognizable and were constantly changing. Some houses belonged to the Russians for a few hours, then to the Germans, and later to the Russians again.

This situation was extremely drastic in the completely destroyed factory area. Here the front line changed from floor to floor. Sometimes the Germans were on the first floor, sometimes on the second, while the Russians occupied the mezzanine. You could hear the enemy talking, but you could not throw them out of the ruins.

Wide-branching sewers became connecting routes, innocent-looking children became border crossers and spies. Casualties were high on both sides, and fear and mutual hatred grew.

Commissars and officers whipped young Red Army soldiers onto the ships. German shells pounded the water around them, sinking one or two ships. When they docked on the opposite bank of the Volga, they were under constant German fire. The Red Army soldiers were mercilessly driven from the ship to fight in the streets and houses. Many of them fell after only a few hours.

Those who wanted to survive in Stalingrad had to adapt and become ruthless. You had to start fighting the so-called rat war. You were forced to become so tough that you would split the enemy's skull without a second thought before talking to him. The men became numb. Many eyes were empty, souls withered. None of them, should they be among the survivors, would ever be able to forget this time.

The icy onset of winter hit the 6th Army especially hard. As in the battles before Moscow, the German troops lacked winter equipment. The Wehrmacht had failed, misjudged the objective and the enemy. Many rightly feared a second "Moscow fiasco," with General Winter siding with the enemy. To prevent the worst, Winter's equipment was quickly sent to the front. Soldiers were even allowed to provide for themselves by having warm winter clothes sent to them from home via the field post.

However, all these measures were a drop in the bucket, and only an estimated 40% of the urgently needed winter equipment reached the soldiers in Stalingrad.

In addition to the biting cold, another plague was spreading. Lice! Every dugout, every bunker, and almost every soldier was infested. Those who were lucky enough to be allowed to enter the stage with their unit for a refresher course and the associated delousing could only enjoy being lice-free for a short time. The rest periods became shorter and shorter, because the front was calling them. Stalingrad was like a hungry juggernaut that fed on people. And it had an enormous appetite. Since the beginning of the fighting, Stalingrad was never quiet, calm and peaceful. There were no breaks in the fighting. There was always fighting, everywhere.

Fate finally threw the cloak of death over the German 6th Army when the Soviet troops, well equipped for winter, launched a large-scale attack with the next bad weather front. Their goal was to encircle the entire 6th Army!

On November 19, 1942, the Red Army advanced with strong armored units on the flanks. The poorly equipped and completely surprised Italian and Romanian units that were supposed to protect the flanks were literally overrun.

Both the 6th Army headquarters under General Paulus and the OKW in Berlin were taken completely by surprise by the magnitude of this Soviet attack. Their reactions ranged from arrogant underestimation of the enemy to tactically unwise inaction. German reconnaissance had also completely failed, as the advance of the Russian troops had gone unnoticed.

Due to the bad and extremely cold weather, the German air force could not be used, or only insufficiently, and within five days the

Red Army managed to encircle the entire 6th Army.

When the two Soviet fronts met at Kalach on the Don, the thermometer showed minus 26 degrees.

In addition to the attacking Red Army soldiers, the lack of supplies, the rapidly spreading plague of lice, and the freezing cold, the soldiers in Stalingrad faced another implacable enemy. Hunger! At the same time, medical supplies such as bandages, medicine, and the ether needed for surgery became scarce. Field hospitals became slaughterhouses. Doctors and medical personnel had to do things they had considered unacceptable before Stalingrad. There was no end to the suffering of the wounded.

Immediate countermeasures were meager. Rations were reduced and it was announced that the air force would supply the kettle. Slogans about the possibility of an escape began to circulate. Breaking out of the cauldron was the small spark of hope that the imprisoned Landser kept in their hearts in order not to be completely disgraced.

Vasily Saizev, the simple hunter from the Urals, who had distinguished himself in the battles for Mamayev Hill and had been discovered by Russian propaganda, began his triumphal march in those days. The Russian's road to success was paved with enemy deaths.

The sniper, considered a hero by the Red Army, trained other snipers during the battles for the factories of Stalingrad. His small sniper school was successful and cemented his reputation more than ever.

The name Saizev spread and eventually became synonymous with the Russian sniper system at Stalingrad.

Vasily Saizev was a man of action. Instead of the forests of the Urals, he went hunting in the ruins of Stalingrad. But his prey were not bears, wolves and deer, but German soldiers.

Saizev hunted them down, tracked them, and developed his own deadly tactics. Together with his observers, he lay in wait, camouflaged himself perfectly, and shot 225 Landser in five months. When he chose a target, he waited for the shot, pulled the trigger, and hit it.

Erwin Koenig spent two weeks in complete lethargy. His mind vacillated between depressive suicidal thoughts and a murderous desire for revenge. He raged against those responsible in the Wehrmacht, the German regime, the Russian regime, the Red Army, and finally the Red Army soldier who had fired the fatal shot at Rolf. He searched for answers to the questions of who was responsible for his son's death and why he had to die.

He wondered if there was a God, and realized that a God would never allow something like Stalingrad, a proxy for wars of all kinds. He thought about the crimes he knew about, committed by German soldiers, and asked himself the same questions over and over again. He was desperate.

Finally, Erwin Koenig asked himself whether he should die or live. He asked himself so many questions to which he could find no definitive answer. The desire to live and to take revenge finally prevailed over self-sacrifice. The melancholy faded and gave way to anger. Anger and hatred. Driven by this fire in his chest, coupled with deep sadness, Erwin Koenig got up one day, went to the mirror and reached for his shaving kit. He knew he had to act, he just didn't know how.

He was discharged from the hospital and assigned to the battalion staff. However, he was not given any special duties there, just helping out here and there. They wanted to go easy on him. He accepted his promotion to major without emotion.

About ten days after he had carried the major's lances on his shoulders, the moment of decision came. Along with the report that another officer had fallen victim to a Russian sniper, came the news from German reconnaissance that on the Russian side a certain Vasily Saizev had repeatedly received an award as the most famous "German hunter".

Koenig took in both reports, recognized the propaganda effect, and leaned back. Thoughts flashed through his mind. The embers that had almost been extinguished with the death of his son finally returned to his eyes. The inner fire of vengeance blazed stronger and stronger, and the officer felt his cold heart vibrate. A fire began to burn in it, even though it was freezing cold and painful, and even though it had no feelings anymore, it began to throb more and more. Each heartbeat had a purpose. And that goal was to hunt!

Koenig reached for the bakelite receiver of his telephone, picked it up, but then decided to pay Lieutenant Colonel Harras a personal visit and put the clunky bone back on the fork.

"I need a bucket truck! Now!" he called outside.

A chair was heard moving. Footsteps followed. A young soldier with an eye patch appeared in the doorway. "Major, it's..."

"Now!" Koenig interrupted, emphasizing the clarity of his order.

The young soldier cleared his throat. "I ... have instructions ..."

"I know you're supposed to take care of me. But that's not necessary. I must see Lieutenant Colonel Harras immediately!"

At the stern tone, the soldier with the eye patch jumped, startled. "Yes, sir, Major. A bucket truck."

An hour later, Koenig stood before his friend and superior, Lieutenant Colonel Harras, and presented his case. He had chosen his words carefully, explained his findings, and finally got to the heart of his testimony: "... and then I got these two reports on the table. The Russians are stylizing this Saizev as a hero. He gives hope to the Red Army. He's not just a successful sniper, he's already an icon. He embodies victory! Do you understand, Richard? He is the backbone of a lot of Russian soldiers. If we break him, we break them.

Harras pondered and finally said only one word. "Propaganda?"

"That's right! Propaganda! His successes are celebrated. Every shot down makes the rounds! He is the hope of the Russian Stalinist fighters."

"And what is your goal? Do you want revenge for Rolf?" the officer asked deliberately to test his friend's reaction. It had not escaped his notice that life and fighting spirit had returned to Koenig.

The new major narrowed his eyes for a moment. "Revenge? Of course, I've thought about it for a long time. I can't give you a definitive answer. Maybe I want revenge, but who should pay for it? After all, I can't directly blame anyone for Rolf's death. But I can fight the system that ordered his death, the Russian sniper system."

Harras believed Koenig and became curious. "How are you going to do that? Fight a war on your own? That's ridiculous!"

"I will become the German Saizev. I'll give our men hope. I'll go out there and get the Russian officers and NCOs and eliminate as many Soviet snipers as possible. And if I succeed in taking out this Saizev, then we have won, we have broken the backbone of Russian hope.

Harras nodded in agreement. Everything the king said sounded plausible. "You know, as a senior officer, you would be an exception. Snipers are in the Wehrmacht ..."

Koenig raised his hand. "At that time I was the officer in charge of our snipers. I'm very familiar with the equipment and tactical procedures. If you send a private on a hunt, that man will be nothing more than another sniper. If I go hunting, people will say we are sending a fighter into the ring who will make his opponents tremble and bring victory.

Harras sat back. The words impressed him. "And if you fail? Will that have the same negative effect on our troops?"

"Whether I'm hit by a sniper's bullet while driving back to the battalion in a bucket truck, or if it hits me while I'm looking for a victim in the crosshairs in the rubble of Stalingrad, what's the difference? Dead is dead! And if I die in battle, a hero is born. That's what men do."

"I don't know," Harras thought.

Koenig looked absolutely sure of himself. "I'm the best man for the job, and if I can raise the morale of the troops and give them hope, that will translate into their fighting power."

Harras was almost convinced. "Morale is nothing to sneeze at. We've been bled dry. This damn city is eating us alive. Little by little!"

"Then authorize me to take whatever I need and to move freely. See to it that the news spreads among the common soldiers that the German sniper of all snipers, the chief himself, is going into battle to take out the Russian chief sniper. You don't have to do anything official. We can still do that if I'm successful."

"I can't officially report this to Division. No one would allow it, and they might question my ability to make decisions. Er-win, you know how that works. Besides, the thought of sending an officer out there as a sniper makes me sick to my stomach," the Lieutenant Colonel argued, gesturing toward the window.

"I just sit here and do nothing. I can act out there. I have no one to go back to. My son is buried here. Shot by a Russian sniper. I am the only one capable of completing this mission in a way that makes the enemy tremble and my own soldiers rejoice. You cannot lose, Richard!"

Harras stood up, paced nervously, and stopped in front of the window. The lieutenant colonel let his friend's last words sink in. Finally he said: "Agreed, even if I regret this decision later. Erwin, you'll get what you want. These Russian snipers are a nuisance. Go out there and finish them off! Bring me that Saizev. Hunt him down and shoot him. Stalingrad is not a battle like any other and therefore requires special means. Winter is approaching fast, and I feel that the worst is coming. I fully support your plan. Special problems call for special solutions.

This was followed by a visit to the weapons master, Sergeant Major Konschewski, a visit to the clothing store, and an audition with the battalion commander. His enthusiasm for the project was limited, but in the end he agreed.

Koenig used the simplest form to spread the first information about his plan among the soldiers. He created what he called a latrine slogan. In the presence of reporters or while eating in the field kitchen, the major would repeatedly drop details about his hunt for Saizev. This particular news spread quickly, because nothing spreads faster than rumors that can be classified as highly classified.

"Koenig challenges Russian sniper chief".

"We're sending Koenig to the front!"

"Koenig will teach the Russians to be afraid."

"The Major will avenge his son!"

"The Russians can pack their bags. They shot Koenig's son, now he'll take all the snipers one by one!"

These and many other slogans actually brought hope to the front lines of the Landser. Suddenly everyone had a story to tell about Koenig. Soldiers dug into their memories and told the strangest things about the former sniper instructor. And the more stories circulated, the more deeds were invented.

"I know someone who was there when Koenig took on two Russian snipers and..."

"Koenig hit at a distance of over 700 meters!"

"I have it on good authority that..."

The legend of Major Koenig was born and spread faster than a forest fire. Since the gist of most of the rumors was true, there was no doubt about their veracity. Each story puffed up like a snowball rolling downhill and arriving as an avalanche in the valley.

The officer did the rest to enhance his reputation as the master of all sharpshooters.

At first, he walked randomly to the front of the line, took the front positions, and drew awestruck glances. Then, with outstretched hands, people told him that everything they had heard was true. After all, they had seen him with his sniper rifle.

Koenig decided to act. He knew the front was not stable. If the Germans were here yesterday, the Russians could be here tomorrow. After the first two days in the combat compartment, he evaluated his findings and focused on his first kill. As Saizev's fighter, he wanted to take out a Soviet machine gun nest. To do this, he moved forward with the food carriers under cover of darkness. The small group of soldiers moved cautiously through the rubble. The silence was broken only by the clatter of dishes or the occasional shovel hitting the sides of the aluminum containers. They arrived without making contact with the enemy.

The outpost was either asleep or otherwise distracted. When the food carriers were at his level, he slid the barrel of his carbine over the wall of rubble, which was about a meter high, and fired. "Stop or I'll shoot!" His voice was tired but determined.

The Landser who had led the troop through the city raised his hand. The men behind him stopped. He replied, slightly annoyed: "Damn you, Hinrichs. It's me, Weber. We've brought your food. Put the gun down!"

"Parole?" flew at them.

There was another voice now. It belonged to the second guard, who hurriedly emerged from behind a pile of rubble and buttoned his coat. He had probably just gotten out. "Shut up, Hinrichs, and put that carbine away. I'm hungry! You know Weber."

A head appeared. Hinrichs recognized Weber, drew his rifle

and said, "You can leave our share right here."

Now the second guard was there. Both recognized that Major Koenig was with the food bearers. This means that the two guards first noticed the rifle with the scope attached, and then the officers' pigtails. They reacted accordingly.

"There's a sniper."

"It's about time, this ..." came after a moment of shock: "Fuck you. That's an officer!"

"That's Koenig!"

"Shut up if he hears us."

The heads disappeared behind their cover again. Koenig heard them whisper, but didn't understand a word. He grinned.

Sergeant Weber, who had joined Koenig, led the food carriers past the posts. At the same level he said: "You can get your food later. Or you can give us your dishes and I'll send them back with the squad."

"No, that's all right. We'll get them later," whispered Hinrichs, embarrassed by the incident.

The farther they went and the more compatriots they passed, the more whispers Koenig heard. "There he is again" or "Here we go!" were often heard. When they reached their destination, the men distributed the food. Koenig, meanwhile, looked for the officer in charge.

"Sergeant Kunisch has taken command," he was told.

"And First Lieutenant Faber?" asked the Major, who knew that this squad was led by an officer. He immediately believed that the lieutenant had become another victim of Russian snipers.

"Our lieutenant had to be brought back. He had terrible stomach pains. The appendix."

Kunisch entered the ruins where the food containers and ammunition he had carried were stored. He recognized Major Koenig, saluted him casually, and made a brief report before Koenig could speak.

"Diagonally opposite, the Iwans have taken up position and set up one or two machine-gun nests. They cover the road and most of the area between the two ruined houses where my men are. We can't take them out from here. There's no blind spot. If we sneak any closer, they will shoot at us. We've been in this standoff for six days. The bad thing is that they're taking over the surrounding houses. When we attack, they

161

start to rattle. When we attack the machine gun nest, they cover us with grenade launchers. They're very accurate. They have an observer somewhere near the machine-gun nest, but we haven't been able to locate his position yet. Lieutenant Faber has already ordered two frontal assaults, but we didn't get further than the middle of the road and had to retreat.

Koenig had listened intently. "Show me where the machine-gun nest is."

The sergeant led Koenig out of the ruins, crouched down and ran about ten feet across open ground, then lay down behind a pile of rubble. Koenig followed. When the officer came to rest beside the sergeant, he crawled up the pile of rubble. He peered carefully over the edge and pointed to a two-story house. "Either they have two machine guns or they keep moving them back and forth."

"Can you be more specific?" Koenig asked.

"Left window, top floor and attic, under the brick rubble.

The sniper pulled out his binoculars, but couldn't see much despite the relatively bright moonlight. He scanned the situation and calculated possible shooting angles. He searched for suitable cover for himself. His gaze lingered on the burned out wreckage of a T-34. It began to rattle in his head.

I should have the best view from there. Risky, but doable.

He weighed his options and made a decision. "I'm going to that wreck!"

The sergeant looked at the bizarre looking pile of steel. "That's downright suicide, Major. The Russians are wide awake. You won't get there unseen."

"I'll go around the ruins and you can make a racket up here. The enemy will be concentrating on the night attack. I'll bypass the skirmish and approach from the other side."

The sergeant looked at Koenig and noted his determination. "Riot is no problem. But if you make it there, how will you get back?"

"They'll attack again! And they'll do it right. If I take out the machine gun, they'll take the building!"

The sergeant swallowed. "That'll cost a lot of men their lives."

"Not if I take out the Russian machine gun. You have to take

162

into account the possibility of grenade launcher fire and get across their field of fire as quickly as possible!"

The sergeant's eyes scanned the building where the Red Army soldiers were holed up. "When will the main assault follow?"

"You will have to watch for my shot. As soon as I fire, you will attack, because when I fire, the machine gun will stop firing. But then it has to be fast."

"How long after the mock attack?"

Koenig thought about it. "I can't determine the exact time, of course, but I'm guessing between 30 and 60 minutes!"

They slid back down the hill on their stomachs and ran crouched back to the safety of the ruins.

Not far from them, a flare shot up. Bright, quivering magnesium light flared up, eerily illuminating the ruined city. A short gun battle could be heard. Screams. Explosions. Long bursts of machine gun fire followed.

The sergeant tried to explain the situation to Koenig. "They're fighting for a house. Sounds like our men were able to repel the Ivan."

Koenig took off the equipment he had brought with him. "We're acting! I'll just take my rifle and binoculars. Take care of these things. I don't want a single man to come closer than fifty centimeters!"

"Don't worry!"

"Good, then let's get down to the details! I want you to conduct two mock attacks before you and your men make a serious advance on the building."

They discussed the procedure for the mock attack and the actual attack. Koenig explained when he was going to shoot and reaffirmed that he would hit the target.

The soldiers sitting with them in the ruins listened in silence and ate the food they had brought. Again and again they looked at the major with hidden glances. When everyone had finished and cleaned their eating utensils, the exceptionally high-ranking sniper stood up, looked at his wristwatch, and said loudly: "Sergeant, let's put the plan into action. We start in exactly ten minutes!"

They took their positions. The faces of the soldiers looked tired and exhausted. Some had sleepy eyes, others seemed wide awake. Koenig had left the ruins. Sergeant Kunisch kept looking at his watch. When the big hand reached twelve, he gave the order: "Attack! Let's wake up the Ivan!"

The bipod of an MG 34 was placed on the windowsill, the rifleman I pressed the stock against his shoulder and pulled the trigger. As agreed, he fired volley after volley, unleashing a barrage on an advancing group of Landsers.

They ran across the road, ducked behind concrete blocks or piles of rubble, and fought their way forward meter by meter in the rising Russian defensive fire. The enemy machine gun also began to fire, bringing the attack to a halt. The tracer ammunition used repeatedly indicated the direction of the projectiles. There was no doubt. The gunner had mastered his craft and was pinned down. Koenig tried to follow the trajectory to determine the position of the machine gun. But he couldn't see it from his remote position.

A red flare shot up.

"Retreat!" yelled one of the men and the mock attack was over.

The Russians could be heard hooting and hollering.

They are cheering!

Koenig was literally glued to the wall. His heart was pounding, his pulse was racing. The major knew that the plan was more than daring, but if he wanted to succeed, he had to risk it. Besides, he was not afraid of death. From his point of view, life was no longer worth living. He had lost all that he loved. He looked around the wall and hoped that all eyes of the Russians were on the mock attack and the retreating Landser.

For Rolf!

With the last slaves of the still barrage firing MG 34 he scurried out of cover and ran towards the wreck. Just before he reached it, the machine gun fell silent. He lay down on the cold ground and made the last meters on his stomach. The diversion had been successful. He reached his destination and disappeared under the wreckage unnoticed by the enemy. There was a pungent smell of burnt oil and something else indefinably disgusting. Koenig had more room under the pile of steel than he had initially feared, and since the front of the T-34 had been driven onto a pile of rubble, the angle of his shot was also correct. Inside he breathed a sigh of relief. He had taken a big risk and assessed the situation correctly. Now came the most difficult part. He had to actually locate the enemy machine gun. To do this, he crawled under the wreckage all the way to the front. The sniper tried to get into position as comfortably as possible. The firefight was finally over and the Russians had stopped cheering. Unfortunately, he had not yet been able to locate the enemy machine gun. There had not been enough time. Then he looked at the fluorescent numbers on his wristwatch.

Another ten minutes until the second, more massive, decoy attack.

Koenig tried to stay calm. Little clouds of breath danced in front of his mouth. It was cold, but he wasn't trembling. The sniper removed his right glove and prepared his rifle for the shot. The bullet was in the chamber and the sight was set at the correct distance. The major fired the test shot and was satisfied.

The moonlight is enough.

He set his rifle aside and picked up his binoculars. As dawn broke, the light improved. Through the binoculars he saw that the roof of the ruins on the back side was almost completely torn off. Half of the tiled roof now rested on three or four heavy beams.

Get moving!

His heart began to pound, he felt the adrenaline rush through his bloodstream. Red Army soldiers were scurrying around on the roof, crouching.

The sergeant was right. They were moving the machine gun from the second floor to the roof after each exchange of fire.

Major Koenig was both relieved and excited. He was sure that he would be able to fire at least two shots from here before coming under fire himself. Assuming the upcoming attack went well.

Then maybe even three shots would be possible, he thought.

The tank provided enough cover, and once the main attack was underway, he had very good chances of retreating unharmed.

The officer put the binoculars aside, raised his rifle and stared through the sight. He knew where the Russian machine gun nest was, but he could no longer see any of the Red Army soldiers. They had positioned themselves at the far end of the roof, facing the street. He would only be able to see them when they moved again or changed positions. That was when he would strike.

If they startle, they're mine!

Koenig held his wristwatch up to the moonlight. This allowed him to see the position of the hands.

Three minutes to the attack!

He suppressed all the thoughts that were swirling around in his head. The Major concentrated on his target.

The MG 34 rattled to the second. The tracer ammunition showed the trajectory of the bullets. They crashed into the wall of the house and into the ruins at the exact spot where the Soviet machine gun nest had been during the first mock attack.

Tracer ammunition ... every seventh round, it flashed through his mind. Stop thinking, focus on your target!

Koenig took a deep breath. He knew that the Landser would crawl out of their cover and advance at the same time as the shelling. He kept his aim, felt the rifle butt against his cheek and breathed shallowly. He was ready to fire.

Go ahead! Fire! You Russians always shoot so fast!

The Russian machine-gun crew took their time. They seemed to be waiting for the right moment. It was a nerve-wracking game of patience. Koenig began to doubt that the Red Army soldiers he had seen earlier were really the enemy machine gunners. Nevertheless, he stubbornly maintained his aim. His right index finger rested on the trigger guard. The gunfire increased noticeably.

Suddenly it started. The Russian counterfire had begun. The major recognized the tracer of the Soviet machine gun. It was positioned further to the left than he had expected, but he could make out the barrel of the gun. So he corrected his aim, followed the tracer backwards, aimed at the rear end of the barrel of the Degtyarov DP 1928, inhaled, blew halfway out, held his breath, and pulled the trigger. The shot cracked. The recoil hit his shoulder. Koenig kept his eyes on the target. Instantly, the Russian machine gun stopped firing.

I hit something or someone. Come on, Ivan, get up!

Indeed, heads appeared and bobbed around frantically above

the gable of the house, which was riddled with holes. The sniper could see three Russians in all. Koenig fired the repeater, took aim at one of the heads, and pulled the trigger.

A hit!

Repeating and looking for the next target was like a single movement. One of the Red Army soldiers seemed to panic. First he fumbled frantically with his arms, then he rushed to the back of the roof. The barrel of Koenig's carbine followed him. When the Soviet soldier reached the point where the German major had a good view, he pulled the trigger. The Red soldier collapsed.

Body hit!

The machine gun was permanently silent, the third helmet was no longer visible.

He must have gone into hiding, Koenig thought, and looked for a new target.

The main attack was in full swing. Koenig's shots were drowned out, so he could not be identified as the sniper.

The barrel of his rifle moved from window to window. When he saw muzzle flashes, he fired.

The first grenade explosions could be heard. Screams, loud shouts, whimpering.

They are in the building!

Koenig retreated under the tank and closed his eyes. Death rode again through the streets of Stalingrad, swinging his scythe. It was harvest time!

When the new day finally pushed aside the night, there was rejoicing. The house had been captured and occupied. Four soldiers had been killed, three wounded, one of them seriously. Twelve Soviets were found dead and two wounded.

Sergeant Kunisch had just received the casualty report by name from a corporal and was writing it down when Major Koenig entered the room. Kunisch saluted. "I don't know what to say. Major, without you ..."

Koenig had already waved him off when the sergeant's hand went up to his headgear in a military salute. "Don't worry about it. That was my job. I have a mission and a specific target. What about the Russians? Are there any prisoners?"

"As it looks, Major, you alone took out at least five of them. The enemy has retreated, but we expect a counterattack at any moment. They are fighting tenaciously for every house. I've already informed the company about the rear guard."

"That wasn't an answer to my question."

Kunisch frowned. He tried to remember the exact wording of the officer's question. "Sorry, that's probably because we're too tired. We're at the end of our tether and urgently need replacements."

"Are there any prisoners?" Koenig repeated. He, too, could see the sleepless night he had had. Dark circles appeared under his eyes.

"Two wounded Iwans. They're sitting in the next room, waiting to be taken to the prisoner collection point."

"Seriously wounded?"

"One was shot through the shoulder, the other took some shrapnel. Nothing life threatening!"

"I'll talk to them, then we'll let them go!"

Kunisch stared at the Major in disbelief. "Let him go?"

Koenig narrowed his eyes. "That's an order!"

The sergeant nodded immediately. "Of course, Major. We'll release him! But..."

"No buts! First, they would only need valuable medical supplies from us, and second, they will deliver a message to the enemy."

"Of course!" Kunisch repeated.

Koenig went into the next room. As he had suspected, the two Red Army soldiers had not yet been treated. At least there were no bandages to be seen. A young soldier guarded them.

The Landser jumped in uncertainty as he saw the senior officer with the sniper rifle enter the room. "Koenig! No one believes me. He really exists. I'm stunned," slipped from his lips. Realizing this, he immediately added, "I'm sorry, Major, that just slipped out."

Koenig paid no attention to him, but walked purposefully and wordlessly toward the two Russians. He crouched down. Then he spoke in Russian. "I am Major Erwin Koenig. Remember my name well. I am not a German sniper, I am the German sniper. I have only five of you today, but the day is young. By evening there will be fifty. I go around the city and get every Red Army soldier I can find. I'm going to get every Russian sniper whose position I can spot, and I'm going to hunt down Saizev. I'm here in Stalingrad to hunt him down. He can't hide from me forever. I'll leave no stone unturned until I find him and put a bullet through his head!"

They both stared at Koenig. His gaze was cold, icy, terrifying. His voice without a trace of emotion. They both felt the coldness the Major radiated. Both felt the death in this man's words.

"You both go back to your men and give them my words. Do you understand?"

They nodded.

"I, Major Erwin Koenig, am hunting Saizev! And he will find my trail, because it's bloody! And now get up!"

The two Red Army soldiers stood up, shaking. The German sniper was an officer. He embodied what they had been told about Germans. He was cold. He was death.

"Repeat my words!" Koenig demanded.

They both stammered out what the Major had said earlier. Satisfied, Koenig pointed outside. "Go away! We won't shoot you. You have been ordered to deliver this message to your officers! Saizev will die. I'll find him, and I won't stop killing Russians until I have him. As long as he is hiding, I will kill many Red Army soldiers every day!"

The two wounded men supported each other. They left the ruins and limped over the rubble toward their own men.

On that cold morning, two wounded Red Army soldiers carried a message for Vasily Saizev. The first sergeant to hear it passed it on to his commanding officer, who passed it on to a political commissar, and it wasn't long before Major Erwin Koenig's words reached Vasily Saizev.

The challenge was accepted. The inevitable duel between Saizev and Koenig had begun. The two hunters armed themselves, each seeking the scent of the other.

With the formation of the Stalingrad pocket, accompanied by

the extreme onset of winter, the suffering of the trapped 6th Army began.

In addition to the daily, increasingly fierce fighting, the temperatures, which dropped to minus 30 degrees Celsius, claimed more victims. To keep the steel helmets from freezing on their heads, they had to cover them with hats or rags. They also had to insulate their hobnailed boots, which were unsuitable for winter. Many soldiers wrapped them in woven straw.

With the cold came hunger. The rations were gradually halved or quartered and still decreased drastically almost every day.

The plague of fleas and especially lice could no longer be controlled. The infestation weakened Wehrmacht soldiers considerably. Conditions in the makeshift field hospitals became increasingly intolerable. Drugs and bandages were in short supply. Surgery could hardly be performed under anesthesia. Amputated limbs were collected en masse in tubs, and this blood soup was disposed of in pits dug outside the military hospitals. Bandages were cleaned and reapplied in the snow. Lice crawled into festering wounds, diseases were transmitted, and death was a release for many soldiers.

The German Luftwaffe wanted to set up an airlift to supply the 6th Army, as had been successfully practiced in the Demyansk Pocket. All available material and aircrews were sent to the Stalingrad front.

In addition to the winterized Ju 52s, converted Heinkel He 111 and He 177 bombers, Junkers Ju 86 and Ju 290 civilian passenger aircraft, and the Focke Wulf FW 200 were also used.

At no time, however, were the 500 tons of supplies needed to keep the troops inside the cauldron supplied with supplies, ammunition, food, and medicine reached.

The distance covered by the supply planes was 200 kilometers, the loss rate was extremely high, and the number of possible landing sites dwindled as the Soviet ring tightened.

At the peak of the airlift, about 50% of the required supplies arrived. This visibly intensified the impending disaster. The death sentence had been pronounced on the 6th Army.

The seats on the returning empty planes were the only way to escape the boiler and almost certain death. They were reserved for selected members of the Wehrmacht and specially marked wounded.

Toward the end of the battle, dramatic scenes unfolded at the airfields. The wounded had to be kept away from the overloaded planes by force of arms.

Major Erwin Koenig went on what he called a daily hunt. He collected reports and noted down any information about the activities of Russian snipers. He talked to prisoners of war and repeatedly sent some of them back to deliver his messages. The name Koenig became the counterpart of Saizev in Soviet propaganda. Koenig embodied the image of the enemy.

While Red Army soldiers cheered Saizev and his men, they told each other horror stories about Major Koenig, the German sniper instructor who roamed the ruins of Stalingrad like a ghost, killing every Russian who crossed his path.

Saizev was given a mission. "Find and kill this Major Koenig!"

The dead soldier lay barely twenty meters from the outpost. His legs were sticking out from under a large section of wall, with iron wire mesh protruding menacingly from the sides. During the last heavy artillery attack, one of the heavy shells had obviously detonated next to the wall. The wall was literally blown apart by the force of the explosion, burying the Russian signalman who had presumably taken cover against it. Instead of protecting him, the wall broke his back, shattering all the bones between his thighs and neck vertebrae.

He had been in his gruesome grave for at least three weeks. In the summer, rats and insects of all kinds would have eaten half of him, but now a few crows occasionally took care of the corpse, pecking flesh from the exposed areas.

The street where the dead Russian lay was relatively quiet. There was hardly any enemy movement to be heard in the entire neighborhood. The HKL had moved slightly. Nevertheless, neither the Russians nor the Germans were able to retrieve the body.

What was the point? thought the soldiers. Either they would break out of the cauldron and retreat to a safe winter position, or a relief force would arrive to blow up the cauldron and finally drive the Russians across the Volga. In either case, Hiwis or POWs would then have the thankless task of recovering the bodies, burying the fallen in mass graves or placing them on meter-high pyres and burning them.

The location of the outpost was ideal. It had a clear view of the last buildings held by the Russians and of the Volga River.

"Don't fire a shot," the sergeant had said. "Otherwise you'll catch a sniper's bullet!"

The outpost's task was simple and yet very important. He had to watch the enemy and report everything that happened in the Ivan. There were two of them, so they could take turns observing, or one of them could immediately bring an important report to the rear.

"It smells better in a slaughterhouse," whispered the Landser, looking down at the Volga through his binoculars. "Even though everything is frozen, I can smell that guy over there."

"What nonsense. Frozen meat doesn't smell," replied the other soldier.

"I just have a good nose," came the snarky reply. The guard raised the binoculars to his eyes and swept his gaze around. "They're crawling out of their holes again."

"Ivans?" the second man asked in shock, clutching his Carbine 98.

"No! Civilians!"

"That's good, then it'll stay quiet," he said with relief. The Landser let go of the carbine. "Damn cold! I'll have a cigarette."

"You still have cigarettes?"

"Machorka! I found them on a dead Russian. The same Ivan from whom I took the felt boots and gave them to you."

"You exchanged them for my bread, and only because your feet were too big."

"First, I already have felt boots, and second, it was a good trade for you. Franz offered me more than a piece of dry commissary bread."

"That's what you give your comrades," came the grumbling reply, followed by, "Man, I'm hungry."

Laughter. "Why don't you crawl over to the guy under the concrete block? Maybe he's got something in his pocket," laughed the other, taking off his gloves and pulling a pouch of coarse Russian tobacco from his coat pocket. He held the tobacco pouch in his left hand, and with his right hand pulled a piece of newspaper out of his other coat pocket. Then he put some tobacco into it. Despite the cold, the soldier skillfully rolled a cigarette.

He looked at his comrade, whose eyes were glued to the small piece of smoking art. "Here, take this," he said, handing it to him. "I'll roll another in a minute."

The guard took the cigarette, put it in his mouth, and tried to get his storm lighter out of his pocket. "Damn, I can't get it," he said with a grin and stood up so he could better reach into his pocket.

The bullet from Saizev's weapon entered the soldier's eye, traveled through his brain, and shredded the back of his skull as it exited. Mortally wounded, he fell and lay motionless.

Major Koenig was informed of the sniper activity on this section of the front two hours after his counterpart's fatal success. The officer sat in the overcrowded bunker, heated by a cannon stove, wearing only his underpants, picking lice from his clothes. As soon as he caught one, he threw it into a bowl in front of him. "That was number 17, these filthy creatures are still eating me."

Sitting across from him was a lieutenant from the second company who was engaged in the same activity. The only difference was that instead of throwing the lice he caught into a bowl, he crushed them between his fingernails or laid them on the table and poked them with the butt of his combat knife.

The messenger who brought the message to the major stood in the doorway, gasping for fresh air. He was used to stale air, especially from overcrowded bunkers, but here he felt as if he had run into an invisible wall. A mixture of sweaty feet, stale air, and human flatulence of all kinds hit him like a ton of bricks. It was warm and stuffy in the bunker, which was designed for six men and occupied by twice as many soldiers. It didn't smell, it stank! It was terrible.

The men had not washed or shaved for days. They had worn their uniforms for at least twice as long.

"Close the door immediately. It's freezing!" was shouted at him.

173

"Excuse me, but I have to stop here. If I come in, I'll throw up!"

"What do you want?" asked the soldier sitting closest to the entrance.

"I have a message for Major Koenig. We have learned of sniper activity."

Koenig finished checking for lice and got up immediately. He walked to the entrance. The cold gave him goose bumps. He didn't care. "I am Major Koenig."

The dispatcher examined the officer from top to bottom with a quick glance, then reported back. Koenig listened attentively, asked two short questions, and then dismissed the simple soldier with a "Thank you. Then he pushed the door, which was made of planks and sealed with newspaper, into the lock, walked back to the table, took the bowl of lice, walked two more steps to the cannon stove and threw his prey into the fire with a skillful toss.

Then he dressed. Under his coat he wore a warm Russian felt jacket. The chest area was still black with the dried blood of its previous owner. Koenig had shot the Russian. It was a scattered soldier who had moved in the wrong direction in the early foggy hours of the morning. Koenig named him after the number he had hit, number 37.

The major had shot this Russian and, three hours later, a signalman and his companion very close to where the Soviet snipers had now struck. With the fourth shot in this section of the front, one day later, Koenig had deliberately drawn attention to himself. He had chosen a direct hit and shot a Red Army soldier in the stomach. His shrill screams and cries for help led to a lively exchange of fire. The Soviets tried to rescue their comrade and lost two more soldiers to head shots. Koenig just managed to get out of his rifleman's nest before it was massively covered by grenade launcher fire.

Yesterday, in the early evening, he shot another Red Army soldier as the sun was setting. This time it was probably a sergeant. The group he was leading stayed under cover for over two hours, crawling out of the concrete rubble only when it was pitch dark.

It's him! He's sending his fighters to get me!

The sniper was sure that Vasily Saizev's men were lying in wait for him. The major alerted his own comrades by putting up large signs

174

warning of Russian snipers.

"Ridiculous," was the comment of the compatriots. "They're already everywhere!"

"And I'll get them!" was the curt reply.

Koenig's plan was simple. First, he had created a sensation with all kinds of shootings and had unsettled the enemy. He knew he would be hunted down. The next step was more difficult. He wanted to eliminate his fighters. Major Erwin Koenig hunting down Russian snipers!

Despite the early morning darkness, the snow provided relatively good visibility. The thermometer had been well below zero for days, and the icy east wind made it feel even colder than it already was to the Major. As he took his first steps onto the pristine white, it crunched. Due to the extreme sub-zero temperatures, the top layer of snow had quickly frozen. The cold also turned the snow to powder. The tracks revealed the sniper's path, and he wondered if and how he could cover them. Koenig had chosen his hiding place carefully a week ago, making it as weatherproof as possible. The officer had set up a total of five such central retreats and ambushes. From a strategic point of view, they were excellently located shelters, each of them well camouflaged and difficult to detect.

Each of them offered the best overview with a wide range of fire. If he was careful with the incoming sunlight, i.e. did not let it reflect in his eyepieces, the probability of detection was extremely minimized.

Koenig was also well aware that his opponents, the Russian snipers hunting him, were well trained. For him, this meant that he could only fire a single shot from each hiding place. After that, the position was useless.

As long as Soviet signalmen or other ordinary Red Army soldiers were his victims, or rather his enemies directly opposite him, he could fire several shots without hesitation before running the risk of being discovered. Hunting snipers was another matter. They worked in teams of two or three. One shooter and his observer. Sometimes a second shooter or observer. And they were masters of their trade. Koenig quickly realized that the observers had the gift of being able to photographically memorize the terrain in front of them. They remembered almost everything at a glance. Every rock, every crater, every hole. If something changed, like someone expanding a firing position, the information was passed on to the shooter. They were masters of camouflage and perseverance as they lurked for the perfect shot. They waited in their hiding places until a window opened and the enemy appeared in their eyepieces. They crooked their index finger and a split second later their target was dead or at least mortally wounded.

Koenig found the trail of the food carriers and followed it a short distance. It was a detour, but it was impossible to follow its path to the sniper's position. As he turned to the right, leaving new footprints in the snow, he unbuckled the warm blanket he was carrying, tied a string around it, and pulled it behind him like a veil.

Better than nothing, he thought, and after a few meters he turned around, satisfied.

He reached his shelter, located between a burned-out Panzer IV tank and a pile of rubble piled up by heavy tracked excavators. Part of the wrecked tank was covered with rocks, chunks of concrete, and roof timbers. Exactly between the pile of rubble and the turret, a cavity had formed in which a man could lie comfortably. The view to the front was provided by two large gaps. The smaller one was just large enough to observe the terrain and the buildings ahead with binoculars, while the larger one was large enough to aim the rifle and swivel the barrel far enough to allow a well-aimed shot. However, Koenig avoided standing in front of this gap and only observed the terrain through the smaller gap in his position.

Looking around, feeling unobserved, he lifted a few stones that he had used to block the entrance and finally crawled inside. The cave was large enough for the Lancer to sit down and turn around with ease. Since the wind hardly blew into the hiding place, it was noticeably more comfortable. Koenig covered the entrance with stones again and crawled two meters forward. There was still the smell of burning. He unrolled the blanket and wrapped himself up to his chest. Then he removed the protective cover from the optics of his rifle, checked the load, and set it aside. Next, he retrieved his sparsely filled pack and binoculars.

Two slices of commissary bread and a can of liverwurst. That was my breakfast six weeks ago, now it has to last me the whole day!

As Koenig scanned the area for a target with his binoculars, he pushed thoughts of hunger to the back of his mind. He tried not to think about anything at all and found himself thinking about his son and his wife again and again. A small pang of melancholy came over him, and as the dark clouds gathered, the sniper came to his senses, shaking his head wildly to clear his dark thoughts. Anger replaced the gloom. Anger and hatred for those who had killed his son. It was dawn, but the sun was nowhere to be seen. The sky was gray and overcast.

Koenig had been in his hiding place for about three hours when he noticed movement. He looked at his wristwatch. It was nine o'clock in the morning. Two Red Army soldiers were throwing signs at each other and scurrying from one concrete mound to the next.

The soldier's binoculars scanned the area, but he couldn't see any more Russians.

Who are you?

The sniper's first thought was that they were reporters or food rations, but he immediately ruled out the latter. They weren't carrying anything. He focused on the two Red Army soldiers and noticed that they were not carrying messenger bags either.

Were they scouts scouting the area?

He panned back to see if he could make out a larger group of Red Army soldiers in the background.

Nothing!

They were cautious and yet conspicuous.

Observers for the Ari? Or even a sniper?

He knew there was at least one sniper in the area. But he couldn't imagine that the observers of a Russian sniper would rush through the area so clumsily.

Decoys?

He swung back to the two Russians. He kept the binoculars trained on the spot where he had last seen them taking cover. Nothing happened for minutes, then one of them lifted his head out of a crater.

He was watching the area, Koenig noticed. Why?

The Russian held up his hand and waved. Then the second soldier, wearing white camouflage over his earth brown uniform, jumped up and ran ten meters forward again.

It would have been easy to shoot the man. The distance was now about 150 meters. As the man in front disappeared behind a pile of rubble, the second one jumped out of the crater and ran forward, crouching.

Rrrrrrrt ... rrrrrrrt

A volley of machine gun fire shattered the eerie silence. Bullets bored into the snow near the running Red Army soldier, crawling forward and finding their target. The Russian soldier threw up his hands and fell to the ground, hit. Koenig only saw the small flash of the muzzle out of the corner of his eye. But immediately after that, the German machine gun fell silent.

There's one! Goose bumps ran through him. The hairs on the back of his neck stood up.

The Russians had actually sent two of their men across the rubble. Poor devils! They were being used as bait. Did they do it voluntarily? Or had they done something wrong and would be rehabilitated by this suicide mission? Oh, he added mentally, what do I care?

He pointed the binoculars at the spot where he had seen the muzzle flash. If the Russian sniper holds his position, he'll show up. His scouts are sitting between him and me, I'm sure of it. But you, my friend, will soon join those poor devils down there.

Koenig put the binoculars away after he had identified the position perfectly and switched to the larger gap. He grabbed his carbine and took aim. Next, he adjusted the scope and rifle to the correct range. The lurking began. The manhunter's heart began to beat faster, then his heart and pulse rate normalized. Ten minutes went by and nothing happened. After another five minutes, the second Red Army soldier emerged from behind the pile of rubble that gave him cover and ran to his comrade. He ran crouching and zigzagging. The German machine gun was silent, but two or three carbines could be heard firing. None of the shots hit.

Koenig stayed on target. The Russian sniper was lying on one of the piles of rubble. He probably had a white sheet draped over him. The movement was barely discernible as the sheet was pushed back a crack. The German major guessed that the Mosin Nagant's barrel was wrapped in the white cloth rather than identifying it as such, but since

178

a face was visible for a fraction of a second, Koenig pulled the trigger and retreated immediately after the shot rang out. He had just seen the cloth turn red.

Blood does not lie! Now you know that I'm not a victim, but an opponent! That was for Rolf!

Koenig did not dare to fire a second shot, but retreated backwards from his foxhole. He bowed and looked for the command post of the troops in position. There was the sound of battle.

When Koenig arrived at the company command post, he was greeted with respect. A lieutenant led the troops and saluted as he faced the unusually high-ranking sniper.

"You are Major Koenig," he said in awe.

"I am!"

"That sniper scared the hell out of us. Thank you!"

Koenig ignored the praise. "You're going on?"

"Yes. We must take the house across the street to shorten the front and protect the food carriers. The sniper has kept us from doing so."

"The next one will take his place. You must advance at least two hundred meters on the right flank to secure the area," the major announced.

"The battalion..."

Rumble

A Russian shell landed just outside the bunker. Dust trickled through the ceiling between the heavy beams.

Rumble

A second followed.

"The battalion," the lieutenant repeated, "will be moving up soon with the other two companies. I'll pass this on immediately."

"Any more sniper reports?" Koenig asked, looking at the lieutenant. The officer was perhaps 22 or 23 years old, but his figure looked like that of an emaciated 60-year-old farm laborer. The sparkle in his eyes, which he surely had at his graduation ceremony or when he received his commission, was gone. The uniform that had once fit him like a glove hung limply on his emaciated body. His face was unshaven. In

Erwin Koenig's opinion, this man did not embody an officer of the German Wehrmacht, he embodied the state of the 6th Army, and he looked anything but good.

The bunker was a hive of activity. Radio messages trickled in and out. Referees torpedoed their young company commander with questions. Again and again Soviet grenades lobbed near the bunker.

"What did you ask, Major?"

Koenig waved them off. He had long since decided to get his information directly from the battalion command post. All reports from the companies were received there.

"How long will this artillery barrage last?" Koenig yelled, trying to drown out the swelling noise.

"Not ten minutes! They don't know where we are."

Koenig glanced at his wristwatch, nodded to the lieutenant, and walked to a corner of the bunker. He sat down on an empty ammunition box and unpacked his meager supplies.

He knew that news of his last hit would spread quickly among the Russians, and Saizev would certainly hear about it. He was one step closer to the duel he had sought.

10

The supplies in Katja and Grisha's cellar were almost gone. They had spoken very little since Boris's death, but they gave each other comfort and support. Katja struggled a lot with herself at first. She took all the weight off her 8-year-old son's shoulders by absolving him of any guilt and looking for it in herself. It was only after two weeks, in one of their few but important conversations, that they both realized that Boris had become a victim of war and senseless shooting. Both quickly found a name to blame for Boris's death. Vasily Saizev, the head of a sniper school and a soldier hailed as a hero of the Soviet Union.

"If he shot himself, he should pay! And if it was one of the men who went through his killing school, he'll pay too!" Katja and Grigory swore to each other.

After their husband and father, they had been robbed of the most precious thing they had. Katja's youngest son and Grisha's only brother. Despair turned into lethargy, lethargy into rage, and rage into hatred. Both Katja and Grisha were tired of being victims of the war. Their idyll was destroyed. Their home lay in ruins. Their loved ones were dead. Life was like hell.

Their cellar hideout was in the part of the dying city occupied by the German troops. Miraculously, it had survived all the fighting, and no soldier, Russian or German, had ever entered it.

Much had changed since that terrible day on the Volga when Boris lost his young life. Katja and Grisha had become even closer. They went hunting together, and Katja taught Grisha how to use a revolver. In other words, they didn't fire a shot, but the boy was able to blindly take apart and reassemble the old army revolver.

"You can point it at someone and pull the trigger," she had said, "I don't have to teach you that. You've played pirate with your brother enough times. You know how a gun works!"

Grisha was aware of the implications of his mother's words. Although he was only 8 years old, he had the mental maturity of a teenager due to the circumstances of his life.

Soon there was nothing left for the raids. The siege was as painful for the civilian population as it was for the trapped German troops. There were far too few food supplies in the cauldron, so the Russian inhabitants left behind were barely able to organize food.

The mother and son had visibly lost weight. Still, they were relatively well off because of the supplies they originally had.

One day, during their daily forays through the ruins, they found a dying Red Army soldier. Katja wanted to help at first, but quickly realized that any help would be too late. The soldier told them about messenger boys who spy for the Red Army.

"They don't attract attention and can move around freely. They crawl through the sewers and report on this and that. They are rewarded with bread, sausages and fish."

The soldier died, his words echoing.

At first Katja didn't want to know and forbade Grisha to go through the sewers, but she knew that without help they were lost and would not survive the winter. She realized that the day would come when she would have to allow her last family member to crawl through the sewers to run errands for the Red Army. The decision was made when, on one of their foraging trips through Stalingrad, they saw a boy only slightly older than Grisha lying in the snow with his emaciated mother. She was dead. The boy did not cry. His sunken face was as cold as the icy Siberian wind. When they passed the place again two hours later, the boy's little sister was lying next to his mother. She had also died of starvation. The boy covered the bodies with a few rags and placed stones at the ends to keep the wind from blowing them away. When he turned around, Katja was shocked by the sad sight and spontaneously thought of taking the boy, who was perhaps twelve years old, into her cellar. But when he saw Grisha, he called to him: "You can go to the sewers over by the old school. There are no Germans there. The Red Army needs us. Come along, comrade! We'll become soldiers and kill the Germans who did this to us!"

"My son won't be a soldier!" Katja replied brusquely, putting her arm around Grishka.

The boy nodded. "That's what my mother has been saying all these weeks. Now I've lost her and Nadja. The Germans came seven days ago. They stole almost everything we had to wear! I'll kill them for it! And if you wait too long, you'll die too. And if I have to die, it will be for Mother Russia and Father Stalin!"

There were two fires burning inside Katja. They blazed hot. One burned for her beloved Pjotr and the other for Boris. She hated both the Germans and the Russians for what had happened to her family. But there was a third voice inside. It said that not everyone was equal. The Russian thought of the officer who had helped her, she thought of the Yenkovas, who had ensured her and Grisha's survival so far by leaving.

"Then become a messenger boy. I've already been there twice and gotten bread and a herring. I curse myself for always listening to my mother and not going through the sewers earlier. You could still be alive," he sobbed and began to cry.

Katja hated herself for it, but if they both wanted to survive, it had to be done. She knew it in that moment. The fate of this family and the boy would also be her fate. Unless they got food.

Two days later she agreed. She took Grisha to the old school after dark, and her son crawled through the small entrance into the sewers.

"Be careful, big boy," she whispered, fighting back tears.

"I may not be back for a day or two, Mom, but don't worry. I'll make it!"

Tears welled up in Katja's eyes. She wiped them away with the sleeve of her cloak. "I know!"

Armed with the courage of desperation, a knife and a flashlight, he followed his instincts.

When Grisha reached the end of the canal, he slowly climbed up the ladder on shaky knees. Carefully, he first stretched his child's hands over the edge of the exit, then pushed his head back. The cone of light from the flashlight pointed to the ground.

The voice sounded harsh and determined. "Come out! Slowly!"

"I'm Grigory Kalikov and I want to be a messenger boy."

"Come out and turn off your lamp!"

Grisha climbed out of the shaft and did as he was told.

"So you want to be a messenger boy?"

183

"I do!"

Another voice was heard. "Take him to the sergeant."

"You think so?"

"You know what the captain said. We need everyone! Only together can we win this battle!"

Grisha heard footsteps, then stood in the beam of a lamp and felt a strong hand on his shoulder. "Come with me, Comrade Ka-likov!"

A bare bulb was the only source of light in the bunker. Grishka had to answer a captain's questions. The officer asked one question after another, and the boy told the story he had rehearsed with his mother. His father is missing, his mother is sick, and his brother Boris is dead. Grisha pretended to want to get food and medicine for his mother.

"What can you offer us?"

"I can walk around the city during the day and memorize all the positions!"

The captain put a drawn map of Stalingrad on the table. Grisha saw a lot of lines and circles. Some had been crossed out several times, and some had been erased.

"Do you know where we are?"

The boy looked at the map. He concentrated, followed the long path of the marked Volga, looked for the school where he had entered the canal, and finally looked up at the captain. "I know where the cellar is where we live. I know where I entered the canal," he pointed demonstratively. "And I know where Mom and I ran into the German officer with the sniper rifle the other day. But I don't know where we are now, because I don't know how the canal..."

"What did you just say?" he was interrupted.

Grisha did not know what he had said. He had only mentioned the German officer because his mother had mentioned it several times when she told him that a German officer with a sniper rifle had protected and saved them from other soldiers. The boy had not said the latter. He just thought it was good to talk about the officer because he thought it sounded important.

"I don't know how the channel works," he repeated.

Captain Oligov looked excited. Grisha thought he saw a change

184

in the officer's face. "No, you said something about an officer with a sniper rifle. I want to know everything about it!"

Grisha's knees went weak. The captain noticed the slight trembling and suspected physical weakness due to malnutrition. "When was the last time you ate?"

Grisha knew he had to lie. There wasn't much left in the cellar, but he had eaten some pickled vegetables that afternoon. "Two days ago. We found some provisions in the haversack of a dead German," he babbled, a little unsettled.

The captain got up and went to the other side of the room. He rummaged in a bag and came back with a hard-boiled egg and a piece of white bread. He placed both on the table. "Eat!"

It was a feast for Grisha. He hadn't eaten an egg since that summer.

Oligov watched him. When the egg was swallowed, he asked: "What exactly was it like when you saw that officer?"

Grisha's mind was crystal clear. "We were looking for food when we saw him. Some Germans wanted something from Mama and pushed her into a ruin, then this man came and scared them away. He had a rifle with a telescopic sight."

The Red Army man seemed to be thinking. For a few seconds there was an oppressive silence. His eyes literally ate Grisha. The boy knew that he had told him something very important. Oligov pointed to the map on the table. "Can you show me this place on the map? And exactly?"

"That's easy," Grisha replied, swallowing the last bite of bread. He looked at the map, picked out a spot he could always find and describe, and put his index finger on it. "This is where it was. Exactly where Comrade Dimitri Solenko's little shop used to be."

Oligov's gaze changed again. The tension disappeared and something resembling a smile appeared.

"I think we can use your services," the captain said, calling for a soldier.

A Red Army soldier led Grisha through the streets. It was almost dusk, and the city here looked just as cold and dead as on the other side of the narrow canal, but instead of German soldiers, it was swarming with Soviet ones. The Red soldier and Grisha joined a group of wounded soldiers.

"We have the same route. If we go through the military hospital, it's safer. The Germans haven't fired continuously since we've been in the hospital," he explained. "And when they do fire, it's mostly in the northern part of the city."

The word military hospital was a stretch. Spread across several ruins, Russian soldiers lay in the cellars, waiting to be transported across the Volga. Moaning and wailing could be heard. Some soldiers had empty eyes staring into space, and many of them were shivering. Some of them from the cold, but most of them from their terrible experiences. There was a strange smell in the air that reminded Grisha a little of the hospital where his father had worked. Grisha was startled when he suddenly heard a long, loud scream. He looked at the Red Army soldier leading him. He grinned. "They're amputating. If you feel sick, close your eyes or just look at the ground. We're about to pass the place where they dump the amputated parts."

Grisha played the strong boy. "That's all right. I've seen a lot," he said, but only half aloud.

The look he cast into the big tub haunted him for a long time. Hands, fingers, and legs were swimming in a kind of blood soup. Two men in aprons reminded the boy more of butchers than medics. They emerged from the ruins and each poured a bucket of blood and body parts into the tub. Grisha gagged, but didn't want to throw up the precious egg, so he averted his eyes and thought of his mother and Boris. He didn't know where he was going, but he wanted to be strong.

Don't throw up, he told himself, and after a while he overcame the feeling of suffocation.

He was taken to a shelter, given a cup of hot tea, and shown a straw sack.

"Get some rest. We'll wake you if we need you."

Grisha was tired, but it took him a long time to fall asleep. The images at the back exit of the military hospital were burned into his memory, but eventually exhaustion overcame his inner psyche and he fell asleep.

"Up you go!"

Someone shook Grisha's shoulder roughly. The boy blinked, rubbed his eyes with his fists, and yawned.

"Come on, get up!" he was told.

The sergeant's face, blurred at first, took shape and contours. The gaze was neither friendly nor fierce, the voice was harsh, almost hoarse, and allowed no contradiction.

"We have a job for you."

"What do I get for it?" Grisha slipped out and immediately cursed himself.

The sergeant frowned. His face darkened. "What a cheeky brat you are. I should slap you for what you just said. It's an honor to fight for your country!"

The eight-year-old intuitively knew what to say. "I lost my father and brother in the war. I'm here to save my mother," said the wise boy. "And to free Russia from the Germans," he added. "And for that I need medicine for my mother and something to eat, or she'll die."

The sergeant's face brightened slightly. "That sounds better, comrade..." he replied in a questioning tone, expecting a name in response.

"Grigory Kalikov!"

The sergeant grinned. "Comrade Kalikov. It is an honor to bring you to the captain. And if your courage is as big as your mouth, you'll get what you ask for in the end. Something to eat."

The order Grisha received from the handsome captain, who wore two medals on his chest, was clear and unmistakable. The order sounded simple, but it was extremely difficult to carry out. Grisha was to find the German officer who was carrying the sniper rifle and, at best, find out who he was and where he was stationed. In short, he was to spy for the Red Army.

Grisha listened attentively and repeated passages of his mission over and over again. In the end, the boy was given a warning to take with him. "Anyone who betrays us will be punished by death. Do not lie! And don't expect any reward if you come back without information!"

The captain then slipped Grisha two slices of hard rusk and a dried fish wrapped in newspaper. The boy quickly tucked the valuable provisions into his coat pocket.

"We want to see you here again in two or three days at the latest. Understood?"

"Yes, Captain!" Grisha replied briskly, clicking his heels together and saluting like a Red Army soldier.

The Russian officer smiled benevolently. Grisha heard the rubbing of a match and seconds later smelled the pungent smoke of a papirossa. He had not yet noticed the second man in the captain's bunker. Curious, he turned around. In the far corner sat a political commissar. The man with the rank of lieutenant had been listening the whole time and hadn't made a sound. The end of the cigarette was glowing. The inspector inhaled and blew out the smoke in puffs. A small cloud had quickly formed from the blue haze, billowing under the bunker ceiling.

Grisha wanted to leave.

"Wait!"

The boy stood rooted to the spot. He immediately felt uncomfortable. The political commissar got up and walked toward Grisha. He stopped in front of him and looked at him. "Where exactly are you hiding?"

Grisha hesitated. Then he answered: "Mom said I can't tell anyone!"

"I'll ask you one last time. Where is your hiding place?"

Grisha shook his head.

The officer took a swing and slapped the boy hard across the face. "Where is your hiding place?"

Grisha's cheek turned red. Tears welled up in his eyes. He was afraid, but he was defiant. "Beat me to death, but I won't betray my mother!"

The officer walked around Grisha once and stopped in front of him again. Grisha closed his eyes in anticipation of a blow, but the hard blow to his face never came. Grisha blinked. The political officer smiled. "Brave!" he said. "Just what I was hoping for. If you had told me where you were hiding, I would have taken the fish from you."

The captain cleared his throat. "Do you think we'll get lucky and the boy will find the German sniper?"

"It's worth a try. Comrade Saizev needs information, and if the boy provides the right information, it won't be to your disadvantage, Captain Oligov."

Grisha got goose bumps. He was supposed to spy for the infamous Saizev, whom he hated. His thoughts were racing.

Saizev is hunting that German. I really have to tell mom. Maybe I can meet Saizev, then I'll take Mom's gun and avenge Boris!

The thought had barely faded when Grisha heard himself say: "Excuse me, comrade officer, may I meet comrade Saizev?"

The captain and the inspector laughed out loud. The political officer patted Grisha on the shoulder. "If you tell him where to find the German officer with the sniper rifle, he'll personally pin a medal on your chest."

Grisha was excited and had to hide it at all costs. He sensed an opportunity for revenge.

Tock tock

There was a knock.

"Yes," barked the captain.

The heavy wooden door opened. A detector stood in the doorway. "A message from the staff, Comrade Captain."

The officer waved the Red Army soldier over, took a piece of paper and pointed to Grisha. "Take him to the canal tonight. He has a mission. And give him a decent bowl of soup first!"

"Yes, Captain!"

Katja was already at the canal entrance at dusk. She looked for a sheltered place to hide and waited for Grisha. She didn't care how long it would take.

And if he doesn't come today, I'll wait again tomorrow from dusk till dawn. And if he hasn't come in a week, I'll crawl through the canal myself.

When Grisha crawled out of the narrow opening, she came running to embrace her son as if she hadn't seen him for weeks. Together they made the perilous journey home. It was not until they reached the safety of the cellar that the boy told her what he had seen, presenting the biscuits and the fish and leaving his mother with two-thirds of the meal.

"I already had some soup. Eat your fill, mother. I'm supposed to crawl through the canal again in two days and bring them some information.

Katja summarized. "So you're looking for the German who helped me?"

"Yes, mom, namely Saizev, the sniper. There was even an inspector there."

Katja thought feverishly. What they were asking Grigory to do was more than dangerous. Should she go with him to look for this German? Should they just go into hiding and never let her son crawl through that canal again? How far could they go? The food her son was getting would keep them alive. The situation was desperate.

After dinner, she got up and fetched a bottle of vodka. She opened it and poured some into a glass.

"You don't usually drink vodka, Mom," Grisha had remarked.

"I need it this time. I need to think."

"There's nothing to think about. We will look for the German and tell Saizev. I can get very close to him."

Katja's eyes sparkled. "And then?"

Grisha wasn't allowed to say what he was thinking, so he said: "And then I'll get a really good reward. Maybe enough to get us through the winter."

Katja knew that Grisha had other plans, and she couldn't blame the young man, but he was a child, her child! And so she had to deny it.

"That's not possible, Grisha. You and I should stay together."

"We will, Mama. We'll always be together. I just have to go through the canal alone. It's so narrow in places, I can barely fit through."

Katja swallowed the vodka and felt the warmth spread from her throat to her stomach. She grimaced. Grisha laughed.

Katja slept very restlessly that night. A thousand things were running through the desperate Russian's mind. She was in the death kettle of Stalingrad. She trusted neither the Red Army nor the German aggressors. She had almost been raped and knew that it could happen again any day. She had seen how miserably civilians died in Stalingrad.

No, they don't die, they die miserably! I don't want Grisha to die, too! Our little family has sacrificed enough. Cursed war!

The next morning, she jumped over her shadow again and let Grisha continue crawling through the canal. She also knew that this meant more marches through the ruined city. They had to get information about this officer named Erwin Koenig. She had memorized the name of the German soldier. On the one hand, she didn't care because he was German, but on the other hand, without this extraordinary man who spoke almost perfect Russian, she would have been raped and maybe even murdered.

The fish Grisha brought home last night was healthy. It's not just food, it's life!

Katja decided to go out with Grisha and gather information. She hoped that they would be able to do this inconspicuously, but at the same time she knew that it was an impossible task. How could they find a single man in Stalingrad? Tomorrow she would send her son through the channel with the name information. She thought of a plausible story how he could have gotten the information and hoped that he would bring back something useful.

Katja's suspicions were confirmed. She and Grisha took long walks through the city, repeatedly approaching soldiers and asking about Erwin Koenig. She said he was an acquaintance of hers. No one helped them, no one knew anything or at least wanted to tell them anything. Katja once mentioned the sniper rifle with her fragile knowledge of German and was briefly suspected of being a spy. An older soldier with a full beard and a kind face defused the tense situation, said that his son was perhaps two years older than Grisha, and sent them both on their way, over the fierce protests of his comrade.

Grisha crawled through the canal on the third day with the only good information they had about the German sniper. Kajta had repeatedly drilled into her son what he had to say. When he disappeared into the canal, she blamed herself. The wait was hell, and when Grisha returned a day later, she never wanted to send him away again.

"The captain was very pleased," he grinned, proudly showing off the dried herring he had received as a reward. "This time it came with four slices of rusk and I even got some toothpaste powder!"

Katja hugged Grisha. The next time he would come without information and without food, she knew. She would have liked to end this dangerous game, but it was a game with no way out. Once in the clutches of the Red Army, there was no getting out. Any refusal to work was tantamount to treason, and treason meant death by execution. Grisha had to continue.

11

The Russian fighters had forced the pilot of the Ju 52 to give his best. But the plane had taken several hits and was barely maneuverable. Now he was forced to descend. Icy winds hit him in the face. The windows were shot out and shattered, most of the instruments had failed, and the co-pilot was hanging fatally in his seat. The last of the daylight was fading and visibility was getting worse. The night mercilessly pushed aside the day, enveloping Stalingrad in a cold, eerie darkness.

Despite the cold, beads of sweat formed on the pilot's forehead. Trying to escape the Russian fighters, he had flown too far and was in the middle of the city. He knew he would hardly survive a crash landing in the rubble of the city. Tracer bullets from a machine gun whizzed by. A flare whizzed upward, emitting its blinding magnesium light. Blinded, he pulled at the stick, but old Aunt Ju was no longer steerable. He realized too late that he could neither bail out nor land the transport plane safely. As the last drop of kerosene dripped from the fuel tank and the fire on the right engine spread from the wing to the landing gear, he knew he was going to die. Here and now.

He let go of the stick, closed his eyes, and raced toward the ruins in the artificial light of the slowly fading flare, which grabbed him like an invisible hand and pulled him toward it. Machine gun rounds slammed into the aluminum walls of the plane from all sides, punching holes in it. The front propeller failed, the left wing engine spun the plane sideways.

A hail of bullets hit the plane. Two or three hit the pilot's left side, but his body was pumping so much adrenaline that he didn't feel the impact.

"Ahhhh" was the last sound he made as he died in the middle of the ruins of Stalingrad. The cockpit crashed into the wall of a house, sending debris flying and stones crashing to the side. Small flames shot from the last functioning engine.

Propeller blades slashed through the air like deadly swords. Wings broke, a huge hole gaped in the fuselage. Crates were hurled out, some hitting rocks and smashing, their contents scattered among the debris. The plane's wreckage creaked to a halt in the bizarre landscape of ruins.

"Holy shit," the first guard of the small barricade had exclaimed. "Did you see that, Heiner?"

The man beside him crawled out from under the frozen blanket. "The whole bird crashed! Of course I saw that. I'm not blind."

"That was one of our supply planes. Boy, that stuff usually comes in the back. Before it gets to us poor pigs at the HKL and we get something to eat, the stagehands have already divided it up and eaten it!"

"Nonsense!"

"No nonsense. Just look at us. You're nothing but skin and bones. Have you ever seen an emaciated general?"

Heiner thought about it. "No! There really is something to it."

"You see, and that's why we get the load!"

"Can we get to it?" asked Heiner.

"If it's completely dark later, maybe we can take the plunge. Ivan has to sleep sometime."

"Where exactly is the stuff?" asked Heiner, who had now crawled out from under the blanket. To get a better look, he raised his head high above the sandbag parapet for a moment.

The Russian sniper's shot tore through his left cheek, shattering his upper jaw and exiting under his right cheekbone. The soldier lay in his position, writhing, moaning, and bleeding profusely.

"Son of a bitch, Heiner! You shouldn't lift your square head over the parapet," the other man shouted at him, unable to cope with dressing the entrance and exit wounds. "Meeediiic .. Meeediiiiic!" he shouted.

Major Erwin Koenig had witnessed the crash of the German plane. The wreckage was right between the lines. To the left were the Russians, to the right the Germans. Koenig had been lying in wait here for two days because a Russian sniper had already shot a dispatcher, two porters, and four soldiers. Koenig had scouted the area as best he could and identified several possible positions for his chosen victim. He had been wrong three times so far, each time costing the life of another Landser.

However, Koenig had achieved partial success. The day before, the most feared German sniper had shot one of the observers of the Russian he was hunting.

The major had identified his position because an iron bar, which had protruded steeply from a concrete block in the evening, stood crosswise the next morning. Koenig had named this position Sundial because of this iron bar. Such word bridges helped him to orient himself quickly.

He had concentrated on the position of the sundial and was lying in position only 100 meters away from it. The German was relatively comfortable and well hidden under a door wedged between a piece of wall and a pile of bricks.

The barrel of his carbine was wrapped in dirty white rags, as was the scope on the rifle.

Koenig knew when the food carriers would come forward and waited patiently. He ignored the cold and the hunger. He had only this one target, and he hoped it was Saizev himself who was in position there.

As the men made their way to the ruins with the sparsely filled aluminum containers and walked along the relatively well-protected hollow path, Koenig noticed that something was stirring in the sundial position.

You have to have at least two observers and communicate by radio. You can't see the detector from there. Damn it, how can I warn my comrades without giving myself away?

He was no longer able to put his thoughts into action. Koenig saw a small flash, knew that the Russians were about to fire, and fired at his target as well.

While the bullet from Koenig's weapon left the barrel and raced toward the target at a speed of more than 700 meters per second, the Russian sniper shot one of the food trucks.

Koenig did not know where the enemy shot came from. All he knew was that he, too, had been hit. Since it was not the sniper, he assumed it was his observer.

We're looking for each other, comrade Ivan, he thought, repeating himself and retreating to another position.

It was from there that he had watched the crash.

After the plane crashed, the sleeping front woke up. Airplanes meant goods, goods meant food or ammunition. Both meant life!

You have to save the cargo. There's no fire in the wreckage, the cargo is lying around there, the Major concluded and stayed in safe cover for the time being.

He continued to aim at the supposed position of the hunted Russian sniper. He called this position "bell tower" because the rubble reminded him of the tower of a church.

Koenig literally forced himself to stay with the rifle in his target, so as not to have to keep an eye on the engine, which was grinding to a halt. He stayed on target even as the Junkers made a spectacular impact. Shortly after, he saw the flash of the muzzle, corrected his aim in a split second, and crooked his index finger. His shot broke, the butt smashing against his shoulder. The Russian sniper did not know whether his shot was a hit or not. The bullet from Koenig's Karabiner 98 hit the Red Army soldier's forehead immediately after firing, shredding the back of his skull as it exited.

"An observer and a shooter. Saizev, if it wasn't you I took out, you'll soon know it was me who took out your people!"

More and more men rose and ran crouched toward the wreckage of the plane. Flares whizzed upward. Machine guns blasted away.

Rrrrrrt..... rrrrrrrt....

Hand grenades whirled through the air and exploded.

Boom!

The Germans and Russians rose at the same time. Both sides wanted to get their hands on the precious cargo. The cheers of the Germans rang out against the roar of the Russians. Koenig had not heard either battle cry for a long time. The so-called rat war was raging in Stalingrad. There were no more big battles, but small groups fought for houses, cellars, floors or even just for trenches or single positions. Close combat was the order of the day. Anyone who hesitated died. You had to split an enemy's skull with a spade or ram a bayonet into his stomach without batting an eyelid before you were hit in the face with the butt of a rifle. Brutality triumphed over humanity.

Koenig gave his countrymen as much cover as he could, but was careful not to be discovered himself. He fired and aimed. As soon as a Red Army soldier appeared in the crosshairs, he pulled the trigger. He fired a maximum of two shots from the same position, then changed positions. After a short time, the sniper saw the men swinging their spades. They crashed into bones, splitting skulls or shoulder blades. Bayonets were plunged into bodies. The Russian machine guns fired incessantly, and their rounds hit more than just enemy soldiers.

Koenig hurried forward. A new fever had seized him. The fever of the hunt for one of the food boxes. They were stuck in a cauldron, their supplies were scarce. Now and here was the chance to eat their fill.

Or maybe I can find some lice powder. "Lupex" or that stinking "Russ-la" for all I care. The main thing is to do something against these damned lice, Koenig thought as he left his position and approached the wreckage from the right flank, which seemed to be less contested.

The sniper took cover behind a concrete block, pressed himself against the cold stone, and waited a moment. Then he cautiously raised his head and surveyed the terrain. More and more Red Army soldiers were jumping out of foxholes, crawling out of ruins, or climbing over walls and running toward the wreckage. Some of them were so well camouflaged that Major Koenig was almost startled when they stood up. He grabbed his rifle, fired and shot two Red Army soldiers with a light machine gun, then slipped back behind the concrete block. He reloaded, took a deep breath, jumped up and hurried on.

Damn it, they won't make it, he cursed inwardly as he realized that the Russians outnumbered his attacking comrades by at least double.

I have to help them!

The distance to the human fighting ball was still about 60 meters. As soon as one flare burned out, the next one shot up into the sky, emitting its trembling magnesium light.

Koenig saw a tall lanser wielding his spade like an old lansquenet wielding his sword to clear a path for the knights through the enemy mercenaries. Two Red Army soldiers collapsed from the blows of the spade. A third shot the German in the body and ran toward him with his rifle outstretched, while a fourth Russian attacked from the side. Koenig shot the Red Army man with his rifle and tried to shoot the other, but both men were already struggling on the ground.

The sniper changed positions again. He skillfully scurried through the cold desert of ruins, using every opportunity for cover to get closer to the action. As more Russians appeared and he heard the first cries of retreat from the German infantry, he realized that the battle for the supply crates was lost.

At least for the moment, Ivan had the upper hand.

Koenig decided not to advance any further. He wanted to avoid direct contact with the enemy. The exchange of fire subsided. Only a German machine gun continued to fire, covering the retreat of the Landser.

Rrrrrrt ....rrrrttt...

This machine gun also began to fall silent.

A voice echoed through the night. It was the call for a medic. Someone answered. Koenig understood only fragments of words: "Hold on ... you ... Ivan!"

The major had to turn around to avoid colliding with the Red Army soldiers, who had magically disappeared from his view. Angry at his failure, he grabbed his sniper rifle, still wrapped in a dirty white sheet for camouflage, glanced over the chunk of concrete he was kneeling behind, and ducked down again. As far as he could see at a glance, two, maybe three Red Army soldiers were running toward him. They were carrying something heavy. Koenig wondered if it was ammunition or a crate from the plane. The latter seemed more likely.

The sniper waited to see if the enemy had seen him. When there was no reaction from the Russian soldiers, he dared to take another look. This time he peered out from behind the cover, registered as much as possible, and quickly ducked his head again.

Crap! They're coming right at me. Two men. They're carrying a crate. From the size, I wouldn't guess it was ammunition.

The machine gun went off again. Two or three hand grenades went off.

Rrrrrrt ... rrrrtttt .... Hum .... Hum

Knowing that the Germans were advancing to rescue their

wounded comrade, Koenig acted quickly. With a practiced grip, the carbine was ready to fire. The sniper swung high enough over the concrete block to aim and fire. The Red Army soldiers were still about twenty meters from him. The first shot pierced the right crate carrier's chest at heart level. He jerked his arms up and fell backwards. The released crate hit the left bearer's leg, whereupon he instinctively dropped the crate and grabbed the painful area. This split second was enough for Koenig to reload and fire a second shot. The Red Army soldier also collapsed, shot in the upper body. Koenig lurked for a moment. It was quiet. Only the bursts from the machine gun could be heard. Koenig was not shot.

The two Ivans were alone, my shots were drowned out by the machine gun fire, he thought, shouldered the rifle, drew the 08 pistol and ran to the two Russians. Five meters from his target, he slowed down, took aim at the bodies, ready to fire in an emergency, and noticed that they were both lying motionless on the ground. Koenig knelt down. Enthusiastically, he read the inscription burned into the crate: Food - below was the Reich's eagle with a swastika, also branded into the wood.

Since the Russian offensive, and especially since the formation of the kettles, the supply had steadily decreased. In the beginning they received about 200 grams of bread a day, the same amount of meat, mostly from slaughtered horses, 30 grams of cheese, 30 grams of fat, and a few cigarettes, which the non-smokers exchanged for food. This was accompanied by a clear soup made from the boiled bones of the slaughtered animals. Some tea and malt coffee, known as muckefuck, rounded out the meager meal.

This portion diminished with each passing day, and some days nothing reached the front. This depended on the weather and enemy activity, especially that of the Russian snipers.

According to Soviet reports, Saizev alone scored 225 hits between November 10 and December 17, 1942, and some of the soldiers he trained as snipers scored even more.

Quick glances. No one to be seen. Koenig slid the 08 into the holster, grabbed the box and lifted it. It was heavier than expected and extremely unwieldy, but he could still carry it. Sneaking through the rubble, however, was almost impossible. The officer's only protection was the darkness. Every meter took strength. He demanded a lot from his emaciated body and pushed it to its limits. Constantly stepping over stones, beams and pieces of rubble was extremely exhausting.

The echo of the machine gun fire echoed dully through the streets. It became more massive again. A flare hissed upward again, casting trembling light over the ruins. Bizarre shadows danced on the ruined walls.

Koenig decided to bypass the disputed area in an arc, choosing the narrow road to the south, only to turn northwest again after a short distance. He knew that he was moving hard along the blurred HKL, if that term could be associated with the center of Sta-lingrad at all.

Everything here is HKL, he thought to himself.

Koenig moved slowly, which took a lot of strength. He had long since changed direction when a group approached him. He quickly realized that they were Soviets and cursed himself for choosing this route. The officer feared that he had lost his way. He hastily pressed himself against a wall and crouched down. He put the box on the ground.

There were five or six Russians, one of whom was carrying something on his back. Koenig knew immediately that it was a combat unit. In this strength the enemy penetrated the occupied ruins, fought the soldiers down or burned them out.

Where there is one of these troops, there are others, he thought.

Single snowflakes danced from the sky. The cold was barely noticeable. Beads of sweat ran down his forehead. Little clouds of breath danced in front of his mouth. Koenig hoped that the Russian soldiers would scurry into one of the buildings. He cursed himself, wondering aloud how he could have been so stupid as to venture so far with a heavy crate.

Idiot, I should have just gone back the way I came! Skirmish or no skirmish!

At that moment, he could no longer follow his train of thought to make a U-turn. Koenig looked around. It was impossible to cross the street without being seen. Even if he got up and ran back the way he came, the Russians would see him. Only in an emergency would he get into a firefight with all five Red Army soldiers. He thought feverishly. A decision had to be made in the next 15 seconds.

Koenig fixed his gaze on the five Russians. His chest was still rising and falling hastily, but he was visibly calming down. Out of the corner of his eye he saw a gap in the wall. He estimated the distance to be seven meters, where part of the wall had collapsed inwards. The gap should be big enough for a man to get through.

Ten more seconds!

The rifle was already in his hand. Should he jump and run? Or should he fire first and then run? Which would give him the greater time advantage? Should he take the food box with him or leave it here?

Five seconds left! The Russian in front of me has stopped. He probably saw my silhouette!

He felt the adrenaline in his body. His pulse was racing. Koenig stopped and tried to stay calm despite his nervousness. He took a deep breath in and half a breath out.

Without food I will die!

His mind was made up.

The stock of the rifle was pressed tightly against his shoulder. The pale moonlight was enough to bring the front Russian's face into the scope's crosshairs.

Asian platoons - Siberians.

Koenig recognized how the targeted Red Army soldier was pointing at him and at the same moment curled his right index finger. The shot shattered the deceptive silence of the street. The bullet entered the victim's head above the root of his nose. Before the mortally wounded Soviet soldier hit the ground, Koenig had fired the repeater, swung the barrel of his carbine around, and aimed at the flamethrower's carrier. There was no phosphorus round in the magazine, but the sniper hoped the regular round would be enough to ignite the burning oil.

The shot cracked. Koenig shouldered the rifle with a flourish, grabbed the box, and ran. A fireball lit up the street. The flamethrower soldier ran around like a living torch, screaming in agony. Meanwhile, the other three Russians ran toward Koenig and fired. Muzzle flashes could be seen. The German rushed forward with the tremendous force of mortal fear and reached the gap in the wall. Bullets crashed against the wall. Ricochets whizzed close over his shoulder. The major threw the crate through and immediately squeezed in behind it. A hard blow struck his upper left arm. Koenig winced and caught the toe of his left foot on a piece of wall as he stepped through. He lost his balance and fell to the floor. His right knee hit the edge of a stone hard. A sharp pain raced through his body and took his breath away for a moment. Stars danced before his eyes.

Don't give in, he reminded himself and tried to grasp the shoulder strap of the food crate with his left hand. He felt no strength. His upper arm grew warm. Only now did he realize that he had been hit. He let his arm hang limply. That was the best way to bear it. King heard loud shouting. The stomping of boots. He feverishly pulled a hand grenade from his belt, bit down on the handle to hold it in place, and unscrewed the breech with his right hand. Then he pulled the safety cord, grabbed the handle, and hurled the grenade through the crack in the wall. He lay down on the ground, hoping it would detonate before his pursuers stood at the opening and fired a few rounds into his back.

Boom!

The explosion was loud. Chunks of stone and dust flew through the gap.

Run or die, Koenig told himself, forcing himself to stand. His knee hurt, but the urge to live was stronger. He grabbed the crate with his right hand and held on to one of the straps. Koenig limped away, dragging the crate more than carrying it. The fatal shots were not fired. For now! Koenig did not know how far he had gone or exactly where he was. All he knew was that he wouldn't last long. In front of one of the many piles of rubble, he saw a fallen lamppost, its concrete base torn from the ground. Above it was a pile of rubble, pushed up by heavy caterpillars. Koenig walked over and discovered a depression in the lamppost's former foundation bed large enough for him to fit into. He pushed the crate into it, looked around again, and slid into the hole. With the last of his strength, he tried to block the entrance with stones so that he would not be discovered. Finally he lay down, completely exhausted. His right knee hurt like hell and his left upper arm was on fire. Koenig thought about self-medicating as best he could, fumbled in his pockets for a painkiller, and felt the last of his strength leaving him.

He closed his eyes.
　　　Only five minutes.
　　　He passed out.

Example photo

PA-0048-zwei Soldaten Wintertarn mit
Karabiner
two soldiers in winter camouflage with carbines
Privatarchiv Author

12

Though he had no information for the captain for the second time in a row, Grisha crawled through the canal again, climbed out of the shaft on the Russian-occupied side of Stalingrad, and demanded to see his commanding officer, as he called Captain Oligov.

"And you have something to tell the captain this time?" the sergeant asked.

Grisha thought about what to say and nodded silently. He had something to say. It wouldn't be the information the captain wanted to hear, but the clever boy had an idea. Maybe it would work.

"And what?" the sergeant asked, leading Grisha to the captain.

"It's top secret. The captain told me not to talk about it with anyone. If I tell you, I have to report it to the captain."

The sergeant scratched his head. He would have liked to beat the information out of the little bugger with a few good slaps, but he didn't want to lose his good post. In the Red Army these days, you were quickly at the front with the poor bastards who had to chase the Germans out of the ruins every night in small groups. The casualty rate was high, the fighting merciless. The sergeant wasn't in the mood for it, so he grated out of necessity: "Then I hope the captain is satisfied with your information, otherwise I'll give you a uniform and send you to the front!"

The eight-year-old took the threat seriously, but he had been through so much in the last six months that he felt cold inside. Still, he didn't want to get into trouble with the sergeant. So he said: "I'd tell you right now, but I'm afraid of the captain and I don't want to be a traitor. I serve our country and do as I'm told."

The sergeant seemed to like the words. He frowned thoughtfully. Then he patted Grisha on the shoulder. "You're a good soldier! Come on, we don't want to keep Captain Oligov waiting unnecessarily."

Grisha followed the sergeant.

There were several men in the room. They were sitting around a table, drinking tea and vodka, and some were smoking machorka.

Captain Oligov stood up as Grisha was led in and bumped his head against the naked, low-hanging light bulb. It began to sway, and long shadows danced on the wall.

"Grisha," he groaned, approaching the boy. "We were just talking about you."

Grisha stared into the faces of the men who were all looking at him. He saluted shyly, which amused the group. Besides Oligov, Grisha knew only the political commissar who had beaten him. Next to him sat a fat officer with nickel glasses. Next to him was a young soldier, and next to him another soldier who was the only one not laughing. He looked closely at Grisha. Their eyes met and remained fixed. Only when Oligov stood in front of Grisha did the boy's eyes leave the man's. Grisha got goose bumps. He felt extremely uncomfortable.

"Well, my little spy, what information did you bring back?"

Grisha swallowed. "I..." he began hesitantly.

Captain Oligov changed his look. The friendliness was gone. "Don't tell me you have no information again?"

"This sniper named Koenig has disappeared from the face of the earth. No one knows him and no one claims to have seen him. He's like an invisible phantom," Grisha squeezed out, feeling the eyes of the group of men on him.

Oligov huffed and puffed his chest. Grisha knew that a roar and a scolding would follow, so he continued quickly.

"And I can't imagine that he's disappeared. My brother and I found a young cat the summer before last. It lived in a woodshed and always hid from us. We knew it was there, but we never saw it. Just like the German sniper."

"Your story is interesting..." Oligov thundered out, but was interrupted by the man who seemed so frightening to Grisha. "Comrade Oligov, please excuse my little objection, but let's listen to the boy first."

The captain turned to the men. The officer with the nickel glasses nodded silently, and the captain became a little more friendly. "All right, go on."

Grisha cleared his throat. "The cat was gone, but it was still there. We were thinking about how to catch it and play with it. Then Boris, my little brother, had an idea. We took a ball of wool from mom's sewing box and dragged it around the shed on a long string. The cat first poked its head out of its hiding place, curious, but eventually it overcame its fear and came out to catch the wool."

Silence.

Grisha continued. "Perhaps this German sniper is like that cat."

The man Grisha found so frightening got up and walked over to him. "Your brother is as smart as a fox. Where is he?"

Flashes of memory flashed. Grisha suppressed them. "He died and my father disappeared. He was a doctor in the hospital."

The man put his hand on Grisha's shoulder. "So you're telling us to play the ball of wool?"

The political commissar rumbled. "This boy takes us for fools! As if we don't know what to do!"

The officer with the nickel glasses raised his hand. "Simple childish thinking gives us insights that we have never seen before because of their simplicity."

Silence again.

Grisha looked at the man whose hand was still on his shoulder. He gathered all his courage and said: "There is only one man who can defeat this phantom. He should be the ball of wool. Saizev. This name is also known to the German soldiers. If I spread the word among them that I know when Saizev is where, Koenig will also be there.

This time the silence lasted longer than the two short pauses before. The soldier in front of Grisha nodded sympathetically and turned to the others. The officer with the nickel glasses lifted the glass of vodka in front of him and took a sip. He put it back on the table and asked: "Comrade Saizev, what do you think of this proposal?"

Grisha's body was instantly covered with goose bumps. His head swam and his knees went weak. Standing in front of him was none other than the famous marksman Vasily Saizev. He, or one of his men, had shot Boris. Grisha felt sick to his stomach and thought he was going to throw up, but he stood firm, not wanting to show any weakness. He fixed his eyes on the face of the man he hated so much.

"Comrades, I am a hunter, and as a hunter I know how to hunt. The task here is to lure a particularly wild, dangerous and shy animal out of its hiding place. I will be prepared, and when I, together with my

207

observers and another good marksman, lie in wait for Koenig in an area I have chosen beforehand, I will shoot him. And if he doesn't come into my field of fire, my co-shooter will shoot him.

Murmurs. The men at the table whispered. Grisha hardly understood a word. After a few minutes the silence returned. The officer with the nickel glasses looked at Captain Oligov.

"Comrade Oligov, you didn't promise too much when you told us about this informer. Give him the promised reward, whatever it was!"

The captain's face suddenly brightened. The permanent grin returned. Oligov winked at Grisha, unseen from the table. "I will," he replied.

Saizev was the next to be approached by the man with the nickel glasses. "How long will it take you to find a good place for this German?"

There was a knock at the door.

"Come in!" cried Oligov.

A detector opened, but stopped in the doorway. He took a stance. "We received a report that a German sniper struck tonight, and we suspect it was Koenig."

"How many men?"

"At least seven!"

Saizev narrowed his eyes. Grisha suspected the sniper had looked just like that when he aimed at his victim and pulled the trigger. Saizev turned to the officer with the nickel glasses and answered his previous question. "I will find this place in three days. Then I'll need another day or two with my men to prepare ourselves there."

A nod from the officer was enough, and Oligov said to Grisha: "You'll get your reward, and then you'll go back and spread the news you overheard about where Comrade Saizev will soon be lurking. In five days you'll come here and find out where it will be. Then you will spread the news among the Germans, so that Koenig will find out sooner or later!"

Grisha's knees still trembled slightly. "I will do that, comrade captain," he confirmed the order, trying to sound as confident as possible.

The Captain gestured to the door. "And now get yourself something to eat. You're already trembling with hunger!"

"Thank you, comrade captain."

Grisha walked to the door without looking back. He knew that the eyes of the men were on him. At that moment, the boy did not realize what he had gotten himself into, but Grisha sensed that taking revenge on Saizev for Boris' death was not nearly as easy as he thought.

Before he closed the door behind him, one of the other men spoke. "It could be two, three, four weeks before Koenig shows up. Do you really want to lie there for that long?"

"Let's wait and see what this boy tells us in five days."

The cold night frost ate through Katja's warm clothes. She froze as she waited for Grisha. She had been sitting here for two hours and was visibly relieved when she finally heard familiar sounds coming from the shaft. This shuffling and scraping along the narrow canal wall, the creeping and crawling, the pushing through and climbing up, was very tiring for her. She suffered great mental anguish when Grisha went to that captain, and she felt a great sense of relief when he finally came back.

Katja tried as hard as she could to suppress the horrible scenario that one day her Grisha would not come back and would stay forever on the other side of the front. These were such dark thoughts that she could come to only one conclusion. If one day Grisha would be taken away from her, she would turn the army revolver on herself. She had to change her thoughts so as not to fall into an emotional hole and become depressed.

My son is a brave little spy between the lines. I'm scared, but I'm very proud of him.

She hated to put this heavy burden on Grisha, but she had to let him do it. It seemed to be the only way to get food at the moment. And if they wanted to live, they had to eat. Of course, Katja was already thinking about selling her body. To German soldiers, but the risk of getting nothing to eat or contracting sexually transmitted diseases was too high.

A strained groan tore her from her thoughts. Now her little hero was crawling out of the sewer and into the shaft leading up. She recognized his voice even as he gasped. Katja bent over the shaft and lifted her hand into it. "Grisha, at last," she whispered, felt her son's cold hand and grabbed it. The Russian pulled the eight-year-old out of the shaft more than he went up.

Grisha was very excited. "Mom, I saw him!" he exclaimed immediately.

"Shh!" Katja warned, raising her index finger to her mouth. "Speak quietly, my boy!"

Grisha nodded, looked around quickly, and whispered in a rush of words: "He was there and spoke to me."

Katja was surprised. She saw her son's eyes wide open and became curious. "Who did you see? Who spoke to you?"

"Saizev!"

The name hit her like a punch in the gut. Everything inside her tensed. Katja felt a shiver run down her spine. Her heart began to race. She knew she could never get proof that this Russian sniper was the murderer of her Boris, but she had declared him responsible on behalf of all Red Army soldiers who shot Russian children and had chosen him as an enemy.

Katja was a peace-loving woman all her life, and her profession as a nurse fulfilled her. She wanted to help people and save lives. But since the day Boris was shot in the head and taken from her, she had been filled with hatred and thoughts of revenge. She trembled as she held Grisha.

"Mama, he's going to tell me where he's lying in wait to shoot the German. You know, the sniper."

Katja hugged her son tightly.

"I can hardly breathe. What's wrong, Mom?"

She took a deep breath, loosened her grip, and wiped a few tears from her eyes. "I don't want to lose you, too. It's too dangerous. You can't work for the Red Army anymore. We must find other ways to get food. The other people in Stalingrad will manage somehow."

"Mama, have you forgotten what we saw? We only have enough food for a few days, and that's only if we starve."

Katja stood up and took Grisha's hand. "What kind of person is that?"

They walked away. Grisha began to tell his mother the whole

story. "...and then the soldier from the kitchen gave me a little more than usual," he finished.

"We'll enjoy it tomorrow, my boy. I'm proud of you, Grisha," Katja said, noticing through the glove that Grisha's handshake was getting a little firmer.

In silence they continued on their way through the freezing cold of Stalingrad. Katja instinctively chose a different route back, always avoiding the most heavily contested areas. The unclear situation on the front in the city made walking through the streets at night doubly dangerous. She did not want to run into German or Russian soldiers. Both could mean Grisha's and her death. She had quickly learned to move with extreme caution and to listen to every sound, no matter how small. She also kept her right hand on the grip of the old army revolver in her coat pocket. When death comes knocking, a man becomes a beast. Someone who used to be a good acquaintance or even a friend could kill you today for a piece of bread.

Katja had told Grisha about the gun. If something really happened to her, he would have to know how to use it. All these precautions had always allowed the two of them to get away without any problems.

The night was starry and cold. They both longed for the warm blanket in their cellar. A few shots were heard in the distance, followed by a muffled silence.

House to house fighting! Will it never end?

Katja closed her eyes for a millisecond. She thought she heard something and pulled Grisha's hand. They both stopped and listened. They could make out a few faint scraps of words. Russian soldiers. Katja tried to determine the direction and crossed the street. They slipped through a ruined house, crossed the rubble-strewn backyard of the former apartment building, and reached the next intersecting street. Again they listened for a while. When they heard nothing, they continued on their way. They had to cross the old wide boulevard, which used to be a great place to stroll, and then turn left into the next one, and then they were as good as home.

Grisha was tired and cold. "Luckily, we'll make it soon," he whispered.

211

Katja had a queasy feeling in her stomach. Wide roads are easy to see. She had the feeling they were being watched, but she was still too tired to walk any further.

They were halfway there when they both heard a low whirring sound.

"What's that?" asked Grisha, looking around anxiously.

Katja was the first to see the silhouette of the double-decker. The pilot was circling slowly and flying relatively low. "Up there! A plane!" she warned, immediately looking for good cover. "Quick! He mustn't see us."

"It's one of ours, Mom," Grisha tried to reassure her, adding, "It's a U2."

He had seen these planes before.

"First of all, it's dark. If he sees us walking, he might think we're German soldiers. Second, he can draw attention to us and thus draw both German and Russian soldiers to us. We must not take any risks!"

The boy could understand.

Another lesson learned, he thought to himself, trying to keep up with Katja's pace.

They both kept looking at the biplane. The pilot made another loop. Katja spotted a heavy concrete pedestal and ran to it. "There!" she gasped hastily, looking over her shoulder again. He would soon be flying along the former promenade. They reached their destination and ducked behind the large pedestal. The biplane whirred above them. Katja was relieved. "Let's wait a minute," she said.

Grisha looked up at the clear starry sky. "Maybe I'll be a pilot too," he said.

A groan made them both jump again, startled.

"What was that?" Grisha breathed barely audibly into his mother's ear.

Katja drew her revolver anxiously. Whoever was here would pay dearly if he came too close to Grisha or her.

Searching glances. No one was to be seen. Listening. They heard another moan. This time it was longer. Katja recognized it at once: "There's a wounded man here somewhere!"

Grisha went to the other side of the concrete pedestal and

recognized an entrance to the largely covered hole from which the pedestal had broken out. "Let's have a look, Mom."

Katja fought with herself. She wanted to get up and leave, but despite the increasing brutalization that Stalingrad was causing in each of its inhabitants, the nurse couldn't get out of her skin. Someone might need help, and she had made it her life's work to save people's lives. She got up and circled the pedestal as well. Meanwhile, Grisha had pushed a few lumps aside and was whistling excitedly: "There's a German lying there. He has a sniper rifle with him."

Regardless of the danger, Grisha pulled out his flashlight and turned it on. Katja jumped as she recognized the officer who had saved her from being raped. "Turn off the light now! Do you want us to be discovered?"

Grisha turned off the light and plugged it in.

Thoughts flashed through Katja's mind. She would have liked to run away, but her conscience intervened. She owed him something, and now she had the chance to make amends. "Damn it!" she cursed.

It was a curse Grisha knew all too well. When his mother hated something or didn't want to do something and then did it anyway, she cursed. Like she had just done.

"We're going to help that man!"

"Why?"

"This man saved me. He's the man the Russian soldiers are looking for. If we leave him here, he'll either freeze to death or be shot."

Katja and Grisha hastily uncovered the entrance. The sister discovered the dried blood.

Wounded.

She put her hand to the soldier's forehead, who was trembling with cold and shivering.

Fever.

Katja spoke to him. "Hello, can you hear me?"

Koenig opened his eyes for a moment. "He...lp," he said, first in German, then in Russian.

"What happened?"

"He...lp," Koenig repeated.

"Can you crawl out of there on your own? If I pull your arm, it will be very painful."

Koenig nodded and began to push himself out of the pit with his legs. Katja grabbed the healthy side of his torso and pulled. When the officer was lying in front of her, she reached for his canteen and poured him some water. "I'll help you, but you have to walk. I can't carry you. Can you do it? Do you understand me?"

Koenig nodded and pointed with his good hand to the hollow where he had been lying.

"Grisha, take his rifle and the backpack."

"Box," Koenig pressed his lips together.

Grisha grabbed the rifle and the backpack in which Koenig carried his small belongings and sniper gear. Only after the German pointed him out did he crawl back into the hollow and discover the box. "Mom, there's something else."

Katja leaned over Koenig. "What's in the box?"

The major replied in Russian. "Food!"

"Grisha, can you carry the box?"

The boy grabbed a shoulder strap and pulled out the box. "I can do it, Mom!"

A few minutes later they were off. Grisha was dragging the box. Katja had put on her backpack and rifle and was supporting the injured major. Koenig dragged himself forward with difficulty. His knee throbbed, his arm ached, and the fever and cold almost robbed him of his last lucid thought. Only the will to survive unleashed a superhuman strength that made the sniper endure every painful step.

Katja knew that if they encountered Russian soldiers, they would have to expect the worst. If, on the other hand, they encountered a German patrol, they would continue to live, but would probably not be able to return to their cellar and would be housed somewhere with the other civilians.

"Where are we going?" Grisha wanted to know.

"Home."

"And the German?"

"We have to take him with us."

"To our hiding place?" he said excitedly. Grisha couldn't understand his mother's actions at the moment. All this time, the cellar had

214

been the most closely guarded secret in the world, and now his mother wanted to take a soldier with her. "Mom, I thought..."

"Save your strength for the box. I trust this man!"

Katja acted purely on instinct. Grisha didn't understand this decision, but he knew that his mother had always done the right thing. If she trusts this man, then he must be a good person.

He saved her, he thought to himself, repeating this several times. Finally, he realized that without this man, his mother might not be alive. Something like spontaneous compassion arose.

"Mom, we'll help him!" he said after a few minutes, determined to help his mother save this German soldier.

For all three of them, these were the hardest miles they had ever walked in their lives. Katja carried Koenig more than he walked. Koenig had to grit his teeth with every step, and Grisha had taken on too much by carrying the crate. After the first third of the way, his arms were getting longer and the crate heavier.

When they were about halfway, the boy hoped they would take a break, but Katja just kept going. She knew she wouldn't be able to pick herself up after a break. She was at the end of her tether and just marched on without thinking. At first, she listened for sounds and possible patrols, but on the last stretch, all she could think about was getting there.

Koenig groaned at irregular intervals, and Katja kept telling him to pull himself together. The officer's strength was dwindling and he was on the verge of collapsing on the last few meters.

"I ... can't ... anymore," he groaned.

"Only ... another ... twenty meters!" gasped Katja. Grisha was still a few meters behind them.

He had never been so happy as today, when they stood in front of the ruins of their house. While Katja put the wounded Major on the ground and looked around to make sure he was safe, Grisha put the box down and sat on it.

"It's all right, we can go in," she said, pushing the tin aside. Grisha went in first, pulling the crate by the straps.

"You have to go through here. Bend over, crawl or creep, however you do it, you have to do it alone. The small passage is too narrow for two people side by side. I won't be able to support you again until you're inside. Grit your teeth one last time and you'll make it.

Koenig understood the Russian woman's words. He forced himself to make one last effort and followed the boy.

Katja covered the entrance behind him and quickly caught up. She assisted Major Koenig by giving him instructions. "This is good! ... Now watch out ... there's a sharp edge on the top right ... only two meters to go .... you're doing very well ... put your weight on your right arm ... kneel down on your left leg ... we're almost through".

The fever seemed to be rising again, and the injured knee and arm felt numb. The pain Koenig felt was no longer localized.

When he finally reached the corridor, the officer grabbed the railing. He staggered. Grisha and Katja supported him left and right.

"Grisha, let's get him down first and get the box later. Give us some light, I'll make it down the stairs. We'll prepare a bed for him in the Jenkovs' cellar."

With Grisha's help, Katja had stripped the German officer down to his underpants and examined him. Thanks to Mama Jenkova's small first-aid kit, she was able to give him at least a minimum of treatment. The trained nurse gave Koenig a painkiller and another tablet to reduce his fever. She cleaned the gunshot wound and was relieved to find that it was a through-and-through shot to the upper arm, so there was no bullet to remove and, after examining the entry and exit channels, no bone had been damaged.

"The iodine tincture prevents inflammation. That's very important," she explained to Grisha, who, despite his tiredness, was eager to help his mother. He only looked away when she sewed the exit wound with two needles and a simple thread.

She applied the ointment from Mother Jenkova's small jar to her knee. "It smells strong, but I hope it will ease the pain," she said. Then she pulled Mr. Jenkow's baggy pants over the German. The legs were too short, but they would keep him warm. With Grisha's help, she pulled a wide sweater over his torso. Then they covered the officer with blankets.

"He'll sleep a lot now."

"Will he make it, Mama?"

Katja's look was kind. She smiled. "Yes, I think so."

Back in their own cellar, they both fell into bed, dead tired.

The next day, Grisha rummaged through Major Koenig's backpack and found an Esbit stove and some burning tablets. He was familiar with the cooking device, as Katja had brought one home from a raid.

"Look, Mom!" he said proudly. "We can eat something hot again."

"It's none of our business what's in the backpack. It belongs to Mr. Koenig."

"How do you know his name?"

"I will never forget his name. He saved me from one of the worst situations in my life, my son. That's the only reason he's lying next door. By the way, he's still sleeping. I checked earlier."

"I'm sure he won't mind. We're cooking for him, too."

Katja nodded. "We'll make some tea. It's good for all three of us. Mother Yenkova has herbal tea for us."

"What's in the box I brought yesterday?" came the excited reply.

"Let's get the tea ready and then we'll see!"

"Oh yes!"

Hungry and with a rumbling stomach, Grisha set the table. On the captain's orders, the Russian cook had given him a good portion. Still, the boy kept looking at the box he had dragged through the nighttime streets of Stalingrad.

Katja prepared the tea and placed a cup with the steaming contents in front of her son. What had once been taken for granted was now something very special. A cup of hot tea. Grisha took it carefully, warmed his hands on the cup and took a small sip. He felt it go down his throat and a pleasant warmth spread through his stomach. Katja poured a cup of tea for herself and one for Erwin King. She took a sip, felt the same sense of well-being as her son and put her cup down. "Grisha, let's carry the tea over together, then we'll eat and open the box."

Grisha took a second sip of tea, went to the flashlight and followed his mother.

Koenig was still lying motionless on the bed. The nurse put the
tea down beside the bed and placed a slice of the rusk that Grisha had
brought beside it. She put her hand on the German's forehead.

"He still has a fever, but it's not as high as it was yesterday."

Koenig opened his eyes. "Spasiba - thank you!"

"Drink the tea. You need to drink a lot. There's also a pitcher
of water here. I put it there earlier. And get some sleep. The wound will
heal. I'll look at it again tonight. The knee is very swollen, but I think
the swelling will go down in the next two or three days."

She held the cup of tea in front of Koenig's mouth. He lifted
his torso slightly, opened his mouth, brought the cup to his cracked lips
and drank.

"Again!"

The procedure was repeated.

"You lie down. Have a drink. And eat the zwieback if you can.
If you need to relieve yourself, use the bucket. Don't leave this cellar.
That's what I'm asking you to do. Do you understand me?"

Koenig nodded. He repeated in a harsh voice. "I'm staying
here!"

Katja smeared some of the ointment on the soldier's lips. "Go
to sleep."

The german officer closed his eyes. The nurse looked at her patient with satisfaction, then she and Grisha left the room.

Back in their own cellar hideaway, they enjoyed their breakfast
to the full. "They rewarded you well this time."

"Yes, the captain was in a good mood."

Both of them had gotten into the habit of eating extremely
slowly. And despite their growing fatigue, they were still curious to know
what was in the box that Grisha had laboriously dragged along. Again
and again their eyes fell on the box.

"Mom, shall we open it before we go to bed?"

Katja grinned. "Yes, my brave little soldier. We'll do that."

Grisha shoved the last piece of bread into his mouth, stood up,
went to the shelf and got a large screwdriver, then sat down in front of

218

the box. "Should I start?"

"Yes, open it," said Katja, and Grisha used the screwdriver skill-fully, levering the wide edge between the lid and the side panel.

It cracked and the boy was able to lift the lid with another lever. Grisha and Katja stared eagerly at the contents.

"Yay," the boy cheered. "That's food! Hurraaaaa. Mom, we have enough to eat!"

Katja could hardly believe her luck. "I'm so proud of you, my boy," she cried, tears of joy in her eyes, and hugged her son.

They didn't know what was in the cans and bags, but they knew they would not go hungry for the next two weeks, maybe longer. The contents of that box meant life.

Koenig slept most of the night that day. Only twice did he wake for a moment. Katja was there once, pouring him tea and making sure he ate at least some of the zwieback.

By the second day, Erwin's health had improved to the point that his body temperature had normalized.

When he awoke, the Russian woman was sitting next to the German's bed with her flat hand on his forehead. "The fever is gone," she said, "and the bullet hole has no red edges. That's a good sign that it's healing without complications. The swelling in his knee has also gone down a bit. It will still hurt for a while, but nothing should be broken. That is very important. I can do a lot of things, but not knee surgery!

Koenig tried to sit up. He recognized Katja in the dim light of a burning candle. His tongue ran over his cracked lips, his throat was dry as dust. Before he could say anything, the Russian woman lifted the cup of chilled tea to him.

"Drink slowly, in small sips."

The German officer nodded and took a sip. It was a relief when the tea flowed down his throat and trickled down his gullet.

"Thank you," he said, first in German, then in Russian. He tried to remember, but it was all a blur. "Where am I and what happened? How did you find me and how did I get here?" he asked, fragments re-turning to his memory.

Katja put the cup down again and took the last third of the zwieback. "You still need to rest, drink and eat."

"They brought me out of this crater." Koenig looked around.

"If you're looking for your weapons, I have them in my hiding place. The box too. Thanks for bringing it to our attention."

The officer started to reach for the mug. Katja beat him to it and held it out. He lifted his torso again, took a sip and lay down again.

"You have a really bad bruise on your knee and a straight shot through your upper arm. No bones seem to be broken and the wound seems to be healing well. They were completely exhausted and hypothermic and had a fever. We only found them because we were hiding from a reconnaissance plane. They were moaning in their fever..."

Koenig listened attentively and did not interrupt the Russian when she paused for a moment.

"... and Grisha was dragging the box. I'm a nurse, and I tended to your wounds. I gave you some of my meager medicine."

"Why are you helping me? We have brought so much suffering to your land."

"Because you saved me. I owed it to you."

"You brought me to your hiding place and took a great risk."

Katja took a deep breath. She looked at the man lying in front of her, whose life she had probably saved. "You are different."

Koenig thought. "What do you mean?"

"You are a German soldier and therefore my enemy, and I should hate you, but you are different. You radiate more friendliness than hostility. I can't explain it."

Koenigg cleared his throat. "You needn't be afraid of me. I will definitely not harm you and I will never reveal your hiding place."

Katja remained silent. Something had changed in her expression. Koenig noticed it and spoke to her immediately.

"Do you not believe me? Do you want to treat me like a prisoner?"

"No."

"Something is bothering you."

Katja considered getting up and just walking away, but then she spontaneously decided to share at least some of her knowledge with the

220

German. She wanted to see how he would react.

"The Red Army doesn't know who you are, but it knows you."

Koenig sat up. "What do you mean?"

"You are feared and hated. You are a notorious sniper and you kill many Russian soldiers."

"How do you know that?"

Katja did not feel any coldness in the wounded major's eyes. On the contrary, she felt a slight attraction, a sense of trust and protection. She liked him.

"Why are you doing this? If you say that you have brought so much suffering to our country, why don't you stop or change sides?"

Koenig lowered his head. "If only it were that easy."

"Nothing that's really worth doing is simple! How many people have you killed?"

"I'm not a good man. At least not since..." He swallowed and his voice cracked. His eyes filled with tears.

"Since what?" Katja asked, almost automatically taking Koenig's hand and holding it tightly.

He squeezed it. Nothing is more beautiful and helpful for a person than to feel the closeness and help of another person when they are in need. He had missed that kind of touch for so long. He had bottled up all his suffering. His soul was filled with hatred and the goal to kill a human being. The one he blamed for Rolf's death. Vasily Saizev!

"I was once a happy man. I was married to the love of my life, and our happiness was complete when our son Rolf was born. I made good money as an engineer. I must have inherited my talent for languages from my mother, because I was able to work for my company all over the world. My life changed when my wife became ill and eventually died of severe pneumonia. I gave up a great career to focus on Rolf. He was such a wonderful boy. The war came and I was called up. I witnessed all the atrocities and felt trapped in that uniform as if in a vacuum. My son was also recently drafted and sent here, to Stalingrad. He had been in the city only a few hours when a sniper took his life. The sniper not only took Rolf's life, but mine as well. That's why I'm wandering through this ruined city as a lone hunter. I'm looking for Saizev. I blame him for Rolf's death."

Katja flinched when Koenig said Saizev's name. Koenig noticed the flinch.

"I'm sorry if I'm robbing you of an illusion. I'm not the kind-hearted man you think I am. I'm bitter and empty. I'm a wreck."

Tears streamed down Katja's cheeks. "He is also responsible for the death of my son Boris," she replied, and now it was King's hand-shake that comforted her. "I hate him and want him dead. I don't know if it's right or wrong, but I hate that Russian sniper so much that some-times I think I'm only alive to see him die one day," she sobbed. "And because of Grisha, of course. The boy is all I have left. You Germans killed my husband, the Russians killed my son."

"Then we have a common goal."

Katja nodded.

"I must confess, I've forgotten her name," the soldier said.

"Katja Kalikova."

"Katja. My name is Erwin."

"I know, because I haven't forgotten your name. Erwin Koenig, you saved me from an act of violence, and perhaps my life. We're even in that. But I have something else to tell you."

"Katja, call me Erwin. If fate has brought us together in this terribly tragic way, we can skip the formalities."

The fact that this German soldier had suffered the same fate as Katja, and that he blamed the same man for it, immediately gave her a feeling of brotherhood in arms. She put all her eggs in one basket and felt closer to her goal than ever before. If she really wanted revenge on Vasily Saizev, this German sniper was the key.

"Erwin, my son Grisha has connections with the Red Army."

Koenig listened, and Katja told him about the canal shaft, the errands, and how her life depended on it, because Grisha was always rewarded with food. Finally, she spoke of her son's last walk, and goose bumps came over her with every word. "...and now you're lying here, and Grisha will soon deliver a message to Saizev."

Koenig remained silent. Katja began to doubt whether it was really right to tell this German everything. She let go of his hand.

"I need a little head start to explore the area where he wants to set a trap for me. And it will be very difficult. Saizev won't come alone,

222

but I have no support."

"And if you return to your people?"

"We are defeated, Katja. The cauldron is choking us. If it isn't broken open from the outside, it will be the downfall of the once proud 6th Army."

The Russian woman stood up. "I'm going over to Grisha."

"Katja, I'll do it. I will challenge this Saizev to a duel. A duel to the death. The three of us will sit down and work out a plan."

Katja wiped the last tears from her cheeks. "We will hunt down the man we hold responsible for the death of our children!"

"Grisha is an extraordinarily brave boy! I won't do anything to endanger him. If it's too dangerous for him, I'll find Saizev without Grisha's help."

"First you must get well. Only then can we talk about a plan."

Koenig had to admit that she was right. He nodded. "As soon as I can move more or less normally, I will ambush this Saizev and kill him. I promise you that."

Katja looked at Erwin in silence, then closed the door behind her.

Erwin Koenig recovered noticeably over the next few days. He was soon able to stand up and move around without help. Even though everything was still a little bumpy and he had to prop himself up, he felt free. The German soldier knew who he owed his life to. Katja! She had taken him into her hiding place, risking her life. Her care, peace and regular meals restored his strength.

They were allies in times of need and used food sparingly. They didn't eat more than they needed. They got to know each other better through long conversations, and Grisha began to like the German officer, too. The boy didn't talk about it, but he liked Erwin Koenig. The German reminded him a little of his father.

Katja enjoyed the escape from the meager and life-threatening life of the Stalingrad population. The officer was a handsome man with manners. She was glad that she had not been mistaken about the nature of this German. The linguistically gifted engineer was a fast learner and improved his already good knowledge of Russian in a very short time.

Another week passed, and Koenig felt his strength returning more and more. Katja was a very good nurse. Sufficient sleep and good food did the rest.

At first, everyone was reluctant to get to know each other. Each gave a little information about himself. They thought things over and spoke carefully. Gradually the ice broke and eventually everyone told their story. Sad and funny.

On the twelfth day, Katja was already extremely nervous in the morning. Koenig noticed immediately that something was wrong. The Russian wasn't as talkative as she had been the days before, and seemed a little distant.

"Do you want to talk about it?" Erwin asked as Katja examined his bullet wound and then put the bandage back on.

"About what?"

"Something is bothering you."

Katja avoided looking at her new roommate. "I don't know if I should talk about it."

"Is it me?"

She shook her head. "No."

"Is there something I can do for you?"

Another shake of the head.

"If you don't talk, I can't help."

She sighed and looked at Koenig. "Grisha must see Captain Oligov again today. The time gap is already much too long. He should have left days ago."

"You're afraid."

"I'm always afraid for him. I don't want him to go."

Koenig's voice became a little more serious, but without losing its sympathetic tone. "We may have avoided the subject the last few days, but for better or worse, we have to talk about it."

"Saizev?" Katja's mouth immediately shot open.

"Right!"

"I'm really afraid for Grisha. It's a dangerous road and we've been lucky so far. There's fighting out there. Every night soldiers roam the streets, breaking into houses and killing other soldiers. If we run into their arms..." Katja didn't finish the sentence.

"I can go with you and protect you. They will not see or hear me."

"Erwin, your wound is not completely healed. You may be able to fire a pistol at a nearby target, but you certainly can't lie in wait with a rifle ..." she paused deliberately and pointed at his legs, "... the swelling on your knee has gone down well, but you'll need at least another week before you can put any normal weight on it. Face it! You can't come with us!"

She was right, and the officer knew it. Erwin Koenig leaned back. A thousand thoughts poured down on him like a heavy downpour. The situation was grotesque. He was chasing Saizev, the stylized Russian sniper, and Saizev was chasing him. As luck would have it, a young boy was able to arrange a duel between the two hunters. A duel to the death. The Russian thought he had the advantage, and that could be a mistake, a fatal mistake. Koenig remembered the words the henchman Sergej had said to him: Saizev is a hunter with the patience of an angel.

Koenig knew that he was challenging an extremely dangerous opponent. And he knew he had no choice. He had to do it. "Many people die every day in this city. Let's make sure that for once it is the one who is responsible for the death of our sons."

Katja stared ahead, lost in thought, but understood every word. She put her hand on Grisha's shoulder and pulled him close. "I lost my husband and one of my sons. I don't want to lose my Grisha as well."

Koenig leaned forward. "And that is why we will be the ones to choose the time and place. And without Saizev noticing. He will always think he has the advantage. This is our best option."

Katja looked into the German's eyes. Her look was cold, her words clear and unmistakable. "If you touch a hair on Grisha's head, I will kill you!"

Example photo

PA-0043-Ju52-Flug /flight
Privatarchiv Author
all rights reserved by the author

13

Koenig's plan had one important goal in the first step. It was to gain time. The major had to be healthy enough to face Saizev. Grisha was to achieve the desired gain of time by reporting to Captain Oligov about the nighttime encounter between the Russian patrol and Erwin Koenig. In order to avoid possible contradictions, everything was specified and discussed in detail.

Grisha repeated the information several times and then asked: "What if he wants to know how I know all this?"

Koenig asked for a pen and paper. Katja stood up and got both. "Here," she said, handing them to the German.

The officer handed it to Grisha and said: "Draw a road here, with a few squares or circles to the left and right to represent piles of rubble."

Koenig was relieved to see that the boy could draw well. Further instructions followed, which Grisha carried out well, and within a quarter of an hour a relatively good sketch had been produced. The officer nodded in approval and satisfaction. "Tell them that here..." Koenig put his finger on a particular spot on the sketch, "... is, or was until recently, a German military base. You've been there and heard the story Koenig told. You can tell them that the Landser and the medics talked animatedly about the German sniper, whom they call the master of all masters. There were also some Russian auxiliaries working in the hospital. They would talk about what the Germans had said. You can also tell them that you heard that the king was slightly injured, but would soon be hunting again, and the Hiwis were puzzling over who was the better sniper: Saizev or Koenig."

Katja raised her hand and objected. "Isn't that too much information? I think the boy is exposing himself to great danger."

Koenig shook his head in the negative. "It's just the right dose, Katja. It's exactly the kind of half-knowledge that people generally talk about. And the fact that Grisha is supposed to have received the information from the Hiwis makes it credible."

Everything was discussed at length. Grisha listened attentively and repeated every word. Koenig also talked about the procedure for caring for the wounded. He wanted everything to be as truthful as possible.

"I'm sure they'll demand that you try to find out my whereabouts through these Hiwis."

Katja looked extremely nervous, "I'm sorry. I'm really afraid it will be too dangerous. It's best if we cancel everything."

"It would be dangerous if Grisha came without any information or didn't come at all. Katja, we're in a cauldron. Stalingrad is surrounded by Russian troops. The situation is precarious. If we want to achieve our goal of bringing the man we hold responsible for the death of our loved ones to justice, we must do it."

"Mom, it's not dangerous," Grisha assured her.

The Russian was still skeptical. "And when are you going to duel with Saizev?"

Koenig took a deep breath. "There is something else," he added somewhat hesitantly.

Small worry lines formed on Katja's forehead. "What?"

"If I want to carry out such an operation successfully, I have to go back to my troops. I need information about current positions, troop movements, planned attacks and so on."

"What for?"

"I need to be able to move freely in our area to find a suitable location. And since I'll probably be considered missing in action, I need to report back, give a report, and state my new intention."

"No!" Katja groaned suddenly. "We can't let you go."

"Are you afraid I'll reveal your hiding place?"

Eyes shifted from person to person. All three remained silent. It was Grisha who finally broke the icy silence and deliberation. "Mom, I trust Erwin."

Katja trembled slightly. "How do I know you won't betray us? You're an enemy."

Koenig slid his hand across the table and took Katja's hands. "I wear the uniform of your enemies. That is true. But it's only the uniform you fear, not the person inside. You both saved my life. Since my son's death, I've been wandering this dead city like a dying wolf, trying to kill

228

the man who killed Rolf. You two have made me my..." Koenig struggled to find the right words, "...friends." He paused and squeezed Katja's hand tighter. "Perhaps more than friends. I would never betray you. Never!"

Koenig's voice sounded slightly raspy at the end of the sentence. He swallowed. His Adam's apple moved up and down. "You are the only people I still care about in this world."

Katja felt the pressure of Erwin Koenig's hand and returned it after his last sentence. "We trust you."

It felt good to hold someone's hand. Katja was a strong woman, but she also longed for security after all the suffering she had been through. This handshake was more than a handshake. It felt like a small piece of security. At that moment, she wanted to throw her arms around the neck of the man sitting across from her and say: "Hold me. Take me in your arms and just hold me. Just for a minute."

"Erwin will definitely come back to us, Mom."

She let go of his hand. "Grisha and I trust you. Please don't let us down."

"You have my word."

Katja grabbed Erwin's hand again. "How long will it be before we see you again?"

The sniper gently returned the handshake. "I don't know. Three or four days at the earliest. But more likely two or three weeks. I still have to fully recover, formulate my plan, and execute it. I have to plan ahead and convince my supervisor. We'll probably only get one try. And we have to be well prepared for it.

Grisha spoke up. "That's too long. What if the captain wants more information in a few days?"

Katja agreed. "My son is right. You're putting him in danger if you wait too long."

"I won't allow Grisha to be put in danger, and that's why we're going to work out credible messages for two more er-rands now."

Two pairs of eyes met. Each of them tried to suppress the feelings that arose. The time and place were wrong and the circumstances catastrophic. Anything could happen, except love. Katja withdrew her hands. She knew at that moment that Erwin Koenig was telling the truth and would come back.

"Take care of yourself."

"I will."

"When a doctor examines you, what will you say about your treated wound?"

"I'll think of something."

A smile crossed Katja's face. "And speak German."

Erwin Koenig smiled affectionately. "I will."

That night, Major Koenig slept very restlessly and woke up several times. He was worried about Katja and Grigory. He would have liked to go with them to protect them, but his state of health made that impossible. He admitted to himself that he was developing feelings. For the first time since his wife's death, another woman meant something to him. Katja was not only extremely attractive, but also extremely courageous. Her character reflected what he was secretly looking for. They also shared the same fate. Grisha reminded Erwin of Rolf.

He's just as cunning as my son, he thought, wiping tears from his eyes.

His nervousness only subsided when he heard them return in the early hours of the morning. They kept quiet so as not to wake him. Reassured, the German officer waited another half hour for them both to fall asleep. Then he got up and slipped into his uniform. Koenig had prepared and packed everything the night before. He slipped quietly out of the cellar. When he left the ruins, he closed the hidden entrance behind him and made sure that no one was watching him.

The cold quickly crept beneath his tattered coat. A few snowflakes announced the beginning of the snowfall. Koenig felt strong enough to make his way to his own ranks. He sucked the cold air deep into his lungs, felt a slight throbbing in his wound, got his bearings, and started walking.

The streets were eerily empty. A light wind blew from the Volga, making the increasingly dense snowflakes dance in the dim light of the rising sun.

"Stalingrad is nothing more than a desolate heap of rubble, in whose ruins the inhabitants and soldiers are entrenched to wait for death, somewhat sheltered from the wind," he breathed out.

The German officer's eyes had lost all their sparkle. When Rolf was alive, he had goals. After the war, he wanted to live a quiet life with his son. Maybe buy a house in the country, big enough for him and Rolf's future family.

"All gone!" Erwin pressed his lips together, wiped a tear from his eye, and thought about everything he had experienced during the war.

There was drill and comradeship. There was sweat and success and laughter. But there were also things that were suppressed. There was looting, called requisitioning. There was shooting, which he could not understand. And there was a racial ideology that he personally never supported, but he did not do anything about it. Although Erwin Koenig was skeptical of the policies of the nationalist government of Greater Germany, he never went on the offensive. Like everyone else, he turned a blind eye. As an officer, he went into a war he did not want, and he was responsible for the deaths of people. He did not see his actions as murder, but as combat, because every enemy he eliminated could not kill another German soldier.

If I had fought this Saizev and his snipers much earlier, my son might still be alive!

Erwin Koenig had a change of heart. Although he no longer embodied the politically correct parade officer, he too was blind in one eye. While they were losing their lives at the front, another war was raging in the hinterland. The racial policies dictated by the Nazi regime were mercilessly implemented, starving the Russian people and rounding up, shooting or deporting Jews. Was it repression? Did they want to know as little as possible about it? Or did they approve of everything? Koenig had a rather liberal upbringing. A person is a person, no matter where he comes from, his mother always said. When did he get caught up in this maelstrom? He was not a Party member. He was drafted and did his duty. He had probably never given it much thought, but had allowed himself to be swept along by the tide of the times. But now, at this very moment, he felt guilty for all the suffering he saw around him.

It had always been said that the Bolsheviks were subhuman. He had never shared that idea, but he hadn't done anything about it either. He had thoughtlessly gone with the flow. And when he was dying, he received help from the people from whom he had taken everything as a member of the 6th Army. He was one of those responsible for death, destruction and torture. And yet Katja and her son Grisha had saved his life and nursed him back to health. It was like an awakening from a life-destroying lethargy.

They are not sub-humans! This war is a crime against humanity and I am a part of it!

A mist of breath wafted from his mouth. The Russian artillery had awakened and sent a few shells across the Volga. The rumble was muffled. Somewhere death hummed with an unmistakable hiss. The heavy and medium shells exploded with a crash in the rubble of the dead city. Here and there, dark clouds of smoke could be seen billowing upwards, only to descend again as a dark fog over the ruins.

Koenig had to admit that he had developed feelings for Katja and Grisha. He didn't ask himself if they could replace his family, because that was impossible, but he did ask himself if he could go into a future with them.

Major Erwin Koenig, who was only a human shell a few days ago, began to live again. His cold heart had warmed up and started to beat again. He was impressed by how confidently this little Grisha ran errands for the Red Army to get information about Saizev. And he was more than impressed by how self-sacrificingly Katja had cared not only for her son, but also for him. After all, he was her enemy. He wore the guise of the German Empire.

These two people who, from the point of view of the Nazi regime, were only second-class human beings and, as such, had less right to life than the so-called Aryan master race according to the nationalist racial doctrine. He was certain that these two people were his future.

If I die, it will be for them!

He thought of the safe cellar where Katja and Grisha lived. It had felt so good not to have to sleep in some foxhole in a wet uniform. It was a relief to hear the voices of a woman and a child, to sit at a table with them and share a meal. The moment he held Katja's hand, the ice that had frozen his soul melted. Erwin began to live again. He felt

232

warmth and emotion. He felt longing and hope.

The officer made a decision. He would bring this one Russian, whom he held responsible for the death of his and Katja's son, to justice. If he survived this duel, he would try to hide with Katja and Grisha in the dead city of Stalingrad and live the life of a mole until this hell was over.

If they had been Red Army soldiers, Erwin Koenig would be dead now. But it was a German outpost that called out to him in warning: "Halt! Parole!"

The sniper flinched, startled. He thought of Katja and was brought back to reality in an instant. The king stopped instantly and raised both arms halfway. He showed his open palms. A steel helmet wobbled out from behind a pile of rubble. Under it, the Landser wore a woolly hat. A large scarf covered most of his face. Stubble extended beyond the edge of the scarf. Across the street, two rifle barrels pointed in the king's direction. He could see them out of the corner of his eye.

"I..." his throat was dry, the word barely intelligible. The officer cleared his throat and started again: "I am Major Erwin Koenig. I have been missing for a few days, I was wounded in battle and have now found my way to you. I don't know the current motto. When I left, it was: Morning dew!

Silence. The guard seemed to be thinking.

Next, the king named his troop.

The soldier stood up and waved. "Major Koenig, come slowly towards us!"

The Landser realized that Koenig was carrying a sniper rifle. "Bloody hell. Are you Major Koenig, the man who teaches the Russians to be afraid?"

Koenig thought for a moment about what this soldier meant, then replied: "I am Major Koenig, and I meet the enemy with the same severity with which he meets us."

The guard turned to his men: "Guys, he's here. He's alive! The master of all sharpshooters is here."

An hour later, Koenig sat in a stuffy but heated bunker, sipping thin coffee. The taste was stale, but it still felt good. A lieutenant was in command. He explained that the casualties from his own ranks had been replaced with scattered Romanian soldiers. "As far as my men are concerned, the feedback I get from all the platoons is that the Romanians are decent men who can be put to good use."

Koenig also learned from the first lieutenant that while the situation in the cauldron was becoming increasingly dire, relief was already on the way.

"Panzer Group Hoth is charging through the Soviet ranks and blowing up the Ring," came the euphoric cry. "We're just debating whether to break out and march on the panzer divisions, or to stay here and tie up the enemy troops. Either way, it won't be long now. We'll probably be celebrating the victory over Stalingrad by Christmas.

Koenig wondered if the euphoria was part of a self-preservation instinct or if the lieutenant really believed in this military miracle. Everywhere you looked, you saw destruction and emaciated faces. The men were at the end of their tether and could definitely not be called combat-ready.

Only the fear of being captured by the Russians and the last glimmer of hope of being rescued from this cauldron kept most of the soldiers fighting. Koenig was sure of it. Cold and hunger had long been a far more dangerous enemy than the Red Army. Everyone could see it, but no one dared say it in public.

"I've heard of you, Major," the first lieutenant finally said, whereupon Koenig changed the subject and asked about his unit. It had been detached for refresher training and was stationed outside the city. According to the lieutenant, however, they would probably be able to move forward again soon, as the Russian was stirring. He offered to take the sniper to the military hospital so a doctor could look at the wound, but Koenig refused. "I have the wound under control so far. I need to get back to my regiment as soon as possible, report back, re-equip and get back to the front!"

The lieutenant nodded and stood up. "With men like you, we will win the war. Heil Hitler, Major."

The german officer wondered how anyone could still be so enthusiastic in this misery and returned the salute by standing up and sa-luting. "Thank you, First Lieutenant."

The fact that trucks were still driving in and out of the city see-med like a small miracle to the sniper. He was less surprised that they were stopped by field gendarmes at the city limits. It was dusk and cold. To the right, a platoon of Landsers marched into the city. A few trucks carrying food and ammunition passed them. A few men smoked ciga-rettes with trembling hands.

The driver rolled down the window, said hello, and tried to make conversation to keep the stop short. Koenig sat in the passenger seat with a tent sheet tucked under his chin.

"Comrade, how far is it to ..." was as far as the driver got. The inspecting field gendarme opened the door of the Opel Blitz, hoisted himself up and shone a flashlight at the sniper, whose rank could not be seen through the raised canvas.

"Where are you going?" came the slightly cynical reply.

"I was about to ask you that. We're on our way to regional head-quarters."

"This is the way to the airfield. Are you trying to get away?"

Baffled, the driver denied it. "What nonsense! Two kilometers straight ahead, then I have to turn right, the airport is on the left."

The beam of light passed over Koenig. "Hey," the sergeant cal-led to him, his distinctive ring collar gleaming silver even in the twilight of the gathering darkness. "What's the matter with you? Papers."

The Major pushed the canvas aside. "Sergeant, if my driver says we're on our way to the staff, then we are! I've just come from the front and I need to see Lieutenant Colonel Harras urgently. If you don't let us go right away, I promise you that in the future you won't stop any more German trucks, but will shoot at Russian trucks further ahead. Koenig took out his pay book and handed it to the field constable. "Here, check me out properly. I am Major Erwin Koenig. And after the check, I want your name, Sergeant, and the name of your superior officer! In times like these we need every man in the HKL!"

The sergeant winced and took Koenig's pay book. You could tell that thoughts were exploding behind his forehead. He was trying to find a balance between his duty as a field gendarme and the power of this officer. Finally, he took a quick look at the paybook, nodded, and apologized. "Here you are, please. You know, Major, the number of desertions has unfortunately increased lately. Everyone wants to get to the airport to sneak aboard a Ju 52."

Koenig took his pay book and said: "Then we can finally get going?"

The field gendarme stepped back, slammed the door of the truck and saluted. "Have a good trip!"

The driver grinned, shifted into gear, and stepped on the accelerator. The engine roared and the truck rolled away. "That was quite an announcement,Major."

"He only does what he's told, but despite all the adverse circumstances here in the Cauldron, I expect respect and courtesy."

"Exactly."

An enjoyable conversation began. Koenig learned from the driver that everyone expected the dance to begin soon. Not from their own troops, though, but from the Russian offensive.

"We drivers get together all the time, of course. Sometimes at the field hospitals, sometimes at the ammo dumps, depending on where you're assigned." He fumbled for a pack of cigarettes and pulled them out of his breast pocket. "Would you like an Eckstein?"

Koenig replied in the negative. In no time, the driver had a cigarette stuck in the corner of his mouth with a practiced grip. He put the pack of cigarettes back in his breast pocket and had a cigarette lighter in his hand. He turned the wheel, the flint sparked and the gasoline-soaked wick burned. He lit the cigarette, which glowed orange with the first puff. A small billowing cloud gathered under the roof of the cab. The driver opened the side window a crack, and the blue haze moved in circles toward the window, finally being carried outside by the suction. "It is suspiciously quiet over there. Too quiet, said Schorsch, who was making his rounds. None of them is making a move. You can feel sorry for them. They're expecting Ivan to attack at any moment. Meanwhile, the neighboring battalion, guarding the flank, is rumbling all the time."

Koenig let the driver chat happily and asked the occasional

question. He learned a lot of trivia, but also some interesting things.

Just over an hour later, they reached their destination without further incident.

"You know your way around."

"If there's one thing you can rely on," the driver said after stopping, "it's German thoroughness. They put up signs everywhere and you can find everything." He laughed. "If the Ivan ever breaks through and has a destination, all he has to do is follow the signs and he'll get there without a problem."

Koenig got out of the car. "Thank you for the ride."

"It was an honor, Major."

The Quartermaster had arranged good accommodations for him. Koenig and a motley crew from the reconnaissance squadron and the battalion staff were housed in a halfway habitable farmhouse. The roof and a room in the back had been damaged by an artillery shell, but the Engineers had managed to patch it up. The stove was burning and it was warm. The beds were made of straw with canvas sheets spread over them.

"You're lucky, Major," the quartermaster had said as he drove him to the house, "we could all be properly deloused again. The beasts stayed at the front."

Koenig was grateful. The lice infestation was enormous. There was hardly a soldier at the front who was not infested. His wound healed well and he felt stronger and stronger. Although he was not yet ready for action, it was that feeling you get when you feel your old strength returning. Koenig was confident that in the next few days he would recover enough to return to Katja and put his plan into action.

Koenig could hardly believe his eyes when the door opened the next morning and his old company sergeant Schmidt stood before him. "Lightning and a thousand thunder, Major, I was afraid I wouldn't see you again."

"Schmidt, you old warhorse!" Koenig got up and went to the door. Schmidt had lost weight, but he still looked strong. Koenig pointed to the spit's belly. "You used to be fuller, too."

"Everybody has to tighten their belt. And when I come home

after this fight, my wife will be cheering. She thought I had a few extra pounds on my ribs anyway."

"You haven't lost your sense of humor."

"We're all clenching our butts, Major," came the casual reply. "And we've taken heavy casualties. But the troops are still standing."

Koenig nodded silently. It was still his company. Would he be betraying them if he simply disappeared after the duel with Saizev? Schmidt chattered on, and the words of the company sergeant snapped the officer out of his nascent thoughts. "... and do you know who's behind the pots in the field kitchen?"

"No."

"Good old Hdromka."

"Hdromka, the man I told to put a vowel between the H and the D," Koenig laughed.

"That's just the pound man. He's simply the best soldier cook in the world. Hdromka turns a dead horse and melted snow into a feast, and no one knows his secret."

"Has he recovered?"

"Completely. He said that such a pneumonia wouldn't let him go. Stalin would have to come personally, otherwise he wouldn't die."

"I thought he was on the stage, somewhere in a fine hospital. In a real bed with white sheets."

Schmidt laughed out loud. "This madman came back here of his own free will. He said we were his family! And he wanted to know if you're really back here, Major. He wants to conjure something special from the cauldrons."

One of the judges shouted from behind. "Then I'd like some of that, too. We only know the thin horse soup, which also gives you a mighty thin stomach."

"A real goulash would be something," said another soldier, and a conversation quickly developed among the men with la-vish menu suggestions.

As the men talked about roast goose, schnitzel, goulash, or biscuits with real coffee, Major Koenig saw the longing in their eyes.

They longed for rest, for home, for peace. Whereas before their eyes had been empty and sad, now they were filled with hope and radiance.

Koenig noticed the change. He knew what the broken look of a dead man looked like. When a soldier fell on the battlefield and breathed his last, his gaze broke and lost its luster. The officer saw this look more and more often in the German soldiers living in the ruins of Stalingrad, fighting for their lives.

They were all passengers on a ferry steered by the Grim Reaper. Depending on which shore you got off, you either lived or died.

Koenig found himself looking at the soldiers one by one. He pulled himself out of his thoughts and said: "Hdromka can't do magic."

"I will resist. Christmas is the day after tomorrow. I'll come here on Christmas Eve with Hdromka and the old warhorse Remmler. And we'll celebrate Christmas together."

"There are twelve of us here," the battalion clerk interrupted, coming over to Schmidt and Koenig. "We've all put something aside for Christmas Eve and literally saved it from our mouths. If Hdromka needs anything else, let him know."

"That's a word," grinned Schmidt. "You're staying here now, aren't you?"

Koenig pointed to the wound. "Tomorrow I have an appointment with Lieutenant Colonel Harras. I will then heal my wound and return to the front as soon as possible."

"Then we'll celebrate Christmas here the day after tomorrow! And I don't want to hear any arguments," the Spike smiled friendly. "Besides, I hope to hear by then that Hoth's first tanks have already broken through."

"To Hoth and our tanks!" came the cheer from the room.

The next day, Major Koenig sat in Lieutenant-Colonel Har-ras' dugout and had a frank talk with his old friend.

Maps of Stalingrad lay on a table. A large map hung on the wall. Points were marked with pins. Strings marked the actual front lines. Small pieces of paper with the names of troop units were attached to some of the pins. Koenig looked at the big map for a while. Harras stood beside him. He pulled out a pin west of Stalingrad and moved it a little farther forward. "Operation Wintergewitter is underway." He pointed to the pin he had just inserted. "This is General Hoth's 4th Panzer Army. The peaks are only 50 kilometers from Stalingrad."

Koenig knew his old friend. He missed the certainty in his words. They said a lot, but sounded empty.

"Richard. What's going on?"

"They were already preparing to receive the weakened 6th Army. In the rear of the front, in the Remontnaya and Salivsky-Generalov areas, protected by three armored divisions, we were to receive food and winter equipment. Company Thunderclap was developed for this purpose."

"When is it?" Koenig asked, thinking of Katja and Boris. He would have to go back to them, not to lose them.

"Not at all! The order to break out has definitely not been given. General Paulus had moved most of his troops to the south of the cauldron and abandoned our positions on the northern edge, but with our resources we would only have made about 15 to 20 km. Hoth's tanks would have gotten no closer than 30 kilometers to the Cauldron." Harras was silent for a few seconds, then said ironically: "But our Führer didn't withdraw his permission because of that, but because he didn't want to give up Stalingrad. Don't make me laugh. He doesn't want to give up that city. As if he himself had fought here for a single day. No matter! But the fact is that our leader is giving up an entire army. And out of stupid narrow-mindedness!"

Both stared dumbly at the map on the wall at the same time. Only a few miles separated them from this deadly embrace.

Harras had more to report. "In addition, the Russians are attacking our relief troops with their 2nd Guards Army and VII Armored Corps near Kotelnikovo. Everything has come to a standstill. Operation Winter Storm has failed! Erwin, they're going to let us die here in the cauldron!"

"Is that fact or conjecture?"

"It's a fact!"

Koenig sat down. Schmidt and all the other comrades were full of confidence. Tomorrow would be a wonderful Christmas, and the hoped-for explosion of the cauldron would be under the tree as a present.

It was all over, he thought and asked: "How long will we go on before we wave the white flag?"

Lieutenant-Colonel Harras went to a cupboard, took out a bottle of cognac and two glasses, and sat down opposite his friend. "There's a little left. I couldn't think of anyone better than you to empty this last bottle from France."

He poured a glass, set the bottle aside, and pushed a glass toward Koenig. Then he raised his own. "Cheers, may we get out of here with our skins intact or meet a quick death."

Koenig squinted at the wall map again. "Tomorrow is Christmas. When will you tell the men?"

"Let them celebrate in peace. We will demonstrate unity once more by celebrating Christmas together and then going down together."

Koenig was horrified. He did not recognize his friend. Gone was the positive self-confidence. "Richard, you seem so disillusioned."

"No wonder. Until this shocking news, I thought we were breaking out. It's like a slap in the face. They're actually abandoning an entire army. This has never happened in German military history."

"That's why the chain dogs are checking so closely," Koenig interjected, reporting on the check on his way here.

"The reports from the airfields are terrible, my friend. The countrymen want to get out of here. They want to be home for Christmas. It's like magic! Hundreds of soldiers are crowding around the Junker planes. They all want to get on and have to be held back by force of arms. Many mutilate themselves to be flown out of the cauldron. I was there a week ago. Good men are being executed. The Cauldron has turned us into animals, Erwin."

"No, my friend, animals are not as sick as we humans. We are worse than animals."

"You know Lieutenant von Klemmstein, don't you?"

"Of course, and you know I don't like him!"

"Last week I was at the Gumrak airfield, accompanied by the field police. We picked up von Klemmstein. He had given himself false papers in order to be flown out."

Koenig was astonished. "Really? Where is this bastard now?"

"He was shot!"

Koenig took another swig of cognac. His inner sense of justice was satisfied. Outwardly, he remained cold. "He deserved it."

"I will have all the sutler's goods at my disposal distributed to the men. Tomorrow they will have their last happy day, as far as one can speak of it."

The conversation now turned to old stories, and it wasn't until an hour later that Koenig spoke of the real reason for his visit.

"I am giving the countrymen something else. I'm giving them hope by killing the most famous Russian sniper. Vasily Saizev!"

Harras stared at Koenig. "His name is actually all over the place. How are you going to do it?"

"I have a plan and challenge him to a duel, so to speak."

"Morale is as important as food and ammunition," the lieutenant colonel replied. "How do you plan to do that, and what do you need?"

Koenig stated his wishes. Harras listened, made a phone call, and eventually the sniper was issued the necessary paperwork to equip himself and move freely anywhere.

Koenig also made a tactical suggestion. The regiment's available sharpshooters should be organized into small squads of three sharpshooters and their observers and deployed effectively. They were to accompany the assault troops, clearing the way for them by eliminating machine gun nests and similar positions, and unsettling the enemy with targeted hits.

"And how are they supposed to get into position?" Harras asked.

"Short bursts from our figure-eights or heavy fire from machine guns and grenade launchers will force the Russians into cover. This phase should be enough for a sniper team to get into position," Koenig replied.

His suggestion was finally approved and the order was given to assemble the snipers in the battalion.

"You lead!" Harras finally said in a tone that brooked no argument.

"Richard," Koenig snapped. "Put me at the head of the squad, but give the command to another officer or a good sergeant. The reason is that I," he paused to emphasize the weight of his words, "jump from left to right like a phantom. We announce that I'm advancing with them, but that I'm only hunting Saizev. This takes the fear out of the men, gives them a sense of security, and provides a positive psychological boost in this catastrophic situation".

The lieutenant colonel made a note. Koenig could see his friend and superior's brow furrow. Finally, he nodded in agreement. "All right. Your suggestion doesn't sound so bad. I'll get the order out right away."

Another hour or so followed, during which they calmly discussed the world, Stalingrad, and the duties of soldiers. Finally, another phone call ended the conversation. Harras was needed.

The friends parted with a handshake that was different than usual. They looked deep into each other's eyes and shook hands for a long time, knowing it was goodbye forever.

Christmas in the cauldron of Stalingrad was a bridge home for most of the soldiers. They were cut off and underfed. Cold, vermin and disease claimed more victims than the enemy. The longing for the distant homeland was greater than ever and Christmas was something very special for the trapped 6th Army. Christmas meant peace, love, family and food. Everything the emaciated and exhausted men longed for. The Christmas spirit pervaded the bunkers from the stage to the front lines. Christmas paraphernalia was made from all kinds of materials. From the silver paper of cigarette packs, from wood and from steppe grass. The men at the front showed a special camaraderie during Christmas and gave each other small gifts. Everyone gave what he could. Above all, they gave each other one thing. A short period of happiness. For a moment, they forgot the horrors of everyday life and escaped home in their minds. Somewhere a harmonica played "Silent Night, Holy Night," and the men gradually joined in. Tears flowed as candles burned and carols rang out from more and more bunkers, trenches and positions.

Schmidt had kept his promise and had come to Major Koenig's quarters with field cook Hdromka and lance corporal Otto Remmler. They brought large containers of food and entered saying: "I have come from the forest. I must tell you, it's very Christmassy here!"

The farmhouse was decorated for Christmas. Ranks did not matter. From the major to the simple soldier, they all sat together and waited eagerly to see what the highly praised field cook had brought them.

Hdromka put down the large food container he had carried alone. "It's nice and warm here, comrades." Helmet, cap, scarf and coat were quickly taken off. "Then get in line, everyone. Bring your cooking utensils. There's horse goulash. I've thought of something for the side dishes. I've collected commissary bread and made bread dumplings. They're not quite as firm because I didn't have enough eggs and milk. And you have to think about the parsley, it's completely missing. But other than that, they turned out pretty good. At least they don't fall apart," he grinned.

At the same time, the soldiers began to clap and cheer. "Hurrah! Hurrah for the cook!"

Hdromka waved them off. "Take it easy, comrades. I suggest we eat first and then celebrate Christmas. Otherwise the food will be cold."

"Goulash, I can't believe it," exclaimed the Landser who had asked for this dish two days ago.

The food containers were opened. A smell that the soldiers hadn't smelled in a long time spread quickly. Their mouths watered.

"That was our last packhorse. The rest was used to make sausage. I kept the meat for the goulash. Your sausages are only half as big," the cook said casually, pointing to a large sack. "But you'll get that later, when the presents are ready."

Koenig closed his eyes as he took his first bite. It tasted delicious. The meat had little flavor of its own, and he wondered where the chef got the red wine he used to make the sauce so fantastic. This meal was not lavish, nor were they sitting at a table set with fine china. But compared to many of their compatriots in Stalingrad, they could celebrate Christmas with the certainty that they would not be attacked by the enemy. After the meal, two bottles of juniper brandy and chocolate were passed around. The atmosphere was cozy. One of the men sang a Christmas carol and everyone joined in. Even Koenig got carried away. They stole away for a few hours of peace and quiet and imagined a sense of security.

A little later the judges set up a radio and fiddled with the antenna. "Comrades, please be quiet. The Christmas program of the Großdeutscher Rundfunk is about to be broadcast."

One of the communications soldiers turned a knob. Hissing could be heard. A sergeant opened the stove to add fuel. The crackling flames ate their way into the dry piece of wood. Everyone listened intently to the hissing and crackling coming from the loudspeaker. Then they heard a voice.

"Attention, I am calling the Liinahamari Arctic Sea Port again," it sounded tinny from the ether. The reply sounded even more artificial. It was as quiet as a mouse in the quarters. No one made a sound. Everyone listened to the transmission.

"This is the Liinahamari Arctic Sea Port."

Finally, they froze when the voice on the radio called Stalingrad.

Noise - crackle, then: "This is Stalingrad. Here is the front on the Volga."

Goosebumps. The sergeant, who had added wood, began to cry. "This is madness! We're sitting here in the boiler, and they're sending such rubbish home. We're miserable and they're trying to make the world look better."

"Heinz, calm down," someone tapped him on the shoulder. "We're about to be saved. That's the real Christmas present."

There was hope in the sergeant's eyes. He nodded silently, sat down at the table, and listened to the music.

Koenig knew that the 4th Panzer Army was already under attack and that Paulus would not give the order to break out. He remained silent. It was the last beautiful evening for the men and he did not want to destroy their illusion.

Overnight, the temperature had dropped again to the minus 30s. The sentimental mood continued on Christmas Day. While the Landser talked about their catastrophic situation and hoped for liberation by General Hoth's tanks, Soviet POWs were dying by the dozen. The food available was not enough to feed their own soldiers. Accordingly, the POWs received little or nothing.

The next morning, Major Koenig got up in a good mood. Schmidt had given him razor blades and soap. The scarce sutler's goods were highly prized, and Koenig had returned the favor with a pack of pipe tobacco and two cigars. A close shave was long overdue, and the sharpshooter was in the midst of his morning ablutions. He was running the blade over his already smooth skin one last time when a detector burst into the quarters.

"Christmas is over for us, comrades. You have until noon to report to your command posts. We'll get ammunition and rations, then we'll move out again. The platoon leaders are to attend the briefing an hour before."

"What?" a lieutenant rumbled. "You said we'd be in the stage until the end of the year and form the emergency reserve."

"We are the emergency reserve and we are needed! The Russian has been active since the morning hours."

"Where is the Ivan attacking?"

"In the northeast with great force! But all the other front lines are also reporting increased shock troops."

Another officer speaks up. "They're afraid we'll rally and head for Hoth. That's why they're tying up the units, but it won't be long, men, then we'll chase the Bolsheviks across the damn Volga with the help of Hoth's tank army!"

Grumbling and muttering could be heard. A few: "Yes, we will!" could be heard.

"I don't think so, Lieutenant," the dispatcher waved off and wiped his dripping nose with the back of his hand. Then he looked at the curious and astonished faces, thought for a moment, and immediately spat out the latest news: "You don't know yet?"

Koenig closed his eyes and took a deep breath. He felt what was about to happen. He finished shaving, reached for the towel, and wiped the remaining shaving cream from his face.

The lieutenant approached the dispatcher. "What don't we know yet?"

"Hoth's tanks have stopped. It's going like wildfire. Ivan is attacking the relief troops. And the escape has been called off! We're supposed to hold the Kettle instead. The fortress of Stalingrad will not fall, they say from Berlin!"

The initial murmur turned into wild chatter. Anger and incomprehension arose. The first lieutenant grabbed the dispatcher by the collar. "What the hell are you talking about?" he shouted.

A crowd immediately gathered around the two men. Koenig went to his sleeping place, took the pistol, loaded it, pointed it at the wooden beams of the ceiling and fired a shot.

Bang!

For a moment there was silence. The major walked over to the dispatcher and stood next to the completely stunned soldier. "Guys, it's been known since ancient times that the bearer of bad news is executed. We don't do that. This soldier is not responsible for the decisions of the OKW. He only has the task to deliver messages".

A shocked silence. Koenig looked around the room. He lowered his voice slightly. "You have heard. General Hoth's tanks have stopped, the order to break out will not come. The Russians are attacking. We are soldiers and must obey! We will pack up, write a few lines home in peace, and then line up and advance to the front positions. If we want to force a chance for the breakout after all, we must hope that Hoth's armored forces are strong enough to withstand the Soviet attacks, and we must hold the fort here! That, my comrades, is our task now. In addition, all available sharpshooters will be assembled and deployed. I myself will seek out and hunt down Vasily Saizev, the Russian sniper whom the Ivans praise as the best lancer hunter of all time, and put him in the crosshairs. That's a promise!"

The first lieutenant let go of the detector and apologized. "The nerve, comrade. I'm sorry."

The men in the farmhouse were still silent. They had all not understood. Everyone's world collapsed as the great hope of rescue died. Still, a faint silver lining appeared on the horizon, bringing a new glimmer of hope. Major Koenig's words could not be shaken. He gave them the hope they needed to keep fighting. Hope was all the soldiers in Stalingrad had left to fight against an overwhelming enemy, lack of supplies, and extreme weather conditions. In short, hope was the Wehrmacht's last trump card to maintain its fighting strength in Stalingrad. Hope was the straw everyone was clinging to. Hope was the last drop of the 6th Army's lifeblood.

"He's right, comrades," the disappointed lieutenant turned to the others. "If we hold our positions and Hoth manages to repel the attack, it can still work."

"Do you believe that?" he was asked.

The first lieutenant looked at Major Koenig. He walked to his seat, picked up his sniper rifle, raised it and answered: "I believe I'm a damn good sniper. And I think that this Saizev, and many other Russian snipers like him, will not live much longer if they get in my crosshairs! The Russians have a saying: In the realm of hope it never winters! I say: My rifle will teach fear to those who oppose us. We are not just anybody, we are soldiers of the 6th Army. So let's do what we do best. Follow orders, clench our ass cheeks, and fight until the Wehrmacht High Command frees us from the cauldron!"

"Hurrah!" came first from two or three compatriots, then this small, almost insane euphoria, which misjudged the facts, spread to everyone. "Hurray!"

Koenig didn't know how or why he had done it, but now he had given hope to a handful of men.

14

The regiment gathered at the staging area and moved to their assigned positions as darkness fell. After only two hours of sleep, Major Koenig had joined a strong assault force whose mission was to reconnoiter a series of ruined houses in order to level the front, as far as one could speak of it in Stalingrad City, and to recapture and hold them if they were occupied by the Soviets. The operation was to take place just before dawn, when the enemy night guards were tired and the other Red Army soldiers were still asleep. Lieutenant Colonel Harras' order had already been partially carried out, and in addition to Koenig, two other snipers, each with an observer, were part of the assault team.

The approach of the Red Army in this battle for houses in the ruins of the city, which had degenerated into a rat war, did not allow the German soldiers to rest. Smaller and larger groups of soldiers kept entering the ruins. They used hand grenades and flamethrowers as well as bayonets, knives and sharpened spades. They came in the dark, protected by the targeted fire of the accompanying snipers. Once a building was taken, the Landser retook it hours later with the same ferocity and brutality. The last humanity of the combatants on both sides died with the soldiers killed in Stalingrad.

The thermometer had once again dropped below minus 35 degrees. The icy air crept under the soldiers' coats. Even the Christmas dinner, which was described as more or less sumptuous but still meager, could not alleviate the constant hunger. The soldiers were simply malnourished.

Koenig had reconsidered his personal plan and stuck to it. He wanted to hold Saizev personally responsible. Whether it was right or wrong to involve Katja and Grisha, and whether it was right or wrong to take off his uniform after this last planned shot, should he survive this duel, he left open.

I feel like I'm climbing a mountain I can't conquer, he thought. I can't look up to the top, I just have to start walking and put one foot in front of the other!

The advance party had stopped. A man from the advance guard came running up, crouching. Major Koenig was standing next to the lieutenant leading the advance party.

The soldier was an older corporal. He pulled a scarf from his mouth as he spoke. He exhaled clouds of smoke with every word. His face was only vaguely recognizable. "We can see a good distance ahead. If we set up a machine gun, we can fight and secure three houses."

The lieutenant listened. "Is there anything to recognize?"

"Negative, Lieutenant. Everything is quiet as a mouse. If Ivan is in there, he's either asleep or giving us a proper welcome."

"Tell Schmittner and Lerch to take position with the machine gun. I'll come forward and take a look."

Before the lieutenant could ask if Koenig was also moving forward, he said: "I'll take a look, too."

The lieutenant now turned to a sergeant. "Take your men to the right flank, Kemmerer is to take the left flank and Schwedt's group is to get ready to attack! I want the two sharpshooters to take up positions on the flanks!"

"Yes, Lieutanant."

The sergeant disappeared. The lieutenant maneuvered his submachine gun into position, checked the magazine, instinctively grabbed the bag with the spare magazines, and nodded to Major Koenig. "Let's go!"

Koenig took off his thick gloves and removed the sniper rifle from his shoulder, exposing the scope wrapped around it for protection. Unlike many other soldiers, he was glad to be wearing a winter uniform and warm boots. He pulled his warm gloves back on and headed out. The lance corporal took the lead and the lieutenant joined Koenig.

The small advance party lay behind a pile of rubble. Koenig and the lieutenant crawled up. No sound was heard except for a small stone that was kicked loose by the lieutenant's boot heel and rolled down.

Three binoculars were trained on the houses. One of them belonged to Koenig. He let it glide slowly from house to house, window to window. The officer paid attention to every detail. He didn't see anything on the first pass.

"All quiet," said the lieutenant, wanting to be confirmed by the results of the other two.

"Too quiet," Koenig whispered, and began to scan the buildings again with his binoculars. "I would leave at least one of the houses occupied. Just as we can control the whole width from here, the Russians can from there. They'd be stupid not to!"

The lieutenant raised his binoculars again. "What do you suggest?"

"Send a man to the snipers. Tell your spotters to keep a close watch. And each of them should watch the building in front of them. The snipers have freedom of action and should eliminate possible targets! I'll take the middle house. Once the machine gun is in position, have three men work their way to each house. At least one with a machine gun. Everybody has to carry grenades. If you can reach the houses without enemy interference, throw in the grenades and go in. The squads will move up accordingly. If we get return fire, concentrate on that and attack as usual!"

The lieutenant nodded.

"But we wait until we get the first feedback from the observers. That usually takes less than a quarter of an hour. Either we hear a shot by then, or we move forward!"

The lieutenant nodded again, patted the lance corporal on the shoulder, and ordered him to pass on the major's instructions. The Landser slid gently down the scree and moved off to the right.

Koenig raised his binoculars again, looking for anything out of the ordinary. This time, however, he concentrated solely on the middle building.

The cold was getting to the soldiers. Every minute they lay still and didn't move, the icy cold crept deeper under their uniforms. They shivered, pulled up their legs where possible to make themselves smaller, or lay close together to give each other some warmth. It was also a nerve-wracking wait. An attack was imminent. Everyone was afraid. They had been through so much, marching through Russia, shooting and fighting. They had seen Red Army soldiers die and comrades fall. They saw the misery of the people, and they took the last pitiful scraps of food to keep themselves alive. But what they experienced and suffered in the last weeks in Stalingrad changed most of them. If they were ever able to escape this hell, the rest of their lives would be marked by their experiences in this city. Some of them already had nightmares. They kept seeing the faces of the men they had to kill in hand-to-hand combat. Even when they were lying in the staging area, some of them would wake up at night, suspecting a spontaneous attack by the Russians because of a common noise. They saw death and misery and lived in a miserable state, hoping to be rescued. More and more of their comrades were unable to fight because of cold and hunger. Nevertheless, the strongest among them pulled themselves together, obeyed the orders of their superiors, and fought. And again, some of them put their fate in God's hands. They themselves had neither the strength nor the courage to save themselves from inhuman suffering with a bullet in the head. But the enemy could! If it was God's will, a Russian bullet could mean the end of all suffering. The end of hunger, the end of trembling, the end of cold, the end of suffering. God's will. Some soldiers found their way back to faith in Stalingrad by taking refuge in the hope of the promises of Jesus Christ, while others lost their faith as a result of Stalingrad, experiencing hell on earth and wondering why God allowed such suffering. Still others realized that they were partly responsible for the misery they had brought to the Bear Kingdom. They were the harbingers of death, the devil's helpers. Hope and self-denial alternated in the soldiers' minds.

Now they lurked among the rubble of destroyed buildings at minus 35 degrees, waiting for the order to attack and take three ruins on command.

The expected and feared shot of a Russian sniper did not come. Nine Landser stalked toward three ruined buildings, apparently unnoticed by the enemy. Koenig had removed his heavy right glove. He was still wearing a thinner wool glove with the index finger cut open so he could remove it to fire. The finger rested long on the trigger guard. His breathing was calm. Koenig concentrated only on the building, paying no attention to the men who had split into three groups.

The first shot rang out on the left flank, followed by a second a split second later. A Russian sniper had waited patiently and killed one of the German soldiers. With lightning speed, he raised his Mosin

Nagant to fire a second shot. However, before he could raise his right index finger, he himself became a victim. The German sniper's observer, almost opposite him, had noticed the position and relayed it to the sniper. With a well-aimed shot, the sniper did his terrible work.

A firefight immediately broke out. More and more muzzle flashes could be seen. A loud "Attaaaaack!" could be heard from the right.

Rrrrrrrt ... rrrrt......

The machine gun rattled. Koenig aimed, fired, repeated, aimed and fired. His targets were easy to find. He stopped at the muzzle flashes that appeared on the windows of the buildings.

Boom!

In the barrage of machine gun fire, a group of three had made their way to the front of the house. The hand grenades they threw exploded. Dust, shrapnel, and a bizarre mixture of blood, skin, and shreds of uniform were thrown around and scattered over the rubble.

A flare shot up from the Soviets with a hiss and cast a bright, shimmering light downward. Men hurried around. A Russian machine gun started firing, stopping immediately when the shooter was hit by the German sniper on the right flank.

Koenig also spotted a target in the flickering magnesium light and fired his fifth shot.

Five shots, five hits!

He pulled a loading strip from the ammunition pouch and inserted it.

The groups attacking the right and middle buildings had already penetrated. The MG 42 now concentrated on the ruins on the left. There the advancing group of Landsers was still under heavy fire, but this was quickly weakened by the massive intervention of the machine gun.

Boom!

Another hand grenade exploded. There was a bizarre flash in some rooms when MP rounds were fired. Koenig fired another shot at the ruins on the left, then the firefight gradually died down. A single shot rang out twice at short intervals, then the three buildings were taken.

Koenig had pulled the woolen finger of the glove back over his clammy shooting finger. He packed up, pulled the cover over the optics of the rifle and stomped off. It took him a few steps to straighten his body, which was stiff from the cold. The wound bothered him from time to time, but only during extreme movements. Lying down and shooting were no problem. In close combat, he doubted he would be able to defend himself hard and fast. His damaged knee, on the other hand, was almost completely healed. Fortunately, it was not broken.

When he reached the ruins, he looked for the lieutenant. Koenig knew that the commanding officer had to make a report and wanted to be present at the radio to hear any further orders.

It was dawn, and the dirty gray of the rising day matched the bloody end of the night. Koenig paused for a moment and stared at the dead city.

This is Stalingrad, the former shining star on the banks of the Volga. Now it is nothing but a pile of ruins, and death wanders through its ruins every day to reap its rich harvest, he thought.

The lieutenant moved about wildly, immediately filling all the important positions. Calls for the medic and a porter could be heard. Two reporters turned knobs. One of them cursed about the cold and the fact that the equipment was running out of power, then there was a hissing and cracking sound.

One spoke into the microphone, the other informed the lieutenant. "We have the battalion!"

At the end of the radio contact, the rearguard was able to report that the front had been cleared. The use of the snipers was also praised. Then came the casualty report: "Four killed, two seriously wounded, and three lightly wounded."

"Hostile?" it croaked tinny.

"No movement at the moment!"

"Got it! Over!"

Four more men dead, Koenig thought, shaking. Another four black-bordered letters home. He smiled ironically. German bureaucracy. We're dying here, but the reports are still neatly typed, the letters written and sent.

The Soviets suffered at least twice as many casualties. In addition, two prisoners were taken and a Red Army soldier lay badly wounded on the ground. His moans accompanied the whole scene. The Russian's eyes were filled with fear. He suspected that he was going to die, but inwardly hoped that he would be saved. His comrades sat next to him, not daring to move.

"The medics are needed here too," said one of the intelligence soldiers, pointing at the Russian.

"Let them take care of their buddy themselves," the lieutenant replied.

Koenig addressed them in Russian. "Tie him up."

They complied.

"Let's give him the coup de grace right away," the corporal commented contemptuously, "and the other two Bolsheviks too!"

Koenig became angry. "Corporal, you're wearing the German uniform. What does it say on your belt buckle?"

The Landser was astonished. "God with us, why ..."

That was as far as he got, then Koenig stood nose-to-nose with him. Pure rage coursed through his veins like boiling blood. He shouted at the corporal, "Then act accordingly. Killing someone in battle is bad enough, but from a soldier's point of view it is unavoidable, but we are not murderers!"

The lieutenant intervened. To prevent further escalation, he placed himself between Koenig and the corporal. "Küster, please take care of securing the right flank. I'll have them disengaged as soon as possible."

Glad to hear the order, the corporal turned and hurried away.

"The war is brutalizing us all," the lieutenant said. "Hunger and cold do the rest."

"We are still human beings."

"People who have too little to eat to get enough to eat. And yet we fight day after day, hour after hour, minute after minute, hoping to be rescued. The men are desperate, and those over there," the officer pointed to the Russian prisoners, "are our enemies and to blame.

"Whose country are we in?" asked Koenig.

"Are you saying that..."

The sniper interrupted the lieutenant. "I'm not saying anything.

We're here to fight, not to settle questions of guilt. As soldiers, we have rights and duties. And one of those duties is to take care of our prisoners, not execute them! You should remember that, Lieutenant."

Hurried footsteps. A soldier came running up. "Right flank secured, Lieutenant. When the left flank is taken, we can move the wounded."

The wounded were taken first to the casualty collection point, then to the TVPl as quickly as possible. A platoon held in reserve reinforced the front line. A Soviet counterattack was expected, but it remained quiet.

Koenig looked through his binoculars at the front line and saw the perfect spot for his plan. His pulse quickened noticeably. Again and again he flew over the spot and the ruins of the buildings opposite.

This is almost ideal, he thought at once.

There were several craters in the rubble of the houses. Bombs from the planes had hit them. Some of them were deep, others more shallow. Depending on the force of the bomb. Some merged into each other. Others were half or almost filled with debris.

Opposite these craters, the buildings were so shattered that the front walls of the houses had collapsed completely or in large sections. There were rubble fields on the flanks, making it difficult for snipers to take up positions. The risk of being spotted there was immensely high because the flanks were in the line of sight of the German soldiers who were entrenched in the ruins they had just captured.

If there was a sniper, he would be in the open ruins, Koenig knew.

His plan matured and took shape. The time had finally come. Tonight he would go to Katja and Grisha. The thought of the Russian woman and her son warmed Koenig's heart. They had become his personal hope in these dark times. They were his future, if he had one.

The Russians had made themselves at home in the basement of the middle building. The ceiling was secured with cross and support beams. Straw sacks served as beds. Some provisions were found, but they could be secured only with great difficulty and by threatening to shoot them immediately before they were quickly eaten. The lieutenant had this coveted booty divided up fairly under supervision and distributed to the men as extra rations.

The Schpagin submachine guns, with their conspicuous round magazines, were as popular as the food. "They work even at minus 50 degrees," said a lanky sergeant, his head bobbing back and forth on a long, thin giraffe neck as he slung one around his neck and searched for extra ammunition.

Major Erwin Koenig waited in the dark for the food bearers to come forward. They brought the men some ammunition and thin, watery horse soup. They were accompanied by a group of sappers led by a bald sergeant. He reported to the lieutenant.

"Sergeant Schulze, Lieutenant. We're supposed to cover the foreland with S-mines to spoil the Ivan's advance," he said very casually.

"That sounds like a suicide mission," the lieutenant replied.

"We'll go out in two-man squads. Their snipers will cover us. If there's too much lead hail, have them radio in with the machine guns."

On the one hand, it was on the tip of Koenig's tongue to criticize the noncommissioned officer's casual manner, but on the other hand, he was neither casual nor rude. On the contrary, the compatriot's manner made the dangerous undertaking seem more feasible than if he had focused on the dangers.

"You know, some of the last supply bombs were filled with medals. The fried egg is still missing from my collection, ha ha," he laughed a bit wickedly, but immediately came back to the point. "Back to the order. The old man told me," he cleared his throat, "sorry. Captain Lederer gave the order. We're supposed to support you, too."

The lieutenant nodded. "All right, Sergeant. Then get to work. I'll brief the snipers and let my men know."

Major Koenig joined the conversation now. "The two snipers will have to do. I myself will go back with the food carriers. I have more missions to lead."

The lieutenant saluted. "It was an honor, Major Koenig."

The sergeant stared and stepped back. "You are Major Koenig? The master of all snipers?"

"Don't exaggerate, Sergeant," Koenig waved him off.

"I'm glad to see you standing before me."

Koenig patted the sergeant on the shoulder. "Good luck, comrade," he turned to the lieutenant. "You will hold this position at all costs!" he said in a stern tone to avoid any misunderstandings and gave an order to the now astonished looking lieutenant. Lieutenant Colonel Harras' carte blanche gave Koenig a free hand. "These positions are more important than just tidying up the front. I expect full commitment. Lieutenant Colonel Harras and I will appreciate your efforts," he added, buttering up the officer. "Let's see what else we can do for you."

Now the lieutenant's eyes widened. "That little conversation you had earlier, that was the heat of the moment."

Koenig waved him off. "That's all right. Like you said, this war in the cauldron, the hunger and the cold. We're all only human."

"Yes, Major."

"I'll be back here in two or three days at the latest. I hope very much that we'll still be here in position."

"We will do our best."

"They call for support and have the Russian positions on the opposite side repeatedly covered with regimental artillery. Our Eight-Eight should not let them rest."

"But we hardly have..."

"Just ask for it!"

"Yes!"

Those who still had Esbit tablets warmed up their horse soup. The others ate it cold. The picture did not show the soldiers of the once so feared and victorious 6th Army. It showed emaciated, hollow-cheeked men in tattered uniforms and blank stares, shivering in their positions and eating thin horse soup with expressionless faces.

Katja jumped when she heard a scratching sound. She had long since become accustomed to the usual noises of the night. She knew at what distance a grenade would fall and where the machine-gunners were, firing their volleys through the night, or when to take cover at the sound of aircraft engines. The war had taught her all that. This scratching was new and didn't belong here. Not at this time of night, and not when she and Grisha were lying here in bed under the warm blanket. Despite the icy cold that had settled over the city, the temperature in their basement was still above freezing. It was cold, but not deadly.

She listened quietly. A few seconds ago she had been half asleep, but now she was wide awake.

There it is again!

Her heartbeat quickened. Fear crawled under her skin. Had the entrance been discovered? Was it German soldiers, Red Army soldiers, or civilians roaming Stalingrad at night in search of good places and food? But whoever it was, it meant death. As a woman, there was always the fear of being raped. Stalingrad, the city of her former love, now stood only for brutality, suffering and death.

Katja grabbed the revolver that had been under her pillow since Erwin's departure and scurried out from under the blanket. Grisha hadn't noticed anything and was sleeping peacefully. She could hear his soft breathing. The Russian didn't need any light to find her way to the door. Once there, she listened. Silence. Then a soft clicking sound. There was no doubt about it. Someone had kicked one of the small stones that now clattered down the stairs. She had scattered some around to warn them. This plan was working. This was good. Someone was here, that was bad.

Katja was more excited and worried than ever. She wondered if she should wake Grisha or not.

Maybe it's just an animal.

Since the many dead bodies and soldiers lay in the city, rats and mice multiplied. The corpses provided them with food. Katja and Grisha also set traps. They fell almost every day. For some Stalingraders this would have been a welcome feast, but fortunately Katja and Grishka still had enough supplies. Quietly, she opened the door and ventured a glance into the hallway. Her heart seemed to skip a beat for a moment as the beam of a flashlight flickered around her. Her palms instantly turned clammy. Her pulse was racing like a train with an overheated boiler. Goose bumps formed at the base of her neck and spread to her toes in a split second.

Someone is coming down the stairs!

Katja gripped the revolver with both hands and pointed it into the hallway. She cocked the hammer with her thumb. There was a soft metallic sound.

A click.

She would shoot.

Her mind raced to weigh all the possibilities. It's just one person. No voices, no other sounds. Then it's definitely not soldiers.

"Katja? Grisha?"

Breathe a sigh of relief. The voice belonged to Erwin Koenig. As quickly as the goose bumps had spread, they disappeared again. Katja's heart was still beating wildly, but this time the cause was different. Joy!

"Erwin?" came the rhetorical reply, and even before the answer came, she went to meet him. The hammer was uncocked and the gun was lowered.

Koenig knew that Katja was in constant danger, and so he had addressed her by name before he saw her. The soldier suspected that she was lurking because he had come unannounced and could be a marauder. To make sure she recognized him immediately, he turned the flashlight on himself and addressed the Russian woman again. "Katja, it's me. Erwin."

"Erwin!" came the joyful cry as Katja recognized the German.

They both ran to each other and opened their arms. They embraced and held each other tightly. There was a moment of silence. They suddenly felt like two children who had been caught doing something forbidden and kept their distance again. Each of them would have liked to kiss the other at that moment, but Stalingrad was no place for a love affair. At least not here and now.

"Come in! You're lucky, I already had the gun cocked!"

Koenig grinned. "That's what I thought."

"You were gone longer than I thought. Grisha and I were afraid something had happened to you."

"I'm here now. And I have found a place where I can and will challenge Saizev."

Katja lit a candle, Koenig put down his gun and sat down.

Grisha had woken up, rubbed his eyes and cried happily, "Erwin! At last!"

"Hello, Grisha."

The boy got up, ran to the table and hugged Koenig. "I knew you'd come back to us. I just knew it."

Katja could hardly believe it. Her son hugged a German officer. The world was turned upside down. How could this have happened? The Germans had come to her country, killed so many people, burned everything to the ground, destroyed her town, and killed her beloved Pyotr. Were they not also the reason why Saizev, or at least one of his snipers, had shot her Boris? Your boy was fetching water for the Germans so they could eat. He just wanted to survive, nothing else. That's why he got shot. But she also had feelings for Erwin Koenig. He was somehow different from the others. Doubts mingled with the budding feelings. Could there be a future? She had thought about it a lot and had found a solution. Yes! A future was possible. But it was dangerous. If it worked, everything would be fine, if it didn't, it would mean death for Erwin and her, and maybe for Grisha too. Katja pushed these terrible thoughts aside and enjoyed the moment. Erwin Koenig sat across from her and he seemed to have recovered well from his wound.

"How have you been?"

Katja said that Grisha had visited Captain Oligov twice during Erwin's absence. The first time, the political commissar Grisha had told him about was there again. According to the boy, the officer listened attentively and asked many questions after Grisha's report.

Katja showed a moment of relief when she said: "Your preparation was just right. Grisha actually had to draw a sketch and pinpoint the location. The political officer also took notes. During the second course, my son was praised by Captain Oligov, because the political commissar was satisfied with Grisha's work. I suppose this had a positive effect on Oligov. Nevertheless, the pressure on Grisha was increased. On the Russian side, your ... um ... how shall I put it ... activities as a sniper were very well noticed and had an effect. Katja paused and looked at Koenig. He sat motionless and listened. She continued: "Oligov told Grisha that this German sniper now had a name thanks to him, and that Comrade Saizev had put this name on his list. If Grisha

261

understood correctly, this political officer wants to publicize the hunt for you as a duel between the great hunters of the Red Army. Of course, the Russians will triumph in this report. Grisha was ordered to find you."

"Yes," Grisha interjected, "but it's not just me. I think everyone is looking for you."

Koenig nodded. His reply sounded level-headed. "But it will be you who will find me."

Katja still had considerable doubts. "Must it be so? I don't know what's right and what's wrong anymore, Erwin. It's much too dangerous. Let's stop this."

"I feel that we must go on if we are to find peace. I know that I have to hunt down and kill this man who is responsible for the death of our sons here in Stalingrad. For Boris and for Rolf, and also in the name of the many other children who were killed."

"What if he kills you?"

Koenig did not answer.

"And how many children have died because of you in this war? How many children died on August 23rd, when your planes opened their bellies and rained bombs on our city?" she said with a vengeance, stood up, went to the shelf and returned with her late husband's identity card. She placed it on the table and slid it over to Erwin. "This is Pyotr." A thick lump suddenly formed in her throat. She swallowed and recovered. "That was Pyotr, my husband. He was a doctor at the hospital and died in the bombing in August. He's been dead less than six months, and I'm full of grief, but I'm also full of hope. Hope that we will survive this war. We have good shelter here, and if we use our supplies sparingly, we'll have something to eat for a while. We are better off than most of the people in Stalingrad. I've seen where they were driven to when they had to leave the city. They live in the barracks, in holes in the ground, and have less than we do."

You could see that Koenig's forehead was rattling. His eyes were glued to Katja's lips with every word. He guessed what she was going to suggest and asked to hear it from her mouth: "What do you want to tell me?"

"Look at the photo. It's not a very good picture, but Pyotr looks very much like you. We can do it. You will get rid of the uniform and hide here with us. We'll find some clothes for you. We say you can't speak, write or read since the bombing. You're in shock! You have scars to show for your fight against the Germans, and you understand enough Russian to react when you're told something, but otherwise you remain emotionless."

Koenig stared at the picture in the passport. Katja was right. There was a striking resemblance. "It's true, I could pass for Pyotr, but what if we meet someone who knows your husband? He was a doctor here in Stalingrad and must have treated a lot of people."

Katja became more energetic. "We'll leave here. Somewhere where nobody knows us and start over. Russia is big. We'll go to Siberia or the Black Sea."

"I want that too," said Grigory, putting his hand on Erwin's shoulder.

Koenig was deeply touched. They both spoke to his soul. The two people he had left behind returned his budding feelings. They offered him something he hadn't had until recently. Hope for a happy future. Despite all the suffering, the struggles, and the painful losses, a silver lining shimmered on the horizon. A smile flickered across the sniper's face. "Just one more shot, then I'll put the gun away forever. I promise you. If I avoid this duel, Saizev will hunt me for the rest of my life. He will not rest until he has captured me.

"And if he kills you in this upcoming fight?"

"I will win this duel."

Katja took a deep breath. "You men are always so stubborn!"

Koenig leaned forward and tried to put some calm into his voice, speaking slowly and in a soothing tone. "Grisha only has to go to Captain Oligov one more time. Just one last time, then we're almost there."

There was a pause. The candlelight flickered slightly. All three of them, even Grisha, knew that this was the moment they would decide their fate. They all felt the invisible, inaudible crackling of this tense atmosphere. Each of them dug deep into his own thoughts.

It was the German who spoke first. He looked at Grisha. "I

know that much, if not everything, depends on you. I know what a burden you carry on your young shoulders. I can never ask you to do this. You have to make this decision yourself, and the three of us will carry it together! No matter how it turns out." He turned to Katja. "And I know how much strength, suffering, fear and overcoming it will cost you to give Grisha your blessing for this last journey. If you do, a new era will begin. After that, the addiction to revenge will be satisfied, regardless of the outcome."

"No!" she protested, "It doesn't matter how it ends! I don't want to lose Grisha or you!"

Koenig was deeply affected. He felt that his feelings were reciprocated. "Don't worry, I'll be prepared, wait for Saizev and fire just one last shot from this gun," he pointed to his rifle. "Then I'll come back to you and we'll hide until the war in Stalingrad is over. I like your plan to pose as Pyotr."

"Me too," said Grisha resolutely, moving demonstratively closer to Erwin Koenig. "Mama, Erwin is a good man, and I miss Papa. I miss Boris. And I would miss Erwin too. He's not my dad, but he's my best friend, and he's the only one I have. And I'm sure he's your best friend too. I'm not afraid to go to Captain Oligov. I remember everything Erwin tells me. Just like last time."

Katja groaned slightly in despair, closed her eyes for a few thoughtful seconds, and took an audible deep breath. Then she said: "All right! But I swear to you ...."

Koenig quickly raised his hand in appeasement, then put his index finger to his lips. "Shh! You don't have to swear anything, we all know what we're up against and we'll carry this burden together. We'll get through it without any problems." He literally stared at her. His gaze was hypnotic. "Katja! We will make it. Believe in it! Repeat it!"

"I believe," came the thoughtful rather than convincing reply.

Koenig raised his voice. "Say it, Katja! Loud and clear, so we can hear and believe you!"

"We can do it!" came louder, then again. "We'll make it!"

Grisha laughed. "Yes, we can do it!" he cheered, thrusting both arms up.

Katja was swept away by her son's enthusiasm. "We can do it!"

she exclaimed enthusiastically.

Koenig put his left hand over Grisha's shoulder and slid his right hand across the table. Katja reached for it. "After this, we are free in spirit. And that means free for the future - a future together."

In the days that followed, they continued to work out Major Erwin Koenig's plan. Grisha gradually received information from the German officer, which he was to pass on. He trained Grisha several times a day and also confronted him with old reports that he had already given to Oligov. He tried to involve him in contradictions and sometimes put him under so much pressure that Katja was on the verge of quitting the company altogether, but the boy put up a brave fight. In the end, the Russian woman was convinced that her son would withstand any questioning.

Koenig returned to the German positions every other day. He had to make sure he could ambush the Russian sniper in that exact spot. Otherwise, the whole plan would be ruined.

The year 1942 ended and the new year 1943 began with an eerie calm on the Stalingrad fronts. Apart from the night assault companies which repeatedly attacked a few ruined houses, took hold and were driven out the next day, sometimes only hours later, there were hardly any serious attacks worth mentioning.

Koenig, who was becoming increasingly aware of the deterioration of the German soldiers, wondered if the enemy was trying to starve the remnants of the 6th Army. Bread rations were reduced first to 100, then by another 25% to 75 grams per man per day. With few exceptions, the soldiers resembled the living dead. Disease spread. Louse infestation was rampant. The weather struck, relentlessly attacking the emaciated bodies with icy cold.

Battle strength was dwindling, yet the trapped soldiers fought each day against the threat of annihilation.

Never before had it been so clear to the Major as it was in those first days of January 1943, what fate awaited the 6th Army, and how unworldly and mercilessly terrible the regime in Berlin, far from the hell of Stalingrad, was letting its own soldiers die a miserable death.

The fine gentlemen decide over life and death and open a bottle of wine while they consider whether to eat a fat goose or a roast beef next Sunday. The 6th Army and hundreds of thousands of people have been betrayed. The whole war is a crime, and we are the tools.

For a moment, Koenig even doubted his plan to kill Russian sniper Vasily Saizev. What finally convinced him to go ahead with his plan was that he was not doing it for Greater Germany or for Adolf Hitler. He was doing it for himself; for himself and for Katja, who shared a similar fate, the loss of a child at the hands of Russian snipers.

Just this one last shot, then I'll be free!

The lack of massive advances by the Red Army was seen as a warning by the compatriots in Stalingrad. Everyone suspected that a major offensive was imminent. The mighty Russian bear stood up and swung his paw to deliver the death blow to his victim.

"You did a good job holding your position," he praised the lieutenant. "Did the Russian attack in the meantime?"

The lieutenant reported proudly that the enemy had launched an attack last night, but had given up and retreated after two S-mines were detonated in quick succession, followed by heavy machine-gun fire. The major thanked him. The ominous lull in the fighting came in handy. He took advantage of the calm before the storm to inspect the craters in front of the position.

As he had hoped, he found a perfect position for his planned final sniper shot. And he found something else. The body of a Russian who had dragged himself wounded into one of the craters and died there alone. While the German officer scanned the area with his binoculars for possible hiding places and shooting positions, he came up with the perfect plan. The body of the Red Army soldier would play a crucial role. He would get everything Koenig needed that night.

That evening, he had given Grisha the go-ahead for his final registration. He calculated a time advantage of at least one day and no more than three days. The first Soviet reconnaissance planes could arrive here within 24 hours of the report. This should be enough time for Koenig to prepare himself, move into position unnoticed by the enemy, and create a hidden access and escape route.

Again and again he raised the binoculars to his eyes and stared at the destroyed house front opposite.

There is a 90% probability that he is hiding there! He positions other snipers and his spotters on the flanks. From there, he can maintain visual contact and has the entire area under control.

The sniper withdraws and returns an hour later with two engineers. "I'll cover you with my rifle. Can you find a connection between these two craters and some kind of trench from here?"

"A trench?" one of the men asked incredulously.

"Not like in the soup, but just a small path where I can get in and out unseen."

The pioneer looked around. "It's not too difficult. The bombs did most of the work for us. Connecting the craters will be done in no time. Assuming we can blow them up. Digging won't work with the frozen ground."

"What do you need for that?"

"We have everything here. However, this is our last blasting cube."

"Use it!"

"By your command, Major."

The other pioneer looked over the rubble. "Are you sure we can work here undisturbed?"

Koenig glanced at his wristwatch. "How long would it take?"

The two pioneers looked at each other. "With blasting, maybe two or three hours."

"That's too long!"

The older of the two soldiers scratched the tip of his nose. Working on the catwalk is not dangerous. We use a few beams or larger pieces of rubble as a screen. I also saw some roofing tarp on the way here. We can put them over the two craters after the blasting. It will be relatively dry here. If it snows again, that's an advantage. But it could collapse in a heavy snowfall.

Koenig liked the suggestion. "I'll have secondary grenades fired when you put the roof sheets over the craters. But the smoke won't last very long in this weather. So you should work as fast as you can."

Again it was the older man who answered. "I was a little queasy, but we'll manage with the fog protection." He raised his left arm slightly and pulled back his sleeve with the fingers of his right hand. A glance at the exposed wristwatch followed. "We can start in thirty minutes, Major."

"I'll go to the judges and give the order as soon as possible. You'll start as soon as there's a rumble over at the Russian."

"Yes, sir."

"How many men will be working here?"

Now the younger pioneer answered. "The two of us and Hans. So Hans Meixner." He improved again. "Private Hans Meixner. He blows up everything that gets in his way. He's the best man for such a job."

Koenig reached into his coat and pulled out an open packet of Juno. "I still have this. There are six cigarettes in it. One for each man. I'll coordinate with the secondary grenades now." He was turning to leave when Koenig stopped abruptly and turned back to the two engineers. "It has to look as natural as possible in the end."

The old engineer laughed. "Look natural? Ha, ha ... here in Stalingrad? It's a big pile of rubble. Nothing stands out." Then he pointed to the dead Red Army soldier. "We'll throw him in front of the crater. As long as it's below zero, it won't stink."

Koenig waved him away. "Leave the fallen man where he is. Just do the work we just discussed."

The pioneer nodded slightly in surprise. "All right, let's get our tools. As soon as the Ivan is fogged up, we'll get started."

"I will also give the lieutenant the order to advance against the two buildings. Then the Russian will be distracted. You must carry out and complete all conspicuous work while the attack is still in progress!"

The engineers looked at each other in confusion. "We'll try."

Major Erwin Koenig next went to the lieutenant and discussed the situation with him. He pretended that the lieutenant was part of a secret project and that he could expect an award if the venture succeeded.

The lieutenant had the order confirmed by his battalion staff. Koenig was present when the reply was received by radio, and the Major's command authority, officially designated as Z.B.V., was activated.

When the junior judge ended the radio communication with: "Understood, over!" said Koenig: "Again, for your information. This is a diversionary attack. Do not advance with full force and withdraw to this starting position after 30 minutes at the latest! I will leave with the food carriers and report to the battalion staff. I will return tonight and expect a full report in the morning.

The last order given to the two snipers was to score as many hits as possible.

"Show the Russians you're here! Shoot anything that moves! Let the Ivan know we have him in our crosshairs. That makes them nervous!"

Basically, Koenig wanted to make sure that the enemy knew about the active German sniper activity on that section of the front.

And you will pass this on to Saizev. You will tell him that I am here, were his thoughts.

Example photo

PA-H-0112-Kameraden – Wintereinbruch
Comrades - onset of winter
Privatarchiv Author
all rights reserved by the author

15

Although she knew that the old army revolver was loaded, Katja checked the loading status of the pistol once more before the cold steel disappeared back into her coat pocket. She had an uneasy feeling as she pulled on the shawl to accompany her beloved Grisha to Captain Oligov for the final report. The streets of Stalingrad had been suspiciously quiet for several days. There was the occasional rumble or the echo of small firefights, but it was no longer possible to speak of constant fighting.

The Russian sensed that something big was brewing. Various thoughts raced through her mind, were discarded and returned.

The Red Army will tighten the ring and advance massively against the German positions. With a little luck, our road will be largely spared, she silently hoped.

Nowhere was safe in Stalingrad, and yet she felt protected in her cellar. It was like a fortress to her. Katja tried to take something positive from the walk to the shaft and Grisha's report to the Russian officer. They needed fresh air and would get a situation report at the same time. In addition, the provisions Grisha was rewarded with after each report came in handy. Despite their frugal approach, their supplies were dwindling. If Erwin were to join them, they would soon be exhausted.

Katja became more and more nervous. She knew from experience that Red Army soldiers were given increased rations of vodka before attacks. If that happened now, and they fell into the hands of a group of drunken Soviet soldiers, they would be no better than the German pigs who had tried to rape her. The terrible moment returned to her memory, then the image of her rescuer appeared before her eyes. She still mourned for Pyotr, and that wound would not heal for a long time, but she was also grateful that Erwin had come into her life. He may have worn the uniform of the enemy, but he was a good man. She was attracted to him, trusted him, and liked him very much. He could be the man she would let into her heart next to Pyotr.

"Mom, we have to go!" Grisha tugged at her hand, snapping her back to reality. "What's wrong with you?"

Katja struggled to smile. "I was just thinking." She stroked his hair. "Do you have your hat?"

"Here," Grisha said and picked it up demonstratively.

"Do you know what you have to say?"

"Mom!" Grisha was annoyed by this question. "I've said it a hundred times."

She buttoned her coat and grabbed her scarf, gloves, and fur hat. "We're going!"

The night was starry and appropriately cold. Every time we breathed, a small cloud of fog blew in front of our faces. Katja and Grisha now knew every secret route that led to the tunnel shaft. They moved quickly and yet with extreme caution. In Stalingrad, it was life-threatening to walk the streets near the battle zones during the day. At night, the risk of losing one's life increased many times over. Reconnaissance units from both sides often took detours to reach their targets. Katja and Grisha were not allowed to meet Russian or German soldiers. Both sides could mistake them for enemies in the dark and shoot them. Marauding soldiers were even more dangerous. They would certainly rape Katja, and if Grisha helped her, they would shoot him, she was sure of it. Nor did she trust other civilians who ventured out into the streets after dark. As a result, she reacted immediately to any sign of alarm. Her nerves were on edge and her senses were working at full speed.

Katja carried a backpack on her back. It contained the last of her bandages, in case something unexpected happened, and a warm blanket. About ten meters from the entrance to the shaft that led Grisha to the Russian-occupied part of Stalingrad, there was an alcove that was sheltered from wind and weather. The blanket would keep her warm while she waited for Grisha.

The worried mother was afraid for her son and was ready to crawl through the shaft with him to protect him with her life. She would stand threateningly in front of this Captain Oligov and hold her revolver to his head while he was interrogating Grisha. And if this Saizev was there, she would ask him if he enjoyed shooting a little boy. Since none of this was possible, the only thing she could do was to wait for her son's return. Thoughts of Saizev brought up anger, hatred, and a desire for revenge. The pain of Boris's death intensified again. It never went away, only the intensity changed. It would stay that way for the rest of her life. She felt as if a part of her heart had been torn from her body. Imperceptibly, she squeezed Grisha's hand tighter. "Are you all right, Grisha?" she whispered as she left.

"Yes," came back quietly.

The hot tea she had prepared on the stove thanks to the remaining Es-bit tablets had long since lost its warming effect.

This damned cold, she cursed inwardly.

They made good progress and only had to hide once for a few minutes. Then Katja thought she heard the clatter of the soldiers' equipment. Only after they had listened for a while and were sure that no one was around, they continued on and finally reached the entrance to the shaft.

Katja leaned down and kissed Grisha on the forehead. "I love you very much. Come back soon."

"I love you too, Mom."

Just as the boy turned to go down the shaft, they were called loudly: "Stoj!"

Russians, it suddenly flashed through Katja's head. She instinctively grabbed Grisha and remained motionless. Her right hand slipped unnoticed into her coat pocket while she held her son with her left.

Two figures emerged from the rubble in front of her. One raised his hand in a gesture, then three more soldiers stood up. One of them pointed a submachine gun at Katja and Grisha. The woman could make out the silhouette of the PPSch 41 with the round magazine. She slowly pulled her hand out of her coat pocket and placed it visibly on Grisha's shoulder. If she drew the revolver, they would both be dead within seconds.

"Who are you? And why are you here at night?" asked the Red Army soldier who had ordered the others to leave cover. The tone was harsh and abrupt. The voice sounded rough.

Katja felt the same as she had the day the German soldiers had tried to rape her. She began to tremble. Her pulse was racing faster than a steam locomotive with its boiler burning hot. She could feel the blood rushing into her carriages. She was nervous, but she wanted to hide it at all costs.

"They're spies! Why else would they be sneaking around her?" said the person next to her.

Katja knew she had to answer quickly and act very confident to keep the situation under control. "I'm Katja Kalikova, and this is my son, Grigory. Captain Oligov calls him Grisha. My boy works for Captain Oligov, and we're on our way to see him!"

The soldiers surrounded Katja and Grisha. Flashlights were switched on. The beams of light swept over mother and son.

"I think she's a spy. Come on, let's get her out, then we'll move on."

One of the men behind them laughed. "I'm cold, I already know how to keep warm. I would interrogate the spy properly and then ..."

Katja interrupted the soldier harshly. She realized that the speaker with the rough voice was a sergeant. She addressed him directly. "Comrade Sergeant. Captain Oligov is expecting my son shortly. He has very important news to deliver. Any delay will cost you your head! And if even one man from your group defends me or touches my son a little too hard, Captain Oligov will see to it that you are all executed, I promise!"

Again she heard the voice of the Red Army man in the background. "Don't listen to this whore! She's spying for the Germans! Why else would she be here?"

"Sergeant, I want that soldier's name immediately! I'm going to report him to Captain Oligov!"

"You won't tell her anything! You listen to me! I think we..."

"Silence!" the sergeant shouted to his men. They suddenly fell silent. He seemed to be weighing his options. The woman's reaction showed that there was a lot of power behind her. The sergeant believed that otherwise she would have submitted, or at least reacted with some kind of fear. It was that tone that he didn't like. It was so single-mindedly certain. She was used to giving orders and commands. That was dangerous. That was what he didn't like. Her tone! He knew that kind of language. She was warning him to be careful. If he reacted wrongly, it would cost him his head. "How do you know Captain Oligov? And who

274

are you? What exactly do you do?"

Katja hesitated for a moment. She thought about how to answer these questions credibly.

Damn, we didn't plan for such a situation!

Grisha sensed his mother's hesitation and just babbled on. "Oligov is looking for Major Koenig, the German sniper. I'm late. They're already waiting for me."

"You?" asked the sergeant.

"Yes, a political commissar is always there. And maybe Comrade Saizev. And there was another officer whose name I don't know. A short, fat one with nickel glasses."

The sergeant pondered and looked a little uneasy.

Grisha continued. "Can you tell me your name, sergeant, so I can tell the captain who stopped us?"

The unpredictable Red Army man spoke again: "You are dangerous. We'll do as I say, then we'll move on!"

The sergeant lowered his submachine gun, which was still pointed at Katja, turned and stood in front of the soldier, who looked ruthless and dangerous to Katja. In a flash, he spun the shpagin around and suddenly jabbed the butt of the MP against his comrade's chest. He stumbled backwards, caught on a boulder and fell backwards. He let out a clattering "Uffz ...", then cursed loudly: "Ouch! Damn it, Fjodor, what are you doing?"

"I'm the sergeant and you disobeyed my order. I ordered silence! You're trying to prevent an important errand with your car. Have you not been listening? This boy has information about the man who shoots some of our comrades every day! I'll report you if you disobey my orders again!"

"But..."

"Shut your mouth," one of his comrades snapped at the man still lying on the ground. "Otherwise we'll all end up in the front trenches when the action starts soon. I know Oligov. He is not to be trifled with."

A fourth person also tried to be reassuring. "This is a Russian woman and her son. They're on their way to see Captain Oligov. Let's move on. I don't want to mess with Oligov. Igor is right. Oligov is merciless!"

The sergeant finally got them all together. "For God's sake! We're not here to argue. I told you to be quiet." He tried to look friendly as he turned back to Katja. "You'll have to excuse me, my men have been in the field for months and are a bit brutalized. My comrade didn't mean it that way," he pointed backwards.

"It's all right, Sergeant," Katja waved him off. "Can Grisha go now? As I said, we have to go to Captain Oligov and be back before dawn."

The Russian sergeant nodded. "Of course!"

Katja let go of her son. "You know what to say."

"Yes, Mom."

The sergeant turned back to his group. "Go on!"

Katja waited until the soldiers were gone. The tension eased. She was noticeably relieved. "You did a good job."

"You too, Mom."

Grisha walked to the shaft and slipped inside. He took one last look at his mother and then disappeared. Katja waited another minute and then went to her alcove as usual. She sat down on her backpack and spread the blanket over her. The waiting began.

This time Grisha was taken to another bunker. Cold, bare walls, thick beams supporting the ceiling. The room where he and two soldiers waited for Captain Oligov was heated. The flue from the small workshop stove led to a skylight half covered with metal sheets. A kerosene lamp provided light. The air was stuffy, and the smoke coming from the pipe of one of the two Red Army men smelled more like burnt horse hair than machorka. Grisha sat with the smoker at a table that, along with four wooden chairs, was the only piece of furniture in the bunker. The other Red Army man stood in the doorway. Everyone was silent. Only when the soldier at the door said that he had to leave, did the other one start a conversation.

"The captain is asleep. He's been expecting you for days, and he's not in a very good mood. The political officer wants to cancel the company," the Russian babbled.

276

Grisha felt queasy. He was glad to sit down because he could feel his knees getting weak and shaking a little. They were almost there. The boy thought feverishly about what to say, then he remembered Erwin's words.

They can use tricks to make you feel insecure. Just stick to what I told you and don't show any reaction if they tell you something else. First of all, it could be a trap because you are a young boy and based on your information, they certainly won't do anything that hasn't been checked, and secondly, if anything has actually changed, it certainly won't be reversed by your information. That's the biggest hurdle you have to get over. You can't let on and you can't believe everything they tell you!

Grisha calmed down.

"Tell me, boy, what took you so long? Why did you come today?"

"Comrade soldier, I want to talk to Captain Oligov. He told me that I'm not allowed to talk to anyone else about my mission or anything related to it. I'll stick to that!"

The Red Army man laughed loudly, took a puff on the pipe, noticed that it was no longer burning, and tapped the bowl against the sole of his boot. The ashes fell to the ground. Then he put the pipe in his pocket. "Look at the uniform I'm wearing. I'm Captain Oligov's right-hand man. You can trust me."

Grisha didn't like the tone of his voice. He felt noticeably uncomfortable. His eyes kept wandering to the door.

"Come on. I'm just curious and I'll find out in a few minutes anyway. I'll make sure you get an extra portion of food later." The voice sounded friendly now, flattering.

The offer was tempting, and what the man said made sense.

"I think we have some chicken left. I could do that and talk to the cook and make sure we can give you a tasty chicken. Imagine, a whole fried chicken. So, what do you say?"

Grisha's stomach growled. Just the thought of fried chicken made his mouth water. He hadn't eaten it since the summer. Summer! Suddenly he saw pictures of Boris and his father. He saw himself playing pirate with Boris and fighting invisible enemies. In a low voice and noticeably depressed, he replied: "What I'm doing here is for my brother and my father. They both lost their lives."

The Red Army man looked at Grisha for a while. Then he said: "Where are you hiding? You and your mother?"

"Mama says we're still alive because we don't tell anyone where we're hiding."

Again, the Red Army man tried to gain the boy's trust. He smiled. "That's true. But I am a friend. You can trust me."

"I trust you, comrade. But I will not reveal our hiding place, and I will speak only to Captain Oligov."

Now the voice of the soldier changed abruptly. The Red Army soldier reached across the table, grabbed Grisha by the collar and pulled him a little in his direction. "You dirty liar. You're full of shit. Nothing you said is true. You're just trying to get something to eat! That's treason, and you'll be executed for it."

Grisha was scared to death. He was shaking all over. He wanted to cry and call his mother. He thought about tearing himself away and running away. He was afraid. Scared to death.

What did Erwin say? Be prepared for anything and stay calm, no matter what pressure you are under. Even if they beat you or threaten to kill your mother, nothing will happen to you or her.

Even with this knowledge, it was damn hard to stay calm. He was just a little boy and helplessly at the mercy of this strong guy. If Erwin hadn't prepared him thoroughly for such situations, he would certainly have started talking at that moment. Grigory Kali-Kov was strong, but he would have preferred to be weak. He would have preferred to hide at that moment. Instead, he repeated what his German friend had repeatedly drilled into him. The Russian spoke to the boy more and more insistently. He even raised his hand to hit him and shouted at him. That was the moment when Grisha gave free rein to his fear, began to cry and scream hysterically: "I'm only talking to Captain Oligov! I may not have a uniform, but I'm in the Red Army. And now you can beat me up!"

"Stop, that's enough!" The voice came from the darkness of the anteroom. It unmistakably belonged to Oligov. The officer entered the room and coughed. "I told you not to smoke your turnip weed in the shelter."

The soldier grinned. "That was part of it, comrade captain. I

278

wanted to make him feel uncomfortable."

Oligov did not answer. He looked at Grisha, who was wiping the last tears from his cheek with the sleeves of his winter jacket. He pointed to him and asked the Red Army soldier: "What is your impression?"

"I think he is what we think he is."

Grisha heard the words and the trembling in his knees returned. Had he betrayed himself? Did he know that Erwin Koenig was their friend? That was impossible.

"Very good."

The officer approached the table and sat down. Without another word about what had just happened, Oligov made a beckoning gesture with his hand. "Get the boy something to eat. A large portion of kasha should satisfy his first hunger."

"Yes, Captain Oligov." The soldier got up and went to the door.

The officer turned to him again and called after him: "Bring another two kilos of buckwheat. And have some milk bottled in the kitchen. That will be the boy's reward, if I am satisfied with his information.

Grisha's eyes lit up. He was about to eat his fill. And two kilos of buckwheat sounded like a lot. He didn't know how much porridge his mother could make with it, but he was sure she would be very happy.

"What can you tell me?"

Grisha followed Erwin's instructions word for word and slowly approached the last topic. Oligov listened attentively without once interrupting the young Russian.

As Grisha spoke, Erwin's words of warning came back to him.

It must not sound as if it has been memorized. Don't ramble on. Tell them that one of the Hiwis used to be a real Cossack, but he joined the Red Army and is only doing this job so he won't starve in a prison camp. Grisha invented a boy to follow him. "I think he wanted to beat me up and rob me, but I hid. Mama was really angry when I came home late."

Now Oligov gave in and asked the first questions. "Let's go back to the two Hiwis. What did one of them say about this Major Koenig?"

Grisha pretended to think. "He said that a sniper of officer rank

279

had gone to the front. He saw him himself."

"Did he say where he was going?"

Grisha heard a commotion in the corridor. Men were shouting. Someone was cursing and moaning in German. There was clapping. The groaning stopped. A scream ended in a kind of gurgling. A Red Army man shouted to another: "Don't beat him to death, you idiot! We need to get more out of him! Come on, get in there with him!"

There was the creaking of a door, then the stomping of boots. "What took you so long? Come on, give me a hand!"

A grinding sound followed, and a door was slammed shut. The voices were now muffled and the words unintelligible.

Captain Oligov noticed that Grisha was startled and nervous by the unexpected noise. "That's just a German. We're interrogating him," he explained, watching his informant's reaction.

The boy felt increasingly queasy in the pit of his stomach. The shaking had increased again. Grisha sat differently to hide the shaking. "What did you ask?"

Oligov continued to examine Grisha with an appraising look, then repeated his question: "On which part of the front is this German officer hunting?"

Now Grisha had to keep quiet. For Papa, for Boris, he thought and concentrated on his answer. "I'm afraid I don't know, but I can tell you where he was and where the men went. That's what the defector told me."

Oligov pulled a notebook and pencil from his breast pocket and placed them on the table in front of Grisha. "I'd also like the names of the defectors, if you know them."

"One calls himself Sergej, the other Vladimir, but that's all I know, why?"

"Because we're going to shoot them after we defeat the Germans. They are traitors!"

Grisha's fear returned. "But they're nice."

Oligov lowered his voice and leaned forward. "Traitors deserve no mercy. Remember that once and for all! Traitors will be shot or hanged!"

The soldier who had questioned Grisha at the beginning came

back with a bowl of kasha, a bottle of milk, and a burlap sack. He put them on the table. "Has he earned his meal, comrade captain?"

"Leave it and go outside. Take care of the German!"

"At your command, Comrade Captain!"

The officer pointed to the pad. "Draw!"

Grisha took the pen. "The paper is a bit small, but I'll try."

With quick movements, childish but easily recognizable houses and streets were created. "Here," the boy pointed out, "was the big department store. I met the Russians right across the street. They cleared the road there so that the German tanks and trucks could pass."

Oligov listened intently.

"The German soldiers and the sniper went that way." Grisha's finger moved along one of the streets he had drawn. "That's all I know. I hope it's enough for the Kasha."

Oligov nodded in agreement and muttered: "Eat!" Then he turned and called the soldier he had sent away a few minutes ago.

It wasn't long before he came back into the room. Oligov pointed at the sketch. "That's the big department store. That's the direction they went. I need the latest reports on operations and German sniper activity."

Grisha shoveled the porridge into his mouth. Less than five minutes later the bowl was empty. The boy looked at the officer and asked: "Can I go see my mom now?"

"Not yet!"

The waiting began. To hide his nervousness, Grisha leaned back and closed his eyes. He was wide awake, but pretended to be asleep.

"Lie down by the stove."

Grisha stood up. "Thanks, but I have to go back tonight. Mama's waiting and it's cold."

"Thousands of brave Red Army soldiers are freezing. Everyone is making sacrifices. We are waiting."

"Yes, comrade captain," Grisha replied, saluted and went to the stove.

Grisha lost all sense of time. It seemed like an eternity, and he was about to fall asleep when he suddenly heard rapid footsteps. Grisha sat up and yawned. The soldier came back. He put a map on the table. He rasped excitedly: "Comrade Captain, we had battles in this sector. The Germans have straightened out the front and once advanced unsuccessfully against the next row of Hou-ses. In the last two days we've lost at least five soldiers there, but probably almost twice as many to snipers. Either there are several, or ..."

"Or it's the best German sniper in Stalingrad in action. We have him! Take this message to Comrade Saizev at once. I'll take care of the rest."

The soldier rolled up the map, saluted and hurried out of the room.

"Is everything all right, Comrade Captain Oligov?" asked Grisha.

The captain took a silver cigarette case from his pocket, opened it and took out one of the cigarettes. He put it in his mouth, put the case back in his pocket and took out a lighter. Seconds later, he inhaled the first puff and blew out the smoke with relish. "Yes, boy, it's all right. You can stay here. We'll wait for the results together. If comrade Saizev reports success, you'll get an extra reward."

Grishka became nervous. His leg began to tremble. "Mom is waiting for me. I'd rather go to her."

Oligov grinned. It was a malicious grin, and it frightened Grisha. The boy was expecting the worst.

"As you wish. I'll take you to the shaft."

"Thank you, comrade captain."

"Divide the buckwheat and hide for a few days. We'll take the city back. Then come back here!"

"When?"

"You'll find out!"

16

Koenig was more than pleased with the work of the pioneers. The entrance to his hideout for the final duel with Saizev was in a place that could not be seen by the enemy. Though the sniper had to make a small detour from his comrades' positions, he was able to approach the entrance between the bullet-riddled walls of a ruin, first upright and then crouching behind a pile of rubble piled next to it. The craters were completely covered with corrugated metal, stones, and beams. They were no longer recognizable as bomb craters. Koenig had to crawl into the larger crater on his stomach. He had pushed his rifle, a second sniper rifle, and his backpack forward and then crawled forward.

The depression had a diameter of at least three meters and an estimated depth of two meters, with debris in the form of rocks and dirt already accumulated at the bottom, leaving a distance of about 1.50 meters to the ceiling. The footing on this rubble was firm. Koenig was able to move around the room in a crouched position.

On the side facing the Russians, i.e. in the direction of fire, the corrugated metal sheets at the edge of the funnel lay relatively unevenly on the rubble. This provided two or three opportunities to get into position for a well-aimed shot.

Koenig went into the crater next to the funnel. There, the height from the ground to the tin roof was an estimated 1.10 meters. Koenig had to crawl on all fours. The light was moderate, and the sniper jumped in horror as he hit the body of the fallen Red Army soldier. His heart pounding, his left hand suddenly thrust forward while his right instinctively reached to his side for the 08 pistol. As his fingers opened the pistol pouch, he realized the bizarre situation and exhaled deeply. He lacked sleep. He was completely exhausted.

Koenig decided to leave his position and ask the lieutenant for a report. Then he would give some orders and lie in wait. He knew he was in for a duel that could not be more nerve-wracking. He suspected that he would have to be patient, and when he fired what was probably the only shot he could fire, he would have to be sure that it was Saizev who lay on the opposite side and fired.

Koenig had worked out a plan and was about to put it into action.

One last shot! Vengeance for Boris and revenge for Rolf! After that, I will leave my life to fate, but I hope to find my way to Katja and start a new life with her and Grisha, far away from all violence and war.

Koenig clung to this dream. He knew it was utopian. He had challenged the best Russian marksman to a duel in Stalingrad, and he knew that this hunter from the Urals would not go hunting alone. The major had to give everything. He needed all his strength, concentration and marksmanship.

I've only got one shot and I'm going to kill you, Vasily Saizev!

When Koenig entered the men's room, he felt as if he were walking into an invisible wall. The room was heated, the windows were boarded up, so there was hardly any air exchange. It was dark, and Major Koenig turned on his flashlight. The bright cone of light flew softly over the covered figures.

In the far corner, a Landser snored loudly. To the right, against the wall, was a man who mumbled a few sentences in his sleep and then rolled over. The lieutenant was right next to him. Koenig walked over and poked the officer lightly in the side. "Wake up! I need a report!"

No reaction. Now Koenig hit him a little harder with the tip of his boot. "Wake up!"

The lieutenant jumped up. "What? ... Who? ... Damn, what's going on?" he groaned.

Someone complained. "For God's sake, keep it down!"

Koenig turned the light on himself. "I am Major Koenig and I need a report immediately!"

As if stung by a tarantula, the lieutenant jumped to his feet. "Major! Immediately..." he cleared his throat and pushed the canvas and blanket aside. "Let's go outside and let the men sleep."

He stuttered out the door. "We came within twenty meters. The twilight was perfect for the attack. I thought we were going to take the buildings, but then the Red Brothers crawled out of all the holes and gave us a real run for our money. I don't think it would have gone well for us if we hadn't had the protection of the rapidly falling night. But

I'm convinced that with this mock attack we were able to forestall a planned counterattack by the Russians. They must have gathered when we attacked!

Koenig was relieved. He knew the Soviets preferred to attack at dawn or dusk. The position was held, his plan could work if Grisha was successful with his last errand. "Casualties?" he asked.

"I told the men to advance at half strength, as it was a mock attack. They were appropriately cautious. One man sprained his ankle and two men were slightly wounded by bullets, but will be able to stay with the troops."

Koenig patted the lieutenant on the shoulder. "Good work. What's your name, by the way?"

"Lieutenant Walter Schaefer, Major!"

"Lieutenant Schaefer, we will hold the position. The two snipers are to be active again today during the day and eliminate any target that appears in their crosshairs. After nightfall, they must withdraw. Your men should stay in absolute cover. I expect extreme sniper fire on the other side, but I'll take care of it!"

The lieutenant stood at attention. "Understood, Major!"

Koenig was amazed at how much fighting spirit this lieutenant still had. Most of the soldiers were shadows of their former selves. Cold, hunger, and disease of all kinds had long since caused more casualties than enemy action could account for. Companies had a fighting strength of 30 to 40 men, sometimes less. Anyone with half a brain knew that the once-glorious 6th Army had long since been defeated and was now reduced to unfounded slogans of hope. If Koenig didn't have a very specific goal in mind, he wouldn't know it unless he was cowering in a lice-infested corner and vegetating. Finally, he said in a firm voice, "I don't want to see a single Landser near the ruins to the left of here for the next day, two days, three days. Tell the men that they will be targeted by Russian snipers."

"Yes!"

"And if the Russians attack, which I don't think they will, then hold this position at all costs!"

"You've said that enough already!"

"I'm just emphasizing the importance!"

"Of course," the lieutenant confirmed.

"I retreat." Koenig looked around again, then whispered: "It's top secret that I'm on the left flank! Do you understand?"

Shepherd nodded. "I understand!"

"Thank you, Lieutenant Schaefer. I will speak well of you. Go back to sleep."

The lieutenant went back to the dormitory.

When Erwin Koenig finally returned to his position, he was overcome with fatigue. He had to force himself to pull his winter gear out of his backpack. He had had a kind of oversized sleeping bag sewn from the hides of slaughtered horses to ward off the cold. Inside this cover, he placed two blankets sewn together and filled the spaces between them with cotton wool. With this he imitated the warm Russian winter jackets and the good old down comforters. The major hoped to find a warm place to sleep so that he would not have to leave his hidden position for a long time despite the extreme cold. He found a comfortable spot, slipped into it, and closed his eyes. Within seconds he was asleep.

A few hours sleep was enough for the sniper. Shortly after waking, he began his final preparations. First, he maneuvered his winterized sleeping bag to the edge of the crater and searched the enemy-occupied ruins with persistence and calm. Gradually, he memorized things like barricades, pipes, the position of stones, and much more. Finally, the sniper put down his binoculars and took notes. Then he pulled a change of uniform from his backpack.

"Now comes the unpleasant work!" he whispered to himself and crawled into the neighboring crater with his uniform. The light conditions were slightly worse than in the larger crater where he had slept. He waited until his eyes had fully adjusted to the new light, then pulled out his knife, crawled over to the fallen, frozen body of the Red Army soldier, and began to cut the stiff clothing from his body. The task proved to be more difficult than expected, and the major doubted several times whether he would be able to do it at all.

When he finally finished, the next difficult part came. He had to dress the dead man in his German uniform. Koenig cursed wildly to himself when he realized how difficult this was. When it was his turn, he had to break one of the dead man's arms to put it on. Koenig was disgusted by his actions, but if his plan was to work, it had to be done.

When he was finally finished, and the dead Russian was more or less dressed in the uniform of a German major, he attached his dog tag. "I won't be needing this dog tag anymore," he thought as he slipped it under the corpse's coat.

Koenig's stomach let out a loud growl. He switched back to the other crater and pulled a can of sardines and a packet of hard cookies from his pack. This was his daily ration. When he was handed three days' worth of cold rations, he asked the sergeant handing them out: "A man is supposed to live on this for three days?"

"Major, the supplies are running low. Unfortunately, we don't have any more food. All hope lies in breaking the cauldron from the outside."

Koenig looked at the sergeant as he tried to justify himself and noticed that the kitchen sergeant and the other soldiers in the field kitchen looked miserable. It was the same picture everywhere. The men had sunken cheeks, some hidden under wildly growing beards. Those on field duty were dressed in whatever kept them warm. Under steel helmets and peaked caps, the men wore knitted wool caps and scarves sent to them by field mail from home.

If you got near the men, you could smell the inevitable lack of personal hygiene. There were no warm baths or showers where you could take care of yourself. There was a general lack of everything.

We live worse than sewer rats, thought Koenig, took the meager rations and wished the men in the field kitchen a good day.

Now he sat in his crater, after he had taken a Russian uniform off a frozen corpse with great difficulty and put on a German one. He was disgusted and hungry. Koenig opened the packet of cookies, took one and bit into it. He chewed slowly and deliberately. Only when the entire cookie was pure mush did he swallow the bite. He reached for his cutlery, carefully opened the can of fish, and began to enjoy his meager meal.

After eating, he crawled back to the edge of the crater on his stomach, watched the position of the sun and the incidence of light, and again scanned the ruins and their apron for changes with his binoculars. He took notes again and compared them to his earlier notes.

A round of gymnastics followed. They were designed to keep him reasonably warm and fit. At the end of one set of exercises, Koenig finally consciously moved all his fingers and toes.

No problem, he noted reassuringly, and then unpacked the other equipment he had brought with him. Two hand grenades that had not yet been thrown, a roll of wire rope, and another pair of binoculars. He moved the items into the small crater, crawled back and retrieved the second sniper rifle.

The major began to prepare the two stick grenades 24 for use. He inserted the tear-off device, pushed the knot of the tear-off loop through the wire loop of the fuse, and finally inserted the tear-off cord with the tear-off button into the handle. He then screwed on the canister with the detonator and fuse cap. He did not screw on the safety cap. This was not necessary. Once both grenades were fully assembled, he carefully placed them in the desired positions and tied them together with a thin cord. As a final step, he attached the cord to the breakaway line and placed it in the crater next to it. He tested his plan to detonate the stick grenades by pulling on the string. It tugged.

It worked!

Koenig held his wristwatch up to the faint daylight. He grabbed his binoculars again, crawled to the edge of the crater, and scanned the area. He didn't see anything unusual, but he had an instinctive feeling that the Russians were here.

Or is it just my imagination?

He slipped back. His heart beat faster. It felt like the first time he shot a person with a sniper rifle. Outwardly, the officer didn't seem to mind, but inwardly it gnawed at him. Koenig countered this growing doubt by convincing himself that his actions had saved the lives of many of his comrades. Then he dismissed all thoughts and tried to focus on his plan again. He crawled back into the smaller crater, grabbed the dead Red Army soldier, and tried to pull him as close to the edge of the crater as possible. He could not be seen from the outside, but he had to be positioned in such a way that a good sniper could score a hit if the barrel of a rifle came into view.

This was the German's last move. He brought the second sniper rifle into position by placing it in front of the dead Russian so that it could not be seen from the outside. Then he attached the wire sling to a piece of wood, passed the wire sling in front of the rifle and around one of the two stones that prevented the barrel, and thus the entire weapon, from slipping to the left or right. He then brought the wire rope over to his crater, walked back, and placed the piece of wood behind the butt of the rifle. He pulled lightly on the wire, causing the gun to move forward a little.

Very good!

He brought it back into position and returned to his crater. As dusk fell, he searched the area several times. Koenig stayed in one place for a long time. He was almost certain that something had changed in the terrain there, but he didn't know exactly what it was. He crawled back, took his notes, grabbed the sleeping bag he had constructed for himself, and crawled headfirst into it. Once inside, he turned on his flashlight in stealth mode. He was sure that no light would be detected from the outside. Koenig glanced over the notes, turned off the flashlight, and made his way back to the edge of the crater.

"Saizev, the duel begins! You will pay," he breathed.

He scanned the area again with his binoculars. He had memorized the suspicious spot. The sniper put himself in the position of his Russian counterpart.

If it was one of your observers, where would you be lurking? And if it was one of your side shooters, where would the observer be and where would you be?

Koenig went through all the possibilities several times. It was like a game of life and death. He and Saizev were the kings. Saizev had a bishop and a rook, he had only one pawn left. It was two squares away from becoming a queen.

I'll beat you!

The longer he lurked, the more the cold crept through his uniform. Koenig slipped into the warmth of his sleeping bag. After a few minutes, he felt able to concentrate on observation again and scanned the area once more. He was close to his goal. He knew that Saizev was lurking somewhere over there. The tearing war of nerves was not imminent, it had already begun.

Night swallowed the twilight. The starry sky continued to make for a persistent bone-chilling cold, but also for relatively good visibility. Koenig slept restlessly. He kept waking up, reaching for his binoculars, searching for Saizev and his helpers. The entire front remained relatively quiet, confirming the theory of an imminent Soviet offensive.

If they raise their vodkaration again, yelling and singing, it's on, he thought and listened. There was nothing to be heard. A good sign that he still had some time. They wouldn't attack yet.

Despite the bad sleep, Koenig felt good. At dawn, he crawled out of his sleeping bag and relieved himself in the far corner of the crater. Then he ate the cookie he had set aside for breakfast and took a sip from his canteen, the contents of which were cold. Koenig crawled back into his sleeping bag and surveyed the area. It was pure coincidence that he stopped at the suspicious spot with his binoculars at the exact moment when something moved for a brief moment.

That's an observer!

The German sniper was sure of it. Now he divided the terrain into specific areas and coordinated them with the observer's position. Koenig's approach was complex, but he hoped it would lead to the best possible success.

Minute by minute passed. Hour after hour passed. Koenig left his sleeping bag exactly twice. Once to get out and once to do gymnastics. By late afternoon, he thought he had pinpointed Vasily Saizev's approximate position.

If I were a sniper with observation and side shooters, I wouldn't position myself in the center, but on the flank. And due to the location of this ruin, I would be on my left side at 11 o'clock!

Koenig demanded everything of himself. The waiting and lurking tore at his nerves. Again and again he was overcome by impatience. He would have liked to take aim at the observer and shoot. Or he would have sent his two sharpshooters after him, but that would have jeopardized the final duel against Saizev. A shot from his comrades would provoke a shot from the Russians and possibly scare Saizev himself into retreating, as he would not trust Koenig to take such an action.

A champion does not shoot at secondary targets, he waits for the main target!

The fact that his opponent had been in position for at least 24 hours and had not fired a single shot confirmed to the German major that it was Saizev himself who was lurking there with the intention of shooting him.

Koenig had long since unpacked his rifle. It lay at his side. He reached for it again and again and looked at the target area through the sights of his weapon.

They want me. The observers report every suspicious little thing. I estimate that there are at least two, probably three guns lying in wait for me. Including Vasily Saizev's.

Koenig put the rifle aside and closed his eyes for a few minutes. His thoughts were with Grigory and Katja. He hoped that the boy had returned to his mother in good health.

Are they both sitting in their cellar thinking about me?

He knew that their nerves would be shattered by the wait. After all, he was not facing an ordinary Red Army soldier, not even an average Russian sniper, but Vasily Saizev, the master of all snipers, the hero of Stalingrad. No less a sniper than Saizev, the hunter from the Urals, who waited with stoic endurance for his opponent to strike with lightning speed and a fatal result, lurked in the ruins of this dying city, waiting for the final shot. In the chamber of the Russian hero's Mosin Nagant, a round was waiting to be fired at Major Erwin Koenig.

When Koenig opened his eyes, it was dark. His stomach rumbled and he felt weak. He was shaking. Nevertheless, he slipped out of his sleeping bag. The icy cold made its way through his uniform to his skin and enveloped him as if he were being held by a cold, icy fist. Koenig felt pain in his lower back and began to do some calisthenics. But he felt so cold that after a few minutes he slipped back into his warm sleeping bag. The warmth did him good. The shivering subsided. Koenig yawned and rubbed his eyes. Then he took off his thick mittens and grabbed his binoculars. He crawled forward and out of the sleeping bag with his upper body. He almost made the mistake of crawling too close to the edge of the crater. It was only because his upper body was sticking out too far from the sleeping bag and he was freezing again that he stopped. He had almost made a fatal mistake. The enemy spotters and snipers had certainly spotted the two craters as possible positions and were watching them just as he was watching Saizev's supposed position.

Damn! I have to be careful, he reminded himself, crawled back into his sleeping bag and decided to sleep. To make a good shot, he needed to be rested and mentally as well as physically fit.

Lurking and watching was nerve-wracking. Koenig lacked exercise and some entertainment. He felt as if he were in a solitary cell.

This time he slept through the night. In the early morning, the wind carried the sound of battle. He sat up in panic.

I hope the offensive hasn't started yet!

He immediately crawled out of his sleeping bag and checked the area with his binoculars. Nothing! Everything lay still before him.

Dead silence.

Koenig emptied his bladder and then ate the last of his provisions with ravenous hunger. He kept only one can of Scho-ka-Kola as an iron emergency reserve. After that, the sniper lay in wait again to finish his gruesome work and finally find inner peace.

The waiting game entered its next round. Koenig hoped to get one last shot before hunger and the piercing cold rendered him incapable of targeting.

After a routine visual scan of the observers' positions with his binoculars, the sniper set them aside and picked up his carbine. He removed the protective cover from the optics and aimed at Saizev's presumed position. The German officer had repeatedly thought about where the Russian would position himself and had gone through all the possibilities several times. Finally he had to make a decision.

If I was part of a group, I would definitely be there!

Although he had already adjusted the sights to the range several times, he checked them again. For him, it was part of the procedure to beat boredom, which was extremely dangerous for snipers.

"When you get bored, you get careless, and when you get careless, there are two possibilities. Either your target notices you and disappears, or you become the target of enemy snipers," he had always preached to his trainees.

He took aim again and looked at the ruins in front of him in the crosshairs. The vertical thick black line was in the target area, the two horizontal thinner lines flanked the small field of fire.

It was hard to make out, and probably impossible for the untrained eye to notice, but Koenig flinched. To the right, behind Saizev's presumed position, he had definitely detected a human movement. His index finger was on the trigger and the pressure point had been reached. He only had to bend it slightly and the shot would have been fired.

Calm down, he reminded himself, and felt the adrenaline rush through his bloodstream. His heartbeat increased, his pulse pounded. Koenig breathed shallowly and stayed focused. He went through his observation again, remembering the image that had been visible for a fraction of a second. What had he seen? Was it real or an illusion? It had happened in the blink of an eye. Still, the sniper was sure.

I know what I saw!

Someone in white camouflage had raised his head for a brief moment, only to immediately lower it back into cover. Koenig was glad that he had not fired immediately, against his hunter's instinct. He knew that a man like Vasily Saizev would not make such fatal mistakes when lying in wait.

Are you trying to tease me? You almost did.

The major suspected that the Russians were getting more and more nervous. It was almost as if they were under time pressure.

Sure, he thought to himself. The offensive is on!

The meager breakfast had not been enough to keep his blood sugar level stable enough for him to concentrate on the target with a steady hand. In the early afternoon, Major Koenig put his rifle aside, leaned back a bit, and dug out the can of Scho-ka-Kola. He opened it and divided the round energy bar into two pieces. Then he cut it into quarters and broke off a piece from one quarter. He put it in his mouth and let it melt slowly. After swallowing it, he ate the other piece of energy chocolate. He did the same with the next quarter. Even though he could have swallowed it all, he was reasonable and put the remaining half away.

He then did a few more calisthenics to warm up and get the blood flowing to all parts of his body. Then he got into position again, but this time with the intention of teasing the Russians to lure them out of their positions. He was ready to play his only trump card. Erwin Koenig wanted to and had to put all his eggs in one basket. Hunger and cold were merciless. The longer he stayed in this position, the harder it would be to shoot. He would either get Saizev here and now or never get him in the crosshairs.

The Major went over his findings and assumptions one last time. He was 90 percent sure that he had identified Saizev's position. And that was where he concentrated.

"It's time!" he said quietly to himself and tied the wire loop around his right leg.

If his plan was to work, he would have to wait for the next possible reaction from the Russians and then pull the wire tight with his leg. The piece of wood attached behind the butt of the second sniper rifle would push the weapon forward a bit, causing the Russian snipers to fire.

Maybe it's just Saizev firing, maybe his side shooters are firing too. Either way, I have to risk it. I can't last another day!

Another half hour of nerve-wracking tension passed without the Soviet snipers making a move. Koenig, who was no longer in his sleeping bag but on top of it, began to shiver again. He glanced at his wristwatch before it disappeared under the thick sleeve of his coat.

He wanted to fire the last shot before nightfall. The onset of dusk was perfect for his plan. During the day, his escape plan was in jeopardy. It was designed for the night hours.

Koenig was feverishly considering when to play his trump card when chance came to his aid. Unexpectedly, something came to life. A single Russian reconnaissance plane had probably flown too low over the area and attracted machine-gun fire. Koenig grabbed his binoculars and noticed a small crack in the snow cover where he thought the Russian observer was almost certainly located.

He seems to have moved to follow the scenario. A German sniper in ambush would shoot him now. Saizev is definitely waiting for my shot. Saizev does not follow the action around him, he lies in wait for his victim with deadly precession!

Koenig had swapped his binoculars for his rifle again and took aim at his target. Without thinking, the sniper raised his right leg. The wire tightened and the piece of wood pressed against the butt of the sniper's rifle positioned in the neighboring crater, pushing it forward a little.

Hopefully they see the run!

The thought was not yet finished when a shot rang out. Koenig had correctly assessed the situation and the position of his would-be executioner. He only had to move the barrel of his carbine a fraction of a millimeter and pull the trigger back. The shot rang out, the butt hammering against his shoulder.

Even before the crack of Vasily Saizev's gun faded, a bullet whizzed toward the Russian. Immediately after the shot, Koenig rolled to the side, took a deep breath, and crawled backward. He had survived the most dangerous moment of his life. That was the moment the shot was fired. If they had had him in their sights, he would be dead now.

A pounding pulse, goose bumps. The officer's nerves were still on edge. He was panting heavily. His knees began to shake. An eerie weight fell from Koenig's shoulders. He began to cry. Major Erwin Koenig broke down inside. For the last few days and weeks, he, Katja, and brave little Grisha had had only one goal: to fire a shot at Saizev. Now he had succeeded. He didn't know if it was really Saizev who was lying opposite him, and he didn't know if he had hit him at all, but he knew that this had been his last shot. Tears ran down his cheeks and seemed to freeze on his skin on their way to his collar. Images raced through Koenig's mind. Pictures of Rolf, pictures of Germany, pictures of carefree times. Koenig wanted only one thing. To jump up and run away. To go to Katja and Grisha and disappear with them forever, to a place where there were no more wars and killing. Erwin Koenig felt like a wreck.

After he had waited a few minutes and his agitated mind had calmed down a bit, he crawled into the neighboring crater. There was another hole in the head of the dead Red Army soldier. Saizev had hit him. Of course, Koenig had known all along how much danger he was in, but it was only now that he realized he was sitting on the Grim Reaper's shovel, and he had jumped off at the last second.

This cunning hunter must have had my position in his sights the whole time. Did I hit him and take him out? It's too risky to check, but I'll find out sooner or later.

Everything happened in a split second. Saizev had already spotted the German's position. He waited for a mistake and pulled the trigger when he recognized the barrel of the gun. At the same moment, Koenig pulled the trigger of his rifle.

The duel to the death took place in a split second. Saizev took cover after the shot, and the bullet fired by Major Koenig raced toward him. Because the Russian sniper had turned to the side in a flash, the bullet of his German opponent missed him by a few millimeters. The bullet from Major Koenig's carbine struck a brick, sending shards of stone flying. Some of them flew into Saizev's eyes. The Urals hunter cursed. For a moment he couldn't open his eyes. They watered and hurt. Instinctively, he rubbed them with his fists.

"You got him," he was told. "The best German marksman is dead!"

"My eyes! Damn it! I can't see! Get me out of here. I've got some shrapnel!"

"Are you hit?"

"No, just shrapnel!"

Koenig threw his sleeping bag into the crater of the dead Russian, removed the wire, and grabbed the string to detonate the two hand grenades. He crawled into cover and pulled the wire. He counted in his mind.

Twenty-one, twenty-two ...

The detonation announced the finale of his plan.

Boom!

He felt the shock wave. Dust, snow and rocks swirled around. The tin roof was lifted and landed diagonally above and partly in the crater. The dead Russian, dressed in the uniform of a German major, lay with his upper body clearly visible. The head was a pulpy mass of bone and brain, unrecognizably mutilated. A sniper rifle lay next to the body. The Red Army soldier wore Koenig's insignia around his neck. Anyone would think he was the major.

The German officer and sniper instructor, Major Erwin Koenig, was officially dead. Shot by the Russian sniper Vasily Saizev.

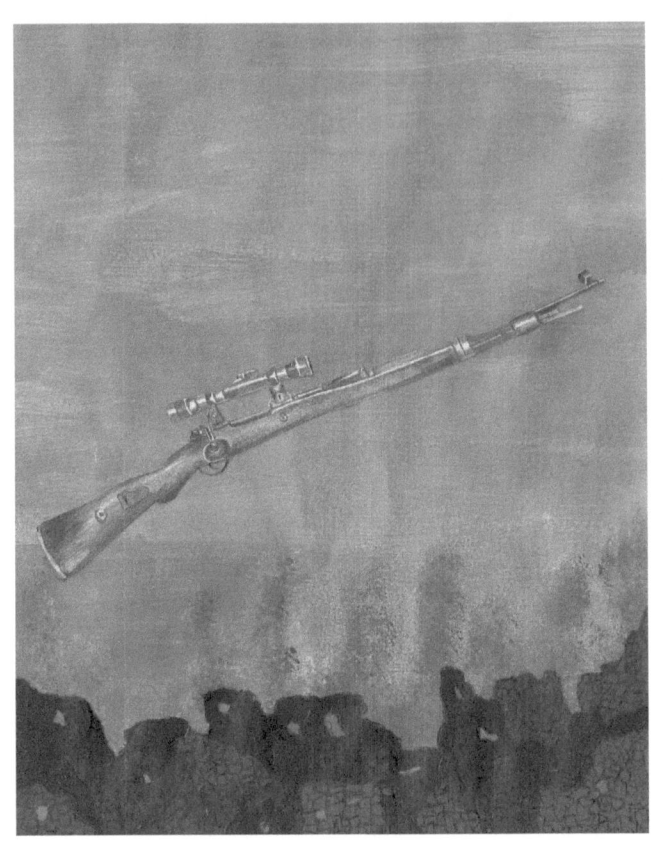

Sophia Wallenda - Stalingrad 2
© W. T. Wallenda
all rights reserved by the author

17

Grishka and Katja were sitting on the bed in their basement. A blanket was spread over each of them. It was still a few degrees above zero in the rooms, and compared to the outside, it was heavenly warm. Two small Hindenburg lamps provided light. Koenig had brought a good two dozen of them on his last visit. He also brought a few packs of matches and other useful things that might be important. "Look, I found this and packed it," he said as he emptied the contents of his backpack. This was a few days ago.

The mood was still low. They were waiting for Erwin Koenig and feared for his life. Katja cursed herself for not expressing her worries more forcefully. They should never have embarked on such a crazy plan. A single German soldier against a Russian hero flanked by other Red Army soldiers. What madness! The death of Saizev would not restore the lives of Boris and Rolf. They no longer existed. They were victims of the war and would never sit next to them again and laugh. They were dead and lived on only in their minds and hearts. You could no longer hug them, you could only think of them and tell their story.

Then came the self-doubt about whether it was right to fall in love with a German. You don't choose love. You hate people and you love people. You can't explain why. It's just the way it is. The love between her and Erwin Koenig was not born under a good star. He was her enemy. The Germans had invaded her country, destroyed her town and killed her husband.

Damn it, Pjotr, I miss you too! Why couldn't you be with us that terrible Sunday? Would you understand that I've developed feelings for Er-win? You've only been dead for a few months, and I have feelings for someone who is our enemy. What's right? What's wrong?

She was supposed to hate the Germans. And yet she had feelings for this man. Katja would have been able to resist the whole thing, if it weren't for Grisha, who had also taken Erwin to his heart. The Russian put Grisha's happiness far above her own. If her son had said a single negative word about Koenig, they wouldn't be sitting here now, fearing for his life.

She continued to talk to her late husband in her mind. Er-win is a good man. Grisha likes him, and the boy needs a role model. My beloved Pjotr. I don't have the strength to stay alone. Please forgive me, but I think it's the right thing to do.

Now Katja was brooding over Oligov and Saizev again. "Grisha, what exactly did this comrade Oligov say to you?" Katja asked again.

"Mama, I've already told you three times."

"Then tell me a fourth time!"

"He said that we would take back Stalingrad and that we should stay in our hiding place for a few days and divide the buckwheat well. After that I should come back to him."

Katja and Grisha knew the power of those words. Oligov had not said them literally, but the Red Army was preparing for the last great offensive. It would finally destroy the dying German 6th Army. Once again a firestorm was imminent. The rockets from the Katyushas, the shells from the howitzers, and the bombs from the planes would rain down on the city before the tank tracks crushed everything that moved. The Red Army soldiers would follow the rolling fortifications, pouring into every house and cellar.

Both were afraid. Fear of destruction, fear of the soldiers, fear of losing each other.

"Did the captain say when we would leave?"

Grisha shook his head.

Katja slid over to her son and put her arm around his shoulder. "He will come. Erwin will make it."

Koenig took advantage of the falling night to retreat from his position. The detonation of the hand grenades had caused a brief commotion. A flare had shot upward, causing the ruins to tremble bizarrely in the cold, artificial magnesium light. At the same time, a few rounds were fired from a machine gun. The Soviets returned fire from two machine gun positions. But as quickly as the brief firefight had started, it was stopped.

A heavy burden fell from the German sniper's shoulders. A burden he had placed upon himself. Suddenly everything was different. But it was not the expected satisfaction. It was quite the opposite. Koenig felt empty. The world around him was cold and desolate. No laughter, no joy, just a somber existence.

The shot at Saizev had been fired, but the pain that had lived in Koenig since Rolf's death, that he had carried around in his soul like an invisible burden, gnawing at him and tormenting him, had not gone away. The longing for human warmth grew. It was like waking from the trance of revenge.

What am I doing here? What have I done?

It was the moment when the soldier and officer Erwin Koenig died. The man is dead, the myth will live!

Major Koenig is dead. Long live Erwin Koenig, the man. Or should I say Pyotr Kalikov?

He thought of Katja. She and Grishka gave him the strength to forget all the hardships, all the suffering, to put it aside and start again. These two people gave him something. That something was called the future.

Without them, there would have been no future for Erwin Koenig. Without them, he would have surrendered to the cold and died in Stalingrad. That city would have been his grave. Now he clung to the small spark of hope that was enough to start a new life. He wanted to go to that future, that unknown future, which was always better than this daily killing and dying in Stalingrad.

Without Katja, I would go hunting every day and shoot all the Red Army soldiers who came into my crosshairs. Until I found myself in the crosshairs of a Russian sniper.

Koenig took the rifle from his shoulder, looked at it, and tossed it aside. He no longer needed it.

The cold that crept under his uniform was nothing compared to the cold that still lingered in his soul. It spread there like the Ice Age did across the Earth thousands of years ago.

He moved carefully so as not to be discovered. Koenig knew the way, knew the hiding places and the frozen corpses he had to pass.

Here lay the starving child, there the raped woman, her skirts pulled up. Her face was covered by her coat. The murderers and rapists had left them there to die miserably after their indignation.

Someday someone will come and take the coat.

A coat meant warmth, and warmth meant life.

How could this happen? How could it happen that two peoples hated and slaughtered each other as they did here in Stalingrad? Am I partly to blame? When was I poisoned by the ideology of the National Socialists? When did my humanity die? When did good become evil? Could we have prevented all this? Are we alone to blame or did world politics also contribute to this terrible war? Where were the beginnings, where should we have stood up and taken a stand? When was I infected by the war? Why did I look through the sights of a carbine? Why was I able to pull the trigger and shoot a man in cold blood in the head? I am an engineer, not a killer! When did I become a killing machine? I don't know!

The officer pushed the thoughts away. The emptiness inside him continued to spread. Hatred and anger replaced self-reproach. He would like to march to Berlin, grab Hitler, Goebbels and all the other party bigwigs and drag them to Stalingrad.

After a while, the anger was replaced by longing. Longing for warmth and love. A yearning for freedom and peace. This longing had a face. It was Katja's face. He saw the image of the Russian nurse before him and his heart began to beat wildly. It was not like the excitement that gripped him before a shot, it was different. This feeling was not driven by the coldness of war, but by the warmth of the heart. It felt good. So good that at that moment Erwin Koenig decided never to fight again.

The longer we fight in Stalingrad, the longer we will suffer.

The officer used the secret routes that he had discovered as a sniper and that had led him to Katja and Grisha more than once. He avoided encounters with soldiers from both sides.

Koenig turned his thoughts to the future. He wondered if he could ever forget. He wondered if the dead would creep into his dreams. Here in Stalingrad, death was so present, and he used to excuse his actions by saying that every shot he fired would save the lives of some of his comrades. Now it was different. Now he knew that every shot he fired would prolong the suffering of his comrades.

"Katja and Grisha. You are my hope. I feel like Saul who became Paul."

Since Katja and Grishka came into his life, his sense of humanity began to flare up. The lethargy of desolation died, the hope for a peaceful future grew. The fighting spirit withered with it. He was no longer a machine looking through crosshairs, searching for enemies to eliminate. The man he thought was dead had been reborn.

"No!" he suddenly said to himself, so loud it startled him. "I am not reborn. Erwin Koenig is dead. Pyotr Kalikov is reborn. In me!"

As Erwin descended the stairs to Katja's cellar hiding place, the Russian woman and her son were running toward him.

"You're alive!"

The embraces spoke for themselves. Three lost souls had found one another.

"Did you...?" Katja didn't finish the sentence.

Koenig nodded. "I took the shot. If I hit him, I don't know."

"And now?" Grisha wanted to know.

"Now it's over. Forever!"

Katja looked at the German. "You have to get out of that uniform. We have to burn it!"

"If the Germans find us, they'll shoot us. And if the Russians find us and identify me as a German, they'll shoot us too. I don't know if I should go. You could do it without me!"

"Never!" cried Katja in horror.

"No!" cried Grisha, holding Erwin's hand tightly.

The Russian woman clenched her hands into fists and put them on her hips. "We cannot change the fate of this city. All we can do is sit here and wait. If we're lucky, we'll reach our destination. If not, the future has no meaning. I've lost my husband, my son and many friends. All I have left is Grisha. And we found you. We have come this far. We'll either die together or go into the future. Assuming you want to turn your back on Germany and can imagine a future in Russia."

Grisha and Erwin looked into each other's faces. Erwin took a step forward, let go of Grisha and embraced Katja. Grisha put his arms around both of them.

"Together!" he said. "We'll be together forever!"

"Then I must get out of this uniform. And when men storm

into this cellar, I'll be Pyotr Kalikov, who has lost his voice," Erwin whispered.

"Yes!"

"And if they torture and torment me. I swear I will die before I say a word!"

Four weeks later, all supplies were gone. Katja, Erwin and Grisha were hungry.

The fighting had stopped. Russian soldiers were searching the cellars and sewers of Stalingrad for the last pockets of resistance.

They came in the morning. An officer led a small group of soldiers into the basement. Erwin Koenig, alias Pyotr Kalikov, was interrogated. The deserted major sat on the bed and looked at the officer.

"Why don't you answer?" he was shouted at.

Katja came in with Pyotr's identity card. "This is my husband, Pyotr Kalikov. He is, or rather was, a doctor at the hospital. When the bombers came, he was buried, survived the inferno and came back to us wounded. Since that day he hasn't spoken a word. The death of our other son, Boris," Katja took out a photo and showed it to the officer, "has added to his shock. I hope that one day he will recover."

The officer looked at her photo and ID, then said: "We have a field kitchen set up two blocks away. Go there and get something hot to eat."

"Thank you."

The officer nodded first to Erwin, then to Katja, then turned. "Men, we're going to the next house!"

When the soldiers were gone, Katja began to cry. She hugged Erwin and whispered in his ear, "We'll make it!

The following weeks were a time of dreams and fear for the scattered family. They planned their future, but trembled at every suspicious sound. Erwin rummaged through the upper floors and took everything that could be used down to the basement. Among other things, he installed a stove. Katja and Grisha were good helpers. He overcame the stairs by building a kind of slide with two heavy wooden planks. When the stove was finally in place and the fire burned for the first time, they celebrated this luxury.

At first, Erwin didn't dare go out into the street, but he was afraid for Katja and Grisha if they went out alone, so he finally accompanied them. This led to a dangerous encounter. They were hauling some firewood and some other lost property on a sled Erwin had built and had to stop at a crossroads. Red Army soldiers had cordoned off the area. Sensing danger, Koenig pulled his fur cap down low over his face and tucked his scarf just under his eyes.

"Come on, look at them!" a Russian soldier laughed, pushing Erwin and Katja forward. "There they go, the proud Germans. They look like a bunch of beggars!"

The long lines of maltreated soldiers had long since passed. So Koenig had stayed in the house all the time. He didn't want to be seen by anyone. Now a Russian soldier pushed him right into the front row.

The procession of soldiers was not too long, but the small line stretched along the entire street. "They should clean up and die here first, instead of just moving out of town," grumbled an old man, bending down and picking up a stone. Then he threw the stone into the line of soldiers. It didn't hit any of the men, but some of them turned to look at it. Then Koenig recognized Lieutenant Schaefer. The fanatical officer had obviously joined a group of resistance fighters. His gaze lingered on Koenig. He raised his hand and pointed. "That's Major Koenig, isn't it?"

The man beside him tugged at the lieutenant's sleeve. "Come on. Koenig is dead. We found his body."

The lieutenant lowered his arm and moved on. "Right."

After a few yards he stopped again and turned, but Erwin Koenig had already retreated to the second row.

"Dawei!" a Russian soldier shouted, urging the prisoners on.

Back in the cellar, Koenig placed a piece of wood on the dying embers. The flames quickly rose again, and soon the oven was crackling with fire.

"We have to get out of here. It's too dangerous," he said.

"Where are we going? We've discussed two options. Which one do you prefer?" Katja wanted to know.

"It doesn't matter. I'll go anywhere with you, as long as it's away

305

from Stalingrad."

Katja stood up. "I have some money. Mother Yenkova gave it to me. It's the foundation of our future."

EPILOGUE

Siberia, 1964. The silence in the forest was almost suffocating. The hunter breathed shallowly. The pack of wild boar he was after was close by. A light snow began to fall. He closed his eyes for a moment. Suddenly thoughts flashed through his mind. He was back in Stalingrad. A head danced in the crosshairs of his carbine. It was a Russian soldier's head. At the same moment a bullet entered the eye of his target. The Red Army soldier fell down, mortally wounded.

He opened his eyes, wiped the sweat from his brow and took a deep breath. The images of the most terrible days of his life came back again and again. They had never left him in peace, and he had to learn to live with them.

Pyotr Kalikov, who used to be called Erwin Koenig, concentrated on the boar again. A shot rang out and the pack stomped off into the undergrowth. A boar had been fatally shot and was lying there.

The former sharpshooter stood up and walked over to the shot animal. With practiced hands, he removed the boar and heaved it onto his sled. If he hurried, he would be home before nightfall.

The wooden cabin was neither large nor small. Bright smoke rose from the chimney. They had all they needed to live. Katja was a good woman. Erwin Koenig had found happiness with her.

As he pushed open the door, he heard her voice. "Take off your boots. I've wiped the floor."

Koenig stamped his foot in front of the door a few times to clear the felt boots of any remaining snow and dirt, then slipped out of them and put them back in their place. Erwin Koenig entered the house and closed the door behind him. "I shot a wild boar."

"That's a good thing. Grisha is coming to visit us. He's bringing Natascha and little Boris."

"What a nice surprise. What's the reason for the sudden visit? He wasn't supposed to come until spring."

Katja came out of the kitchen. Her graying hair was hidden under a headscarf. She was still very attractive. Katja was beaming with joy at her son's impending visit with his young family. Erwin took the hunting rifle from his shoulder and set it down. Katja helped her husband out of his coat. "He's got the job as head doctor at the hospital in Tomsk. They can finally leave Novosibirsk and move. They've assigned him a large apartment along with the post. Isn't that great?"

"That's wonderful."

Katja blurted out the next words. "Now they can visit us more often and we can see little Boris all summer. I'm so happy."

Erwin hugged his Katja. "I'm very happy too. His father would be proud of him, and so am I. The brave little boy has become a smart and brave doctor. And he has done his brother a great honor by naming his son after him.

Although Katja smiled brightly, there was a moment of sadness in her eyes. Erwin hugged her tightly. "The wounds from that time will never heal, but we've learned to live with the scars. I also see my Rolf in Grisha, and you see your little Boris in his son. That's good for us, my darling."

Katja returned the pressure from the man she loved and with whom she had fled the dark juggernaut of Stalingrad. "Yes, it feels good. And I hope that mankind never goes to war like this again."

"I think they have learned. The next war would destroy all mankind. We must defend ourselves vehemently against all beginnings."

Katja released their embrace, smiled at Erwin and said: "Now we'll have a hot cup of tea and then we'll get to work and carve the boar. I want to prepare a good roast for our guests."

They found a new home in the solitude of the Western Siberian lowlands, a few hours' drive from the city of Tomsk. It was an area where many Russian-Germans had settled. Here no one asked uncomfortable questions. Here they were free and happy and could live in peace.

Erwin Koenig never knew that his shot had ended Vasily Saizev's career as a sniper, and Saizev never knew that he had not won the duel with the former German sniper instructor Major Erwin Koenig.

None of them could forget the Stalingrad period. There were always nights when they woke up in a cold sweat and remembered the hell in which they lived and killed.

In war, the devil opens the gates to his kingdom.

End

GLOSSARY AND CREDITS:

STALINGRAD

The Battle of Stalingrad began on August 23, 1942, and officially ended on February 2, 1943, claiming the lives of some 700,000 people, most of them Red Army soldiers.

A few thousand scattered soldiers continued to resist until early March 1943. Of the estimated 100,000 prisoners of war, only 6,000 returned home.

VASSILY GRIGORYEVICH SAIZEV

According to Soviet sources, Vasily Saizev killed 252 German soldiers during the Battle of Stalingrad. He was honored as a hero of the Soviet Union in Moscow in February 1943.

The legend of the duel with the probably fictitious German marksmanship instructor Major Erwin Koenig probably originated in Soviet propaganda.

Saizev himself only briefly recounted in an interview a fatal duel he had won against a German sniper. The sniper reacted incorrectly when Saizev jumped out of a trench and was shot by the Russian.

In January 1943, Saizev was wounded in the eyes by shrapnel. He spent three weeks in the hospital and was then transferred to an ophthalmologist in Moscow.

Saizev was questioned about his sniping activities in Stalingrad. He stated that he had been wounded three times, had a nervous condition, and had been trembling ever since. When he was reminded of the battles, the trembling increased.

Most of the passages from the interview with the Russian hero of the Soviet Union were published many years later. The man who was depicted as an icon on posters was not supposed to show any weaknesses. He was and should remain a figurehead of the Red Army.

(Source: The Stalingrad Protocols, Jochen Hellbeck, Fischer Verlag GmbH Frankfurt am Main, ISBN: 978-3-596-19522-0, pages 429 - 450)

MAJOR ERWIN KOENIG

The historian and author Antony Beevor writes in his book: Stalingrad, Pantheon Verlag / Verlagsgruppe Random House GmbH, 2nd edition, December 2010, ISBN: 978-570-55134-9, page 241:

According to some Soviet sources, the Germans ordered the head of their sniper school to Stalingrad to hunt down Saizev, but this proved to be a failure. After a chase lasting several days, Saizev apparently discovered the hideout ... and shot him.

It is also mentioned in the same paragraph that Saizev considered the scope of the killed German to be his most valuable trophy. This scope is on display in the Museum of the Armed Forces in Moscow.

According to Beevor, however, there is absolutely no mention of this in any Red Army report, although otherwise every aspect of sniping was portrayed favorably.

In fact, the existence of a Major Erwin Koenig, who is said to have been a sniper instructor in the Wehrmacht, is not documented.

The use of officers as snipers was not common. Sharpshooters, also referred to pejoratively as "Scharfschützen", did not have a good reputation, and it was not honorable for an officer to be used as a sharpshooter.

All known snipers of the Wehrmacht and Waffen-SS came exclusively from the team and sergeant ranks.

GLOSSARY FOR THE NOVEL:

Arko	Artillery commander
Degtyarov DP 1928	Soviet machine gun caliber 7.62 x 54 mm, conspicuous by plate magazine (filling: 47 cartridges)
iron ration	The survival rations as emergency rations for German soldiers in the First and Second World Wars were officially called eiserne Portion (iron ration). If the regular rations failed, the specially packaged emergency rations were only to be opened and consumed on the express orders of the commanding officer. However, this reservation of orders could not be upheld during the course of the war. Two iron portions per soldier were carried on the field kitchen or in a convoy vehicle. For the Wehrmacht, this iron portion consisted as standard of 300 g of bread (*a packet of hard cookies, crispbread or rusks*), a 200 g tin of meat (liver sausage, ham sausage, etc.), 150 g of ready-made food (e.g. *canned vegetable stew or pea sausage*) and a 20 g sachet of coffee powder.
Concentrated load *(original)*	Prefabricated explosive in cuboid form, dimensions: 7.6 x 16.4 x 19.5 cm, weight with carrying ring: 3 kg explosive

concentrated charge *(several hand grenade warheads are tied around a stick grenade)*	Emergency aid for blowing up obstacles, shelters or for defending against armored vehicles *(the latter usually for blowing off chains or when attacking immobile vehicles)*
He 111 *(Heinkel)*	Standard bomber *(alongside the Ju 88)* of the German Luftwaffe in the Second World War, bomb load: 2000 kg, armament: 3 MG, crew: 5 men
HKL	Abbreviation for main battle line
Yak	Yakovlev Yak-1 was a single-engine Soviet fighter aircraft
Reich Labor Service (abbreviation RAD)	According to the Reich Labor Service Act, all young Germans of both sexes were obliged to serve their nation in the Reich Labor Service. As a rule, young men were called up for labor service for a period of 6 months before their military service. Women also made their contribution. The assignments of the RAD varied. (e.g. in agriculture or road construction)
Me Bf 109 *(Messerschmitt)*	Single-seat German fighter aircraft. Standard fighter of the Luftwaffe. Number built: approx. 33,300 units
MP 40 *also called "Schmeisser", as the name of the weapon's designer was affixed to the magazines.*	Submachine gun 40, successor to the MP 38, standard submachine gun of the German Wehrmacht and Waffen-SS, bar magazine, 32 rounds, 9 mm Parabellum
Muckefuck	noun for coffee substitute *(grain coffee, chicory coffee or malt coffee)* or for thin, stretched coffee

Pervitin	Stimulant - Manufacturer: *Temmler (1938 - 1988)*, Pervitin suppresses tiredness, hunger, pain and anxiety. Side effects: psychoses, personality disorders, risk of addiction. Initially often distributed to soldiers in the Wehrmacht as a miracle cure, distribution was greatly reduced after the side effects became known. Nicknames: *Armored chocolate, Stuka tablets*
Political commissar, political officer in the Red Army	Each *Red Army* unit *(down to battalion level)* was assigned a political commissar who had the authority to rescind orders from commanders who violated the principles of the CPSU. Although this was counterproductive from a military point of view, it ensured the political reliability of the army vis-à-vis the party.
PPSch 41 *(Pistolet-Pulemjot Schpagina)*	Russian submachine gun, (year of introduction in the Red Army 12/1940), very reliable, caliber 7.62 x 25 TT, Drum magazine (71 cartridges) and curved magazine (35 cartridges), developed by *Georgii Semyonovich Shpagin*
PM 1910 *(Pulemjot Maxima obrasza 1910)*	Russian machine gun based on the development of the manufacturer *Hakim Maxim*. Use with protective shield on wheeled carriage.

	Weight: approx. 24 kg - with carriage: 66 kg Caliber: 7.62 x 54 mm Cadence: 500 - 600 shots min.
OKW	Abbreviation for: High Command of the Wehrmacht
Mosin Nagant	Russian bolt-action rifle, caliber 7.62 x 54 R, magazine filling 5 cartridges with loading strip. The rifle was also available in a version for snipers, the standard rifle of the Red Army.
K 98	Mauser Model 98, German bolt action rifle, caliber 7.92 x 57 mm, 8 x 57 IS, magazine filling 5 cartridges with loading strip. The rifle was also available in a version for snipers, standard weapon of the Wehrmacht and Waffen-SS.
Scho-ka-kola	round chocolate containing caffeine, packed in a tin can.
Sanka	Abbreviation for ambulance
Sturmovik	Ilyushin Il-2 "Sturmovik", single or two-seater, single-engine, heavily armored combat aircraft of the Soviet Air Force
TVPl	Abbreviation for: Military medical area
UvD	Abbr. for: Sergeant on duty *(usually a special service to supervise the internal service, the UvD followed the instructions of the company sergeant (Spieß) and ensured compliance with military order after the end of the service. Among other things, he was responsible for waking up the soldiers, supervising the performance of cleaning duties and*

	ensuring that the night's rest was observed)
VB	Abbreviation for forward artillery observer
WuG	Abbreviation for: Weapons and equipment Sergeant, *usually a member of the combat team*
z.b.V.	military abbreviation for: for special use

FROM THE GENERAL LANDSER JARGON:

Eight-eight	German anti-aircraft gun (FlaK), caliber 88 mm, which could also be used for ground targets
Age	Nickname for: Superior officer (usually company, battalion or division commander)
Acja	Tub sledge (Nordic means of winter transportation)
Barras	Barras is the soldier's term for '*the military*'. To be conscripted means to be drafted (compulsory military service). The word probably goes back to the French statesman *Vicomte de Barras (1755-1829)*. He was one of those responsible when France introduced compulsory military service. The term is particularly common in southern Germany and Austria. A number of soldiers from Napoleon's *Grande Armée* during his Russian campaign came from these regions.
Germanic booty	Slang term for ethnic Germans *(people of German origin with non-German citizenship)*
Thunderbolt	Latrine / field toilet
Frozen Meat Order	East Medal
Goulash cannon	Field kitchen
"Sore throat"	someone would like to receive an award *(Knight's Cross, Iron Cross, etc.)*
Hindenburg light (named after Paul von Hindenburg)	A small bowl filled with fat or tallow into which a wick was inserted. It was used as emergency lighting. Its modern successor is the tea light.
Assumption mission	particularly risky and dangerous assignment, the execution of which is

	highly likely to lead to death (*albeit unintentionally*)
Hitler saw	MG 42 = powerful German machine gun
Dog tag	Identification tag (*usually worn on a chain around the neck*)
Taxiway	Important road/supply route, e.g. for supplying troops, but also for rapid advance
Intelligence strips	Tucks on the pants of members of the general staff
Ivan	Nickname for Red Army soldiers (*Russian soldiers*)
KdF (Strength through Joy)	Nationalist political organization with the task of organizing leisure activities (*hiking, vacations = land and sea travel*) for the German population. The society was based in Berlin.
Chain dog	Nickname for: Field gendarme, recognizable by his metal sign hanging around his neck (Military Police)
puzzle cup	nailed soldier's boots
Suitcase	Nickname for: heavy grenade
Bucket or bucket truck	Light, all-terrain military car (Volkswagen)
Kitchen bull	Nickname for: Cook
Landser	German soldier (*Landsknecht = mercenary fighting on foot 15th/16th century*)
Tinsel	Medals/other also rank insignia
Latrine slogan	Rumor
Napola	National political college = boarding school leading to university entrance qualification / elite school for the training of young National Socialist leaders
Skewer	Nickname for: company sergeant (*usually a master sergeant in the position of*

	a sergeant major - recognizable by two sewn-on piston rings on the uniform sleeve)
Fried egg	Nickname for: *German Cross in Gold.* The *German Cross* was a German military decoration and was established by Adolf Hitler on September 28, 41 in the gold and silver divisions. It has the shape of an eight-pointed star made of gray-tinted silver. On it is a laurel wreath made of gold or silver, which encloses a swastika. Silver: *(awarded for: repeatedly proven exceptional acts of bravery or multiple outstanding merits in troop leadership)* Gold: *(awarded for: multiple exceptional merits in military warfare)*
Stalin organ	Soviet rocket launcher *(proper name in the Red Army: "Katyusha")*
String-puller	radio operator
S-Mine	Abbreviation for shrapnel mine, fragmentation mine or spring mine. When triggered by a kick or tripwire, the mine body is thrown up to about hip to shoulder height and explodes with a fragmentation effect. This weapon was so effective that it has found many imitators to this day.
Aunt Ju	Nickname for the Junkers Ju 52, an aircraft type manufactured by Junkers Flugzeugwerk AG, Dessau. The most successful model was the three-engine Junkers Ju 52/3m from 1932, which evolved from the single-engine Ju 52/1m model.
Twelve-ender	Professional soldier *(period of service was at least 12 years)*

BOOK RECOMMENDATIONS

War Diary of the High Command of the Wehrmacht 1940-1945 (1961 - 1965)

Special edition, Berdard & Graefe Verlag, Bonn,

Edited by Prof. Dr. Percy Ernst Schramm, explained by Prof. Dr. Andreas Hillgruber, Prof. Dr. Walther Hubatsch, Prof. Dr. Hans-Adolf Jacobsen and Prof. Dr. Percy Ernst Schramm, ISBN 3-7637-5933-6

Wikipedia according to the inserted links.
The license terms can be viewed under the following link
http://creativecommons.org/licenses/by-sa/3.0/deed.de

Infantry Weapons Yesterday (1918-1945) Volume 1
Reiner Lidschun, Günter Wollert, Brandenburgisches Verlagshaus, 3rd edition 1998, ISBN 3-89488-036-8

Infantry weapons yesterday (1918-1945) Volume 2
Reiner Lidschun, Günter Wollert, Brandenburg Publishing House, 3rd edition, 1998, ISBN 3-89488-036-8

Das Handbuch der deutschen Infanterie 1939 - 1945, Edition Dörfler im Nebel Verlag GmbH, Eggolsheim, ISBN: 3-89555-041-8, Alex Buchner

German Uniforms 1939 - 1945, Motorbuch Verlag, Stuttgart, 4th edition 2004, ISBN: 3-613-01869-1, Jean de Lagarde

Stalingrad, Antony Beevor, Pantheon Publishers,
2nd edition 2010, ISBN 978-3-570-55134-9.

Waffen-SS Snipers on the Eastern Front - In the Crosshairs of the Hunters, information, original photos and a gripping novel, Books on Demand, ISBN: 978-3-7347-3984-2, January 2015, 132 p., € 8.90, Wolfgang Wallenda

Sniper Mission Voronezh - information, original photos and a gripping novel, Books on Demand, ISBN: 978-3-7357-5629-9, July 2014, 120 p., € 8,90, Wolfgang Wallenda

The Stalingrad Protocols, Fischer Verlag GmbH Frankfurt am Main, 2012, ISBN: 978-3-596-19522-0, pages 429 - 450, 14.99 euros, Jochen Hell-beck

and

Memoirs and records provided by veterans and contemporary witnesses (in writing or in personal conversations with the author) and the author's own knowledge.

More books by the author

"Sometimes I can still hear them screaming," Josef Altmann said more than 50 years after the Battle of Monte Cassino, lost in thought. He instinctively flinched, ducked to the side, apparently seeking cover from an imaginary approaching shell.

As a member of Regiment 361, the former foreign legionnaire witnessed the merciless fighting on the Gustav Line and around Monte Cassino. The war had reached an unimaginable level of cruelty, and death struck mercilessly every day.

Altmann was quickly trained as a sniper and immediately sent to the front. He recognizes the faces of his victims through the telescopic sight. His hands start to shake, his heart races. Goose bumps covered his body. Fear, misery, the loss of his closest comrades and the screams of the dying made him pull the trigger despite his initial doubts.

Josef Altmann tells his story without pathos, free of heroism and frighteningly close to reality.

This book is an unflinching factual account and should serve as a memorial against war.